G000081349

Corrupted Kingdom

Casbury Prep - Book 3

A.L Maruga

Corrupted Kingdom

ISBN: 978-1-7782508-6-6 Paperback

ISBN: 978-1-7782508-5-9 Ebook

Copyright © 2023 by A.L Maruga

All rights reserved.

No part of this publication may be reproduced, distributed, or transmitted in any form or by any means, including photocopying, recording, or other electronic or mechanical methods, without prior written permission of the publisher, except in the case of brief quotations embodied in reviews and certain other non-commercial uses permitted by copyright law.

This book is a work of fiction. All names, characters, locations, and incidents are products of the author's imagination. Any resemblance to actual person, things, living or dead, locales, or events is entirely coincidental.

Cover design provided by: Cady Verdiramo of Cruel Ink Editing + Design

Formatting & graphic design provided by: Mark Suan of WeLoveWriters Design Studio

Editing by: B&R Edits

Contents

A Note from A.L Maruaga   VI

Dedication   VIII

Author's Quote   IX

Introduction   XI

1. Mia   2

2. Theo   11

3. Carter   21

4. Mia   29

5. Diego   40

6. Finn   46

7. Mateo   54

8. Mateo   62

9. Mia   69

10. Carter   77

11. Mia   86

12. Theo   93

13. Carter   106

14. Carter   114

15. Mia   124

16. Theo   133

17. Theo   141

18. Stella   150

19. Mia   159

20. Finn   164

21. Carter   169

22. Mia   176

23. Mia   185

24. Carter   194

25. Carter   202

26. Mateo   212

27. Mia   226

28. Theo   242

29. Mia   251

30. Carter   262

31. Mia   274

32. Theo   292

33. Mia   301

34. Finn   311

35. Mia   317

36. Carter   328

37. Mia   338

38. Mateo   350

39. Mia   360

40. Theo   369

41. Mia   375

42. Carter   379

43. Finn   385

44. Mia   392

45. Theo   399

46. Mia   407

47. Theo   421

48. Mia   431

49. Epilogue   439

About Author   450

Come Stalk Me!   451

Also By   452

Acknowledgments   455

Resources   458

A Note from A.L Maruaga

Hello, my lovelies,

This book is the last book in the Casbury Prep series. You would have had to have read **Reign of the Queen and Fall of a King for** this to make any sense.

If you read the other two books, then you already know we have descended into the rabbit hole of depravity and darkness. <u>**This book is darker.**</u>

It is a deep black void that will leave you gutted, in emotional turmoil, and wanting to run screaming into the night. I'm sorry for the roller coaster you are about to ride. *Please forgive me and come back intact.*

This series follows a reverse harem of characters filled with possessive and destructive tendencies, supercharged emotions, and controlling alpha-aholes that can't seem to help themselves.

All characters are over the age of eighteen, and none of the main characters are blood-related.

<u>**This is an adult, dark romance and is strictly a work of fiction**</u>. I do not condone or approve of any behavior, actions, or scenarios that take place between these characters. **This book is intended for 18+ only.**

Many potential triggers are waiting to rush forward and bring you to your knees in this book. Please, for your sanity and mental health, heed my warning. I have placed international resources at the end of the book for those that may need them. **PLEASE**, I beg you, read my warnings.

It may contain scenes of violence, pain, primal behavior, suicidal thoughts, self-harm, struggles with mental health issues, BDSM, sexual manipulation, corruption, depravity, breath play, knife play, gunplay, gun violence, bullying, and blood play. If any of these may be triggers for you...**STOP**. *This is not the book for you.*

Content in this work may contain graphic scenes of physical, sexual, and/or emotional abuse, captivity, Child S.A. (A memory), r*pe, sexual assault, consensual, non-consent, and dubious consent, and inc*stual assault. If these may be triggers, **please STOP here! Go no further, I beg of you**.

There will be explicit profanity throughout the pages of this book. The characters are unreasonable, morally questionable, lack self-preservation at times, and cause each other harm. If that will cause you distress, **this is not the book for you**. *I am not the author for you.*

Don't say I didn't warn you, and give you an opportunity to get off this ride.

For those who want to take the return journey, welcome back to the world of Casbury. This book almost had me in the fetal position writing it. I have left my sanity inside its pages. I hope you return with yours.

A.L. Maruga xoxo

Dedication

To all those that love the dark.
Forget the flashlight.
We don't need it.

Author's Quote

I awoke with treachery,
their sins reflected on my soul,
and yet, they still called to me,
pleaded with me for forgiveness and mercy.
It was then that I knew the one to betray me
and hurt me the most was my own heart.

A.L Maruga

Introduction

They say when your heart breaks, all the shattered pieces make the same sound. A sound that is so devastating that it fragments your very soul and changes you forever. After all, songs, poems, and stories are made about the awakening and destruction of heartache. The word they use to describe those sentiments is *love*.

Love is the most destructive force on the planet. Not greed, not envy, or even hate. *Love*. It causes a rational person to change their own way of thinking, whether that be for good or for evil.

In my experience, love does damage that is irreparable. It brings with it pure chaos that makes you lose sight of your goals, your mind, and even your self-preservation. It blinds you, beats you bloody, and then leaves you in a shallow grave to rot. Alone. Abandoned.

The love spoken about in fairy tales consumed Amelia Hamilton. It took a young girl with rose-colored glasses, and it broke her of mind, body, and spirit, and then it spit her back out as Mia Stratford. A woman filled with the need for vengeance and destruction and the desire to repay those that had scarred her past.

Yet despite my need to avenge that girl that I once was, the one that was easier to kill than this new incarnation. I fell in love with the same monsters from my past. Villains who tried their best to hide their true natures and intentions with professions of love. Love, there's that pesky word again.

I was deceived, discarded, and abandoned once more by the kings of Casbury. My heart led me into peril at their hands and those of their enemies when I should have stayed my course. I should have taken my revenge when it was presented to me. Instead, I let love sway me on a different path. *The path of fucking love.*

Now here I sit in darkness, lost in a world of horrors. Ones that threaten to take my very sanity and destroy this new version of me. The only thing that keeps a fire lit from within is the thought of my vengeance.

My revenge will be righteous. I will spill the blood of my enemies and watch as it coats my hands. I will paint my walls red with the blood of the kings of Casbury.

We are almost at the end now. The end of the fairytale that was indeed a nightmare. They say at the end, you will find peace. Where is my peace? All I have left now is rage.

Have you discovered whether I am the villain or the victim? Do my decisions make any more sense to you now that we are at the finale? Do you still fucking *love* me?

One thing is for sure, there will be nothing left of us when I am done. This is the end of this corrupted kingdom. It's time I burn it all down to the ground.

I hope you forgive my sins as I bury them in a shallow grave at the very end of this tale.

Mia

xoxo

CHAPTER
Mia

"That's the problem with letting the light in — after it's been taken away from you, it feels even darker than it was before." Kim Liggett, The Grace Year

"**Y**ou really are a difficult little bitch, aren't ya?" The rage in his voice has the hairs on the back of my neck standing on end. He grabs onto both of my ankles and drags me across the seats and out the pickup door. When he manages to force me out, he swings me over his shoulder in a fireman's hold and slams the door—turning and heading towards the porch. *No! Fuck no!*

I sway back and forth, making my head pound and my stomach nauseous. I try my hardest to hit him repeatedly with my tied-up arms, but it's like he doesn't even feel the impact. Screams leave my lips, the sounds immediately swallowed by the deep darkness and the cold air. He's massive with broad shoulders, and I can feel all the hard-packed muscle underneath his clothes. Who the fuck is this lunatic who has taken me? Fear is an animal trapped inside my chest. My heart races even though I try my damndest to calm it down. *Breathe, bitch; we can't fall apart now!*

The air around us is cold, with a biting wind that suggests we may be at a higher altitude. The clean, fresh air doesn't have a hint of brine to it, so I know we are far from the ocean. It's so utterly silent and eerie out here, causing terror to race across my mind. As he walks, I can hear his footsteps breaking twigs and crunching on loose debris. There are no calls from birds or other creatures. We are entirely alone out here in the middle of nowhere. The trees taunt me with an escape I cannot grasp. *I'm going to die a painful death.* The thought is a drum beating in my mind causing my heart to gallop in my chest.

If I can't get out of here, my only hope is that he kills me quickly. I don't think I could survive what June, Mateo, or Theo have been put through. I wouldn't be able to live with my broken mind if he raped me repeatedly. I'm weak, after all, not the vengeful deity I pretend to be.

Shut the fuck up! My mind yells. I need to stay sharp and focused on a way out of this situation. I can't give up. I can't be weak now; no matter what happens to me, I must be strong. I must continue fighting to get free and back to my family. The knowledge that Stella will burn the whole world to find me fills me with a shard of hope. *I need to be Stella. There is no way she wouldn't survive.*

What about the kings? Will they search for me when they discover that I'm gone? *Why would they bother?* They hate me now that they know I'm Amelia Hamilton. Besides, I sent that text message to Raegan; no one will suspect that I haven't run off with my tail tucked between my legs to avoid the hurt the kings were putting me through. I am ashamed of my weakness. I fucking ran away instead of fighting. Look where I have ended up.

This is all their fault. No, it's ours; we let them in. We believed that they had changed. That they had real feelings for us when all it had ever been was lust, infatuation, and manipulation on their parts. Once again, the kings of Casbury have hurt me and gotten what they wanted. *I allowed that.* I deviated from my plan and let emotions control me. I fell for their deceit, and when they were done with me, they discarded me like I was nothing. *We are not nothing; we are a fucking Stratford!*

I will make them pay. Yes, if and when I survive, they should suffer untold horrors at my hands. I will see their blood splattered across this miserable world while I set fire to everything they desire and love.

Raegan and Issy will only discover something is wrong when Trevor and the wrecked vehicle are found. Then the alarm will go off that the Stratford princess has been taken. My grandmother will wage war to get me back, and when she discovers the reason for me leaving my property to begin with, I fear what she will do to the kings in retribution. *Don't worry about them. They deserve whatever fiery hell she is about to rain down on them. Traitors!*

Fuckhead climbs up the two steps to the porch, and I hear the electronic lock of the door opening. It makes a sharp beeping sound, and then we are moving forward, my head bouncing against his upper back. He reaches for the rope around my legs, pulling it taunt, but I can't see what he's doing from my position on his shoulder. I feel my legs suddenly being released from their confinement, and I start squirming on his shoulder until he's forced to put me down or drop me. He releases me so suddenly that I lose my balance instantly and fall on my ass to the floor with no way to brace for impact with my arms still tied.

"Fuck, you asshole! That hurt!" I scream up at him from the wood floor. The hard impact on my ass and back stinging. Tears fill my eyes, but I fight them back, refusing to give this guy any sign of weakness. I hear him mumble to himself about divas, and then he slams the door and the same electronic beep sounds. *Shit, he's locked us in.*

He moves past me further into the space, and then a bright light blinds me. I turn away and raise my bound hands to try to block it out until my eyes can focus properly. Once the light is no longer causing my brain to shout in extreme pain. I survey my surroundings. It's a small rustic cabin, the walls all made of timber and the furniture all pine and leather. A large cowhide is on the ground, acting as an area rug, and several deer heads are mounted on the walls. *Shit, it's a hunter's cabin, and this guy is hunting one thing right now...me.*

A noise captures my attention, and my head turns to the room's far corner. There's a door partially shut, and a thumping and whimpering noise is coming from that direction. Oh my God, I am not the only one he has captured. Someone else is in here with us. "Who else is here? What have you done?"

Fear skates up my body. What if he has taken one of the guys or, worse, my sister or Raegan? I try to push myself back to my knees, ready to headbutt him and cause as much damage as my confined limbs will allow.

I turn my glare back at him, prepared to cuss him the fuck out for his mistreatment and for kidnapping me, but what greets my sight has the words trapped in my throat. The air leaves my mouth in a whoosh, the sound bouncing off the walls in the space. I can't fucking breathe looking at him.

I can't fucking breathe! *Oh my god! This can't be.* This is one of my worst nightmares. This can't be right, can it?

He stands there tall, staring down at me with an arrogant look on his broad face. He's enormous with wide shoulders and tree trunks for legs, dressed in black jeans and a thick black hoodie. The baseball cap has been pushed back so I can see more of his facial features. He has high cheekbones covered in brown and gray whiskers, a thick pink bottom lip, and a thinner top lip, currently rocking a menacing scowl. Dark brown bushy eyebrows are raised questioningly over blue eyes with just a hint of green.

I watch as amusement crawls across his face at my horror. His intense eyes meet mine, eyes that I am intimately familiar with because I see them every single time I look in the mirror. *No! No, no, this can't fucking be!*

"James?" The name leaves my trembling lips. *Is it really him? Am I seeing things?* My body trembles like I'm a little girl once again. My heart is pounding so quickly in my chest that it's causing me to feel light-headed. I can't breathe, my mind struggling to process who is in front of me.

"Don't you mean daddy?"

Rage fills me at the word, daddy. *This monster is no father of mine.* My father is dead. Jared, my stepfather, was my only father. This asshole in front of me is just a sperm donor. A fucking monster from my most profound and scariest nightmares. One that caused so much destruction to my early childhood that he did irreparable damage, and I still struggle with scars left on my soul. Scars that are so deep and painful that they helped break Amelia Hamilton but shape

Mia Stratford. Now here he is before me, having kidnapped me and forced me into this cabin of horrors.

"You are not my father, asshole. You're a fucking monster from a nightmare. My only father is dead. He was nothing like you, an irredeemable demon from hell."

I bare my teeth at him as the words leave my lips, my sharp breaths causing my chest to heave. I try to force myself to my feet, wobbling a bit as I do but compelling myself to face him with all the indignation I can muster. My spine rod straight, and my head held high. I am a mother fucking Stratford, and before me is a cockroach who has crawled out from under a rock. *Whatever he wants from me won't be good.*

Anger flashes across his face, and his large body goes rigid. I watch as his eyes glint with malicious intent, and his fist clenches with suppressed rage. Fear skates down my spine and fills my limbs with adrenaline, ready to fight him off at the first sign of violence.

"That pansy-ass weak fucker, Jared. That's who you cherish as your daddy? That fucker is worm meal now, princess."

His words cause rage to incinerate inside my veins. A roar leaves my lips as I try charging at him, my teeth bared and snapping to try to capture any part of him that I can. The need to maim him, make him bleed, fills me. No one gets to talk about my father like that.

Just as suddenly as it appears, the anger disappears from his features to be replaced by an amused chuckle. One that leaves his lips as he watches me struggle and try to control my emotions. My stomach clenches painfully, and cold shudders run down my spine, my fight or flight activated. My mind screams at me to escape and run, that this man will hurt us.

"My blood would say otherwise, princess, but you go on right ahead and tell yourself whatever you want."

I don't hesitate, my vision seeing red at his expression of disdain directed at me, as if I was nothing but a pesky fly in his way. Once I'm steady on my feet, I charge the fucker again, catching him by surprise and slamming my shoulder into his stomach. The contact is jarring to my body, but I ignore the rush of pain and dizziness. I use my teeth, my only available weapon, to bite at whatever skin I can reach. I lock my jaw onto his forearm, and I bite down as hard as I can until the taste of copper fills my mouth. He loses his balance with the impact and stumbles backward, crashing into a small table and taking me down with him.

I don't release my teeth's grip, even when his large hand grapples painfully in my hair, ripping out strands and causing tears to cascade down my face. "YOU FUCKING WHORE!"

His giant fist comes flying at the side of my face, crashing into my cheekbone and forcing my teeth to lose their grip on his flesh. He shoves me off of him and backward. My body lands awkwardly, my tied arms are pinned below my body, and he's rising above me, a look of psychotic rage across his features. "You try that shit again, and I will end you, you little cunt!"

"FUCK YOU!" I scream, spitting his blood that's coating the inside of my mouth back at him. Some of it lands on his chin and neck, the rest landing back on me and sliding down my chin. His large booted foot lifts, and before I can move away, his foot impacts with my side. Instantly it feels like fire is rising through my ribs, the sharp pain forcing my air to get trapped and choking me.

"You need to learn some manners, little girl. It's obvious your momma hasn't done a good job!" His foot raises again, and this time lands a kick to my upper thigh as I try to squirm away from him.

More muffled noises are coming from behind that door, louder now. My eyes dart in that direction before returning to James. He rolls his eyes toward the sounds and mumbles to himself, but I don't catch his words. I can see the anger still on his face. His chest rises and falls with labored breaths, and his lip curls sinisterly, showing me a view of his large teeth. He looks like an enraged bull ready to charge at me and beat me to death.

For a moment, I almost welcome the thought of him killing me in his fury. For just the briefest of seconds, my mind whispers that is precisely what we should do, force him to kill us. Whatever he has planned will no doubt be a fate worse than death.

"Why have you brought me here?"

I don't expect an answer. In fact, he takes a step away from me, pausing to stare at the bite mark on his arm that is trailing his blood down to his fingers and dripping onto the floor. He moves so fast that I don't even get a scream out before his bloody fingers are in my hair, and his other hand is wrapped around my throat. He yanks me back, dragging me across the floor, my body sliding and my shoulders being painfully wrenched behind me.

He pushes the door open wider that the noises are coming from with so much vehemence and savagery that it slams into the wall behind it. His grip on my throat is bruising, preventing me from getting any air in, and spots of light are starting to appear before my vision. If he doesn't release me, I'm going to pass out. The grasp on my hair has tears dripping from my eyes and down the side of my face. He shoves me hard and then suddenly releases me, so that I fall on my side with a hard impact that has my teeth cracking together. I quickly gulp a mouthful of air and try to back further away from him, scrambling across the floor.

The sounds are louder now; as I turn my head to see where they are coming from, an unbelievable sight meets my eyes. Lying on his side, confined to a wooden back chair, dark blue terrified eyes meet mine in a face that is so swollen and bruised, at first, my mind struggles to make sense of what it's seeing. Muffled screams are leaving his mouth, which is confined with a dirty and bloody fabric. He thrashes in the chair but barely moves an inch. His limbs are tied tightly with a black rope around the frame and the legs of the chair.

"I brought my daughter a gift. I have gifted you vengeance. Isn't that what you crave, Amelia?"

Before me, looking pitiful and broken, is Vincent Saint-Lambert. The monster from all of my recent nightmares. The man that has caused so much harm to this world and to the men that I love. The psychopath that took Theo from me, then Carter, and finally Mateo. The man that destroyed his only son before attempting to take his life. *A life that was not his to take because it belongs to me!*

He barely left him alive, the harm to his physical body taking a toll on him and almost succeeding in ending his life. What is so much worse than the physical damage inflicted is the mental and emotional harm that he caused. He sentenced

Theo, Mateo, and Carter to a lifetime of waking nightmares. Where they relive their torture over and over again. Where they are constantly looking over their shoulders for the monster that will finish them off. He caused so much mental anguish to my Theo that he preferred to retreat into himself. Into darkness, totally devoid of light. All that was left in his place was this wounded animal desperately fighting off monsters in his mind and trying to protect himself from further pain.

Pure bloodthirstiness and a murderous rage that I have never felt before fills me, as I force my body across the floor in Vincent's direction. The desire to end and destroy his life fills me, and it cannot be stopped.

"You fucking devil! I am going to send you back to hell." I lunge, my head banging into his face hard, and I hear the crunch of his nose or cheek breaking. My teeth snap at his face, getting his chin, then his jaw before landing on the skin of his neck and biting down. *He will die at my hands! Retribution and vengeance will be mine!*

CHAPTER

Theo

"When she had died, his anchor was gone and the world had burned from his untethered insanity." Cedric Nye, Jango's Anthem

*C*arter is sniffling and trying to hide his tears. His jittery movements are starting to really irritate me, especially since my dad keeps giving us that look. The one that means a belt is going to make my skin welt up and burn after this. I grab onto his arm and squeeze as tight as I can.

"Stop, fucker! You have ants in your fucking pants or something?" A groan leaves his lips at my tight hold, no doubt pressing on some of the bruises he already has. I watch as he finally settles and wipes the back of his hand across his nose. Ugh, fucking yuck!

My gaze returns to the dark, blood-red, open casket with beautiful white roses trailing across its surface. The overwhelming scent in the air is cloying and suffocating, making the back of my throat itch and my nose wrinkle. The smell of flowers, trying to hide decay and death, not only from my mother but from the living inhabitants in the room.

The beautifully polished casket taunts me from its short distance. It currently holds the only person who has ever shown me an ounce of love in my short, miserable, painful life. My mom looks like a sleeping beauty from the fairy tales we read in school. She's so much prettier than all those princesses they described. Her skin is pale, almost the same color as the roses that adorn her casket, and her dark brown eyes are closed, finally at peace.

Her face is no longer streaked with tears from all the torment she was in or my father's harsh words. I should be happy that she's no longer in pain, no longer suffering both from her illness and at the hands of the man standing a few feet away from me. Finally, she has some relief from this world and from him, but now...now I am all alone. You were always alone; her presence didn't change that, my mind whispers.

The thought makes my heart thud painfully in my chest and my hands sweat. I know my father hates me. He's never made it a secret, even though I try my best to be the son that he wants. To stay out of his way. To obey without question, to never cry out when he's hurting me or the others. The latter being the hardest thing I always have to endure.

It's never enough, though. It never stops him from harming me or, worse, harming others around me. Why does he always want to cause me pain? Am I really that bad? He says I am the son of the devil, but wouldn't that make him the devil? He tells me that he needs to make me strong, but I don't know what that means. Strong for what? What does a ten-year-old need to be strong for?

The things he does, the way he has behaved since my mother got ill, terrifies me. The horror movies Carter and I watch aren't anywhere near as scary as my dad. He's a real-life monster, dripping with evil and creating nightmares that you can't escape from. It's like a door has been opened, and whatever bit of restraint he had, has disappeared. The leash is gone, and in its place has been left a rabid dog who only wants to cause damage and inflict pain.

Will he be even more violent now that she's gone? Will he hurt me even more than he already does? Now that he doesn't have to pretend to be the doting husband of a dying woman? The worries and fears I carry, no boy of ten should have to even think about. A shudder runs through my body, and I think about running away from home once again.

Where are you going to go? There is nowhere to run to. He will find you no matter how far you try to go. The reminder is painful and causes my little chest to rattle with the suppressed breath. The one that wants to strangle me with my own fears.

My eyes return to my mom once again. Why couldn't you have taken me away from here before you got sick? Why couldn't you have saved us both? Instead, you have left me in this hell to face this monster alone. I try to push down the unfair rage I have at her leaving me, at cancer taking her away from here and abandoning me to suffer. Alone. With no one to protect me.

From the corner of my eye, I watch as Mateo shuffles towards us, his large green eyes downcast and his shoulders hunched in on himself. His long, dark, wavy hair covers his face and hides his eyes from us. The shaking in his body tells me the fucker is once again crying. Fucking hell!

Doesn't he know that our fathers hate that? That they see that as a sign of weakness? They are like a pack of vicious hyenas preying on a weak animal. Right now, he is that defenseless animal, unwillingly luring them to attack. I often wonder if something is wrong with him. If that's why he can't try to behave the way they expect like Carter and I do.

Not that Carter does a great job of it. If anyone gets more beatings at the hands of their father than I do, it's him. The boy chooses to learn his lessons in the most painful and antagonistic way possible. Constantly pushing back against Mack and behaving with defiance.

A defiance that Mack enjoys trying to break him of, to no avail. They are both locked in a battle, two stubborn stags, neither one refusing to cower. Fear often runs through my mind that one day, Mack will go too far with his rage, and Carter will end up breathing his last defiant breath at the hands of his father. Right now, his hand is once again in a cast from another 'unfortunate and clumsy' fall. That's code for, he pissed Mack off, and he broke it for him.

My father angrily decreed that we will be kings when we start Casbury Prep next week, just like our fathers before us. His tight fist around my throat when he let me know of his expectations, and the punishment if I failed him, has panic seizing me from the inside. How can I keep Carter and Mateo safe from our fathers? I can't even save myself.

Carter is constantly getting into trouble and finding new ways to aggravate his insane father, and Mateo...fuck, Mateo is weak. He shows his feelings, emotions, and thoughts, wearing them on his face so everyone always knows how to hurt him. I don't want anyone to hurt him. He's my best friend. "Remember to protect those who are weaker than you, my little knight. Leave the world a better place than you found it." My mom's words circle through my mind, causing a sharp pain to race across my chest. I wish she was still here. I wish she hadn't left me to face this world utterly alone.

"Thhhh...Theo... I'm so sorry...about your momma." Crystal tears cascade down his face, his startling green eyes connecting with mine. Sorrow fills me with his words, which I know come from his heart. He, too, lives in a hell of his parents' making. Abandoned and unwanted. Now I am all alone too, no parent that loves me left. Will I become weak too? Mateo is not weak, fucker! He is untarnished by Vincent's evil! My mind yells in his defense.

My fists tighten painfully at my sides, the need to punch him in the face at his kind words filling me. No, fuck I don't want to hurt him. Mateo is my friend; everything about him is always genuine. He has a kind heart that others use against him. I don't want to be like my father and hurt those that I'm supposed to love.

Fuck! How am I going to protect him? I ask myself again. How will I protect the three of us when I can't even protect myself? Should I just cut ties with both of them? I'm sick of getting beatings from my father for Carter and Mateo's weaknesses. He wants me to rule, to be the leader, to be a king of Casbury. He says I must control them, but how do I do that? They are my only friends. I don't want to hurt them.

"Protect, cherish, and love, Theo. That is what will make the world a better place. Do not forget my words." My mother's voice echoes through my mind.

When Carter acts up, my dad has started letting Mack slap me around. He tells me that if I cannot control him, that I will pay for it with my own hide. I now suffer the painful consequences of Carter's actions, uniting us further in misery. Why the fucker can't keep his mouth shut and just behave, I don't fucking know.

I shift to the side, and a searing pain radiates up my backside, a reminder of my father's wrath last night. The lashings I took with his thick leather belt for having the audacity to question whether we should have female guests and a party in our house on the night before my mom's funeral. It's just one more painful reminder that no one should question Vincent Saint-Lambert, not ever.

My father's deep voice carries over to us as I move my slight body to block his sight of Mateo's tear-streaked face. "Jack Barrie-Chelmsworth apparently has found himself a new whore, one he plans on marrying. Some pretty gutter trash from the other side of the tracks."

"Oh? A new plaything for us?" Mack smirks at my father, causing the hairs on the back of my neck to rise. He enjoys hurting women as much as my father does. I hear their screams in the night, begging to be freed from my basement. The one I avoid at all costs. There are monsters lurking down there, and they all answer to my father's commands.

"No, I don't believe he will share. He has never been a part of our games. He is still the weak asshole that he was in our youth." The distaste and rancor across my father's face tells me all I need to know. He doesn't respect whoever this Jack Barrie-Chelmsworth is. He can't control him like he does Mack and Mateo's dad, Salvando, or any of the other jerks that follow him around like he is the devil himself, doing his evil bidding.

A dark-haired woman enters the room, her head bent low, her face shadowed behind her thick wavy hair. Her body is so slim that you can see some of her ribs against the fabric of her worn and shabby black clothing.

She stands out from the rest of our wealthy and bejeweled guests, especially all the women here, who look like they are going to a party rather than visiting my dead mother. Not that any of them even bothered to approach my mother's casket to pay their respects. No, my mother's funeral is a social event for these cockroaches.

The dark-haired lady approaches my mother's casket, a yellow daisy clutched in her hand. I watch with interest as she murmurs something to my mother that I can't hear. The melody in the tone of her voice is soothing to my ears. Tears cascade down her face as she stares intently at my mother's still and silent form.

I watch with pity and a dull ache in my chest as she reaches for my mom's clasped hands, gently laying the daisy across them. She leans forward, tenderly placing a kiss on my mom's cold cheek. "Rest in peace now, beautiful Chelsea. I will see you in heaven." Her voice shakes as she speaks to my mother. Her words are beautiful and bring me a wave of sadness but also peace. Someone here truly loved my mom besides me.

My eyes never leave hers as she wipes at the moisture on her face; with one last look at my mother, she straightens her posture. Her head raises and meets my eyes with a sadness I feel from a distance. Who is she? I have never seen her before, was she a friend of my mother's?

She shifts towards my father, hesitation clearly evident across her frame. Her arms wrap tightly around her abdomen, almost as if she's trying to protect herself. Maybe she knows he's a monster like I do. Like my mom did.

"Vincent...I...I am sorry for your loss." Her voice is soft and guarded, her eyes meeting my father's shoulder rather than his eyes. I watch, riveted to the spot and with trepidation skating down my body as she gets his attention and that evil spark of interest enters his eyes. No! I don't want him to hurt the nice lady that brought my mom a flower.

"Cathy, how lovely of you to come and pay your respects to my Chelsea." The words leaving my father's lips are strung together to sound kind, but I hear the genuine humor behind them. He doesn't mean a single word. He's playing with her. He always reminds me of a lion, playing with his food before he eats it.

"Yes...well... we were friends once." The woman named Cathy stumbles over her words, looking more uncomfortable by the second. I watch Mack move in closer, cornering her like a hyena and pushing her into the circle of men surrounding my father. Mateo's dad licks his lips as if she was a tasty treat he would like a bite of. Gross asshole.

"You still look really great, Cathy. The years have not been unkind to you." Mack stands behind her and sniffs her hair like a deranged animal while his wife watches from a distance. My small fists tighten at my side, and my body trembles *with anger. Why can't they leave her alone? I don't want them to hurt her. To do the bad things they do to other ladies. Monsters, evil monsters, are what all of them are.*

Her body stiffens, and she steps to the side, trying to put space between herself, my father, and the men surrounding her as if she were a weak deer about to be eaten by hungry predators. She's not wrong; that's what they are. The type of ravenous animals that will take enjoyment from ripping into her flesh. I should know; I hear the screams in my house.

Out of the corner of my eye, I watch as Mateo and Carter's moms observe the scene going down with anger painted across their plastic features before they move closer to their husbands. Giving the pretty lady an opportunity to escape. One she takes immediately as she rushes from the space without a look backward. I let out the breath I was holding. She's gone. Safe, at least for now.

"Mack, we really should be heading home with Carter." Alice Pemberton utters, a look of displeasure across her pretty features. I watch as Carter stiffens next to me with her fake concern for his welfare.

Where is she when Mack is beating on him? Where is her concern, then? My mom told me she used to be a beauty queen like Mateo's mom, but I see how she has always treated Carter. She's ugly on the inside. The outside is just a mask. Everyone in our world seems to wear one, except for the pretty lady that just escaped.

"In a moment, Alice, go back to speaking with your friends." Mack dismisses her without even bothering to look at her. His eyes honed in on the dark-haired woman scurrying from the room as if her body was on fire or she was being chased by monsters.

"Cathy still looks delicious, doesn't she?" Mack stares at my father with a raised eyebrow. A knowing look passes between them that has my throat tightening. "Heard she ended up keeping that brat; James put it in her belly. What a fucking pity."

"Heard James is doing a few years upstate. Not really surprised with his special tastes." Mateo's dad mutters, his face showing a hint of disgust.

A chuckle leaves my father's lips. "Brat or no brat, maybe I should be paying Cathy a little visit. Especially if she's all alone. She always did have the prettiest *lips when they were wrapped around a cock. Maybe I'll even follow that fucker, Jack's lead, and get myself a new bride from the gutter. I'm sure she would be more receptive to our needs than Chelsea was. Maybe we can tie her up in my playroom and have some fun."*

"What about the daughter? You planning on playing stepdaddy?" Salvando grins. The skeevy asshole makes my skin crawl. You would think he's not as bad as my dad and Mack, but there is just as much evil underneath that charming facade. He wasn't a king when my dad and Mack were growing up here in Casbury. They met him later when they were all in college together. He's always trying to make up for lost time with his nose shoved up my dad's ass. Fucking brown noser, cunt.

"If she looks anything like her momma, she won't be a hardship to play with, now will she? Maybe we can give her over to the boys, so she can learn to be an obedient slave, and they can get advanced lessons on how to tame a dirty cunt."

All of the men chuckle together, and bile fills my mouth at their words. I know what they do to women at my house, down in the basement. They're evil monsters, worse than the ones in the fairytales we read about in school. Most of those monsters have reasons for the way they are or can be redeemed, but not these ones. There is no redemption for my father and his friends.

The thought of that woman who showed my mom kindness when no one else here did, living in my house, being my dad's new wife, or plaything, fills me with revulsion. She has a daughter, they said, one that they will hurt or make me and the guys hurt.

No, no, I can't let that happen. I can't let that woman anywhere near my father. I don't know what to do to stop it, but if I ever meet this girl, whoever she is. I am going to make sure she runs screaming from us before he makes me hurt her. I don't want to be like him, taking pleasure from hurting those weaker than him. He's a monster.

"Theo...bro, are you ok? You're shaking like a fucking leaf and look green." Carter grabs onto my shoulder with his hand. His fingers digging into my skin has me returning to the present and pulling my mind from all the nightmares I have had to watch my father star in, in the last couple of months.

"Whoever that woman was, the one who gave my mom the flower. We need to make sure she, and whoever her daughter is, stay away from mine and your dad, Carter." A small whimper leaves my lips at the thought of how my father will hurt that lady who was gentle with my mom.

"I got you, bro." Carter nods, his disturbing husky blue eyes meeting mine before he elbows Mateo. *"Yeah, I...I'm with you."* Mateo replies with trembling lips.

I wake with a start, my heart pounding in my chest, the sound deafening to my ears. Cold sweat coats all of my limbs. My neck cracks as I move from the position I am in on the floor. I release my tight hold on my knees and stretch out my legs. It was just another nightmare, the same one that has played on repeat the last couple of times I have been able to close my eyes. *FUUUCK!*

He's not here. He can't hurt Catherine or Mia anymore. He can't hurt me anymore. He's finally gone, sent painfully into hell by someone's hands other than mine. The knowledge that I never got to repay him for all the harm and pain he inflicted on me is like a cancer eating away at me. I wanted to make him suffer and feel even a minuscule amount of the terror that I have lived with for years, but someone took that from me. Someone took their own revenge on him before I could. *Robbing me of mine in a horrific way.*

I drag my hands through my hair, pulling on the strands, a groan leaves my lips, and my body feels all the aches from sitting too long on the floor again. My thoughts return to where they always do once I am awake. *Mia.*

It's been over two weeks, and we still have no actual leads on where she is or even who took her. How can she have just disappeared off the face of the planet? I rub my hand across my chest, the pain that radiates a constant companion. Where is she? I need her back. *Come back to me, Mia.*

"THEO! You better come quick, asshole! Carter is fucking at it again and trying to leave! My grandmother will have him shot if he doesn't stop!" Issy screams and pounds on my locked door.

CHAPTER 3

Carter

"I'd always secretly believed that a love as fierce and true as mine would be rewarded in the end, and now I was being forced to accept the bitter truth." Alma Katsu, The Taker

"**G**et the fuck out of my way, asshole. I don't want to hurt you!" The sound of my blood rushing in my veins is a thunderous pounding in my ears. A deep thudding sound, like war drums being pounded on, over and over. It calls to me, begging me to do something, anything to relieve the pressure they are under. The neverending blackness that wants to seep out and envelop me. *She's gone.*

I watch as Finn crosses his thick muscular arms across his broad chest and plants himself in my way, trying to stop me from leaving out the front door. He thinks he's an obstacle that will deter me? *Fuck that shit.* I'm here for him, even trying. The angry monster that lives inside of me is stirring once again in his cage, demanding to be let loose. He desperately wants to rain fire down on the world, inflicting as much pain as he can. The one person that soothes his wrathful soul is gone. Taken from us.

The look of fury on Finn's face and how tight his jaw is, tells me he will fight back if I try to force my way out once again. *Fuck this asshole. I'm done caring.* He wants to stand in my way of finding Mia. I will go right through him. A slight thrill fills me at the prospect of feeling anything other than the terror that resides in my body now.

Out of the corner of my eye, I spy the rest of them creeping up, little ants ready to follow the queen of Manhattan's command. They are readying to once again try to restrain me. *I guess they haven't learned their lessons yet.* It seems it's time to cause some more damage.

"Carter, man. Calm the fuck down, brother. Please."

"Fuck you, Finn. Get out of the way!" Spittle flies from my lips at my snarled words. I'm losing control again. The anger that consumes me heating my blood, and causing me once again to see the world around me through a tinted lens. *Red.* Everything is always red.

I am not allowing anyone to prevent me from going after her anymore. Don't they understand I can't breathe in this house, not knowing where she is and who has her? I can't close my eyes without replaying the last time I was alone with her. When I hurt her, breaking her heart and mine.

The image of the look in her stunning ocean-blue eyes of pain are my constant tormentors. All these images threaten to decimate me. To tear me to brutal razor-sharp pieces. To drown me under their harsh weight of knowing that she's gone and I had a part to play in her leaving. *I can't fucking breathe.* I need to get out of here. *She's gone.*

My fists clench at my sides, and I launch my right one into the wall next to me in an attempt to prevent me from hitting one of my best friends. I don't want to hurt them, but I can't stop. Can't pull myself back from the edge. My precarious control is slipping. The drywall caves in with a hard crack, and my hand goes right through it. I wish I could tell you it hurt, but the truth is all of me is numb. The only thing I ever feel anymore is the pain radiating from my chest that tells me I pushed my heart to fucking leave me. *She's gone.*

"You dirty, rotten maggot! You better stop breaking shit in Mia's house!" Raegan puts herself in front of me, anger flaring from her livid emerald-green eyes. I gaze at her with compassion. She, too, is suffering and devastated. Mia disappearing has broken her like it has us. Her eyes are filled with a chasm of pain. One that I can relate to; after all, she loves my girl too.

Dark deep shadows stain the space underneath her eyes, signifying the knowledge that she doesn't sleep any more than I do. Than any of us do. We are all walking zombies, waiting for the end of our regretful and useless lives. I hear Rae's anguished cries in the middle of the night. The sound, wounded and dismal, calling to my own devastated heart. It's a thumping in my mind that never seems to leave me. *She's gone.*

Rae stopped eating days ago, and no one has been able to get her to take more than a few bites of anything since. One of Mia's shirts hangs off of her thin frame. Her curly hair is limp at her side, unwashed and tangled. I'm pretty sure she's been wearing the same dirty clothes for days since the last time Issy forced her to take a shower. She's a wreck; a part of her is missing. The same part that has my own heart in tatters.

We are all a shattered mess in this house. Ghosts, lost and broken without their spark of life. Our spark being that of a dark blonde-haired, ocean blue-eyed temptress with a temper and penchant for violence. *She's gone.*

"Rae-Rae, please don't get in my way. You...you know I have to find her...I can't go on like this." Understanding and sorrow flicks across her face. I tear my gaze away from hers and meet the dark blue eyes of the other fucker moving toward me. He, too, has a look of sympathy and understanding painted across his features that causes my blood pressure to rise.

Rise because before me is the mastermind of my destruction. The asshole that needed control so severely that he ripped my bleeding heart in his fist and caused me to hurt my girl. Like the fool I am, I allowed him to convince me to follow his lead, and now here I stand without my fucking heart. *She's gone.*

Bitterness and animosity flare again through my body at his approach. The monster inside of me rattles his cage, forcing the confining bars to let him free. I lunge before he can get more than two feet from me, my clenched fist catching his jaw and making his head smack back with the impact. *Yes! Fuck, yes! I need to fuck him up and break that ugly jaw of his. Damage, we need to cause more damage.*

He grabs onto me, trying to grapple and wrap his arms around me to stop the impact of my motions, but naw, I'm not having it. This motherfucker needs to bleed. I slam my fist into his stomach, and the air whooshes from his chest as he bends forward with the contact.

I don't hesitate, slamming my knee into his groin and head-butting him as hard as I can. Pure satisfaction fills me with the sounds of his pain, and when I pull back, I see the gash above his eye that's streaming bright, red blood into his eye. *MORE!* More, my mind begs. *Make him bleed even more! Hurt him, destroy him! He is the reason that our heart is gone. She's gone!*

I lean my face closer to his ear as he hunches forward, trying to brace himself from my force. My voice is pitched low, so my words are only for his ears. "I will fucking end you. Every part of you will bleed when I'm done with you, Theo. No one will stop me from wiping you from this miserable earth and sending you to hell to meet your father." I bite down hard on the top of his ear and punch him in the chest as he tries desperately to pull away from me.

"FUUUCCK, CARTER STOP! Finn's voice yells as he tries to restrain me and pull me off the miserable creature in front of me. The one that never fights back, despite me inflicting violence on him daily. *Fuck him.* I want him to fight back. To show some sort of fucking emotion other than the constant darkness that trails him like wisps of smoke. *Fight me, motherfucker; fight back!*

"Carter Pemberton! You stop this goddamn insanity right this instant!" Stella's voice rings out over the space as Clark helps Finn pull me back, restraining me with his large body as Stella approaches.

My chest is rising and falling, panting breaths leaving my lips as I struggle in their tight hold. The feeling of being restrained doing absolutely nothing to calm me down.

Stella stops before me, anger across her features. Her hand rises, and she grabs onto my chin, clutching it tightly in her grasp. Her nails dig into my whiskered face. Her cold blue eyes glare into mine, a grimace across her pale face. "What do you think you'll do that we haven't already, Carter? You think somehow you are going to go out there recklessly, and what? She will suddenly appear?"

Her words are harsh to my ears, her tone biting and causing me to flinch. Her nails sink further, causing a pinch of pain to race across my skin. The sensation is welcome right now. Fuck, any sensation other than this constant pain that feels like my heart is slowly dying is welcome. "I have to find her. She is mine. I will not allow anyone to take her from me."

My words cause a streak of pain to cross Stella's face before she tries to hide it. "I know you love my granddaughter, Carter. It's the only reason I haven't put a bullet through your miserable, disturbed head for the way you've treated her."

Her grip tightens painfully on my face, and the pain causes the monster to retreat back into his cage, recognizing a scarier monster in front of him. "She is not yours, Carter. She doesn't belong to any of you. She is a Stratford; she is mine." Her blue eyes are lit with a fire, and in its depth, I see rage. One that, too, wants to be let loose. A deep sigh leaves her as she releases her grip on my face. "We are doing everything we can to find her. I am tearing the world apart section by section. I will leave no rock unturned in my efforts. I love her too, Carter."

"Please..." My voice sounds pitiful even to my own ears. I am not even sure what I am begging for. I just know I need to go out there myself and look for her. I can't handle this confinement anymore, sitting here hour after hour, waiting for news that never seems to come. *She's gone.*

"Clark, give him your gun." Stella's gaze centers on mine, and I see acceptance and understanding there.

"No, Stella, what the fuck. You can't give him a gun and let him leave here alone." Theo's furious voice rings out in the hallway filled with shocked spectators.

Stella's cold gaze turns menacingly towards him, and I watch as he swallows painfully and takes a step back. Theo cowering before anyone has my hands clenching at my side. The need to be at his back, to protect him, trying its best to call me forward, but I resist. I'm no longer his brother or his fellow king. Those sentiments left when Mia did. *She's gone.*

Stella is incredibly frightening when she's angry. Who the fuck am I kidding? She's terrifying even when she's not furious. She's the boogeyman of grown men's nightmares.

We came to find out a week ago from Tom that Stella actually killed three people. Three fucking people, herself, when she first married into the Stratford family. Mind you, they were apparently trying to kill her, but the fact remains. Stella is a killer and a force to be reckoned with.

Her hand snaps out and slams into Theo's face, the slap loud, skin meeting skin. His head turns painfully on his neck, and gasps ring out from Raegan and Issy's lips.

"You, Theodore, don't tell anyone what to do anymore. You are the reason for my granddaughter leaving the safe confines of her home." She snarls like an angry wolf close to his face.

"The only reason you are still breathing is because I know she would never forgive me if I put a bullet in between your eyes. Do not try me, though, young man. My restraint only stretches so far. I would love nothing more than to see you bleeding at my feet or inhaling your last breath."

Theo doesn't utter a word in response, but I see the devastation across his face at her painful but truthful words. A knowledge that he is excruciatingly aware of. It was his idea to push Mia away. To make her think we didn't give a shit about her, even though that was the furthest thing from the truth. I want to feel sorry for him. I want to intercede on his behalf. After all, he is one of my best friends and the brother of my heart, but that's the thing. He shattered my fucking heart and decimated it when Mia ran from us because of his need to control everything. *She's gone.*

I can no longer stand by his side. I can't forgive him. Even being in the same space with him, seeing his mournful eyes, makes me want to make him bleed. Where there was always love and loyalty, now all that remains is disdain and rage.

Clark hands me the gun and a set of keys. His eyes meet mine before nodding towards the door. I don't hesitate to open the door and walk out without a backward glance. The need to get out of the mansion and look for my girl filling all of my limbs.

The sunshine glares down over me as I cross the courtyard towards the armored Land Rover that Clark drives. Welcoming me into its warm, radiant embrace, but there is no warmth without Mia. She took all the light and warmth with her when she left, and now my mind and heart are in perpetual darkness. *She's gone.*

As I climb in, my only thought is to find her. My gut and the gaping wound in my soul tell me that she is still alive. I start up the engine and move down towards the locked gates of Mia's estate, breathing deeply now that I am not locked behind those walls. *I'm going to find my girl and bring her home.*

CHAPTER 4
Mia

"Life could do nothing for her, beyond giving time for a better preparation for death." Jane Austen, Sense and Sensibility

A booted foot nudges my thigh as I lie on the dirty hardwood floor in the fetal position, trying to make my body as small as possible and keep myself warm in the frigid temperature of the room. Aches radiate through my numb limbs as they wake up from being in their confined state for too long. A moan leaves my parched lips, and my head lolls on my shoulder with no energy left to hold it up. My dirty hair drags across my features and pools in matted knots and tangles on the floor below me.

"Wake up, you worthless whore." The punishing heavy boot presses harder into my leg, and pain ricochets from the many deep bruises and cuts along my skin. I want to jump up and punch him in the dick. That would involve moving, however, which I don't have any strength for right now. It's not like I could use my fist anyway. James made sure to break my wrist days ago when I tried to fight him off. The swelling in that hand has just continued to increase until I can barely move my fingers anymore.

I crack my crusted eyes open and meet his rancorous ones. His meaty jaw grinds back and forth on his ugly face, and his lips snarl in my direction. A monster straight from my worst nightmares stands before me.

"Leave me...alone...you piece...of shit." The words leave my dry mouth with a vibrating soreness. I'm not sure if my jaw is bruised or fractured from the kick he gave me to the head last night when I refused to do his bidding right away as instructed. Was that just yesterday? All of the continuous beatings are starting to blur in my mind.

The reminder of what he forced me to do has the acid from my empty stomach rising and coating the back of my throat. I gag from the taste, and he steps back, not wanting to get vomit on him again.

Nothing would give me more satisfaction than to puke on this fucker, but my stomach is caved in on itself and painfully empty. My throat is sore and raw from my screams last night and all the nights before it. I have my doubts about whether I even have enough energy to spew vomit at him at this point.

A water bottle and a granola bar drop by my face, the water bottle smacking me in the forehead before rolling a small distance away on the wood floor. "Eat and drink, cunt. That's all you're getting today. You need a fucking shower. You smell like piss." He stomps away from me, and I hear the door of the room I'm confined to slam and then lock. *Motherfucker, one of these days, I'll have the energy to end your miserable life.*

I stare longingly at the water bottle, my mouth so dry I can't even make saliva anymore. I reach my uninjured hand out towards the bottle and groan as I have to stretch my painful limbs to grasp it. Once I manage to grab and pull it towards me, I force myself to sit up. My core protests immediately and throbs as sharp pains shoot across my back and sides.

They cause cries to escape my lips as I try desperately to silence them. *Be strong bitch, silence.* I bite down desperately on my bottom lip until the taste of copper once again fills my mouth. I don't want to give that fucker the satisfaction of hearing me cry or scream. He seems to get a perverse joy in hearing both.

My head spins, and white dots flash before my eyes as I manage to make it into a crouched sitting position. I know I'm dehydrated and starving slowly to death. I can see my bones pushing against my flesh, fat, and muscle wasting away without nourishment. He ensures I only get a bottle of water a day, and that's only on the days when I have cooperated the night before. *Fucking psychotic monster.*

Food is always just one protein granola bar. I'm pretty sure it's to guarantee I don't have the vigor to fight back against him. I am not a hundred percent certain how many days I've been here. There were days where I didn't wake from unconsciousness and the beatings he enjoyed giving me. But I think it's been over a week, maybe even two. Time in this hell has no meaning for me.

I stare lifelessly at the walls of my prison. Nothing but yellow-toned wood logs make up the walls. The ceiling is paneled in the same wood with a small black flush mount fixture too high up for me to reach. The one window in the room barely gives off enough daylight so that you can't see if it's sunny or not. Metal bars are placed across the glass surface from the outside, stopping any possible attempt at escaping from its depths.

Other than a broken wooden chair, there is no other furniture or items in the room. Nothing I could use to fight James off or harm myself with to end this miserable captivity. *I'm going to die here...but only after he's used me up.*

The smell coming from the room I'm forced to spend most of my time in reaches my nostrils. It smells rank and stale, like piss and death. I am sure I don't smell any better. I haven't had a shower since the day I left my house. When I was running towards Manhattan and freedom from the mistreatment of the kings, James the monster ran me off the road. Capturing me and bringing me to this hell on earth.

My eyes trail across the room, as they always do when I am forced awake into this nightmare that is my new existence. They meet with the broken wooden chair that is still on its side and the large dark stain below it. It almost looks like some grotesque application of abstract art. Its meaning is nothing I want to decipher as I know the truth of how it came to be. *We could use the shattered pieces of the chair, maybe end our own lives with it?* Just the thought of touching any piece of that wood has a shudder racking my thin, pitiful body.

The memory of that day tries to crawl back across my mind, the images of what happened once we got to this cabin trying to once again accost me. A cry leaves my lips, and a pitiful tear slides down my face. *NO! Please, NO!*

James yanks me off Vincent's body by my hair, making my neck bend backward at a painful angle and a cry leaves my blood-filled lips. The taste of Vincent's blood coating them, doing nothing to soothe my rage. The need to destroy him is a fire lighting from within my dark soul.

"You want your vengeance, don't you, Amelia? You're more like me than you think." He forces me to meet his eyes, ones with madness and hunger in their depths. A blade cuts through the ropes confining my wrists, and then they are released. The feeling of blood rushing back to my fingers causes tingles to spread, but I disregard the sensation. I will not allow anything to distract me from my rage. Not even the knowledge that I am playing into whatever sick game this is that James has brought me here for. "Go get your revenge, little girl."

Vincent sits there, confined to the chair, frightened, dark midnight eyes staring at me with horror. The scream attempting to leave his mouth is muffled as I move back across the floor toward him. My rage is a wildfire burning through me, ready to decimate everything in its path. It consumes me and begs me to cause as much harm as possible to this demon before me. The asshole behind me momentarily forgotten in my need for vengeance.

My hand slams out and grabs onto his hair in my tight grip, forcing his body to lift from the upturned chair and causing chunks of hair to be ripped from the roots where they are now stuck between my fingers.

With my other hand, I dig my fingers into his jaw, forcing his face to turn in my direction and his frightened eyes to stare into mine. "I'm going to repay you for every injury you inflicted on them. Every. Single. One. You are going to suffer so much pain that you will beg me for mercy, one that I will not grant you. You tried to take what was mine away from me in pursuit of capturing me. How does it feel now to be the prey, asshole?"

James hands me a small sharp blade with a thick dark wood handle. My eyes meet his, and I recognize the resolute confidence within their depths that shows he knows that right now, my will to fight him is overshadowed by my need for revenge against Vincent. You are as much a monster as he is, Mia. Why hide it? Let it out. Let it consume you. Destroy this demon that tried to take them from you. Vengeance is ours; take it, feel it.

I bend down to my knees behind Vincent's restrained form. His hands are bound tightly to the chair with thick black rope, but his fingers are loose and trying frantically to pry at the confining knots. No motherfucker, you will not escape my anger. I press the sharp edge of the blade against his forefinger and slice. The blade cuts through skin and tissue like butter. A muffled scream rents the air simultaneously as a satisfied chuckle leaves my lips.

My stomach lurches, threatening to reintroduce me to everything I consumed earlier. Stop this madness, Mia, my heart begs. NO! Fucking take your vengeance; feel its darkness deep in your soul. This man is a demon. Remember what he did to Theo. Remember the condition Mateo returned to you in. The image of Mateo in that forest when we first found him enters my mind, followed by the animalistic sounds of Theo thrashing in his room, plagued by terrors that this man caused him.

I press harder, pushing down with all my might on his digits and repeatedly slicing until it cuts through bone and his finger falls to the ground. Disgust is replaced with satisfaction. It fills me at the sight and the sound of his garbled screams. Screams that will rival the ones I heard from Theo's mouth. Only nine more to go, fucker.

How I can still cry is beyond me, with all the hell I have been through in the last couple of days. *Don't fucking cry, Mia!* My mind demands. Yet there it is, the symbol of my weakness, *one lonely tear.* I brush it quickly off my face. I will shed no tears for that demon or my loss of control. A groan rips from my lips when my fingers trail across the cut on my cheek.

The one I received last night from the thick belt that James used on my body to force my obedience. The lashes and welts across my back, shoulder, and neck wake up with a burning sensation at even the most minor movement. Even then,

I fought him with everything I had, but in my current state, that fire is starting to slowly diminish. The small amount of determination to survive that I have stoked within me is dying, just like my soul.

A reminder that there might still be a worse fate than the one I am currently living, even though I don't think that's possible. That one can lose their soul to madness and become the very monsters that they hate. I am a monster now, too. The blood of a beast flows through my veins, corrupting my very cells every moment that I breathe.

Regret is a devastating thing. It overshadows and consumes you like rot taking over all of your dreams, memories, and hopes, and poisoning them. It causes you to lose sight of who you are and leaves nothing but utter tragedy in its wake.

Death would be a blessing to me now, one that I do not deserve. It would relieve me of my burdens and the knowledge that perhaps what I am suffering is recompensation for my own actions. For the evil that lives within my blood. That suffering will cleanse me of deeds, of the hate in my heart. *You're insane just like he is, if you believe this, Mia.*

A snort leaves my busted and blood-caked lips, my mind filled with ill humor. *If you still believe that death is a worse fate than what we are currently surviving, you have finally lost your ever-loving mind*, my mind snarks back at me. It might be right. At this point, death might be a blessing rather than having to endure one more day at James' hands in this hell. Even my evil actions and blood-soaked soul don't deserve what I am being forced to undergo.

The only thing that is keeping me here, preventing me from trying to find that death, are the pictures and videos that James shows me daily of the kings, Raegan, Issy, Stella, and my mom.

He uses them to torment, taunt, and control me. Images somehow taken from the hacked cameras in my house and the ones placed in the home in Europe where my mom is blissfully unaware of what is happening in North Carolina. He's been watching us all along, one step ahead of everyone else.

He lets me watch a few minutes every day so that I can see that the people I love the most are still living, still breathing, and going about their days without me. It's both a torment and a vicious blessing. There's no sound, so I can't hear them, but I get to at least see their faces. It helps to keep my sanity from escaping me, from running off and flinging itself off the edge I am straddling. Every day, drawing closer to losing the battle and letting my demons win.

I know that they have realized that I am missing. Stella is in my home, holding court and commanding her forces to find me. Every day I beg the universe to let her find me with one breath and let me die with the other so she doesn't see the weak, pitiful creature I have become.

I crack the bottle of water open and let the blessed coolness gulp down my parched throat. Taking a mouthful and swishing it before spitting it to the side. Trying desperately to rid myself of the taste of copper and vomit that coats it.

I rip open the granola just as my stomach lets out an angry sound, demanding nourishment. I take the first bite, chewing slowly and painfully with my sore jaw, and then force myself to take another two bites, swallowing a sip of water to push it down. My hand trembles and water spills down the oversized gray T-shirt that I am wearing that barely covers my upper thighs. James took away my blood-soaked clothes that first night, ripping them from my body by force until I stood before him naked and shivering.

Fear paralyzed my limbs as his disgusting eyes roamed over my body, making my skin crawl as he inspected me. For what? I wasn't sure at that point, but the look on his face terrified me. He was assessing my body as if I was a fine cut of meat that he wanted on his plate. When he threw me the shirt, I let out the trembling breath I was holding. I should have known that there would be no mercy or relief. Look at all the man did to get his hands on me.

I now know that James was the one who killed all of Vincent's vile associates. The men that kept appearing brutalized and dead in an act of suppressed rage. We thought it was someone with a grudge against Vincent, and I guess, in a way, we were right, but that was never his only motivation.

He was the one that managed to capture Vincent, despite Diego and Stella's attempts to find him. For what reason, I wasn't sure at the beginning of this ordeal. He brought me Vincent, as a deranged gift for my vengeance. A gift he wanted me to have and enjoy tearing apart. A lie that he wrapped up in a pretty bloody red bow. He made me believe that it was a prize he willingly was providing me, and I had a pathetic hope that he would release me after I committed my horrific crime.

The memories of how I lost control try to rise again in my mind, and my stomach lurches, threatening to bring up the sips of water and the granola bites. "No, nope, stop that shit right now. Be strong. Be Stella." I whisper my daily pep talk to myself out loud to try to force myself to keep going, to keep enduring the unendurable.

I finish the last bite of the granola and drink down the last of the water just as the door opens, and James stands in the doorway. His glare searches me out and roams over my body with blatant possession across his features. "Get up and move towards the door. Don't be trying anything, Amelia, or it will go twice as hard on you tonight."

The image of him forcing me to do more than he already does and the enjoyment he gets from hurting me makes a whimper leave my lips. I force myself to my swaying feet, the room spinning around me as I stumble, and slam into the wall at my side, almost falling back down. My eyes rise and meet his, and I see nothing but impatience and cold malice across his features. He waits, tapping his booted foot at the doorway before grabbing on hard to my arm and pulling me from the room.

I'm shoved hard, almost sliding on my bare feet across the hardwood flooring. My knees threaten to buckle as I take rushed steps in the direction he is leading me. My eyes quickly dart across the open space of the large living room, eating area, and kitchen, trying to map out a possible way to escape this hellhole, just like I do every time he pulls me from my room. The front door would be the easiest, quickest way, but it's locked with a fingerprint recognition lock that only registers James' thumb.

The windows in the living room and kitchen area are covered by metal bars from the outside, just like the room I inhabit. So even if I could open the window, I wouldn't be able to slip between the bars. I stare across the expanse of the tiny kitchen, hoping to see anything I can use to hurt him with, but the counters are entirely bare.

I've never made it that far into the room, so I don't know where he would keep a cooking knife or that blade I used on Vincent. *It's hopeless.* He has ensured that there is no escape. There is nothing for over a hundred miles in any direction except forested area and thick red Cedars and Sassafras trees. *I'm going to die here...*the constant whisper from my mind makes me bite down hard on the inside of my cheek to prevent the sob that wants to race up my chest. *Be strong. Be Stella!*

He shoves me through the door that leads to the small bathroom. I can hear water already running in the space. Before I can protest or even try to loosen his grip, he shoves me inside the running shower. Freezing cold water pelts my skin, feeling like a million little knives are stabbing me all at once.

"Get cleaned up real good, Amelia, and don't be wasting my water." He stands back in the doorway, watching as I turn my back on him. The soaked shirt plastering to my malnourished body. I grab the bar of soap and try to wash below the shirt as best as possible, keeping my body covered from his filthy eyes.

My teeth chatter in my mouth, causing my jaw to ache and goosebumps to rise across my icy skin. I rush through, just getting the barest amount of shampoo into my hair and not even getting all of it washed off before he reaches across, shuts off the water, and pulls me from the shower.

Frigid water pools at my feet, creating a puddle as it slips down my body and from the soaked shirt. "Take it off." He barks the order with impatience, his stance rigid as my body is wracked with more shivers. "Give me a towel first...please," I beg, hating myself. Hating that I am reducing myself to actually begging this monster for anything.

"You don't get to make demands or requests here, Amelia." He grabs the shirt's side, yanking as hard as he can on the material, and I hear it tear as it's ripped from my frame. He stares at my body, his eyes moving over my parts and all the bruises and cuts that adorn it now. "Guess you're getting it twice as hard tonight since you can't follow instructions." He shoves me hard, and I fall back, crashing into the shower wall, losing my balance, and hitting the tiled floor hard.

He throws me a towel, and it lands across my cold body. "Get that mess cleaned up and dry yourself, girlie. You have five minutes to be presentable, then you better come outta there, you little worthless whore. We got some entertaining to do."

CHAPTER 5
Diego

"You either die a hero or live long enough to become the villain." Aaron Eckhart

I fist my short dark hair as I once again pace back and forth on the side of the two-lane highway where Vincent was found. My eyes desperately search the grassy and wooded terrain for something that we missed. Nothing but dried grass, cedar trees, sassafras trees, and asphalt greet me for miles in either direction.

The fucker was dropped right fucking here, where my dad has driven a wood stake into the ground as a marker. The only thing that will remain as a marker of the psycho's passing. His body will never be found, gone for all eternity. Both Stella and my dad made sure of that.

The question now is not where he was left but how the fuck did he get here and where he was before whoever took him, brought him here, and dumped him. Whoever it was did a vicious number on the psychopath. The wounds and state of his body indicate rage over a short period of time.

Someone inflicted a lot of damage, ensuring that he suffered horribly before he died. I almost want to shake the hand of the person who did it. They seem like my type of people. A monster much like me with no sympathy for predators like Vincent Saint-Lambert. A devious grin crosses my face. Looks like old Vinnie met a bigger predator to his painful demise.

Fuck, the guy had his severed cock shoved down his throat, was missing his tongue and fingers, and had an "X" carved into his chest near his heart. One very reminiscent in placement to the mark my cousin Mateo will sport for the rest of his life.

Almost every bone in his depraved and evil body was broken or bruised. Hell, they even went as far as to poke his eyes out, talk about savagery. His throat was sliced open from one side to the other, making him a macabre joker figure. That was what killed him; at least, I hope the fucker suffered extensively before he breathed his last miserable breath.

Whoever took him clearly hated that motherfucker and used that hate to ensure he suffered horrifically before they sent him back to hell. Who could have had that kind of rage other than the stupid rich prissy fuckers sitting in Mia's house right now?

I know for a fact it wasn't any of them. My money was on Stella Stratford, but she swears she had nothing to do with it. Though, I'm not a hundred percent sure if I believe the Stratford queen. I've heard some shit recently about her that has me playing it safe, trying not to get back on her radar and staying the fuck out of her way. *Well, at least for now.*

Vincent's appearance, just as Mia Stratford goes missing, has to be connected. This smells of dirty, foul play. Who would have benefited from ending Vincent while also taking the Stratford princess? It just doesn't make sense; he was her biggest enemy.

He's the one that took her precious useless, wannabe *kings* and tortured them while trying relentlessly to capture her. Then all of sudden, the fucker shows up dead and tortured, and she's gone. *I'm missing something here, something that is hidden just out of my sight.*

There has to be another player on the board, but who? My phone vibrates in my pocket, and I pull it out to see Issy's name on the screen. *Fuck! What does the other Stratford fucking princess want now?* I should just decline the call. She's been nothing but a frigid bitch to me for days.

If the little bitch thinks I've forgotten that she threatened me with a knife to my throat a few days ago, I haven't. These Stratford women are nothing but *jodidas locas.* I don't have the energy nor the time to deal with any more of their shit. I should be back in Columbia, getting ready to take my place as head of our new enterprise.

Then why are you out here on the side of the road, looking for clues to help you find Mia Stratford? It's not like you can marry her now. Your deal is done. You can't even avenge Mateo anymore. The fucker who took him and tortured him is already dead.

"What the fuck do you want, *Princesa?* I bark into the phone as I accept the call.

There's silence on the other end for a moment. I can hear her deep breathing, no doubt trying to calm herself down before speaking and taking my head off on one of her tangents.

Isabella Stratford is a colossal walking contradiction. She looks like this beautiful prim and proper china doll. Small, delicate, and exquisite to look at with all that luscious long dark hair that I crave to wrap around my wrist while I force her to her pretty knees.

Beautiful arctic blue eyes, red pouty lips, and a small ripe body that just begs me to ravish, consume, and control her like the devil and tyrant that I am. Yet she opens that vicious mouth of hers, and I swear she could give a few of the gangsters I know a run for their money.

"Listen, you fucking snake! Don't speak to me like that. I'm not one of your little whores, Diego!"

I pinch the bridge of my nose, feeling a headache coming on, and I'm just done with Issy's constant shit. I'm just about to hang up on her spoiled ass when her next words give me pause and make me groan in irritation.

"Stella gave Carter a gun and let him out of our prison to go search for Mia. The guys are worried he's going to do something reckless."

Fuck my miserable life since I came to this godforsaken town. Has Stella lost her damn mind giving that deranged fool Carter, with no fucking brain Pemberton, a gun and letting him out of the house?

Carter's fucking middle name should be "reckless." The guy is utterly psychotic on a good day. He has a penchant for violence and bad decisions. A sigh leaves my lips as I start walking back to my armored, blacked-out Audi parked on the side of the highway.

"What do you want me to do about it, Issy? He's not my problem. If your grandmother let him out, she's responsible for the destruction he causes."

"Don't give me that shit, Diego. I see right through you, and I know that you actually like the guy, despite pretending that you don't. Besides, my sister loves the fucker. She would be crushed if something happened to him because he was out there searching for her."

"*Princesa,* you do remember that your sister is missing, right? That she has no way of being crushed because we can't fucking find her. She might not even be alive, Issy."

The minute I say the words, I want to kick myself in the ass. I can hear her broken sob even through the phone. Shit, why am I so fucking heartless sometimes? It's not like she doesn't already know that we may never find Mia alive, but she for sure as fuck didn't need me to throw it in her face. I am a fucking asshole.

"Issy...Issy, I'm sorry, *Princesa.* I didn't mean to...FUCK!" The words leave my lips and taste like shit. It grates on me to be soft with anyone. That's just not who I am. I'm cold and ruthless. I could slit your throat one minute and fall blissfully asleep the next without the slightest bit of remorse.

I open my door and slide into my vehicle, starting it up and turning the car around in the opposite direction as I hear another sob cross the line. Fuck, that sob does things to me, things I don't want to look too closely at. Things that cause small fractures to start to appear in my solid shield of emotions.

"You're a heartless piece of shit, Diego. Find him or don't. What does it really matter? At the end of the day, you don't give a shit about anyone but yourself. But if something happens to him and you could have stopped it, my sister will never forgive you, and neither will I."

The line goes dead as I slam on the brakes hard, stopping in the middle of the road and slamming my hands over and over into my steering wheel.

How the fuck did this become my life? Chasing after wealthy and fucking spoiled princesses, tracking down deranged, psychopathic serial killers, and now fucking having to babysit one deranged and reckless rich, prissy white boy. *Esta mierda apesta.*

Someone up there really fucking hates me. This must be punishment for all the sins I have already committed that have blackened my soul. Doesn't the *puto* upstairs know that there is no redemption for any of them, and I'm not seeking it anyways, even if there was.

They are what have made me the ruthless survivor that I am today, and I am a hundred percent ready to meet the devil. I'd give him a run for his money any day. Fuck, I would bet any money the fucker is one of my ancestors.

A la mierda mi vida ahora mismo. Now, I have to go and stop a wealthy boy from getting himself killed or thrown in jail and then try to make it up to a woman I'm not even sure I like but that my body and mind crave. Yay fucking me! *Esto chupa grandes bolas peludas...*

CHAPTER 6

Finn

"Because what's worse than knowing you want something, besides knowing you can never have it?" James Patterson, The Angel Experiment

I stare at Carter's retreating back as he walks out the door. Fear races down my spine. Dread that it might be the last time I ever see him alive fills me. I move in his direction, ready to fight him and beat his maniacal ass to a pulp, if I have to, to bring him back inside. To keep him safe from his own demons, the ones that plague his mind constantly. Before I can, Clark puts his large body in my way, which has me stopping short and staring up into his dark eyes. "Let him go, Finn."

"Are you fucked in the head? We can't just let him go! He's going to get himself killed out there."

My fists tighten at my side, and I crack my neck loudly as I look disparagingly at the large man before me, shaking his head. I can feel my nostrils flaring as my breathing picks up with the strength it's taking me to try to remain calm.

The temper I keep tightly leashed is about to explode from its rigid confines, and when it does, it's going to level everything around it. I can't take much more of any of this shit. It feels like I have been on a destructive and deadly roller coaster for months. My heart, soul, and mind are battered and singed with the fires of my regrets. *You did it yourself,* my mind reminds me with disdain.

I shove my chest into Clark's, daring him to hit me. Egging him on to throw a punch my way, so I can finally lose control and show them all what darkness lies beneath my own exterior. The one I hide behind being the peacemaker of the group. Everyone always worries about Carter being insane. I guarantee you, my demons and the rage I keep squashed down would give Carter's a run for their money.

"Young man, you had better leash that attitude." Stella's sharp voice rings out behind me, but it doesn't stop me from chest-bumping Clark again, trying to force him out of my way.

"Finn, he has to do this on his own. He has to try to find her himself, or his demons will eat him alive." Clark's words rumble from his chest and into my face bringing with them the further need for violence.

What about my demons? Does he not worry that mine will destroy me? What about Theo, who has retreated into the dark hole in his mind, becoming increasingly estranged from us as the days pass without the slightest inclination of where Mia may be.

Don't they understand that he is shattered of body and mind? That Mia was the only thing keeping him sane, and now she's gone, he's blaming himself. His actions, the trigger, sent this whole flaming fireball of shit rolling forward into the dark abyss we now find ourselves trapped in. *You are as much to blame, if not more. She was our friend first.* My mind seethes, calling me out for being a Judas.

Out of the corner of my eye, I watch as a visibly pale Mateo slides down the wall, wrapping his arms around his knees and pulling harshly on his shorn dark locks. A cascade of clear tears trails down his face in a river of misery. He doesn't even attempt to hide the sobs leaving his chest as Raegan crouches down and wraps him in her arms, speaking soothing words into his ear.

Fuck, I am so worried about him. All the shit he just survived and then Mia going missing is wrecking what was already left of his sensitive soul.

The memory of the blade I pulled from his hands a few days ago as he tried to slit his wrists makes a shudder run down my body. Terror tries once again to rise at the image of my best friend, hurting himself. He almost succeeded in ending his own life. If I hadn't been worried about him and gone looking for him because of this sinking feeling in my gut, the unthinkable could have happened. *We have to protect him, even from himself.*

The image of his blotchy and tear-streaked face and his distraught words run on a vicious cycle through my mind. *"I betrayed her, Finn. I hurt her, when all she did was love me. She did everything to find me and when she did, I refused her. I broke her heart with June. I deserve to die! I should have died in that cabin in the woods. You all should have let me die. You should have never come looking for me."*

His tears and the action he almost completed have essentially destroyed what was left of me. Those images haunt my waking and sleeping hours. Not that I fucking sleep; no one in this godforsaken house does. How can I sleep when she is still out there?

Theo's silence was deafening when I told him what had happened and how we had to keep a closer eye on Mateo. He had no words of encouragement, no answer on what to do. He didn't make any move to demand that Mateo stop that shit. I was stunned and hurt at his cold state. Is there really nothing left of my best friend and brother? Has he really turned off his emotions and humanity? Perhaps it's because he, too, is contemplating his own demise? Does he, too, wish we had never saved him?

All the fight leaves my body, and I step back, looking over Clark's shoulder and watching as Carter peels out of the driveway with a loud shriek of rubber on asphalt. The car speeds towards the gate like a madman is driving it. *Fucking hell! He's gone now. I'll never catch him and stop him.*

I don't understand what Stella is doing and why she is allowing this to go down. She knows he's the most reckless and mentally unbalanced out of the group. Does she want him to die? Is she stacking the board so each one of us will perish? One by one, will we all self-destruct before we find Mia? I wouldn't put it past the fucking vicious queen of Manhattan to be plotting ways to get rid of us without having to sully her own hands.

The truth is Carter has been losing his mind daily here at the estate. The walls of this house now show the evidence of his uncontrollable rage in every room. Not to mention Theo is sporting so many bruises and injuries across his body from going toe-to-toe with Carter constantly.

Carter can't even be in the same room with Theo anymore without attempting to bloody him. Their friendship and brotherhood has been tested daily, and right now, I don't think things will ever go back to the way they were between them. He will never forgive Theo if Mia is not found, and even then, I am not sure their relationship can be salvaged.

I get it. I do. My anger towards Theo and this whole situation is just right under my skin, ready at any moment to boil over. I want to hurt the fucker just as much as Carter does. This was all his doing, not that we are innocents. We all played our parts, me more than anyone else other than Theo. His need to control the situation, to dictate what he thought was best, was the cause of all this tragedy.

My words, however, were the catalyst. I should have never told them who Mia was. I once again backstabbed the girl I love. My best friend growing up and the owner of my heart. I knew the information I was sitting on was a ticking time bomb. One that would explode and cause catastrophic damage.

Did I choose the girl I love and protect her? I tried in my own way to protect her, but once again, my actions caused irreparable damage. I was a coward who should have confessed to her that I knew who she was. One that should have immediately fallen at her feet and pleaded for mercy.

I was right, of course. Telling my fellow kings that Mia Stratford was Amelia Hamilton was devastating to them, but to my fucking astonishment, none of them seemed to really care after processing the information. They still wanted her, needed her with the same ferocity as they do air.

It didn't change their feelings for her. If anything, it cemented them further. Knowing that she was always ours, even when she was younger, and we put her through hell. The girl we tortured and abused came back for vengeance. One that we all wholeheartedly deserved. Not one amongst us disputed that fact. Mia was owed her avengement for what we did to her when she was Amelia.

The part where all of this gets even more fucked up is the danger we ultimately put her in. The one we convinced her into by bringing an overdosed Carter into her house, consequently putting her on Vincent Saint-Lambert's psychotic radar. The deranged fucker got one look at our powerful queen and immediately got a hard-on for her.

He saw Mia in her powerful, unapologetic element when she refused him access to Carter and Theo. Her demeanor showed him that she didn't fear him and would fight him to keep us safe. That was an aphrodisiac to a sadistic psychopath like Vincent, who enjoyed breaking women. He got a taste of her power, and it made him hungry for more.

That one moment in that room led us down this path of no return. My three best friends and brothers suffered horrifically at his insane hands as he tried to get to Mia. Just as things were calming down slightly and becoming our new crazy normal. I gave my brothers the flint that would light the match. I let them into the secret I had been holding for weeks, the one that should have stayed locked in my heart.

Our need to protect her and keep her safe from Vincent forced us to do the unthinkable. Push the girl that each of us loves, the one we would all die for, away.

Did we tell her about our fears and expose our hearts to her, like normal fucking functioning human beings? No, of course not. That would have been too easy. No, the four of us decided, led by Theo's fucking idiotic controlling mind. To use the fact that she lied to us and came here with motives to hurt us and destroy our reign as kings of Casbury, to push her away. *What fucking useless idiots we are, doomed to make the same mistake over and over.*

We once again used vicious tactics and damaging words against her like weapons. We turned our backs on her and made her believe that we never cared. That we used her, and she was nothing to us. In actuality, we wanted her to leave us behind and return to the safety of the Stratford compound. To go back to

Stella's fortress, where an army would keep her safe from Vincent. *We knew we couldn't protect her ourselves, from that psychopath.*

Did we ever even stop to think that our actions and words would make her run from us the way that she did? *Not even once.* We thought we would drive the wedge between the five of us, and she would just leave of her own accord. She would cut ties with us but make us painfully regret our existence.

A punishment all of us were more than willing to pay if it meant our little queen was safe. The hope was that once the threat of Vincent was eliminated. We could return to her on our knees, through no doubt, the broken glass she would make us trudge through.

My Mia has a craving for sweet revenge. I wouldn't have put it past her to throw us out on our asses in wrath at our words and deeds and risk Vincent getting his hands on us, especially after the way we treated her.

Unfortunately, that would have been the better outcome. The one all four of us, would have gladly taken and endured rather than what did happen. Mia left, unable to take any more of our abusive and callous behavior, to return to Manhattan, but she did it without telling us. What was she afraid of? Her own lack of willpower or that we wouldn't let her go? That thought constantly circles in my mind and haunts my nightmares. *You're to blame, asshole.*

She left us here, in her house, and ran. Behavior so out of character for my warrior queen. Somewhere between here and the private airport strip, she was run off the road by some unknown force and taken.

Then fucking Vincent shows up, giving us the blessing and the mercy of his death. Only for us to realize that while she was now safe from one demon, another monster had captured her. We have been grasping at straws ever since to try to find her, not knowing who even has her. That not knowing makes vivid nightmares run through our minds on autopilot nonstop.

"If he dies, if something happens to him, Stella, Mia will never forgive you." I meet her ice-cold blue eyes, the lines of strain clearly evident across her forehead. The woman has aged a decade in the weeks since Mia's disappearance. The cold queen exterior is a facade, and we are beginning to see the fissures with every day that Mia is missing. I turn toward her, squaring my shoulders and bringing myself to my imposing six-foot-three height.

"If he dies, you better pray I get to you first, queen of Manhattan. I'll give you an easier death than she will."

I see Theo from the corner of my eye, trying to move towards us, to stop my words and actions before Stella does me harm. *Fuck that shit; I am not afraid of Stella Stratford.* The fucker is always trying to protect everyone but himself. I wish he had more self-preservation. Right now, he should worry about keeping his damn self alive and Carter from killing him slowly, piece by painful piece.

I don't wait for anyone's response, pushing through Clark and Theo's rigid bodies and making my way out the front door. I can't breathe in this fucking house, surrounded by the memories of the girl I love and knowing I helped destroy whatever future we could have had. *I betrayed her. I am a monster.*

CHAPTER 7
Mateo

"So it's true, when all is said and done, grief is the price we pay for love." E.A. Bucchianeri, Brushstrokes of a Gadfly

I watch as Finn disappears out the front door, and Theo turns on his heel and takes the steps back into his room at breakneck speed. A sigh leaves my lips as I drag my hands across my face to remove the tears that are like unending rivers. Raegan moves away from me, the heat of her embrace leaving me cold once again.

My body feels like it has had permanent permafrost since Mia disappeared. My heart beats only for the girl that is missing, leaving a gap that can't be plugged without her. The feeling of desperation runs through my body, causing a cold sweat to once again break out across my skin. We have to find her. I need her back. I have to somehow make it up to her. Make her see that I never wanted this. She is my everything; without her, I might as well be dead.

I feel like a panic attack is about to crest, the tightness in my chest a constant companion. There's buzzing in my ears, and my stomach tightens and then lurches. I stumble to my feet and run down the hallway, making it to the guest powder room, where I am brought down to my knees, emptying the meager contents of my stomach into the white toilet bowl. Once nothing is left to purge, I stumble backward, landing on my ass. My limbs feel weak and useless. My head tips back against the vanity, and once again, thoughts and memories plague me and run through my mind.

June rises to the tip of her toes, and my head bends toward her. "Mateo, I know you love her, but I need you. I...I can't do this without you."

June's words are spoken with fear and desperation, tears slipping down her battered cheeks. Our lips touch, and mine open for the sweep of her tongue. A relieved gasp leaves June while my heart pounds in my chest and my mind screeches that this is not right. Allowing this to happen will destroy what we have with Mia. My Mia, the only girl who has ever understood my anxiety and can see into my heart and soul.

The sharp realization that this is not what I want despite everything I experienced and lived through with June. She would never be the girl for me. An ocean-blue-eyed vixen captured my heart from the moment I laid eyes on her in the courtyard of Casbury prep. She owns the heart that beats painfully in my chest. She is the keeper of my soul, and I cannot give it to June or anyone else. Move away from June; my heart begs me.

A noise at the room's entrance has me turning my gaze away from June. Instinct has me grabbing her and pulling her into my body to block her from whoever might attempt to hurt us. A pained cry leaves her lips at my rough treatment. My heart pounds in my chest, fear riding me as my grip tightens and my body prepares to fight.

My fiery, determined gaze meets devastated blue eyes. The look of shock and pain across her features before she schools her face and constructs the mask she wears that hides all her thoughts from me. Mia is standing there in the doorway of the room. She's so still, her body locked tight.

My heart skips a beat, clenching painfully and causing all my injuries to be felt throughout my body. All the hairs on my arms stand on end at the stern look emanating from her. She's displeased, no fuck that; she's more than just displeased. If I wasn't injured and a pitiful creature right now, I have no doubt my little queen would be beating me into the ground and ripping out my beating heart. She should do it, we just betrayed her, my heart seethes in the chamber of my chest.

June shifts herself from my grasp and places her hand on my chest in a demonstration of possession. One that has my hackles rising as I shift from one uncomfortable foot to another. A moment of heavy silence fills the air, feeling weighed down and ominous. A bead of sweat trickles down my back at the cloying unease in the room.

I watch as Mia tracks the motion, her jaw clenches, and her eyebrow rises as she meets my gaze. Fuck, I am on dangerous ground here. Would Mia attack June in her present condition? She's a lioness ready to attack; she will take back what is hers and give no quarter to anyone who infringes on her possessions. I am hers.

Mia doesn't fucking share. She has warned us time and time again of that fact. Now here is June trying to lay claim to me. Right in front of my violent and destructive queen, a claim that I am now positive I don't want. My heart only beats for the blonde in front of me.

"Mia...thank you for saving us...and the medical care." June's voice comes out unsteady and hesitant. She leans her body closer to mine, and I watch as Mia's nostrils flare. Ah fuck!

Mia tilts her head in consideration of the sight before her. Her jaw tightens, and the vein in her neck does jumping jacks before my eyes. Is she contemplating violence right now? Will she attack me, June, both of us? I don't know whether to be horrified, frightened, or turned the fuck on. Get it together motherfucker; this is serious! My mind bellows.

"Mary says you can leave the medical room, that your tests are back. Each of you will require further rounds of antibiotics to...recover...from what you have experienced...and caught in captivity."

Mia steps further into the room, the picture of power with her head held high and her posture stiff. My unbending queen, the one that takes no prisoners and gives as good as she gets. Her lips are in a tight grimace, and her clenched fists give away the fact that we hurt her. What she saw when she walked into this room has cut her deep, but she will never give anyone the satisfaction of seeing how much, especially not me.

Her words bring an immense and immediate feeling of shame within me. I feel heat rising up my suddenly slick back as prickles of heat erupt across my neck and scalp. Damn it! She knows that both June and I have caught not one but two sexually transmitted diseases from Vincent and his lackeys.

Pure disgust at myself and what we endured fills me and threatens to have me purging my stomach of all its contents. Fuck, there is no doubt that she is aware that June and I were intimate. Even though it was coerced and nothing but torture at Vincent's hands. Maybe she knows or suspects that I was raped too? The thought brings a tinge of shame to my mind and heart.

I want to beg for her forgiveness, even though there was no way for me to stop what happened to us. The desire to appeal for her understanding rises within me, but my words are a giant boulder trapped in my throat, refusing to be released. Say something, say anything, you fool! My mind begs, but not a sound leaves my mouth. Even though my heart pounds painfully in my chest.

I'm a fucking irredeemable cunt. I don't deserve Mia's forgiveness or even her understanding. I'm no longer locked in that room with June and under the presence of Vincent's threats and violence. I'm free, and I know what I'm doing and what I am allowing to happen here.

Mia just caught me standing in a room in her house, kissing another woman while she's being treated like shit by my fellow kings. I deserve whatever comeuppance she serves me.

"The staff has prepared a room for you, June."

I watch with horror as June lifts her chin, her fear-plagued eyes meeting mine. She's still scared, and I know being here hasn't put her at ease. Despite all the security around us, she is still afraid. I am not sure if she's worried Vincent will get to us here or if it's the knowledge that Mia owns my heart.

"That's okay...I will stay with Mateo." Ah fuck, June has no idea that her words are baiting a bear right now, or does she? She wouldn't be so reckless to try to start something with Mia, would she? Does she not understand the danger that Mia represents?

I watch as Mia tries to restrain herself, the strain on her face showing me how hard she's trying to control herself. Her hands clench and unclench at her side as her jaw tightens, and I can tell she's grinding her teeth from a distance. Her eyes are filled with blue fire, promising a world of hurt to both June and me. Holy fucking shit.

She's jealous? Jesus, wow! I never thought I would see the day Mia would be jealous over me. Honestly, I never thought I would be stupid enough to give her a reason to be but look at where I am right now, like a complete dumbass.

Damn it. Mia, filled with jealousy, is a sight to behold. If this goddamn situation weren't so messed up, I would even tease her about it. But right now, I don't have the balls or the right.

"I see." Mia grits out the words between clenched teeth. "Is that what you think is best, Mateo?"

The question cuts through me like a knife. Her words, intentionally laced with venom, cause a shiver to race down my spine. My mind begs me to tread lightly here; Mia is one moment away from raining fiery hell down on us.

Mia's leaving it in my court to decide between the two of them. This is not about a room or even where June ends up staying. It's a declaration of which girl I'm going to be with. I'm a fucking chew toy between them. My anxiety is rising inside of me. I don't want to fight with Mia; that is a battle I will not win. I also don't want to hurt either of them. What the hell do I do here? Mother fucker, no matter what you do, you're going to hurt both of them.

Theo's deep voice slips through my mind. "It's the only way to protect her, to push her away." No, fuck, there has to be another way. I can't do that to her; it will devastate her. It will fucking crush me. I won't survive her loss. Theo always leads, and we just follow, but my heart is telling me not to follow this time. We are going to lose her. Think about this! My mind urges. What if something happens? What if Vincent gets his hands on her?

My heart aches and starts to rip apart with the knowledge that I am about to hurt her to try to save her. No matter what I might desire, I have to put Mia first. She's my everything; I can never let Vincent Saint-Lambert get his hands on her. Especially not after the hell June and I just survived. The thought of Vincent and his evil minions hurting and using Mia the way they did June brings a sense of profound dread to the pit of my stomach.

"Yes, it would be best if June stayed with me in my room." I see the satisfaction cross June's face from the corner of my eye. She got what she wanted, regardless of the intention behind my words.

Nausea threatens to bring me to my knees. I just lied to the girl I'm in love with. To the one that is my everything and owns my heart. I also just misled June after she helped keep me alive. If there was a hole I could crawl into that would allow me to disappear, I would gladly do it.

I watch as my words register on her face, hitting her like blades with an accuracy that terrifies me. Then her mask slips across her features, her eyes trail across my body, from the top of my head to my feet, and I feel blistering cold and anger in their wake. My mouth opens, the words on the tip of my tongue about to beg for her forgiveness, pray for her mercy, and throw my brothers under the bus with the truth of what is going on here.

I don't get the chance, however, even to utter a syllable. With one last scathing look in my direction, Mia turns on her heels and leaves the room. Her head is still held high, her posture rigid, and no doubt images of murdering me and June are running through her mind.

I push away from June and put much-needed space between us. My skin burns from her contact. My heart squeezes painfully as my mind warns that we have just ended our very world with our deceitful words.

"Fuck, what have I done?" The words leave my lips as agony fills my limbs. All the shit Vincent put me through, all the terrors I survived, nothing hurt as much as crushing my girl like I just did.

I pull the shaving blade I pilfered from Clark two weeks ago from my front pocket. The cold, sharp metal surface helping to bring my thoughts back to the here and now. I grab the back of my shirt and pull it off my body. The body that is still emaciated and scarred from my time in captivity. My eyes traverse over the lines that now mar my flesh in a macabre geometric pattern. The sight of them helps my heart rate slow down to a more manageable level.

The first slice with the blade brings a sting, a moment of pain, before euphoria hits and brings with it a sense of grounding relief. The pain helps to clear the ghosts of my mistakes from my mind. The first drop of blood that wells on my skin has my breath stuttering in my chest and then leaving my mouth in a harsh gasp. This has been the only way that I have been able to manage the last three weeks.

Especially after Finn stopped me from slitting my wrists in a moment of deep desperation and ending my life permanently. Although I am grateful to him for pulling me back from the edge, the pain and overwhelming panic are still there every second of every day. Every moment without Mia is agony and another step into the dark hole that wants to claim my very life.

The feel of momentary sharp pain, just a payback for the anguish I caused Mia with my actions. It's never enough, though, hence all the different lines that mark my skin. Will I ever be able to make amends for what I have done? Will Mia ever be able to forgive my actions, words, and the hurt that I caused her?

You are weak. The thought races through my mind as I make another line.

CHAPTER 8

Mateo

"Hearts can break. Yes, hearts can break. Sometimes I think it would be better if we died when they did, but we don't." Stephen King, Hearts in Atlantis

You *don't deserve another chance.* The thought pushes through my mind, giving me no peace. No, I probably don't. Hence I need to live in my memories of the good times with my girl. The places in my mind that no one can take from me, not even her. They will be all that I have left of her, whether she is found or not.

"Mateo!" Her voice is high-pitched as a giggle escapes her lips. The sound brings rays of sunshine with it to my heart. A melody I crave, just like I do the feel of her skin. I push her further into the darkened kitchen pantry, lined with white shelves and food, and silence her with a kiss, forcing her lips to part for my tongue. A groan makes its way out of my mouth and is swallowed up by her own needy moans.

We haven't had a moment alone without one of my fellow kings in days. My need for her is at a crushing level. Ever since I fucked her in the bathroom, reclaiming her sexy body from Theo's primal chase through the house. I haven't been able to stop the overwhelming nonstop hunger for her. It's a blazing fire through my veins, one that has my cock hard and weeping pearls of cum.

I slip my hand in between our bodies and thrum her hardened nipples through her pale blue shirt. A low growl leaves my lips when I realize she's not wearing a bra underneath. Fuck yes! I pull on her stiff nipples between my two fingers until a cry leaves her mouth. Pulling back from the passionate kiss, I slide my fingers inside the bottom of her top. My fingers ghost over her soft, warm skin, leaving goosebumps in their wake.

"Mateo..." Her moan calls to me like a siren's call, beckoning me to come closer and worship her with all my breaths. The light is dim in the small room, provided by a motion sensor that illuminates the shelves. I pull her top up higher, ripping it from her skin so her gorgeous round breasts are in my sightline.

"Fuck, you are so beautiful. You take my breath away, Mia."

I lean forward, taking one of her stiff peaks in my mouth, my tongue lashing it over and over. Her nails dig sharply into the skin on my arms, the pain adding another level of heat to our embrace. She holds onto me, her limbs trembling as I lick across her warm flesh, leaving open-mouth kisses in my wake.

"Are you wet, mami? Does this sweet pussy need my thick cock? Do you crave a hard fuck, my little reina?"

My fingers drift down to the waist of her black leggings. Pulling the fabric away from her skin and pushing it down over the round, firm globes of her ass. My fingers meet the warm flesh, and my cock twitches in its confinement in my pants. Fuck, I would love to run my length between her two firm asscheeks and watch as my tip peaks out as I cum all over her back.

Drenching and painting her with cum is one of the hottest things that she lets me do to her. My little slut of a queen likes to be covered in all of our cum. She enjoys it when I possess her and force her to take my hard cock in all her holes. Stretching her tight pussy and puckered hole with my girth and forcing her to take all of me until I'm balls deep inside of her. Her cunt is perfect, made to take mine and my best friends' cocks.

"*Mateo, I need you.*" *Her voice is soft and filled with passion, the sound making my heart rate speed up inside my chest until it feels like a bunch of Stallions are racing in there.*

"*Mami, pull down these leggings, so I can feel that drenched pussy.*"

I skate my lips over her neck and up to her jaw, where I graze my teeth and listen to her breath hitch in her mouth. She slides her hands down her body, pushing the tight leggings over her toned thighs and down to her ankles. I slide my hand to her waist, helping to steady her as she steps out of the tights and stands before me in just a scrap of pink silk.

A wet spot visible on the material, even in the dim light, right over her plump lips. Fuck, I need a taste of her. I need to rub my face continually on her flesh and drench myself in her scent. Every part of me wants to be owned by Mia and to possess her in return. She is mine, and I need to claim her again.

I lower myself to my knees as one of her hands makes its way into my long, thick hair. Her fingers stroke my dark tresses before she gets a firm grip, pulling my head closer to her core. Her other hand trails up her abdomen and reaches her breast, kneading the warm, soft flesh as a whimper leaves her lips. Fuck, she is the sexiest woman that I have ever seen. Watching her bring herself pleasure has pearls of precum sliding down my throbbing cock.

I grab her calf, forcing her leg to rise and push it over my shoulder so that her body is open before me. A feast for a starving man and one I plan to ravish. "*Baby, I'm going to eat this sweet cunt, but you need to be quiet. Otherwise, the others will find us.*" *Fuck, I hope those bastards stay away so I can enjoy my fill uninterrupted. I'm all for sharing her tight pussy, but right now, I want it all to myself.*

I swipe my tongue over the wet spot on her panties, getting my first hit of her tangy and musky taste. Hell, she tastes delicious, an aphrodisiac to a deprived man. If I could have her numerous times a day, it would never be enough. I wish we had room in this small pantry so I could lie below her and let her ride my face with abandonment until she cummed, suffocating me in her juices and scent.

My cock is so painfully hard in my pants that it's pressing relentlessly against the harsh zipper, demanding to be set free from its confines. I use my finger to slide her panties to the side until her plump bare lips are exposed to my waiting tongue.

My tongue slides over her folds, licking up every drop of wetness before moving up to her hard little nub. Her sweet moans are going to be my undoing.

I suck hard on her tight little bundle of nerves, and a cry leaves her lips. I watch from below my lashes as her head tips back on her neck and her dirty blonde hair cascades down her back, while her eyes close, and she enjoys my mouth's ministrations. I slide my pierced tongue through her wet folds and impale her tight hole, thrusting in and out like my cock is desperate to do.

"Fuck, Mateo...feels so...good!" She pants, her breathing sounding ragged to my straining ears.

"Shhh baby, I want to enjoy this pretty cunt without the others," I mumble into her delicious skin. Her scent is making my eyes want to cross with pleasure.

My hand trembles as I move it up the back of her leg, enjoying the softness of her warm skin. I slide a finger through her perky asscheeks and over her puckered hole. Rubbing and then slipping the tip inside as she clenches down hard on my tongue.

"More...Mateo...I need...more." She begs between soft moans.

My thumb slides inside her tight channel alongside my tongue, stretching her hole and thrusting in and out as my forefinger mimics the same motion inside her puckered hole. In no time, her grip on my hair tightens, and her body seizes up tight. I watch as goosebumps break out across all her beautiful flesh, and a pink blush streaks across her chest and neck. Fucking beautiful!

She comes with a gush that wets my face and drips down my chin and a loud cry that has me coating the inside of my boxers with thick creamy precum. I lap at her skin, wanting and needing to capture every drop of her essence. Mine. She is all mine!

Once the waves of ecstasy have subsided to small aftershocks, I pull my fingers from her sweet body. Standing up, I grab the back of her neck, twisting her around and forcing her to bend forward and grasp one of the shelves. "I'm going to fuck you hard and fast, Mia. My dick is going to leave a permanent imprint on this pretty pussy."

"Fuck, Mateo, stop talking and slip that huge cock inside me." She gasps as she struggles to hold herself up. She's boneless and gorgeous and, for this one moment in time, completely mine.

I unbutton and unzip my pants slowly, torturing both of us. Her body is a live wire, thrumming with electricity, and I can't wait to plunge myself into her so we can both burn. My cock head is protruding over the waistband of my blue boxers and is covered in pearls of cum. I yank my boxers down, freeing it from its confinement and stroking it firmly in my grasp. A moan leaves my lips. I'm already so worked up that it won't take me long once I'm inside of Mia's tight heat.

Pulling her asscheek aside, my mouth salivates as both her tight holes clench, awaiting the pounding my hard dick is about to give them. Fuck, I hope I can hold off long enough to fuck both. I rub my cock through her wetness, sliding the throbbing head through her folds, over her clit, and back down to her tight hole. My grasp on her neck tightens as I pull back and slam inside her, bottoming out in one ruthless go and forcing her to brace or fall on her beautiful face.

"Mateo...fuck...too big!" A cry of pain leaves her lips, but I don't wait for her body to adjust. I pull out almost to the tip and slam inside again, my heavy balls slapping against her swollen pussy lips and clit. Her whimpers are causing my nuts to tighten, and all I want to do is desperately flood her tight pussy with my seed. I'm fighting the urge to cum. I pull back and try to regain some control. She feels so good, so tight and wet.

"You will take all of it, mami. This pretty cunt was made for fucking hard and rough." A grunt leaves my lips as I hit the end of her and push her ruthlessly into the shelves in front of her. "This sweet pussy is mine. You're going to show me that you're my good girl, and it belongs to me."

I fuck her hard and fast until incomprehensible words and moans are leaving her lips. My thumb slides across her clit, stroking and rubbing it in deep circles. Her pussy clenches and strangles my cock.

Fuck! I take deep breaths through my nose, trying to slow the galloping of my heart. I want to cum, but I need her to go one more time before I do. "That's my good girl, strangle my cock with this tight pussy. Milk me, my little slutty reina. Your pussy was made for taking a pounding."

I stroke her clit and pinch it between two fingers. The combination of my dirty words, my hard strokes, and the pressure on her clit, has her pussy clenching me in a tight vise grip as she explodes. The spasms in her core are my undoing and push me over the edge as they strangle my cock right into heaven, and I cum hard and deep inside of her.

"Fuck, Mia!" I grunt, my mouth latching onto the side of her neck and biting down until my body is depleted. Pleasure rises and continues to fill me with the thought that she will be sporting my mark, where the other fuckers can see.

She's mine, all fucking mine right now. Her sweet pussy is coated in my cum. Fuck, I'm already hard again. I need to pound her tight ass next and flood it too with my cum until it's dripping out of her.

The door to the pantry opens without warning, and light floods inside. I use my body to block whoever is standing there the view of Mia's body, only allowing them to see my bare ass instead. These fucking assholes have the worst timing.

"You dirty hound! My damn cereal and treats are in there!" Raegan screeches! "Mia, you are nasty girl! There's food in there!" Raegan's disgusted voice greets us and has both Mia and me laughing as I slip from her body.

Banging on the outside of the door startles me from my daydreams of Mia. "Mateo, what the fuck are you doing in there? Are you okay?" Finn's loud, deep voice penetrates through the solid door.

I stare down at the drying blood streaking my skin. The blade is still clutched in my hand, awaiting the next cut across my skin. The loss of the memory makes my chest ache. I need her back. I can't live without her.

What if she never returns? What then? My mind questions with an agonized whimper.

Then there is no point in living another day without her. If she doesn't return, I will make sure I don't breathe another moment longer without her on this miserable earth.

CHAPTER 9

Mia

"The bravest thing I ever did was continuing my life when I wanted to die." Juliette Lewis

"**B**end forward, you dirty cunt, grab those ankles and show our audience that wealthy pussy!"

When I don't cooperate fast enough, the leather belt crosses my left arm with a harsh lash. I bite back the scream that tries to leave my throat, refusing to give these fuckers what they want. Another lash strikes in the same spot, and the flesh gives way with a searing pain. The feeling of wetness lets me know he has once again broken the skin, and I'm bleeding. *Motherfucker!* He's going to run out of flesh to rip open.

"I'm going to fucking kill you, you sick bastards!" I shout between clenched teeth, forcing myself to bend until my face is between my legs. The unbearable pain racking my body as I lower my head causes my vision to get spotty and my head to spin. Laughter greets my threat just like it has every day that I have had to perform these degrading and horrific tasks for these sickos.

Perverts that want to watch the Stratford heir be degraded, abused, and assaulted on the dark web. Fuckers that I am sure are also my grandmother's enemies, as well as being vile creatures.

James the fucker is charging two hundred and fifty thousand dollars for one of these shows, so it's not your average pervert watching. No, it's rich, privileged men that like the idea of bringing a Stratford woman down low.

A safe fuck you to my grandmother hidden behind the safety of their screens. They may think they're protected, but whenever I get out of here I am going to make sure to track each and every one of them down and murder them myself. Everything I am enduring will have retribution. I swear it on my blackened soul.

"Make her spread those cheeks and show us that gaping hole, dirty whore that she is!" A garbled male voice shouts from the laptop.

"You heard the man, princess Stratford, spread those sweet cheeks and give them what they want."

Humiliation fills me once again at having to perform not only for these sickos on the web but also for James. The man is my fucking blood. I always knew he was an evil man.

After all, my mother had him charged and incarcerated for what he tried to do to me and her when I was little. Those memories were buried deep inside my mind, inaccessible under lock ,and key until over a week ago.

Every new traumatizing moment in his company has new disturbing images appearing in my mind, causing me to lose another sliver of my sanity. Now under the constant abuse he's subjecting me to, they fill my waking and sleeping thoughts, and I can no longer block them out.

"Amelia, sweetheart, come here, daddy needs his sweet girl to help him with something."

I slowly skip up to my father, excitement and fear all meshed into one at what my daddy may want. He's being extra nice to me today. He even brought me some new books and brand-new crayons to color with. I drag Molly, my dolly, with me, holding her tight against my chest.

Sometimes daddy pretends to be nice to me, but he hurts me. He tells me I'm his big girl and that I have to listen and do what I'm told if I want to be his princess.

I'm not sure if I want to be his princess. I thought princesses didn't get hurt, but daddy hurts me sometimes. I have never seen a princess get hurt in the movies by her daddy.

Momma had to go to work early today, and Mrs. Simpson, our neighbor, wasn't back yet from her trip to her sister's house. Momma looked so scared when she left. She told me to stay in my room with the door locked and away from my daddy, but he came looking for me with my gifts, and I unlocked the door.

I wanted to go across the street to my best friend Finn's house, he's six just like me, and show him my new gifts. He likes to look at all the pretty pictures in the books; we don't know how to read yet. I wanted to go color with him, so we could draw momma a nice picture and make her smile. She's so pretty when she smiles. She hasn't smiled in a long time since daddy came back from being gone. All she does is cry now. Daddy said I had to stay in the house and be his good girl, though.

I hug Molly tighter as I move closer to him, but he grabs the front of my blue dress, dragging me roughly into his big lap. I lose my grip on Molly, and a cry leaves my lips as she falls to the ground. He pulls me into his chest, holding me too tight.

"That's my sweet girl. Don't you want to help daddy? Don't you like the books and crayons daddy brought?"

I nod my head slowly, not sure if I really want to, but too afraid to say no to him in case he smacks me. A tear skates down the side of my face, and snot starts to trickle down my nose. I want to wipe it with my hand, but he's taken both of my hands into his much bigger one, and he's holding them tight.

"Daddy...you're hurting me. I want Molly!"

I feel something warm and slippery underneath the skirt of my blue dress brushing up against my thigh and bum, and a cry leaves my lips. I don't like it when daddy's worm touches me. It feels gross and dirty.

I start to squirm, trying to loosen my grip from his hands, and a harsh grunt leaves his lips. His mouth lands on my neck, and I can feel his warm breath against my skin, and my tummy doesn't feel so good anymore. I think I'm going to be sick, and I want my momma.

Tears trail down my face, and my chest rises and falls quickly. Huge sobs are leaving my lips, and I can feel my face and neck getting really hot. Daddy's breath is too hot on my skin. I don't like it. I want him to stop! I don't want the crayons or books no more.

"That's it, sweetness, just a little more. Pretend you're on a ride at the fair, slide back and forth for daddy." He grunts.

"I want momma!" I try bucking against him and screaming, but his hand comes around my face, covering my mouth and part of my nose as I thrash in his lap. I cry, the tears making their way down my face and soaking the front of my pretty dress.

A groan leaves his lips just as the front door slams open, catching his attention and mine. Momma stands there shaking and pointing a gun at us. A river of tears down her bruised face as her busted-up lips tremble. Her eye is really purple now, a color I don't like, and she can't open it so I can see her blue eyes.

"Let go of my daughter, you fucker, or I will end you right here."

The sound of sirens can be heard in the background, getting closer. Daddy's hand releases from my mouth and nose. I let out a scream as loud as I can, "MOMMA!" I'm so scared that I pee my pants right where I am on daddy's lap and over his worm.

I have never seen my momma with a gun before. Is she going to hurt me? Have I been a bad girl like daddy always says? Is she going to spank me now and send me to my room? I want to get away from daddy. I don't like these games he needs help with. I...I don't want to play anymore!

"Amelia, move away from daddy, my love. You come right over here where momma is." I try pulling away from daddy, but his hand wraps around my throat tightly, and I can't breathe.

"I'll kill her, Cathy. I'll snap her fucking neck if you try anything!"

"How could you do this to your own child, James? You're fucking sick! Do you know that? You're going to rot in hell for what you have done to Amelia and me."

My chest is tight, and I can't keep my eyes open. Daddy's holding me too tight, and momma is scaring me with her screams. Just as my eyes start to close, I hear shouts from the front door behind momma. I think I see a police officer, and then there's a large bang, but I can't keep my eyes open anymore, and I slump in daddy's lap.

The memory overtakes me and has my legs buckling and me falling to the ground. I try to catch my breath, my breathing is ragged, and not enough air is making its way into my lungs. My head spins some more, and before I can stop it, I'm vomiting up all the granola and water from earlier all over the floor in front of me.

"Fucking weak whore!" I hear James shout behind me before he grabs onto a fistful of my hair and pulls my neck painfully back.

"MAKE HER LICK IT UP!" One of the voices on the laptop yells to the cheers of others.

"You heard them cunt, lick up the mess you just made on my nice floor." He forces my face to rub in the puke on the floor. "Clean it, Amelia, or I'll make it hurt even more." His fingers pinch my nose, and I'm forced to pry my lips open to get air. He uses that moment to push my face into the vomit, and I get a mouth full of my own puke again.

"TEACH THAT WHORE A LESSON, FUCK HER WITH THE DIL-DO AGAIN!" A deep voice cheers from the laptop.

"FUCK HER ASS, TEAR THAT HOLE OPEN TILL IT BLEEDS!" Another voice yells.

My whole body seizes up tightly, and I start to thrash wildly, not caring that thick strands of my hair are being ripped out in his fist. "NO, PLEASE, NO! I'll clean it up, please," I beg as wretched sobs sound in the air around us, and in the background, cheers rise from the sickos watching. Even though I try, I can't stop them from leaving my throat. The fear seizes me tightly, and I can no longer control my panic. It washes over just as desperation fills my body. *I need to get out of here. I need to kill all of them.*

"You heard the paying customers, Amelia! They get what they want." His hold on my hair doesn't release, but he bends my neck at an awkward angle until I feel like it might actually snap and end my miserable life. God, I hope he kills me right now. I don't know how much more of this abuse I can take.

Theo and Mateo survived much worse, and for longer, you can too. I want to be strong like Stella, but the truth is I'm weak, and I know it. As much as I try to fight back, it only worsens the abuse. It makes them enjoy hurting me even more. They get off on my refusal to submit, viewing it as a challenge to break me further by any means necessary. Soon enough, there will be nothing left of me to fight back with, not my body, sanity, or soul.

He pulls a vibrant green, long, thick monster dildo from the rough stone counter above me, next to where I am chained like a rabid animal to the floor.

"Please, James..." I beg as desperation fills me. An evil chuckle leaves his lips, and before I can get another word out, the hard length is shoved inside of my pussy, and a scream leaves my lips.

A burning pain sears through my core as my vagina tries desperately to expel the object. The fucker never uses lube, purposely trying to inflict as much hurt as possible. The desire to choke him with the offending dildo and force him to stop breathing fires through my blood. I try once again, in vain, to pull on the chains binding my arms and legs to the anchor on the floor. It's useless, though. They don't budge.

"Look at that pussy; swallow that monster!"

"Yes! Fuck that whore!"

"Fuck her pussy hard!"

"Make her scream! Fuck her ass too! Make the cunt bleed!"

"Fuck her asshole next, fuck that stupid bitch!"

The shouts ring out across the room, but my mind has retreated back into the dark hole that I have been hiding in for what seems an eternity since I was captured and forced to be here.

Confined like a pitiful, damaged animal while real animals torture me sadistically. The dark hole that helps to shield me from this nightmare that I am living in. That helps me forget that my biological father is raping me over and over with sex toys and beating me for a paying audience.

"Fuck, look at those plump lips, Amelia. Daddy might need to get a taste of those."

A scream leaves my lips as the thick leather belt wraps and tightens around my throat until I can't take a breath, and ribbons of light are all I see. Fuck I hope he squeezes so tight that I never wake up. It would be a blessing to die instead of having to endure any more of this abuse.

An image of four men appears in my mind before I'm pulled into blessed darkness.

CHAPTER 10

Carter

"Remorse is the echo of a lost virtue." Edward G. Bulwer-Lytton

I press the button to roll all the windows down and let the clean North Carolina air into the Land Rover. Inhaling a deep breath and then releasing the scream that has been choking me for days. The sound vibrates through the confines of the vehicle and out the windows, disappearing into the view of the ocean and the grassy hills around me. I still can't believe that Stella let me leave Mia's estate and gave me a gun. That was fucking sick ass of the O.G. queen and also really disturbing.

I hit the radio, trying to drown out the sounds of my own breathing and my monster stretching and pleading to be let loose. Drake's *"Laugh Now Cry Later"* croons to me and makes a chuckle leave my lips. *Fuck, yes, that's what I'm talking about.*

If I'm honest with myself, I'm a bit confused as to why she did it. Maybe she's completely sick of my shit and just wanted me gone. Hoping that someone out here ends my miserable life before they find my Mia, and then she never has to put up with me again.

Fuck that shit, I plan on finding my girl first, and when I do, they will have to pry her from my dead hands. I'm about to be a damn koala where Mia is concerned. She is never leaving my sight again. Mia is fucking mine, now and forever. Stella will just have to welcome me as her new grandson, whether she wants to or not. *I'm about to put a ring on it and a ball and chain.*

I know I have made things in the house even more intolerable for everyone since Mia disappeared without a trace. *Days that we have all spent in anguish over our missing queen.* I have done some serious damage to all the walls in Mia's house, letting my anxiety get the better of me, and my fists fly with frustration. It was either that or I was going to kill someone with my bare hands. Two specific fuckers come to mind right away, both that could use a little death.

The lump on the back of my head throbs as a reminder from Raegan to act right and stop breaking shit. That little spitfire took a wood chopping board to my skull last night with no remorse for almost cracking my damn head open! After I put my fist through Mia's pantry door.

In my defense, though, it was either the door or Diego's miserable cunt face. *I should have hit his face. No one would have been angry at me then, but him.* Well, maybe Issy, but she also would have high-fived me.

The fight in RaeRae reminds me constantly that I am missing my vicious queen. It feels like one of my limbs has been ripped from my body, and no one bothered to cauterize the wound, and I am just slowly bleeding out. Her scent surrounds me in the house, the ghost of her in every single space, and there is no escaping it. The shared memories of places where we kissed or where I held her close to me overwhelm all my senses and bring me to my knees over and over.

I can't sleep, fuck I can't even close my eyes without seeing her face. The hurt that I helped inflict across her beautiful features. The image torments me and has me unable to function. My body is tightly wound every minute of the day and night, constantly in fight or flight mode. All my thoughts revolve around finding my girl.

My beast rages inside me, demanding that we find her. That we wrap her in our arms and painfully kill anyone that touched her. He wants me desperately to set the whole world ablaze, in a massive raging fire because she's gone. The only person that can bring him peace, that holds him back, is gone.

Then there's seeing Theo in Mia's space, living and breathing when I don't know if my girl is still doing the same. The fucker is wholly destroyed, his soul and heart in tattered pieces since she went missing. His whole world has crashed down around him in mere weeks. He barely survived the abuse Vincent put him through.

He was still having nightmares and recovering when Mia disappeared. Then we get the news that his psychotic father has been found brutally murdered on the side of the road, and we don't know who to send a bottle of champagne to in thanks. *That's some shady-ass shit right there.*

Not to mention he's being held semi-hostage in Mia's house by *fucking evil Queen* Stella, with the constant reminder that he no longer even has a pot left to piss in. That the wealthy, proud, and entitled Theo Saint-Lambert, the leader and king of Casbury, is penniless thanks to Vincent changing his will and ensuring Theo can't access any of his funds. Fuck, I know that has to feel demoralizing and like someone took a bat, and rammed it up his asshole *sans lube.*

Most importantly, though, and what is really breaking him apart, piece by piece, is the knowledge that he is the one that talked us into pushing our queen away, and now she's gone. Taken hostage by some unknown lunatic out there. That was the end of Theo Saint-Lambert, as the world knew him. He is now just a broken, tarnished shell of himself. Barely breathing and just waiting to die at my hands or someone else's. I have no intention of granting him absolution or a moment of peace. He can survive in hell just like the rest of us. *Drowning in his pain and his misdeeds.*

All of those facts should make me hold on tight to my brother and best friend, wanting to be by his side and supporting him. After all, I went into the devil's dungeon and almost died to fucking save that motherfucker. I shot and murdered my own father to try to get him out. At least that was a blessing in disguise and I rid this world of one more psychotic asshole.

Yet, I can't stand to look at him. I can't even be in the same room with him anymore. I have no mercy left for him. The minute I lay eyes on him, all I can see is the memory of him urging me to hurt my girl. To push her away and force her to leave us, to leave me.

I become a crazed animal whenever he tries to speak with me. My beast demands satisfaction and revenge. All I want to do is hurt him, to inflict more pain on him, because my pain is scorching me from the inside and overflowing.

I tighten my hands on the steering wheel as I fly down the highway back toward where Theo's house used to be. The images of Theo letting me beat on him, letting me tear him to pieces, and making him bleed, crosses my vision until I am not even seeing the road in front of me anymore.

No, he wasn't the one to kidnap her and take her away to god knows where, but he was the reason she ran. I drag my throbbing hand through my hair and grip the strands. Fuck, that's not right, either. We all share responsibility for that. He wasn't the only one that hurt her. The four of us did a number on her. Again. We did a number on her again! We learned nothing from our past mistakes with Amelia. Fuck, I tried to force her to her knees, to force her to suck my cock in anger! *How could I have done that to her?*

"WHAT THE FUCK!' My thoughts are quickly interrupted when I notice a black SUV with tinted windows racing toward me on the wrong side of the road. I blare on the horn in warning, but this fucker speeds up rather than slowing down and moving over. As the SUV gets closer, I recognize the vehicle's model and make.

This asswipe is just trying my fucking patience and restraint to send him to see his maker. I blare one more time on the horn and switch over to the other side of the highway, which, luckily, is empty. The fucker makes the same move, putting himself once again on a direct collision course with me.

"You want to play chicken with me, dickhead? Let's play chicken!" I scream at him through my open windows. Adrenaline runs through my veins, and just for this moment, I feel alive again. My heart pumps rapidly in my chest, and my nostrils flare with a desire to fuck him up.

I slam my foot on the gas, accelerating rapidly and gunning for him. His blacked-out Audi is looking more prominent and larger as it approaches, but I don't hesitate or back off on the gas. If Diego wants to die in a fiery crash of metal and glass, who am I to deny him? I already told the fucker I would return him to hell, where he crawled out of. *Time to go meet your maker, motherfucker!*

Just as we are about to have a head-on collision, he shifts slightly to the left, and the front of his car sideswipes the Land Rover. The sound of screeching metal against metal is so loud that my ears feel like they are going to burst. Both vehicles slide as we smash together, and I end up spinning and doing a one-eighty. My heart thuds painfully in my chest, and my eyes feel too large in my head. This crazy fucker could have killed both of us.

When my car finally comes to a loud and sudden stop with the smell of burning rubber. I'm right smack in the middle of the two-lane highway, sideways, and Diego's Audi is down the embankment on the other side of the road, its hood currently wrapped around a goddamn tree.

"MOTHERFUCKER!" I slam the car into park, race my ass out of the driver's seat, and run towards him. My heart slams in my chest, and sweat pours down my back, making my shirt cling to my frame. I rush down the embankment and to the driver's side door. When I reach it, it opens with a metallic groan, and I can hear loud laughter from inside of it. *What the ever-loving fuck is wrong with this guy?*

I stand back, shock and disbelief making their way across my mind. "Are you insane, fucker? I could have killed you!" I grab his forearm and forcefully yank him from the vehicle until he stumbles and almost falls to his knees. My hold on his arm is the only thing preventing him from face planting. *We should let him hit the dirt.* The fucker is a menace to every living thing on this planet.

More laughter leaves him in a rumble, and tears slide down his face. The scar looks more prominent as it pulls up grotesquely on the side of his face. Once again, I wonder how he got it. He's very closed mouth about it, and Mateo doesn't know cause I already asked him.

"Fuck, I...I didn't think you had it in you." He huffs out as he tries to contain his laughter. He rubs his hand down his bleeding face, a cut above his eyes, tricking blood into his left eye. He stares at the blood on his fingertips and lets out another demented cackle. His face is going to be sporting a large bruise come tomorrow from the impact with the airbag. It's already red and swelling. *Eh, fuck it, it might improve his ugly mug.*

"You didn't think I had it in me to what? Kill you? Fucker, I have been warning you over and over for days."

"I thought it was all for show, that you weren't really insane. I didn't think a prissy rich fucker like you had the balls of steel that you apparently do." The look on Deigo's face is fucked. A wide grin strikes across his features, making his green eyes sparkle with maniacal enjoyment. He really is nuts, I always thought he was, but now I am one hundred percent certain. *This guy needs to be locked up somewhere.*

"You do remember I committed patricide, right, fucker? I shot my own fucking father in cold blood and ended his psychotic life." I raise my eyebrow at him, unsure what to make of him.

Diego's grin grows even wider, if that's fucking possible, and the fucker waggles his thick dark eyebrows at me. "Shit, I had forgotten about that. You're a stone-cold killer, motherfucker! Not just some prissy, rich fuck."

I roll my eyes at him, completely done with his dramatic ass. "I'll send your stupid ass back to hell any time you want." I pull away from him and let him stumble forward, more laughter leaving his lips.

I don't know why this fucker keeps mentioning me being a "prissy rich boy". It's not like he grew up poor. The fucker grew up with just as much privilege and wealth as we did, albeit in another country. Diego is a contradiction breathing. A rich, educated Latino, filled with cunningness, malicious intent, loyal to a fault, and a heart of gold, the fucker hides like he's working for the CIA.

A metallic groan has both of us turning to stare at his car; smoke is coming from the hood in a thick wave. The front is completely wrapped around the tree, and the metal is all caved in like something out of a *Looney Toons* cartoon. I stare through the window at the deployed and blood-streaked airbag and shake my head. They all think I'm the one that's insane. Do they realize that this fool walks around looking for death?

Diego starts walking back up the embankment without a look back, heading towards my vehicle. "Where the fuck are you going?" I race after him, wondering if he's concussed or something? There is no way that the impact from that airbag hasn't fucked him up.

"Move your ass, Carter. We have places to be!" He shouts over his shoulder at me.

I drag both my hands through my hair, wondering if I'm the one with the head injury. This guy is not making any sense. *We have places to be?* What the hell does he mean by that? I finally catch up to him just as he rounds the side of the Land Rover and opens the passenger side door.

Another vehicle comes flying past us, blaring its horn, the driver screaming profanities out his window at us. I give him the finger and slide into the car just as Diego slams his door. Fuck, Clark is going to beat our asses for damaging this car. A shiver runs down my spine. Clark is one scary dude, especially when he's angry. I wouldn't want to meet that fucker in a dark alley. It's no wonder he's Stella's number one protector.

"Where the hell do you think we're going? I have to find Mia, Diego. I don't have time for these fucking games." I meet his gaze, and I watch as all signs of amusement disappear. The look of cold indifference, the mask he always wears, reappears. It's like a switch being flipped; once again, he's the cold, ruthless, manipulative asshole he always is.

"I know. I'm going to help you find her." His dark green eyes sear into mine.

"Why would you do that?" My voice is cold, and anger is once again starting to seep in. "If you think you still have a chance of trying to force her to marry you, I'll smash us both right now into the next fucking tree and end both our miserable lives." Fury seethes through me, and the desire to lay hands on the fucker fills me. My beast paces behind the bars of his confinement, asking to be released and do damage to Diego's face.

A devious smirk graces his face, and I watch, perplexed, as he straps on his seatbelt. "I knew I liked you for a reason, you unhinged motherfucker. Naw, I'm not trying to marry that Stratford princess. She's all yours if you can keep her. I have an idea of where to look, though, so let's go!" He nods his head towards the highway in front of us, and I shake my head, aggravation filling me at his enjoyment of the situation, and put the vehicle back into drive.

I notice he didn't say he wasn't trying to marry a Stratford princess, just not that one. Joy and relief fill me with his words. Let's face it, he never really had a chance of getting Mia to the altar. I've already killed two men in cold blood, and I wouldn't even blink at killing Diego. Then there's the matter of Stella Stratford. There is no way on this earth she would let this asshole marry Mia. He wouldn't be breathing thirty seconds after he tried.

An evil grin crosses my face. I might still get to put a bullet in his head or at least get a front-row seat to Stella murdering him. He might not be after my Stratford princess, but he is still after a Stratford princess, and the only other one in existence is Issy. *Diego has a death wish, after all.*

"Where are we going?" I question with curiosity as the fucker turns on the radio, and *Post Malone* starts singing about hoes and enemies being at your back.

"Back to the beginning, Carter. Where it all started."

CHAPTER 11

Mia

"Your hope is the most beautiful and the saddest in the world." Naomi Benaron, Running the Rift

A sharp pain in my side has me groaning and trying to move away from whatever is hurting me. "Wake up, you useless whore!" I feel something wet spray across my face before my hair is yanked back, my neck wretched painfully to the side, and my eyes are forced open with the pain.

James' ugly face greets me. His eyes, the ones that are identical to my own, are filled with malicious intent and rage. He hawks up phlegm and spits in my face. I feel it dripping down my cheek to my jaw, where it disappears into my neck. Revulsion and rage fill me, but I force my body not to react, not to give him what he wants. Another reason to hurt me. To take pleasure in abusing me. *Not that at this point, he even needs a reason the sick fuck.*

I groan and shift my body, trying to force myself backward and away from him. "Where do you think you're going, princess? You cost me money, little cunt. We had to end the show early."

I want to spit into his face and laugh at him. *No, fuck that. I want to scratch his damn eyes out.* He's upset he had to end his abusive, degrading, and disgusting show early for those perverts. The ones that are taking pure, sick satisfaction in watching me be raped with objects. *Fuck him and fuck them too. May they all burn in hell.*

"I'm going to make you sorry you were ever born, princess!" He drags me up to my aching knees by my hair.

"Too late, fucker, I already am. Your mother, whoever the poor bitch was, should have swallowed instead of having you. Then neither of us would be here!" I screech, pain burning across my scalp. He releases his hold on my hair and pulls away, swatting at the loose strands of hair tangled in his fingers that he ripped out.

"Harhar, the princess, has a sense of humor. Let's see how much you're laughing when I shove a dick down that tight throat of yours." His words give me pause, and I stare up at him with fear racing through all of my limbs. *He wouldn't?* He wouldn't go that far with this already sick situation. There has to be some level of evil he won't subject me to. *Please, God, let there be a line he won't cross.*

"Oh, I can see that you understand where I'm heading with this little princess. See, you're only good to me if you're making money. If you're not, I'll slit your throat like I did to your buddy Vincent and drop you on the side of the road like a dead animal."

The image of Vincent before he took him out of the cabin, tries to force its way to the forefront of my mind, but I immediately push it back. I can't let it seize me in James' presence. The damage it does to my mind leaves me vulnerable. *What the fuck do you think we are now?* My mind whimpers.

"Why? Why are you doing this? Why go to all this trouble to hurt me? Is it really just about the money? You could have ransomed me to Stella. She would have paid whatever you demanded to get me back!" My throat is raw as I shout at him. All the aches and pains throbbing painfully across my body. My core feels like it's on fire from his latest abuse with the dirty toys he uses and the infection I know I have. *Fucking gross bastard.*

He lets out a laugh that sounds unbalanced and dangerous and has me wrapping my arms tightly around my chest. I am trying desperately to make myself a smaller target for his fists and feet. The knowledge of what I am doing both scares me and makes me angry. It's a sign of weakness on my part. *I am not fucking weak. I am a Stratford.*

"It's not just about the money, Amelia. It's about all the years you and that whore mother of yours stole from me." He trails his meaty hand across his whiskered jaw. His knuckles are red and swollen from all the constant abuse he's inflicting on me. *This piece of shit enjoys hurting me, just like he did my mother all those years ago.*

"While I was locked up in that hell, you two bitches were living the life of freedom and wealth." His fist strikes out and hits me on my cheek, causing my head to slam back against the side of the island next to me. Dizziness hits me hard, and my mouth fills with blood.

A wave of nausea threatens at the foul taste of copper in my mouth. "I was stuck in a six-by-nine cell for twenty-two hours a day while you two cunts were off living a life of luxury for twelve years. Twelve fucking miserable long years, Amelia."

"No one told you to molest your own daughter, you sick fuck! Never mind beating my momma and almost killing her. You got what you deserved, and it wasn't enough!" I scream and spit the blood in my mouth at him.

His fist lands hard again against my face, this time getting my jaw and forcing my neck back. I try to shield myself with my arms when his foot slams forward, and he kicks me in my hip with his heavy boot. "Oh, you think what I did to your momma was bad, Amelia? You won't survive what else I have in store for you, girly. I'm never letting you go!" He rains down punches, and kicks on me until, once again, merciful darkness takes me. My last thought is how much I just want to die.

My head is pounding, and I can't stop my stomach from lurching. It wants to purge itself, but it's completely empty. The taste of blood fills my mouth and coats my teeth. My jaw aches as I try to wet my bleeding and torn lips with my tongue. I attempt to take a deep breath through my nose, but it's crusted with blood, and I get the taste of blood and snot down the back of my throat.

I force my eyes open, and semi-darkness greets me. I'm not sure if that's just because where I am is dark or if I'm seeing everything in a fog again. I shake my head slowly, trying desperately to clear my vision, forcing my groaning body into a semi-sitting position. My arms protest, my broken wrist useless, and my shoulders screaming in pain. The darkness abates, and I can see bright moonlight trailing through a small window, casting eerie beams of light across the dark space.

I glance around the room, trying to figure out where I am. The space seems smaller and more confined than the room he usually keeps me in. I stare in front of me, a shape appearing out of the darkness. It's then that I realize I'm sitting on the floor of the small shower, the toilet just past my sightline.

Awareness of my body has terror racing through me, and a garbled cry leaves my lips. I can feel wetness seeping out of the inside of me between my legs. I close my eyes and beg it to be blood, hoping that I am bleeding to death rather than the alternative.

I force my trembling fingers down my naked abdomen, over my abused and raw flesh, and between my legs to my swollen and painful core. I trail two shaking fingers down to my opening and feel the pool of wetness coating me and below me on the shower floor. The residue feels sticky between my fingers as I press them together. My stomach lurches once again, and I force myself to turn to my side and vomit nothing up. My stomach is painfully empty, but my body won't stop trying to purge itself.

Tremors race down my body, causing all of my limbs to shake. My head moves back and forth on my neck like a rag doll in vicious denial. I try to crawl to my knees and stumble into a beam of moonlight. Once I can see my hand clearly, I trail my fingers down again to my core, quickly rubbing them through the moisture and my swollen heated flesh, a whimper leaving my lips as I raise my hand to the light.

Whatever is inside of me is streaked with a bloody tinge. Maybe it's just discharge from the infection. *Please, just be discharge, please.* My mind begs in desperation. Even as I try to convince my mind that is what I am seeing, I can smell the sharp, sour smell of semen through my one working nostril. Horror and devastation rips through me, threatening to take what's left of my sanity.

He's raped me. James has raped me while I was unconscious and left his semen inside of me, so there would be no doubt that I knew he had done it. So that last vestige of hope that he wasn't a complete psychotic monster was destroyed instantly.

Shudders rack my body, causing all of my limbs to tighten and spasm painfully. I wrap my arms around my legs as I bring them to my chest. I need to force him to kill me in a blind rage. He won't stop now that he's crossed that line. He's going to rape me over and over now, whether I'm conscious or not. I can't survive that. I won't survive that, not with my mind intact. *I am not Stella. I am not strong enough.*

We need to get out of here! My mind screams. That little voice inside of me sounding so small and defeated. There is no way out. We've tried. *The boys will find us. Stella will find us!* No, if they were going to have found me, they would have done it by now. It's been weeks since I have been confined to this hell. By the time they discover me, nothing will be left of me. My body, mind, and soul will be tarnished entirely and laid to waste.

I need to save myself. The thought races through my mind. Immediately followed by the realization that I am never getting out of here alive. *I know that now.* James will never let me go. I have to force him to end my life now, and if there is any mercy and justice in this world, I will take James to hell with me when I go. I lay myself down on the cool tiled floor as tears trickle down from my eyes and soak my dirt-ragged hair.

Images of Raegan, Issy, and Stella race through my mind. Each of them speaking words of encouragement to rest and be still. To let my mind escape this hell I find myself trapped in.

The images switch, and I'm faced with husky blue eyes begging me to survive, to come back to him. His demand is forceful and angry. They switch to dark chocolate brown eyes that command that I fight, that I not give up. As the image changes to Mateo, more tears trail from my eyes and down my battered face. He begs me to not leave him, to come back to him.

Then dark blue eyes that always remind me of the Atlantic Ocean at midnight fill my mind. There's unrelenting rage in his eyes. A ravaging fire within their depths insists that I fight. That I not lay down and die. That I pull everything that I have left within me and use it to relight my own fire.

"You are mine, Mia." The words sear through my mind, fierce anger and possession in their undertones. They fill me with a fiery blaze, one that swells through my limbs and mind with the need for escape, revenge, and bloodlust. *We will kill him, end this damn monster's life, so he can never hurt anyone else.* Save us! My mind demands.

Out of the corner of my eye, a fluorescent green stick catches my eye. I drag my body to the small plastic wastebasket beside the toilet. I reach my hand inside and pull out a used toothbrush, the bristles worn and bent. I clutch the handle in my tense hand and hope again swells inside me. We will survive at all costs, my mind screams with a battle cry that urges me on.

The memories of a movie Carter made me watch slip through my mind. The male lead filed down a plastic toothbrush in jail to use it as a shiv and stabbed one of his cellmates. I wonder if that would work in real life? Could I somehow file this down without James seeing it and use it to stab him with it? What's the worst that could happen? He kills me in a blind rage for trying to kill him? *That would be the second-best outcome and one I am fully prepared for.*

A spark of hope starts deep inside me, buried under all the pain and torture I have endured. Hope is dangerous. It breathes life back into my mind and forces me to once again take my fate into my own hands. If I am going to die here, I am going to die fighting like a Stratford and not this man's disgusting blood.

CHAPTER 12

Theo

"Sometimes your very existence seems nothing, sometimes it's your shadow I yearn for or a glimpse of it." ehddah

"**Y**ou are mine, Mia. Admit it. I want to hear you shout it to the whole house." *My grip on her throat tightens as her blue-green eyes meet mine. Her face is in that mask that she wears, the one that tells me nothing of her true feelings and aggravates me to no end.*

Mia and I are the same in that way. Both refusing to bend to anyone else's will and hiding our thoughts and feelings deep inside of us. It makes us both dangerous and frustrating to those around us.

I lean forward, allowing my tongue to trail a path along her cheek to the shell of her ear. "You want me to fuck this sweet, needy pussy? The way only I can? Forcing you to cum nice and hard until you drench us both?"

I pull back and meet her gaze again; her eyes are dilated, and her breath has picked up. She's aroused and wants what I am offering, but she's being defiant. Really, would she be my little queen if she wasn't?

I slip my hand down the front of her tight workout shorts. Warm skin meets my touch and has my cock throbbing painfully in my track pants. I slide my hand

down inside of the band of her panties, and my fingers meet her plump, bare pussy lips. The smooth skin is an aphrodisiac to my senses. A groan leaves her lips before she can swallow it, and has a smirk pulling across my lips.

She's trying to suck in oxygen, but my fingers tighten further on the column of her swan-like neck. "No air for you until you give up control and admit you are mine."

I swipe the slick moisture already sliding out of her across her folds and up to her hard little nub, rubbing the pad of my finger over and over and causing shivers to race through her body. The look on her face and the sweet feel of her pussy has me completely enthralled. Fuck, she is my everything. She has me so profoundly in her clutches that there is no way out for me. She will be mine for all eternity; together, we will go from this life to the next. I will never let her go.

I slide one finger inside of her tight hole, and her body instantly clamps down on it. Holding it hostage in her warm grip. I loosen my stiff fingers on her neck as more of her face starts to go a shade of scarlet. Her beautiful eyes are prominent in her face and bugging out. I would bet my fucking massive pride that she's seeing spots right now, but her stubbornness refuses to ask for my mercy. My vicious little queen will never bend for me.

As much as I would like to force her to admit what we both already know. I don't want her to actually pass out. The need to be deep inside of her, to claim her, is riding me hard, and I can't do that if she's unconscious. Well, I could, but it would be a lot less fun. I enjoy her willing participation. When she's driven by need and meets me stroke for stroke.

I slip a second thick digit inside her as her head tries to thrash back and forth in my grip. She's soaked. Her arousal drips down my fingers and pools in the palm of my hand and has me salivating for a taste of her delicious cunt. The one that belongs to me despite her need to try to fight that fact.

Every nerve ending on my body is a live wire right now, and the source of the electricity is the beautiful blonde in front of me. Prickles of heat are making their way down my spine and begging me to fill her with my cock. Which is painfully hard in the confinement of my pants. It throbs against its restraints and demands access to plunder her wet pussy.

I release the hold on her neck and remove my fingers from her soaked core. A whimper leaves her lips and has my lip tugging up in amusement. She can fight all she wants, but her body will never be able to lie to mine. I use both my hands to frantically pull her shorts and underwear down her ass and thick thighs.

Thighs that I constantly dream about being wrapped around my head while she rides my face and drenches me in her taste. I force her to step out of the clothes that are blocking my much-needed access to her warm core as I pull my pants down below my ass and free my hard cock.

I force my eyes away from her beautiful luscious pink folds and quickly look around. We are down in the above-ground basement of her house, in the home gym. She was running on the treadmill when I came in to do the same and burn off some of my restless energy.

One look at her in the tiny workout outfit she's wearing had all my good intentions going straight to shit at my feet. Fuck, she really is the most beautiful girl I have ever seen. No one else can compare to her, even in something as mundane as a pair of dark blue spandex shorts and a tight sports bra. A bra that has those perky tits of hers standing at attention and begging for my lips to suck and bite them. The need to wrap my hands around her throat and take her breath while I fuck her hard is a blast of electricity soaring through my veins.

Anyone can walk in here and catch us. I should show some restraint and take her somewhere else rather than this giant glass fishbowl with all its exposure and windows. I can't, though. My need is overpowering my rational thought process, and all I want is to sink to the hilt inside of her. Bury myself balls deep inside of her and never pull back out. To possess and consume her. Show her body, mind, and soul that she belongs to me. That I am her master and own her, just like she owns me.

I've been trying to stay away from her since I gangbanged her with Finn and Carter in the garage, but it seems utterly futile. I need and crave her, and depriving myself of her touch only pushes me further into my darkness. She is my salvation. She calls to a part of me that only she is able to reach. The darkness within my mind, heart, and soul answers only to her command to release me into her care.

"Wrap your legs around me," I demand gruffly as I slip my hands under her thighs until I have lifted her from the ground and forced her core close to mine. A moaned gasp leaves her lips as the swollen crown of my cock brushes against her folds and bumps her clit. "Slide me inside of you, Mia."

Her soft, warm fingers wrap around my thick length, constricting their grip as she strokes me a few times. The sensation has my balls tightening painfully with the need to blow my load. Hold the fuck on. We are not letting go until we are deep inside her warm depths. I grit my teeth and try to slow my breathing down. My eyes threaten to roll to the back of my head at her touch. She brings my tip to her tight hole, and I immediately plunge inside, needing to feel her wrapped around me more than I need blessed air right now. Fuck, she is perfect!

"Theo...holy shit." The words are garbled from her lips as her head leans back against the glass wall. I thrust forward, meeting the end of her before pulling back to the very tip and slamming home, again and again, as my thrusts increase in savagery.

They make the glass vibrate loudly behind us. The sound meeting both our harsh breaths and the loud slapping sound of flesh meeting flesh. I want to own her and mark her up so that she sees me when she looks at herself. A constant reminder of the ownership she refuses to acknowledge. She is mine.

I lean forward and wrap my lips around the skin of her neck, sucking hard and leaving the first mark; a whimper escapes her mouth at the sensation. I remove my lips and skate further down, leaving another spot, and then my lips find where her neck and collarbone meet.

I graze my teeth over her exposed skin before I leave a perfect imprint of them behind. The sight brings me an overwhelming sense of satisfaction. Mark more of her, leave not an inch of her skin exposed without a brand. She belongs to us, my mind urges in carnality.

Her pussy tightens harshly with the ministrations of my mouth and the hint of pain I'm providing, forcing a panted breath out of me. I'm so close. If she keeps squeezing me like that. I won't be able to wait for her to find her release before mine takes me in a chokehold. No, she comes first. Always.

"Play with your clit, baby. I need you to explode before I paint this tight cunt with my cum." I breathe harshly, my forehead meeting her shoulder as I watch her fingers skate across her flesh as my cock penetrates her. What a beautiful sight it is to see my cock coated in her juices and sliding in and out of his favorite home. A home that belongs to me and my fellow kings, even if she won't utter the words.

Her fingers circle her clit, rubbing over and over on the swollen flesh as her body tightens before me. The vein on her neck becomes more pronounced as she gets closer and closer to her own detonation. I let my tongue peek out and drag over the top of her breasts that are heaving in her purple sports bra.

Fuck I want to leave my teeth marks there. All over the decadent flesh of those golden globes. I make sure I tighten my hold as I bend forward, never losing the precious connection between us, and suck in the soft flesh before biting down hard. Her body detonates around me. Mia's pussy clenches tightly and grips my cock like a tight fist. Heaven, this is what heaven must feel like.

"Oh my God, oh my God, oh my God!" Leaves her lips as she continues to come, and I quicken my thrusts, wanting to go with her into bliss. I'm so close. So fucking close to paradise, I can taste it.

"THEO!" A bang on the door has me pulling out of my erotic daydreams about Mia's amazing cunt and returning to the darkened room that has become as much of my sanctuary as my prison.

"Yes..." I clear my throat and try again. "Yes!"

"Stella wants to see all of you now." Tom's gruff voice sounds from the other side of the wooden door. I stare down and realize I had pulled my cock out during the memory and was stroking myself. The large vein that graces my long length is pronounced, and the tip leaks tears of precum that meet my finger's tight grasp. Fuck, I lean my head back against the wall as my balls tighten painfully, demanding rapture and refusing to be denied.

"Fucking hell," I mumble as I stroke myself harder and faster. I need to come. I need to feel my balls tighten and empty out so that I can try to release some of this nonstop wrath and pent-up energy within me. My cock misses Mia just like the rest of me. He, too, is suffering her loss.

I picture her swollen pussy in my mind, dripping with my cum, while her puckered hole gapes for me, begging to also be filled. Her eyes blaze as they tease me to fuck her harder, to fill her so completely that her end will be my beginning.

"Did you hear what I said, Theo?" Tom bangs his fist against the door again.

"Yeah, I'm coming!" With one last harsh stroke, I do cum all over my hand as I hear Tom's footsteps retreat from my door. *Fucking hell.*

I walk into Mia's home office, dragging my feet with my head down. My gaze firmly planted on the ground, preventing me from meeting anyone's eyes. I can't stand to see my fellow king's hate shining back at me, Rae and Issy's misery and condemnation, or that mask that fucker Diego wears. The desire to be anywhere but here is a drum beating in my veins. The last thing I want or need is to be in Stella's overbearing and harsh presence. The woman absolutely loathes me with a passion.

One that I completely understand, as I hate myself even more. I know that the only reason I am still breathing is not because of Stella's mercy. She has very little of it where I am concerned. No, I am still living because she knows that if she were to murder me, like I deserve, Mia would never forgive her. Even though I doubt that belief myself. Could Mia still want me after all of this? Maybe she will do the honors of killing me herself.

Right now, I would rather Stella put a gun to my head and pull the trigger, ending the misery of every minute of missing Mia and worrying about what she is enduring. We both know that Stella is more than capable of it. Yet, she persists in allowing me to breathe. To breathe and live with the memories of my stupidity and devastating choices. With the knowledge that my arrogance is what set all of this into motion. She's making sure I suffer, minute by minute, hour by suffocating hour.

It no longer matters what I want, though, not anymore. I am captive here in Mia's house. Being held by Stella's iron will, whether I want to be or not. *Can you blame her?* The question glides through my mind sharply.

No, I can't blame her. I deserve everything she does to me. Every punishment that she sees fit to inflict, I will readily take. I won't fight her. *What would be the point?* I want to end my miserable life as much as she wants to take it from me. Theo Saint-Lambert is nothing now, not a man filled with pride or power. Just a shell of a man that destroyed himself and all those he loves.

Stella is determined to break me and bring me to my knees. The strong and proud Theo Saint-Lambert, broken and bowing before her. What she fails to see is I'm already on my knees. I'm already broken and festering inside, the wound poisoning me one minute at a time. The one piece of my heart and soul that survived all the hell I lived through is gone. She's gone, and she took what was left of me with her. I am empty and lost now, bleeding out the last vestiges of the man I thought I would be. The man that planned to stand by Mia's side.

My eyes greet Finn's as he turns around to face me. His face is haggard, with dark shadows and puffy bags pronounced under his eyes. Dark brown eyes that are filled with remorse, pain, and self-recrimination. I know that he regrets telling us the truth about who Mia really is. He believes that if he had just kept his mouth shut, she wouldn't have left, and some unknown malicious fucker out there wouldn't have taken her.

Maybe he's right. Perhaps it wouldn't all have played out as it did. But he's not to blame here. I am. His words weren't the determining factor for us pushing Mia away so that she could return to Manhattan and the safety of the Stratfords. They were the opportunity.

The nudge we needed to use to distance ourselves from the girl each of us loves in order to prevent her from being hurt by my deranged father. A heinous man whose attention I brought her way. I am solely responsible for what is happening here now. That weight lives on my shoulders like a herd of elephants crushing me to the ground.

"Theodore..." Stella utters my name with distaste and an icy countenance.

The villainous queen in all of her glory, except she's as broken as we are. The last couple of weeks have been just as devastating for her as they have been for us. While the guys and I have lost our girl, the one that each of us loves, she has lost her granddaughter.

The only family Stella has left on this earth are Mia and Issy. Knowing that Mia is out there somewhere in the hands of an enemy is crushing her bit by bit. Every day that we don't hear any word of Mia's whereabouts is another crack in Stella's armor. Soon she will be as shattered as the rest of us. Even the cold and calculating queen of Manhattan has a heart, it seems.

My gaze leaves Finn's that pleads with me. *What is he asking me for? To live? To keep going? To fight?* Who am I fighting? Stella, who is determined to punish me for my trespass against her granddaughter and the missing piece of my heart?

Maybe he's asking me to fight my demons. The ones that are ripping me apart from the inside out. I have no answer for him. I am lost in a void of darkness, one I don't see any way out of without my light, my Mia.

"Sit down, Theodore." Her command irks me, and because there is still a little asshole left in me, I meet her cold blue gaze with my own. "I would rather stand."

Stella's fist makes contact with the top of the glass desk, the sound vibrating loudly through the room and causing my hackles to rise. "I would rather that you weren't breathing, Theodore Saint-Lambert, but neither of us are going to get what we want today."

Fuck, there it is. Stella never sugar coats shit. She would strangle me with her bare hands if she could. If she thought that for one second, Mia wouldn't hold it against her. I'm betting that she's wrong, though. After what I did to her granddaughter, I'll bet she helps her end my life.

I hold her glare for a moment before relenting and taking the seat in front of the desk. As much as I want to defy her, what would be the point? She's not going to put a bullet in my brain, and I can't escape this reality without knowing that Mia has returned and is safe. Even if she never wants to see me again. We are both stuck with each other for the time being.

Stella's menacing glare meets mine, and I watch as she takes deep breaths, trying to calm herself down before sitting behind the desk. The frigid queen's mask is thawing, and her control slipping. Her fingers trail over her charm bracelet, an action I have noticed her indulging in more and more since Mia's disappearance.

"Finn has just confessed to me that it was, in fact, him that divulged the knowledge of my granddaughter's background to you worthless cowards." Her eyes slide from mine to glare with suppressed heat over in Finn's direction. From the corner of my eye, I watch his Adam's apple rise and fall as he swallows with uneasiness. *Damn it to fucking hell!*

Why the fuck would he confess that to her? Does he, too, have a death wish? What am I saying? Of course, he does. All four of us do. I wait for her to go on. She hasn't called me here just to reveal that information. No, the viper has something else in mind. Pain and punishment are always her preferences.

"I believed the culprit to be you, Theodore. I was mistaken. Yet that changes little. You four are all equally responsible for what has happened to my granddaughter." A pinched look crosses her mouth, and a sour expression graces her face. It must grate on her to have to admit she was wrong about something. I have a feeling Stella Stratford doesn't ever admit to failure.

"Is that all, Stella? You called me in here to what? Rake me over the coals some more? Trust me, nothing you could do or say to me is worse than the hell I have already lived through and am reliving now."

"Theo..." Finn mumbles through clenched teeth before grabbing on firmly to my forearm and preventing me from rising out of the chair and storming out of the room.

"If you think I can't cause you more pain and anguish, Theodore, I am willing to show you what lengths I can go to." She shakes her head and clenches her fists tight, and I watch transfixed as a bit of the fight leaves her. Maybe it's just a ploy to get me to let down my guard, but for a moment, pain shoots through my chest at all the suffering she too is feeling.

"No, Theodore. I called you in here to lay out my terms." Her jaw tightens, and I can see the muscle twitching.

"Terms? What terms, Stella? Terms for what exactly?" I question her with a sardonic tone and a raised eyebrow.

"When my granddaughter is found." She slams the palm of her hand on the desk. "And she will be found. I assure you it will happen even if it takes the last breath from my body and me setting this whole world on fire. The four of you will disappear from her life. Not a single one of you is worthy of her. I will not allow you to continue to hurt her."

"Stella, we love her," Finn utters with devastation.

"It doesn't matter if you love her. Your type of love is poison to her. You have been hurting Mia for years. You four are destructive and cause her to forget her own self-preservation and good sense. Once she has been found, I will never allow any of you near her again. If you truly love her, as you claim. You will release her. You will leave this house and town and stay as far away from her as possible."

"And if we refuse?" I question with a deliberate eyebrow raise and a tilt of my head. I'm trying to project defiance, but my heart is pounding like a stallion in my chest. How could she demand this? Does she not realize how much we love Mia? *She's ordering it because you love her, fool!* My mind scathes back at me.

"If you refuse, I will end all four of your lives. I will ensure that your bodies are never found and that every trace of your miserable existence is wiped from this earth." The look on her face is frightening and cold, like the plains in the arctic. She means it with all her heart. She will have us eliminated.

A gasp behind us catches all of our attention, and Finn and I turn sharply in our chairs towards the doorway. Mateo stands there broken, unshaven, and disheveled. A tear slides down his blotchy face. He is a fuckin' mess. If I think I'm taking it hard, Mateo is barely breathing.

"Then you might as well end it now, Stella... because I can't live without her." He begs, his arms wrapping tightly around himself.

"I would love nothing better, but unfortunately, my granddaughter would never forgive me. However, the four of you will break ties with her once she returns. You will do this in order for her to heal, not only from what she is experiencing now but from your relationships with her. Relationships that are toxic and cause her relentless pain."

Not one of us opens our mouths to dispute her charges. We are toxic to Mia. Our relationships with her have done nothing but hurt her and us. And yet, there is no way I would go back to a time when I didn't know her. Nothing I wouldn't give to have her back, including my very life. I would give up everything except her.

Stella pulls a folder from a drawer below the desk, opens it, and sets the contents in front of Finn and me as Mateo moves further into the room to stand behind Finn's chair. I give her a severe glare as I look over the first couple of paragraphs of the documents, and my breath gets trapped in my throat with shock. *No, this can't fucking be.*

"As you three can see, I have now provided you with the means to stay far away from my granddaughter."

The document in front of us outlines the release of all our inheritances, including Finn's. Stella has had not only my father's will overturned but all my assets from my mother unfrozen and released to me.

Carter's trust fund and inheritance has also been relinquished to his name. Ensuring he and his younger brother, Foster, are the sole owners of his family's enterprises. I'm sure Carter's bitch of a mom is going to love that.

Mateo's family's company and assets have been reverted solely to his name, and all the funds are accessible to only him. Even though we believe his disgusting and traitorous parents to still be alive. How she managed to accomplish all that is insane. Stella really is a force to be reckoned with, and nothing is beyond her reach, it seems. Except for killing us right now, it's why she is going this route.

"Jack will provide you with your trust fund now and ensure that you are able to access your family's funds, but only under the condition that you remain at a bare minimum, across the country from Mia at all times. The minute you disobey that directive, I will have your family's company dismantled and sold off piece by piece, Finn."

"You think it's wise to threaten a man that has nothing left to lose, Stella?" I clench my hands tightly to prevent myself from reaching out and wrapping them around her fucking neck.

"I will protect Mia from everything that means to harm her, even if that harm is you."

CHAPTER 13
Carter

"There are moments, if you look for them, where a decision is made that alters the contents of your life and how it ends"
Eric Overby, Hourglass in Grace

"Do you remember where Mia used to live when she was Amelia, and you were kids?" Diego questions, turning in the front passenger seat to stare at me, his dark green eyes boring holes in my skull without any indication of his thoughts. *Fuck, he's a creepy bastard.* The hairs on my arms are standing up with that look from his serpent eyes.

Confusion is racing through my mind at where he's going with his question, but if he has even the slightest possibility of a lead on Mia's whereabouts, I will follow him anywhere. Even right into hell, no doubt, to meet some of his relatives and greet my father.

Do I trust the fucker not to shank me in the back once all of this is done? *No fucking way.* Right now, though, he wants to find Mia too, at least I think for Issy's sake. She's falling to pieces over Mia's disappearance, and if the fucker has feelings for her like I believe he does, that has to be hurting him too.

"Yeah, she lived in a rundown house on the other side of town, past the train tracks. Finn used to live across the street from her. What of it?" I pry my eyes again from the road to see if his face will give any of his thoughts away, but much like Theo and Stella, Diego wears a mask that hides his thoughts from those trying to decipher them.

I have never been able to master that blank, emotionless mask, despite my dad beating me daily for it. In all my years on this earth, I have never been able to hide my anger or contempt. Most of my irrational thoughts readily display themselves on my features for the whole world to see and fear. It makes me both reckless and dangerous. I don't hide that I want to kill you. You know it at that very moment.

"I'm just rolling with a thought that has been niggling at the back of my mind this week. Something doesn't feel right about this whole shit, with Vincent appearing brutalized and Mia being taken simultaneously. I'm positive the two things are connected and that both are related to someone's retribution."

"Okay, so where do we start?" A kernel of hope starts to rise in my chest. At this point, I will take even the smallest possibility if it leads me in the direction of where Mia might be. "Mia hasn't lived there for almost twelve years. You think someone out that way knows something?"

I watch as he rakes his fingers through his dark hair, and his other hand drags across his eyes. Diego is just as exhausted as the rest of us. The fucker has been searching from the very beginning for Mia along with Stella's men. I would never admit it to him, 'cause you know, he's an asshole that tried to manipulate my girl into marrying him, but I was somewhat relieved to have him out there searching for her, especially since Stella had us on lockdown at gunpoint at the house.

Diego is relentless and ruthless. I know if he found Mia, he would kill whoever had her, but before they died, he would make them regret their very existence. If it couldn't be one of us that delivered the killing blow to whoever took my girl. At least I know Diego would send them to hell torn apart.

We are more alike in that way than I would like to admit. Neither one of us shies away from our crazy. We are both unhinged and quick to anger and violence. Both of us would do anything necessary to protect the ones we love. If someone hurts someone we love, neither of us would hesitate to destroy that person painfully. Fuck, the way my mind is going on and on, you would think the fucker was my long-lost soul brother. *Maybe he is?*

"Let's just make it out there and see what we find. I could be wrong. It could be nothing. At this point, we have nothing to lose except our time in each other's company." He grimaces, that scar on his face pulling on the skin near his mouth and giving him a fierce look. Fucker makes it sound like being in my company is distasteful to him, but I know he gets a kick out of going toe to toe with me. *Like I said, we are more alike than we are not.*

I take the exit on the highway that will lead me to the other side of town. The side that I haven't really visited in years, since well...Amelia Hamilton and her mother disappeared without a trace. There was no reason to return there after she was gone, and we couldn't find out where she went.

I remember when we went looking for her after weeks of not seeing her or her mom around town. The need to see her, to mess with her, was all-consuming. I couldn't figure out then why that was. Every time I needed to hide from my dad, I would find myself going back to that house alone, without the guys, to spy on Amelia Hamilton.

The girl I was supposed to help Theo bully and torture to make sure she never made it into our world like Finn did. The one we tried to make sure Vincent, my dad, and their friends never got their dirty hands on.

The disappointment and loss I felt at finding her gone and all of her belongings missing was devastating and painful. I was just a stupid kid dealing with his own shit at home, but that empty room in that rundown house made my chest hurt. Made me feel like something was taken from me, something I desperately needed. I spent hours just sitting there, breathing in her slight scent with dust molecules in the air around me as my only company.

Looking back, the reality is that Amelia Hamilton was a distraction from the misery of my home life. She might as well have lived in an alternative universe to the guys and me. She was dirt poor, living in a house that was falling down around her.

Her mom worked hard at low-paying jobs trying to make enough to support them. They had nothing, while the guys and I were surrounded by all the riches you could imagine. We never had to worry about not having enough to eat or getting evicted from our homes. I never worried about what would happen to my brother and me if my dad lost his job. Thoughts like that never flowed through our young, rich, privileged minds.

Yet they would have been an everyday occurrence for Amelia and her mother. Her mother worked so hard to provide for her, and instead of not adding to their lot in life, the guys and I made it so much more challenging.

With how hard life was for the two of them, you would think that Amelia's home life would be rough and worse than mine and Theo's. While I am sure it wasn't a walk in the park for her and her mom, she had something that no one in my world had.

I had never seen or experienced anything like the way Amelia's mom loved her and the way she loved her mom in return. How protective Catherine was of Amelia. Everything she did was to sacrifice for Amelia and ensure she was safe. Catherine never beat her or called her names. She never took her frustrations out on her or showed up at home loaded from alcohol or high on drugs and smacked her around.

It was addicting for me to watch it. To bear witness to the love a parent is supposed to have for their child. When I knew my mom didn't give a shit about me and my dad hated me.

The guys' home lives were just as bad, except for Finn. His mom cared about him, but not like Amelia's mom. I found myself craving to be a part of that, and when I couldn't, I used it to fuel my anger and jealousy because I felt less than.

Punishing Amelia was like punishing myself at the same time. Becoming a monster so that her world sucked just as much as mine did daily. So that she lived each day afraid of what could happen to her, just like I did.

Yet, if I'm being honest, every time I hurt her, I felt like shit. The more we frightened her and bullied her, the more I started to feel like I was becoming the monster that resembled my father. I didn't want to be like him. When I questioned Theo on why we couldn't stop hurting her after her mom got fired, he snuck me into his house and I watched terrified from a closet as his father did terrible things to a young woman who must have been just a little older than us. How she cried and begged for him not to hurt her, but her pleading only seemed to egg him on. How he laughed at and rejoiced in her pain. It was at that moment I knew that he would do the same to Amelia's mom and maybe even to Amelia. I never questioned Theo again, we just became more determined to hurt her to make sure she was never a part of our world.

Mateo followed our leads, even though he never had the stomach for it. Every wound we inflicted on that girl was one more cut on his skin and made him retreat more into himself. He acted tough in the moment but would completely shut down after the damage was done. Our actions changed him and hardened that sweet, caring boy. The one that would have never hurt a fly and used to love to commune with nature.

It was shortly after that both he and I started smoking weed, doing heavier drugs, and dabbling with alcohol. We needed something to keep the nightmares out of our heads. It was already so hard to look in the mirror knowing you came from shitty parents, but then to hurt an innocent just because we had this misguided need to stop our dads. Misguided because we were never powerful enough to stop them. Just little boys playing at being kings. Now look at our kingdom in a pile of rubble.

We never divulged to Finn right from the get-go all those years ago why we were bullying Amelia in the first place. He was an outsider that was let into our world, and we didn't know if we could completely trust him. It was only much later, after months of torturing her and him losing his shit with us anytime we hurt her, that he started fighting against Theo's demands. Then, we had no choice but to tell him and trust him with the secret of what we knew. That was just before she and her momma disappeared.

When he found out the truth, he was devastated, crushed under the weight of the world that we live in. He was dragged into darkness right along with us when all he wanted was a better life. When he was trying to protect her, his lifelong friend, instead of hurting her. I felt sorry for him.

While he never actively participated in our physical bullying of Amelia, he didn't stop it once he discovered the truth behind our actions. It didn't mean he went along with it willingly after he knew. In fact, it caused huge problems between him, Theo, and me. Mateo, I think, was just happy someone wasn't hurting her.

Anytime we approached her, he would tell us to stop. Any cruel words to her were met with one of his fists fighting against us in private, even though Amelia never saw it. She always thought that he actively betrayed her when he didn't. He never tried to dissuade her of that belief either, much to my confusion.

The fucker punched Theo in the face the very first time he saw us bullying her. That day we played street hockey out on the road, and she ran away when we were teasing her about her weight. I'm not going to lie. I enjoyed watching Theo get knocked down a peg. My heart hurt inside my chest when we were mean to her.

When we physically hurt her, Finn would lose his mind afterward, vomit and even cry. He would threaten us with bodily harm. Tell us he wanted nothing to do with us. That he didn't want to be our friend if we were going to hurt her. That's when Theo's threats started. He forced Finn into being silent and looking the other way; how I'm not sure, but I have my theories.

Theories that all lead back to Finn's mom, Lori. Who entered our world through Jack, but yet couldn't let go of her old life and tended to make mistakes, like cheating on Jack at the beginning of their marriage. We knew Finn was desperate for a father figure. We knew he loved Jack and that Jack treated him like his actual son.

I think Theo, the manipulative bastard used that as a weakness and forced Finn's compliance. Even then, with the threats against him, we couldn't force him to participate. I could always tell that Finn was torn up about what we were doing. He never seemed to recover from what he helped us do to her. She was his best friend for so many years, and while he didn't physically hurt her, he never managed to stop us, either.

When he finally found out about the reasoning behind our horrific actions, he was devastated. He didn't speak to anyone for weeks. A silent giant, lost inside of his mind. Then Amelia and her mom disappeared, and I think he was finally able to breathe a sigh of relief that she was out of our hands. By then, it was too late. He was a king of Casbury and had become one of us.

I can't even imagine how he feels now, as he once again watched while we bullied and hurt her. If he felt for her then, even just a little bit of what he feels now, I don't know what has stopped him from killing all of us.

CHAPTER 14

Carter

"The past is never where you think you left it." Katherine
Anne Porter

"H ey fucker, you zone out or some shit?" Diego slaps the side of my
face hard and brings me back to the here and now and out of my
memories of a time gone by. One that I cannot change and will always be a stain
on my soul. *Fucker, our soul is so stained that it's black soot.* My mind snickers at
me.

I release a deep breath, trying to make those ghosts disappear from my mind
and welcoming the distraction. I waggle my eyebrows and quirk my lips. "So,
Issy?"

"Shut the fuck up, asshole!"

"Naw, fucker. I want to know what you're doing with Mia's sister." I hold my
hand up quickly, feeling the anger instantly radiating off of him. "Not like that
asswipe. I don't want to know the kinky shit you two get up to in the backyard
or down by the beach."

His eyes grow large and meet mine before I turn mine back to the road. "Yeah
fucker, we all knew where you two were slipping out to. You're not as slick as

you think you are." A laugh rumbles through my chest, and for just a moment, I feel lighter than I have in weeks.

"Oh, you mean like you four fuckers all up in Mia's cunt, twenty-four-seven? Sharing her with each other? Cause that's not kinky."

He has a valid point, I guess. The guys and I made it no secret that we were not only willing to share Mia with each other but that we were actually determined to, and we did.

"We are not talking about that shit right now. I just want to know if this is all a game you're playing with Issy and Mia? Also, think real hard about the way you answer that. I can still wrap this car around a tree and ensure you don't take another breath." I huff out an agitated breath.

This asshole likes to push my buttons just to get a rise out of me. I'll end both our psychotic lives if he fucks around. There is no world in which he would end up with my girl and still be breathing.

I take the next turn down a residential street, the train tracks visible at a distance. The feeling of nostalgia tries to roll over me, but I push it back. There is nothing here to remember with fondness. This place holds some of the darkest sins I carry on my soul and heart.

"I'm not playing with her." He mumbles his words, and I almost don't make them out.

"What about Stella? There is no way she's going to allow you two to be together. Hell, I doubt she's even going to allow us anywhere near Mia ever again, and she likes me. Well, maybe "like" is too strong of a word."

"Let her try to take Issy from me." Diego breathes harshly, his fists tightening in his lap and his whole body going rigid. Well, look at that, another possessive asshole. Diego fits right in with us. He just doesn't realize we are kindred spirits.

I'm about to answer him, giving him a friendly warning not to take Stella lightly, when I spy Mia's old house and pull the car up to the curb. The whole thing is dilapidated and boarded up. There's a sign on the door warning you to keep out and the word "condemned" written in red spray paint across the boarded-up front window. Well, shit, there goes that idea. Before I can open my mouth to speak, Diego is getting out of the car and moving towards the structure.

I groan out loud, letting my head hit the headrest for a moment. The ghosts of my past are trying to make a reappearance in my mind. I take a deep breath and then another. I then pull myself out of the car and walk to where Diego is already looking around the side of the house for a way inside. *Shit, I guess we're doing this one way or another.* I reckon I should prepare myself to once again come face to face with my past.

We move around the perimeter of the building, pulling on rotted wood boards. When we have a few boards pried off, we climb through a broken window and make our way slowly inside Mia's old house. The both of us turn on our phone flashlights so we can see what's inside.

The space is a complete wreck. You can smell mold, rot, and animal feces in the air. The water-logged floor groans with our combined weight, letting us know that it could cave in. *Fuck, I'm going to die or lose a limb following Diego's stupid lead.*

I don't even know what the hell we are looking for here or why he's so determined to have come here in the first place. Diego is keeping his thoughts guarded, and I don't like it one bit. I don't want to end up stumbling into a trap, and this asshole likes to venture into danger as a fucking hobby.

"Fucker, what are we looking for?" I question as I move carefully over the cracked and peeling pea-green linoleum of the kitchen floor. Dingy, dirty white cabinets scrawled with graffiti greet me, some of the doors barely hanging on. The counters are all worn and peeling gray laminate, the kitchen sink is long gone, and you can see rat feces everywhere. *Fuck, the smell in here is nauseating and starting to trigger a headache.*

"She really lived here? Like, was it this bad a dump when she and her mom lived here?" Diego questions from what used to be the living room. I follow the sound of his voice and meet him around the other side.

I take a sorrowful glance around the pitiful space. Their old worn sofa is still there, looking soggy and destroyed by animals. The image of a young Amelia lying on it reading makes its way into my mind, and I clench my fists tightly.

"It wasn't this bad then. They kept it clean and tidy, but yeah. They didn't have much." My eyes trail down the short hallway to where I know Mia's old bedroom is. I broke in here once and wandered through the space, touching all of her precious books. That was before she moved them to the metal shed and before we recklessly and maliciously burnt it down to the ground.

The other guys don't know this, but after we made it across the tracks heading back to our side of town and split up to go our separate ways, I turned back around. I needed to see her face. My chest felt tight, knowing we had destroyed the one place that gave her peace from us.

It was such a shitty thing to do. Finn refused to have any part in it and hid at home that day. Threatening Theo with physical violence if he went through with it.

Mateo pleaded with us not to do it. That it was going too far and something bad could really happen, but Theo and I didn't listen to him. He came with us but sat there staring off into space with tears silently sliding down his face and causing Theo to lose his mind further. Our menacing actions ensured we destroyed another piece of that girl that day and that we terrified her mom.

Diego starts moving down the hallway toward Mia's room, and my hackles begin to rise. An irrational sensation of jealousy and possession fills me. I don't want him in her room, in her space. *She belongs to me. She did even then.* Even though neither of us knew it. She was always mine. Mine to love, but also mine to torture.

I force myself to breathe in the gross scent around me and realize she's long gone. That girl doesn't exist anymore. We made sure of it, after all. Unsurprisingly, the one that replaced her came back here to seek vengeance for all the shit we put her through. We fucking deserve everything she had planned to do to us. Taking our kingdom from us didn't even begin to even the score between us.

"Fuck, this place is sad. I knew Mia came from a humble beginning, but I didn't realize what her life was like." He stares at me over his shoulder, and I see the disgust across his face. "You fuckers made her life even harder, and she was already dealing with all this shit."

I don't bother to open my mouth to defend myself or to tell him why we believed our actions back then were righteous. Looking back over that time, I know there is no justification for our behavior. We didn't need to destroy her the way we did.

We weren't protecting her by turning her life upside down. Making it harder for her to survive. We could have approached Catherine at any time and told her what our dads were planning. We didn't because we were idiots.

No, we were more than idiots. We were bullies who took our pain out on someone, an innocent girl, and hid behind the illusion of putting her best interests first. Eight years later, we committed the same exact sin. Instead of talking to Mia, we came to the conclusion that hurting her so that she would run away, was the best option.

"Let's get out of here. I don't think we are going to find our answers here."

We make our way back out the same window and into the fresh air. Just as we are starting to move towards the car and away from the offending structure, a woman's voice calls out.

"What are ya two numbskulls doin' climbin' in that window? Y'all got no sense? That building be ready to fall down around y'alls ears!" Her southern drawl is thick, and her voice is filled with reproach.

I meet her glare and angry scowl from across the dried-up grass, and a spark of awareness flies through me. This is still the same old neighbor who lived here when Mia and her mom did. She took a broom to my back once when I was here bullying Mia.

I move closer, Diego right on my heels. "Ma'am." I nod respectfully. She squints her eyes so she can see me better. She was old eight years ago, now she's ancient. I'm surprised she's still living here.

Fuck, I'm surprised she's still breathing. She's tiny, with pure white tresses cut short along her pink scalp. Her back has a pronounced stoop to it that is visible as she moves. She's wearing a worn black and pink striped robe that has seen better days and oversized slippers shaped like Dalmatians on her feet, duct tape holding the majority of them together. Her face is so lined that you can't see any skin that doesn't have a deep wrinkle in it.

"Don't ya ma'am me, boy! I recognize those demon eyes. They ain't ones ya forget. Why ya back here, boy? That girl been gone a long time."

She gives us her back, and we watch as she shuffles slowly back into a white plastic lawn chair on her porch. Diego gives me a look and a head nod. We communicate without words, something I have never been able to do with anyone but Theo. Together we move towards her porch and up a step, both trying not to look threatening to the little old lady before us.

"You remember me?" I question softly.

She lets out a cackle that makes her sound like a witch from a movie. "Hard to forget eyes like yours. Never seen another pair in my long life that be the same. Thank the lord for that."

"Do you remember the woman and her daughter that used to live here?" Diego questions, moving closer to her but trying not to look menacing. *Good luck motherfucker. Menace* secretes from his pores.

"Boy, who done that to your face? What demon done that to ya?" She leans forward, getting a closer look at Diego, and I have to bite down hard on my bottom lip to stop the grin that wants to break across my face. He looks like he swallowed piss.

"A demon that is no longer breathing." He replies and stops a few feet from her, staring into her cloudy eyes.

"Well, thank the sweet Lord Jesus for that, don't be needin' demons walkin' the earth that do things like that. Amen to that." She harrumphs. "Yes, boy, I remember my sweet Amelia and her mama. What's it to ya?" She questions with a look of suspicion.

"Do you remember if she or her mom ever had any problems with anyone? Anyone that maybe wanted to hurt either of them?"

She raises an eyebrow at Diego's question and turns her cloudy gaze back on me. "Ya mean other than him and his little devil friends?"

"Yes, other than us." I try not to feel the slight at her calling us devils. She's not wrong. We were horrible to Mia and her mom back then. Not that much has changed since, I guess. We are all sons of devils except for Finn's stepdad, so name-calling is only fitting.

"Lemme see here. It's been a while since I thought on those two. They disappeared from here real quick when Miss Catherine got that boyfriend."

As she thinks back, I take a look around the state of her porch. The wood is rotted through in some sections. Her front window is cracked and taped together with duct tape. The plastic chair she's sitting on looks worn and cracked. If she wasn't so small and slender, I'm pretty sure it would have lost its leg a long time ago. Fuck, I have to come back here and try to do something for her. Fix this shit up somehow. She shouldn't be out here living like this at her age.

The thought stuns me. I have never given a shit about other people other than my fellow kings, Mia, my brother, and maybe Raegan when she's not beating on me. Perhaps it's the despair of Mia's old house or my past sins catching up to me, but I feel bad for this lady.

"Well, there was that no good daddy of Amelia's, but he be run off by the lawman years ago. He used to beat on that angel Miss Catherine and do unspeakable horrors to my little Amelia. A demon that he was. Someone should-a put him in the ground instead of lettin' him breathe behind those bars."

I see the look of excitement on Diego's face at her words. "What was that demon's name, ma'am?" He questions.

"Well, now lemme see here...been a long time. What was that demon's name?" She rubs her little head with her tiny hand that has all her bluish veins showing underneath her thin skin. "Ah yes...a demon named after an apostle, if ever there was a crime. Lord, have mercy and save our wretched souls. James...James Hamilton. That be his name."

James Hamilton. I know I have heard that name before and recently. I try to rack my brain for where I heard that name while the lady continues to lament the fact that the demon was named after a disciple of Jesus to Diego, who is busy staring at me. Where do I know that name from? *Come on, Carter, think! This could help find our girl.* My mind begs.

The memory of us all sitting in the family room a few weeks after Theo returned home pops up in my mind. We were all forcing ourselves to do schoolwork because Stella cracked the whip. I was trying my best to entice Mia to disappear upstairs with me so I could study some of her anatomy.

When one of the guards came into the room and announced, someone was at the gate looking for Mia or her mom. Mia played it off like she didn't know the dude, but I saw her eyes widen, and then she gave Issy a look. What was the fucker's name that was at the gate?

I trail both my hands down my face, pushing my mind to play out that scene again. I watch it play once more through my mind, slower, and then the name pops into my head. *James Hamilton.*

"Fuck! It's him." I catch Diego's eyes simultaneously, and a broom comes flying at my head.

"Boy, ya ain't got no manners! None of those words on my porch!" She screeches and hits me again. Diego lets out a belly laugh and holds tight to his abdomen. *Har Har, motherfucker is totally enjoying me getting beat by this old lady.*

"Beg your pardon, ma'am. I'll be taking my mannerless self right out of here!" I make it off the porch as quick as I can before she lands another hit, and Diego follows me, still laughing. We make it back to the car, and I'm flooring it before he even has the door closed all the way, never mind a seatbelt on.

"He came to the house a few weeks after Theo was released from the hospital looking for Mia or her mom, but she pretended like she didn't know the name. He was looking for them. Could he be involved?"

"Anything is a possibility. It can't be a coincidence that, right around that time, Vincent's little minions started showing up dead. I don't see the connection to Vincent, but maybe if we dig, we will find one."

Diego's cell starts vibrating in his pants pocket, and I take my eyes off the road as he pulls it out and accepts the call. "Papá, qué está pasando?"

There's silence in the car as Diego listens to the person on the other line. "WHAT? Are you sure? Holy fuck! Yeah, I will meet you back at the house right now."

He hangs up the phone and turns his gaze in my direction. The look on his face has me slamming on the brakes and almost crashing into a parked car. *No...no...please no! Please, they can't have found Mia dead...please!*

"We need to head back to the house right now. My dad found some shit about Mia on the dark web. He's heading straight there. Fuck, Carter, it's bad, bro, it's really bad." Diego looks pale, sweat breaks out across his face, and he looks like he wants to be sick.

A tsunami of dread fills me at his words and the look on his face. I close my eyes for a moment, trying to force down the red rage that wants to take over and drown me. "Is she alive?"

"If she is, she's wishing she were dead."

CHAPTER 15
Mia

"No one saves us but ourselves. No one can and no one may. We ourselves must walk the path." Gautama Buddha, Sayings of Buddha

I don't know where James is. There hasn't been a sound outside the locked bathroom door for hours. I've taken the opportunity to drink as much water from the sink as possible and wash my body thoroughly of the ghost of hands that I still feel touching me. The ones that make my skin crawl, even now after scrubbing myself raw under the freezing cold water.

I'm lying on my side next to the toilet, wrapped in the only towel that was in the room. One that is too small to even cover half of my body. I'm pretty sure the infection I have is giving me a fever, but my skin is slick with sweat, and shivers keep wracking my body. My skin is both chilled and feverish at the same time.

Maybe I'm in shock? My hand is aching and throbbing from me grinding the plastic toothbrush handle across the ragged bolts holding the toilet to the floor. At first, I didn't think it would work, but I kept trying until some of the plastic started to wear away, and I could start to see a blunt point happening on one side. I turned it around and filed down the other side until soon I was beginning to see that point turn into a sharp one. I run my finger across it once again. It's getting pointier and sharper. It could almost pass for a thin plastic blade.

I know I will only have one chance of attacking him with this. The minute I try to ram it into his skin, the plastic is going to snap. I have to make it count when I do. My legs and core throb from my position on the floor and whatever James did to me when I was unconscious.

Large dark bruises appeared after my shower, the imprint of each of his fingers across both of my breasts, hips, and thighs. Just the thought of what he subjected my body to makes me want to vomit up all the water I have managed to force down. *No, we are getting the hell out of here. Be strong, and keep going.* My mind begs me.

Images of my childhood with my mother accost me, how beautiful she was, and how much she sacrificed and endured for me. It's like all the pieces that my mind held back to protect me have now flooded my brain. The images have me grinding the plastic harder against the metal, determined to kill this son of a bitch for hurting me and for hurting my mom all those years ago.

When I get out of here, I am going to wrap her in my arms and beg for her forgiveness for the way I have treated her since Jared died. I can understand her need and fears about landing back in that same hell she dragged us out of. I have been unfair to her in my grief, forgetting that she loved me first.

A sound from the other side of the door has me freezing. Was that the sound of the front door opening? Is he back from wherever he was? He will come for me and drag me out of this small reprieve to hurt me. He will never stop hurting me unless I make him.

Panic seizes me, and my chest tightens until I can't breathe fully. I can't let him find the toothbrush. I refuse to let him take my only chance away from me. Where am I going to place the plastic shiv? I can't leave it hidden here. I need to somehow have it on me so that I can attack him with it. How am I going to disguise it on myself? There's no way it will stay hidden in my hair, not with how he's constantly grabbing it.

There's only one place I can hide it that he won't notice until it's too late. I hear movement outside the door. I cringe, biting hard on my bottom lip to suppress my cry of pain as I slip the thin plastic, up and inside of my vagina, with the pointy end pointing outwards. I'm going to have to try to clench and hold it so it doesn't slip out. Right now, I am so sore and swollen down there that it might just work in my favor.

My thoughts are stolen from me with fear as the sound of the solid wood door unlocking from the outside brings me back to the here and now. I close my eyes and pretend to be passed out, letting my body become completely lax and even allowing a little spittle to slide from my lips and down my cheek.

"*Fucking whore*," I hear him mumble before the sound of his heavy footsteps approaching me becomes louder and closer. He groans as he reaches down and rips the towel away from me, exposing all my skin to his eyes. "Hope she washed that dirty cunt. It was starting to smell ripe." He groans and bends down to slap my cheek.

I play possum, not moving an inch, not even flinching as he slaps me harder on the face. *Stay calm; stay still.* It's a mantra inside of my mind. I feel his rough hands grabbing at my shoulder and hip before I'm lifted into the air and thrown across his body like a saddle bag. My body makes a hard impact with his. A whimper leaves my lips before I can stop it as I clench my core as hard as possible. His heavy footsteps take us from the bathroom back out to the living room area, where I'm sure my next round of torture awaits.

He throws me down on the sofa, my body bouncing against the cushions, but I remain boneless like a rag doll being thrown around. I hear him mumbling to himself and open my eyes a crack, spying on him from below my lashes.

He's moving around, setting the tripod and his phone up. I spy the laptop off to the side, ready to be used for the live streaming. The minute he turns his back, I reach down and slip the toothbrush from inside my inflamed pussy. I hide it in my fist, pressed against where the back and seat cushions meet.

My whole body seizes up, adrenaline rushing through me. I can feel my eye twitching and my heartbeat pumping loudly in my ears. I have to stay strong. I have to hit him as hard and as quickly as I can. *Aim for his eye or throat, and do as much damage as possible!* My mind screams instructions at me.

The sounds of him clicking buttons on the laptop and the telltale sounds of it connecting to the chat reach my ears. Going forward, I will forever associate those sounds with demented perverts watching me be raped from behind a screen.

He shifts closer again, his scent filling my nose and his body giving off heat against my frigid flesh. He creeps his fingers up the inside of the arch of my foot, then over my ankle and up my calf. His fingers tighten on my knee, pulling my legs apart until my most intimate parts are exposed to him. I can hear his breathing picking up. He's getting aroused, the sick psychopath.

His thick fingers drag up the inside of my thigh, pressing firmly on the bruises in his path heading towards my pussy lips. I hear a groan leave his lips, and it makes me want to scream. I can smell his body odor, a mixture of sweat and the outdoors. The scent causes my stomach to cramp painfully as the need to purge fills me once again.

I beg my body not to respond, not to flinch and give away that we are conscious. I force my features to remain slack as James' fingers trail in between my swollen slit, and he dips one inside of my pussy roughly.

Revulsion fills me, and the desire to scream and tear him apart is almost unmanageable. *Just a little longer. You can do this. Just keep still.* "Dirty cunt. Use this swollen pussy. It's going to be so tight." I hear him mumbling to himself. "Pay me back for all the hell I went through in the clink."

He pumps his finger in and out of my core, and I hear the telltale noise of a zipper being pulled down. *I can't! I can't let him do this to me. I can't let him rape me again!* Just a little longer, patience. We have to hold until the right moment. We are only going to get one chance. His finger leaves my core, and I hear the sound of him stroking himself closer to my face, his hand moving over his flesh in a quick rhythm and the hitch in his breathing. Fucking parasite. I'm going to fucking kill you!

The tip of his cock rubs against my closed lips, precum coating them and smearing across my mouth, cheek, and chin as he drags himself across my skin.

"Pretty whore." He pushes the tip between my lips, and I force them to remain soft. There is no way he would dare risk putting his cock in my mouth if he thought I was conscious. The fucker knows I would try to bite it off. He has let his guard down in his eagerness to abuse and use me. I need to use that to my advantage. I am going to make this fucker regret ever breathing in my direction.

He slips his dick in and out, pushing against my lips until more of him is inside my mouth and moving against my tongue. My mouth is filling with saliva with the disgusting taste of him. The urge to vomit is rising and trying to overtake me.

I pinch myself hard in the back to stop my body's natural response. He pumps in and out a few times, but the angle must be awkward for him. I hear him swearing under his breath. He crouches down further, bending until he's almost on his knees. His cock slips further into my mouth, almost hitting the back of my throat. His hand trails across my exposed breast until it reaches my sore nipple, and he pulls on it, forcing the tip to extend.

I simultaneously swallow the cry that tries to leave my mouth as he pushes further inside until my nose almost reaches his disgusting pubic bone. He pulls back and groans as his cock slides almost entirely out to the tip and slides back in, rubbing against my tongue.

I feel his face bending closer to me, and I risk opening my one eye a sliver to see what position he's in. He's trying to lean his chest over me so that he can get my nipple in his mouth while he fucks my mouth.

He's distracted and hasn't noticed that I have moved my arm a little forward. His cock pushes against the side of my cheek, and he lets out a hoarse grunt, his eyes lowering to half-mast as his tongue licks the flesh of my breast. *NOW!* My mind screams.

I let my mouth open wider, and he slips in further, then I bite down as hard as I can. The taste of blood coats my mouth as my teeth penetrate the skin, and I force my jaw to close tightly. He releases a high-pitched scream and tries to pull back, stumbling and almost losing his balance on his bent legs.

I force my broken wrist and hand to grab a firm grip on his shirt and clutch it tightly. My other arm comes flying towards his face with the sharp end of the toothbrush, and I stab him in the eye, shoving it in as hard as I can until the thin plastic snaps, three-quarters of it still intact.

His screams are getting louder as he tries to fight my hold and pull away from me. "FUCKING BITCH, I'M...GOING TO...KILL...YOU!" He garbles between incoherent shouts.

I release his shirt and cock at the same time, and he stumbles backward, the back of his body making contact with the thick wood coffee table and forcing him to slip to the side, his feet losing purchase with the ground.

He's trying desperately to reach up to his eye to remove the toothbrush, his hand trembling and missing it. I rise quickly from the sofa and slam my palm into the broken end, pushing it further inside his eye and causing more blood to pour from the socket.

At the same time, I let my other fist fly with the pent-up rage I have inside, and it lands with a smacking sound on his other eye. With a harsh thud, the impact knocks his head back against the coffee table. He goes down hard, his body sprawling across the floor, and the only sound in the room is my heavy breathing.

I look around, panic seizing me. I have to get out of here, but I need to make sure he can't follow me. I rip his belt off his pants and tie his hands together, strapping them to the thick wood coffee table leg. I frantically search for something I can use to break the door, panicked whimpers leaving my lips, the sound too loud in the wooden cabin. *Breathe; you have to calm down and breathe!* My body instructs me in a calm voice.

Fuck! I suddenly remember that it will only open with his thumbprint pressed against the electronic reader. I race to the kitchen and open all the drawers until I find a steak knife. I hold it between my swollen fingers like a dagger.

I reach over with my throbbing swollen hand and grab a small empty pot off the wood stove. I force my broken wrist to carry the weight, tightly grasping the black metal handle in my sweaty and turgid hand, and rush back to the room. I can hear him starting to shift, his legs starting to move. Why won't he just fucking die? My clasp on the small pot tightens, pain radiating up my arm as

I swing it as hard as I can against his head. The sound is loud in the air as it connects with his scalp.

Die, motherfucker, die!

Rage fills me as he lies there with his bleeding dick hanging out of his pants. I smash the pot against his face, over and over, his nose crunching and gushing blood. We need to get out of here! My mind reminds me. The pot slips from my hand, tumbling to the floor with a loud bang. I bring the knife up, staring at it for a moment in my hand before I look down at his flaccid cock.

I grip the organ that has tainted me and caused my soul anguish and nightmares from my youth. I slide the sharp side of the blade across the skin, where it connects to his body. The knife is not sharp enough to cut right through, so I slide it repeatedly over the slimy skin until my hands are slick with blood and I'm cutting through thick tissue. He's bleeding like a stuck pig, and his body is twitching. *We don't have time for this, Mia, my mind screams at me. We need to get the fuck out of here.*

My breathing is ragged, and my skin is covered in his blood which is not helping the feeling of revulsion crawling across my body. I release his dick, leaving it half dismembered and rapidly pooling blood down his legs.

My grip on the bloody knife tightens, and I grab his hand, using my knee to force it flat against the hardwood floor. I slice the blade across his rough skin below his first knuckle. It takes four or five tries before it cuts through skin, bone, and tissue. My hands, arms, and knees are covered in blood as I grab onto the digit and almost drop it in the process. A low cry is leaving my lips over and over. I need to calm down. I can feel my chest tightening like I am about to have a panic attack.

I turn frantically and search for his car keys everywhere, but I don't find them. FUCKING HELL! I have no time. I have to get out of here. I don't know if he will wake from the beating I just gave him, and I'm too scared and shaking too badly to see if he still has a heartbeat. *Get out! Get out of here!*

I race across the room to where his heavy jacket hangs from a hook on the wall. I check the pockets, but the keys are not in them. I spy the shoes I wore when he first kidnapped me, thrown in a corner off to the side. I slip them on, my hands shaking so badly that I can't even do the laces properly, and I end up tying them into knots.

I slip the oversized, heavy black puffer jacket over my naked body, and it reaches down to my knees. It takes two attempts to even get the zipper to connect and then pulled up all the way to my chin. We have to go; we have to go right now!

I sprint back into the kitchen and open all the cupboards until I find a bunch of granola bars, shoving them in my pockets. I spy a bottle of water and slip it into the other pocket. I dash back towards the door and pick up the knife and thumb.

I'm getting ready to escape, but I spy the laptop with various squares open, showing different subscribers live on the screen. I walk back over, place my face close to the camera, and hit the mic button. All the faces are shadowed or distorted, none of them visible to me. *Fucking disgusting cowards!*

"Be forewarned, I'm going to find each and every one of you fuckers and kill you just like I did him. A Stratford never forgets or forgives. You better run."

Then I close the chat window, throw the laptop against the wall, and hear it smash with my brutality. The sound brings me a lick of satisfaction. I run back to the door with one last look at James. An animalistic snarl leaves my lips at his bleeding form. I spy his cell phone still attached to the tripod and still in video mode. I grab it quickly and shove it into the pocket of the jacket.

I want to make sure he's dead. *Fuck I want to set fire to this cabin of horrors, but there is no time.* I don't know if those others fuckers who were watching understand where we are. I don't even know if someone else might be coming after me.

I need to get as far away from here as fucking possible. With one last look back, I press his thumb to the reader, hear the beep that signals my freedom and pull the door open, racing out into the fresh air and towards the thick tree line.

CHAPTER 16

Theo

"Anger is a killing thing: it kills the man who angers, for each rage leaves him less than he had been before – it takes something from him." Louis L'Amour

Mateo, Finn, and I are sitting in the kitchen when the front door slams open with a crash, and we hear loud, heavy footsteps thundering toward us. I grab the largest knife from the butcher block and place my body in front of Mateo, only to have the fucker shove me aside and move up beside me with his own knife clutched in his fingers.

I watch as Finn hefts one of the counter stools in his large hands, getting ready to throw it at whoever comes through the doorway. The look of readiness and violence on his features.

Diego's large frame is the first to appear through the doorway, with Carter and Manuel fast on his heels. I release the breath that I was holding, and my grip on the knife loosens. Diego gives all three of us a scathing eyebrow raise and a look of menace before moving closer to the island. This motherfucker pretends like he isn't scared of anything. One of these days, I'm going to show his psychotic ass he should be scared of me.

"STELLA! STELLA!" Carter yells frantically, his body filled with energy. His face is pale, and fear is clearly evident on his features. His husky blue eyes look too wide for his face. Manuel enters the space with quick sure strides behind them but refuses to meet anyone's eyes. His face is an unreadable mask. *What the fuck is going on here?*

My heart thumps wildly in my chest, not knowing what to make of the three men standing before me. A trickle of unease skates down my spine. Something has got all three of them spooked. Have they found Mia? Is she dead? My heart constricts painfully at the very thought.

"WHAT IS THE GODDAMN MEANING OF THIS!" Stella storms into the room, hands on her hips and a look of menace across her features. Tom is right on her heels with his gun drawn, looking dangerous and ready to kill everyone in the room at the slightest indication of a threat.

"We might have found Mia." "I have some news." "We have a possible lead." All three men shout out different things in response to her demand. Mia's name is the only thing I hear through the buzzing in my ears. My body moves forward before I even realize I have taken a step, my grasp clutching to a fist full of Diego's shirt and pulling him towards me.

Finn reaches out and swipes the knife from my distracted hand, probably trying to stop me from bloodying Diego.

"Mia, you have found Mia?" My lungs feel tight, I'm not getting enough air, and my vision starts to see spots. I tighten my hold and stumble back, taking Diego with me as he reaches out to steady me.

"Yes, no, fuck. We are not sure, but we think we might have a lead." Diego tries to pull back from my hold with an angry scowl. His fingers reach up to dislodge my hold on his shirt, but I don't release him until he wraps his fingers around my wrist and tightens his grip until my hand goes numb.

"*Tio*, please tell us what you know!" Mateo begs from beside me. His hold on the knife is forgotten, but his fist still holds the blade.

"Hijo, no es bueno." Manuel shakes his head, and I immediately notice that he looks pale and sweat coats the collar of his black long-sleeve shirt. His eyes glance away from Mateo's and meet Stella's fierce blue ones. *"Lo siento reina, ojalá viniera con mejores noticias."*

Mateo sways next to me at Manuel's words, and the knife crashes to the stone floor with a loud bang. His hands are clenching and unclenching at his side, and his breathing has picked up. He's mumbling the word "no" over and over under his breath. Whatever Manuel just said wasn't good fucking news.

"Is she alive?" I swallow the rancid bile that races up the back of my throat as the question leaves my lips. I'm pretty sure the only thing keeping my knees from giving out on me is my hold of Diego's shirt and his grip on my wrist.

Diego and Carter meet each other's gazes before Diego releases my wrist, and he pulls back angrily. The sound of material tearing is loud in the air around us. He manages to dislodge my hold and takes a step back, putting space between us.

His face is filled with a vortex of emotions. Rage, despair, and pity are the most prevalent. With all the emotions crossing his features, the scar across his skin looks even more pronounced and monstrous. *Diego is feeling empathy? Fuck, what have they found?*

"What in the name of baby Jesus is happening in here?" Raegan and Issy rush in from the backyard to join in the chaos.

"They think they have a lead on Mia...." Mateo utters, but his voice doesn't sound confident; it sounds scared. He's biting down so hard on his lips that I can see the flesh tear and a drop of blood welling on the surface.

One of Manuel's men races into the room with Clark, both their faces solemn and filled with an emotion I can't read. Is it anger, sadness, or a combination of both? Clark's face is usually made of stone, and no feelings are ever visible unless he wants you to see them.

Right now, he's not even trying to hide them. *Fuck, what have they found? Where is my girl?* Different possibilities race through my mind, all of them horrid and threatening to cause my madness to overtake me.

"Put it there, Jorge. Connect to the site." Manuel indicates the large island, and the stocky, dark-haired man moves forward carrying a high-tech-looking chrome laptop in his hands. He sets it up with efficiency, never taking his eyes off the task and avoiding all the pairs of eyes that are glued to his every movement.

That small piece of metal against the white and gray marble countertop with its dark screen taunts me with malevolent energy. Whatever is going to appear on that screen, has Manuel behaving like it's the forthcoming of the apocalypse. Cold sweat is breaking out across my body, and nausea is racing through me. *She has to be okay, please, fuck, be okay.*

"It would be...best if the young ladies...left the room." Manuel's gaze never leaves Stella's, and I witness a crack in her icy facade. Her eyes scroll over to Raegan and Issy just as they both yell that they are not leaving. Issy clutches tightly to Raegan's hand, but her blue eyes meet Stella's and implore her not to send them away.

Stella closes her eyes tightly and takes a deep breath, nodding her head as her arctic blue eyes meet mine across the room. We speak without words being uttered to each other. Whatever we are about to see will be devastating for all of us in this room.

Her gaze promises me a painful death if the news is that Mia's gone. I stare steadily back at her, letting her see that I am more than ready to die. If Mia is truly gone, I will have nothing left to live for. Her head tips in acknowledgment.

"Is she alive?" The question is so painful to utter. The words feel like shards of glass slicing me open with each syllable. My mouth fills with bile for even asking it. *No*, I refuse to believe that there is a world where I could still be breathing and Mia isn't.

Jorge's gaze leaves his fancy machinery and meets mine. His dark brown eyes are filled with compassion and fear. *What is he afraid of?* Does he know what has happened to my queen, to the owner of my heart?

"She's alive...well, we believe she was alive as of a few hours ago." I watch as his Adam's apple moves up and down with his words. "I managed to hack into some dark web chatter that was making mention of a Manhattan princess being punished."

Punished? What the fuck does he mean by punished? The monster that lives inside of me, the one that thrives off darkness and desperately wants to shed his cage, rattles inside my head at the thought of someone out there hurting Mia.

Jorge wipes the sweat trickling down his face with the back of his hand. "I...I managed to hack one of the subscribers. It was for a live chat on a hidden website." His nervous eyes meet Manuel's before returning to mine.

"Ummm..the buy-in to watch was steep, two hundred and fifty thousand dollars for a session, so it was only available to a select few. This guy I hacked had managed to somehow save the live feed as he was watching it...."

"What was happening on the live feed?" I demand, stepping towards him, the threat of violence in my demeanor. *Let me loose; the monster inside me rattles against his bars.*

"Ahhh..." Jorge's golden and tanned skin seems to pale before my very eyes as he nervously swipes at more sweat, and his shoulders rise close to his ears. He turns his gaze back to Manuel, who nods. "It...it was...*la niña.* The girl, Mia...she was on the live show. She...she was being abused."

"What do you mean she was being abused? Someone was beating her? Who was hurting my sister?" Issy demands, her voice rising with every word until she's shouting the words to an already terrified Jorge.

"No...well, yes, but not only being beaten. She was being assaulted...sexually for a paying audience. The man was taking...requests from the subscribers to hurt her."

"WHAT THE FUCK!" I shout, pushing the guy hard against the island. Red rage crosses my vision until I can't see anything clearly.

"You...I..." I can't get any words out. Vile images of someone abusing my girl are trying to push their way into my brain. Images of things my father used to do to women. My stomach lurches and threatens to empty itself right now. I have to force myself to take deep breaths, to try to gain some control.

"No! No, no, no. This isn't happening," Mateo mumbles over and over. His color turning green, and sweat breaking along his hairline and upper lip.

"Show them, Jorge." Manuel's voice sounds defeated and broken. I force my eyes away from him to Stella, who is bracing her hands against the top of one of the barstools. Her knuckles and fingers are white from how hard she is gripping it. Raegan and Issy are holding each other tightly next to her. Tears are a crystal river flowing down Raegan's cheeks.

Jorge turns, meeting each of our eyes, and releases a jarring breath, one that I feel deep in my own soul. He has already witnessed the evil he is about to show us. It will no doubt leave scars on all of us like it has on him.

He hits a button on the laptop, and the screen lights up with an image of a rustic wood cabin. Deer heads are visible and attached to the wall facing the camera. The walls look to be all made of yellow-toned wood logs. There's no other *art* in sight, just a hint of a window in the right corner of the screen where daylight is streaming in. The sounds of worrisome whimpers can be heard off-screen.

Is that my Mia? She sounds like an injured animal. A bowling ball size of dread fills my stomach. I brace my hands on the side of the island to keep from grabbing the laptop or losing myself to my rage.

My glance meets Carter's, and I see the hint of insanity in his eyes. He's losing control of himself by the second, and soon we will be in this room with an uncontrollable lunatic. I have to ensure that I am the only one he hurts when his fit of rage boils over.

I glance at Mateo from the corner of my eye. His arms are tightly wrapped around himself, but his body is still trembling. His lips are pressed so tightly together that they are almost bloodless. He's been barely keeping it together for days now, falling further and further into his depression and anxiety. What will this do to him? *What will this do to him? What about us?* My mind questions.

A sound on the screen has my head turning back in that direction and captures my rapt attention. The angle on the small screen tilts down, and my breath leaves my lips in a loud exhale. My mind wars with what it's seeing...no it can't be. *Can it?*

Mia...my Mia. The woman who pulled me back from the darkness, fought and sacrificed for me, and holds my battered heart in the palms of her hands. My Mia is chained to the floor by one leg and arm like an injured animal, naked. Her beautiful face is all swollen, beaten, and battered. One of her eyes is black, and she's barely able to open it. Her nose is swollen, and even in the image, you can see her nostril is filled with dry blood.

No, fuck no. This isn't real. This can't be real. A whimper from the Mia on the screen sounds loud in the air. The silence of the kitchen is almost deafening as everyone watches the screen with devastation.

She is almost unrecognizable. An image straight out of a horror movie. I wouldn't believe that it was her, except my heart will always know its mate. That right there, on that small screen, is my mate, my heart, and my warrior queen.

Her long dark blonde hair hangs limply down her back in tangles. As she shifts, you get a glimpse of her skin. She's black and blue, and her ribs are clearly visible and protruding from her skin. Whoever has her is starving her. Her once lush curves are now mere skin and bones. More cuts and bruises mar her arms, chest, and legs. Until they are all you see, rather than untouched skin.

Find whoever is hurting her and kill them. Kill them all, and get our girl back! The monster inside of me rages at the image of our Mia so injured and broken.

CHAPTER 17

Theo

"The agony of my feelings allowed me no respite; no incident occurred from which my rage and misery could not extract its food." Mary Shelley

"Tell them you're a dirty Stratford whore." A thick voice instructs off-camera. Her ocean-blue gaze stares back in defiance. "Fuck you!" She spits, yanking on the chains. They rattle against the large hook in the floor at the same time as she tries to swallow the cries the painful movements must cause her.

"Fuck her pussy again with the dildo!" A gabled voice sounds from the screen. "No fuck her ass!" Another voice shouts. The sound echoes as if they are not in the room. We can see dark square boxes of other viewers who are hiding their identities along the top of the screen.

Deep, dark rage swells inside of me at their words. Out of the corner of my eye, I watch as Carter takes a few steps away from the group and puts his fist through the kitchen wall. No one says anything to him, and Stella's eyes remain glued to the screen before her. Diego takes a step back, placing his body between Carter's and everyone else's.

"Do you hear that, princess? A paying customer always gets what they want." A large man moves into the frame, grabs something bright green off the counter, and moves toward Mia.

"Please...no...please." We hear her beg as she thrashes wildly. The sound of her pleading rips at my heart and soul.

With horror and disbelief, we watch as he wraps his large hand around the back of her neck and forces her upper body to the ground and her ass up into the air. All the while, her ravished and battered body tries desperately to fight his hold. He takes the sizable green dildo and shoves it inside of her core violently as she screams and begs.

A scream echoes in the kitchen, and my eyes tear away from the screen to see Raegan rushing across the room to the kitchen sink, where she empties her stomach loudly. No one else moves, everyone frozen like statues as we listen to Mia screaming in pain and watch her trying to fight off the man's hold while garbled voices cheer in the background.

Jorge stops the video and turns back to us. The scream frozen in time, showing my girl being raped by an unknown man, taunts me, taunts the crazed beast inside of me.

"I'M GOING TO FIND THAT MOTHERFUCKER AND SLICE HIS THROAT OPEN!" Carter yells and pushes against Diego's body as he tries to restrain him.

"How many? How many of those videos did you find?" Finn questions with icy rage. "Are they all like that? He uses only toys on her...or...?" He doesn't finish his question, his intent clear to all of us in this room.

"Twenty-five videos. That is a more recent one from a day or so ago." Manuel replies with the promise of violence in his voice. "Jorge managed to find twenty-five of them on this guy's account. I wish that was the worst of it, Finn. He...*maldito monstruo*...he raped her with his own cock while she was unconscious in one of the last videos and beats her bloody. *La pobre princesa.*"

"No...no, this can't be real." Mateo's voice is so small that I barely hear it through the commotion in the room. Issy wraps her arms around his waist and pulls him to her body. All the while, Diego watches both of them while trying to keep Carter from causing more damage to the room or racing out of here in search of the fucker that has my Mia.

"Do we ever see his face in any of the videos?" Stella's voice rings out, but there's no firmness, only desolation in its sound. Her queen facade is shattering before us at the image of one of the people she loves the most being abused.

"How do we know she is still alive?" Finn demands. His death grip on the top of the stool indicates he is mere moments away from throwing it through the window.

"FINN!" Issy screams. Her mind cannot even comprehend that our Mia might not still be alive after suffering these horrific tortures. Part of me, the part that knows exactly what it's like to be taken against your will, beaten for some sick demon's satisfaction, partially hopes that she's not. I don't want her to live with the waking nightmares.

The evil thoughts that never leave you and cause you pain with every single breath you take. The revulsion at your own skin. The feel of hands touching you even when no one else is in the room with you.

"There is a new video. Jorge didn't have a chance to watch it before I had him come straight here. It's only a few hours old, so we believe she is alive. Show us the last video, Jorge." Manuel requests, as his body locks tight for what we are about to see.

I close my eyes and try to take a steadying breath, knowing that whatever I am going to see next will have me unleashing my darkness. I just hope that I am able to get to this psychotic, deranged fucker before Carter does. There will be nothing left for me to avenge myself on if I don't.

"I'm going to murder him slowly. I will make sure he feels every inch of pain that she did before I tear his fucking throat out." Carter shoves against Diego's tight restraining hold, and Finn has to lend his strength, holding Carter back.

"Carter, she's alive. She's out there, fighting. You saw her. She's a fighter. We have to focus on that. We have to find her, then you can mutilate and kill that son of a bitch, and I will help you." Finn grasps Carter's face, and they both take angry, panting breaths.

Diego's enraged gaze meets mine, and I see the promise of violence in their depths. Is he picturing Issy in my Mia's place? It could have been her on that screen. These fuckers wanted to punish a Stratford princess. He nods to me, and silently I read him loud and clear. He will help us kill these psychotic pieces of shit to make sure they never target any of them again.

"Grandmother." Issy reaches out and grasps Stella's arm, pulling her into a tight embrace. It's then that I notice the tears cascading down Stella's cheeks. "She's alive, grandmother. She's a fighter, just like you taught us to be."

Jorge clicks a few keys, and another video starts up. In the video, we can see Mia lying naked on the cushions of a dark brown sofa. Her body looks like it's been thrown onto the surface. Her neck is at an odd angle, like a discarded doll.

Her thick hair drapes across the sofa arm, down to the floor, and across parts of her face. She looks to be unconscious. Her slight frame is so still and silent that it has my heart rate skyrocketing. Is she even breathing right now?

Mia's whole body is riddled with more cuts and bruises than in the last video. How that's even possible, my mind can't comprehend. My eyes wander down her torso on the screen, and I can see deep purple bruises in the shapes of fingermarks displayed across her breasts, around her neck, and on both of her thighs. My heart aches at the image before me. The vision of the girl I love so incapacitated, small, and damaged by the hands of a maniac.

My eyes meet Stella's. I know she has noted what I have. I can see it in the panic on her face. Mia has been brutally raped by this man on the screen. He not only raped her, but he also made sure to inflict as much damage as possible. There is not even an inch of her that is unharmed.

"I will kill him, Stella. She is mine. No one will ever hurt her again, not even me." The promise lies between us. A promise of violence yet to come.

We watch as the grotesque muscular male moves into the frame, mumbling to himself, but the camera doesn't catch his words. My fists tighten painfully until my short nails are digging into the skin of the palm of my hand, and sweat pouring down my back. My hackles rise as he runs his fingers up her leg, forcing her knees apart and slipping a rough digit inside of her. *NO! Fuck NO!*

A wretched cry leaves Issy's lips as she burrows her face into Stella's shoulder, refusing to watch her sister being sexually abused by the fucker on the screen. The desire to look away fills me; I wish this was just one of my nightmares and not actually happening. *She is enduring it, surviving it. You will watch so that you know who to kill. She is not a coward, so you don't get to be one, either.* My mind chastises me with vehemence.

Finn loses control of himself at what is happening on the screen, and the stool before him crashes into the kitchen window. He's breathing heavily, and his eyes look crazed.

My eyes turn back to the screen. Mia's body never responds, not even a twitch, even with the invasion of his thick digit. He thrusts in and out of her core. Which, even from the short distance the camera is placed, we can see is really swollen, abused, and red.

His groans are the only sound playing on the video. He leans closer, and we watch as he unzips his pants and strokes himself. All the while, his finger is inside of Mia. He swipes his hard dick across Mia's face, running it across her cheek, chin, and lips before pushing himself through her closed lips. Forcing her to take him in her mouth as she lays there unaware.

A loud, angry growl sound goes off in the kitchen eating area. My eyes are ripped from the screen just in time to catch Carter flipping over the round dark wood table. He picks up one of the kitchen chairs from the breakfast nook in a fury, and throws it at the nearest wall. It hits, smashing a substantial hole in the wall, as he begins to pace back and forth, fisting at his own strands of hair and refusing to look at the screen.

I turn back to the screen, my heart in my throat, just as a loud scream is heard. The cry isn't coming from Mia, though. No, it's rough, angry, and deep. I watch as the man struggles to pull away from Mia's face. She has regained consciousness and bitten down hard on his cock. He tries to slap at her with his meaty paws, but one of her hands is fisted tightly in his shirt.

My eyes lock on the screen, mesmerized as her other arm lifts, a bright, thin green item catching the light before she strikes forward hard and embeds it into the guy's eye. Harsh screams are coming from her assailant as he tries to remove whatever she has shanked his eye with. *Fuck yes! There's my warrior queen!*

"Jesus fucking Christ!" Finn shouts from next to me.

Her bloody mouth releases its hold on his cock, and she moves quickly into a standing position. She hits the slender green item protruding from his eye again with the palm of her hand before cracking her small fist back and punching him in the other eye.

We can hear the guy screaming and swearing at her. Her face and chest are covered in his blood, and there is a crazed look in her ocean-blue eyes. A fire I have never seen before that both terrifies me and exhilarates me. Yes, my fucking queen. Look at how powerful she is. She will not allow anyone to bring her down low.

We see her crouch down in front of him as he panics and stumbles down to the ground, his body twitching. Everyone is silent in the room, the only sound coming from the screen as we all hold our veritable breaths.

Mia struggles to remove his thick leather belt from his pants in jerky motions. Then she's rising, forcing his hands together behind his miserable broad back and tying them tightly to the leg of a heavy-looking wood coffee table.

She leaves the frame, and panic fills my body. All we see on the screen is the fucking guy lying there but twitching and still breathing. That belt isn't going to hold for long if he decides to get back up. We can hear banging noises in the background, and then Mia is rushing back into the frame, still naked but now holding a small metal pot and a kitchen knife.

I observe with satisfaction as she slams the pot down on his big head. The sound is loud through the screen. His head jerks back before she slams it again, this time onto his face. Causing blood to gush out of his nose, over his lips, and down his chin.

Worry immediately fills me. Is this guy the only assailant, or are there more there that she has to worry about? Fuck, I need to get to her, to protect her from anyone trying to hurt her. *Like us, you mean?* My mind hisses the thought, and my breath becomes trapped in my throat.

"FUCK YES, BLONDIE!" Carter bellows from behind me.

We don't get a good view of what she's doing next, but we can see her kneeling, giving us a more thorough glimpse of her back which is covered in welts, lashes, deep bruises, and what looks like an imprinted boot mark and cuts, so many fucking cuts. We can hear rapid pants and grunts as she moves around. Her hands come away bloody, the knife still clutched in her tight grip. What the fuck is she holding? *Is she holding one of his fingers?*

"Jesus, Mary, and Joseph!" I hear Raegan mutter loudly.

Mia leaves the screen again, but we can hear her rushing around and more banging happening in the background. The guy on the screen lies there passed out. His cock is a bleeding mess, and you can clearly see she attempted to cut it off as it lies half attached to his body, and blood pools below him.

The gruesome display causes my beast to crow with enjoyment. He wants to destroy that fucker piece by piece. The knowledge that our vicious little queen has already begun this guy's destruction only soothes him a bit.

A minute or two go by, and my heart beats painfully in my chest. A look at Stella shows me she's pale, and more tears are streaming down her face. She's so pale that you can see veins underneath the skin on her cheeks and neck.

Stella is holding Issy's hand tightly in her own, and Carter has his arms wrapped around Raegan, who is trembling and has her face tucked against his chest, refusing to watch the video. Finn has a tight hold on Mateo's shoulder. Mateo is visibly shaking as tears slide down his face. *She's alive! Look, fools, my queen is alive!* I want to shout at them.

Mia reappears on the screen, now wearing a huge black puffer jacket that trails all the way down past her knees and makes her look like the *Michelin Man*. She looks straight at the camera, blood streaked across her cheeks, chin, and lips. Her beautiful blue eyes are thunderous, the wrath swirling and visible even through the camera. They call to my monster, and he wants to answer. *To bow at her wrathful feet.*

"I'm going to find each one of you fuckers and kill you just like I did him. A Stratford never forgets or forgives. You better run." Her voice comes out strong but hoarse. Then the screen goes blank.

"What the fuck!" Finn screams at the same time Mateo yells, "Did she make it out?"

I turn my gaze to Manuel, who has moved up next to his son, both of them looking like generals ready to start a war. "That was saved six hours ago. We only managed to hack the videos within the last hour. We can't pinpoint their exact location, but another one of our hackers has managed to triangulate an approximate area, but it's miles and miles of forested area two hours from here."

"Clark, I want helicopters in the air now. As many as we can get, and personnel immediately diverted to ground search. Find my granddaughter!" Stella screams.

Mateo is already pulling away from Finn's grip and racing for the kitchen entrance. He turns back around as Clark and Tom push ahead of him, both speaking into their phones and rushing for the front door. Honestly, I had forgotten the two fuckers were even here. "What are we waiting for?" Mateo shouts.

"*Reina*, my men are armed and ready outside your door. We will find her, and I promise to you, on my honor, I will capture and kill all of the men that paid to watch that happen to her." Manuel stands before Stella and reaches out, wiping one of her tears from her cheek.

"Bring me their heads, all of them." Stella inhales a deep breath at Manuel's touch. His dark eyes meet her icy blue ones. They share a moment, one that a bond forms between them. A bond forged between the ruthless queen of Manhattan and the violent criminal arms dealer. Right now, they are unified in destruction and in the task of finding Mia Stratford.

CHAPTER 18

Stella

"Life can only be understood backwards; but it must be lived forwards." Søren Kierkegaard

R age. All-consuming and desperate rage fills me. It flows through my veins like lava, threatening to smother everything in its wake. My granddaughter, not of my flesh but of my heart, was captured, abused, and raped by a madman.

All done in retaliation for being a Stratford heir, no doubt. Done to punish me for my own sins. For my unrelenting and unwavering grasp of power. She is paying the price for the strength of our empire. The tears slide down my face like a river of misery, and it feels like the cavern of my heart is about to split open and shatter what pieces were left after the loss of my Jaxon.

The screen taunts me, frozen at the sight of my granddaughter's defiant eyes. She has survived. She has fought back without mercy against those that would hurt her. Just like I taught her. The anger and strength within her empowering her to refuse to cower, to give up, to be a lamb to the slaughter.

Her blue-green eyes meet mine through the small screen, and they demand a war be waged against our foes. *One that I will give her.* There will be no mercy for those that hurt my Mia. No rock left unturned, no place safe to hide when I am done. Even if it takes my last breath, I will rid this world of all of the men that did this to her. *"Kill them all, my little viper; protect our girls."* Jaxon's voice runs through my mind, filled with unyielding wrath and the ferocity of an alpha wolf, ready to do damage to anyone who threatens his pack.

The sound almost brings me to my knees, my heart aches for the loss of the love of my life. The man that I had planned to spend eternity with, yet eternity was never promised. Our years spent together, while too short, were filled with so much love. *Those boys love Mia the same way Jaxon loved you,* my heart whispers. *They will set this whole world on fire for her. They will protect her when you are no longer able.*

Will they? They have hurt her over and over again. *I hurt you too, my little ice queen.* Jaxon's whispered words cause a shiver to go down my spine and goosebumps to rise along my skin. He's right, he did hurt me, but he was also my fiercest protector. My champion and knight, even though I never needed one. He stood by my side while we navigated this world together.

Mia doesn't need a knight. She doesn't need a king. She is the queen I have raised her to be. Strong, intelligent, capable, and ruthless. She is a survivor, unable to lie down and just let the world take her in its miserable grasp. She will fight back each and every time it tries to bring her down. She is a Stratford.

She may not need them, but she wants them. She loves those four assholes. I saw it the moment she bargained her freedom for them. One I never had any intention of taking. I will not repeat the sins of my father on my own children and grandchildren.

No, the Stratford line will be filled with love. My Jared grew up with love, and so did Isabella. When Mia arrived in our household, we all ensured to smother her with all the love we had. Jaxon and I wanted them to always know how much we cared about them. To grow up in a loving home, one that neither of us really had the full experience of.

Although it chafes me to admit, those four fuckers will love her until the end of their days. All four of them add a different dimension to my Mia; they bring her to life in different ways. Helping to further shape the strong and powerful woman she is meant to be.

Carter, the disturbed, maniacal criminal. He reminds me the most of my Jaxon. That boy will set the world ablaze, watch it burn at my Mia's feet, and do it with a smile as he bows willingly to her power. She will never have to question his loyalty to her. I know in his eyes, there is no one else for him. *He loves her with a madness that is as frightening as it is invigorating.*

That controlling power-hungry asshole, Theo. The one my granddaughter seems to react more intensely to than the others, even if she doesn't realize it herself. How I long to tear that misguided fool apart, one piece at a time. Unfortunately, my granddaughter will never forgive me if I do. Theo brings out this fierceness in her with his abrasive personality and controlling tendencies. *Much like my Jaxon did with me.* Mia and Theo battle with each other strategically, one trying to outmaneuver the other, but the truth is they love it. The fight, the challenge, brings both of them to life.

He was the mastermind behind their bullying in her youth. The idiot didn't learn from his previous mistakes and led them right back to committing the same crimes. He reminds me the most of me. He is a born leader; the others look to him to make decisions and to help keep them safe. Even though he tends to lead them straight into danger with his need to protect them.

It broke my heart when he sacrificed himself to return to that monster, Vincent Saint-Lambert, to keep the other three safe and Vincent away from my granddaughter. I knew the treacherous fate that awaited him. So did he. I wanted to save him myself, yet even knowing he would be tortured till his dying breath, he still went back. The courage he displayed in doing so won my respect, something that is increasingly hard to come by.

My heart almost stopped as I listened through the phone as Mia put that gun to her mouth on my plane to force my hand. Frigid, spiraling fear that she would actually end her life to protect them ran through my veins. Gone was my little girl with fierce eyes and a stubborn streak, now in her place was a woman determined to do what she needed to in order to save the man that she loved. *Men, Stella. She loves all four of them equally.* Yes, four assholes, because only one wouldn't do.

The other two are so different from Carter and Theo, yet their demeanors have a distinct quality that places them in the same circle of darkness and violence. Links them together to form a chain, one that wraps around my Mia in protection.

Mateo is the charmer and kind soul of the group. I can see that he feels things deeply. His love for his fellow kings and, more importantly, for my granddaughter, is forged from the strongest steel, unbending and all-encompassing. He brings out a softer, more genuine side to my Mia. One that she doesn't like to show through the cracks in her facade. While he fights with the demons that plague his mind, he finds peace at my Mia's hands. He places his battered and soul-weary heart at my granddaughter's feet with a devotion that I can understand. I once had the same passion from my Jaxon. Some might call him weak, but they are fools; there is nothing stronger than fighting your own demons.

The last one is a contradiction. Finn. He was Mia's best friend, grew up with her in poverty, and loved her first. A childhood love that blossomed into more upon reacquaintance years later. Yet, even with that love, he has allowed horrendous things to be done to her on more than one occasion, including the most recent attempt to push her away. That knowledge brings with it the need to hurt him more intensely than the others and punish him for hurting my granddaughter. There is almost nothing worse than betrayal. He carries it on him like a thick skin that he cannot shed.

He has confessed to me his past actions, indiscretions, weaknesses, and the thoughts behind them. Ready to take the punishment for his sins, even if that meant that I take his life. I was tempted, so very tempted to rip his beating heart from his chest for his part in hurting my Mia. Though I must admit, the fucker had some courage divulging his secrets and awaiting his execution.

I now know his deeds were all done with the intent to protect her, even as a child, from that psychotic sadist, Vincent, and his lackey, Mack. Unfortunately for him and for her, his actions had unprecedented consequences. Not only with Mia being captured now by this unknown assailant but even back then when she was a child. Can I forgive him for his trespasses against my heir? Can she ever forgive him for his betrayal? *Only time will tell, I suppose.*

Finn is a guardian in the night, standing firm against the evil that would attempt to hurt my granddaughter. A wall that all others will break themselves against in their efforts to reach her. While the other three stir fiery emotions inside of Mia, Finn brings her the respite of a safe harbor. The comfort that she once knew as a child. Even though she fights against those emotions rekindling. I see it in the way he speaks with her, the genuine emotion in his voice, words, and deeds when he is not following that fool Theo's orders. Also in the way she sometimes forgets herself and his betrayal, yet reacts before those thoughts slip back in and remind her of his transgressions.

A shuddered sigh leaves my lips as my eyes refocus on the image before me. My beautiful girl. *I am coming, Mia. You will have vengeance, my love.* How I long to wrap her in my arms like when she was a child. To hold her tight to my chest and whisper to her of all the power and glory she will attain. That she is a warrior that will continue to defend the Stratford line.

A noise has me turning rapidly on my feet and preparing for violence. I may be older now, but I have never lost my instincts and self-preservation. Over the years, the various attempts on my life have taught me hypervigilance. One that I tried to instill in both Mia and Isabella.

Diego Cabano stands before me, his dark green eyes meeting mine unwaveringly, without repentance or fear. Just that one look from him makes my hackles rise, and the desire to plunge a blade into his manipulative heart rises within me.

He is a dangerous predator, and what he's hunting for is power, glory, and my granddaughter. Just not the original granddaughter he and his father bargained for. He thinks I don't know about his infatuation with my Isabella. Fool! I know everything that happens with my heirs. *Yet Mia was taken, your highness.* The snarky cunt within me stabs me deep with the knowledge of my failure.

"Stella, there is something you should know." Fear slides up my limbs, and my heart painfully constricts in my chest. I force my hands to unclench, my back straightening, and my head to remain high. I am a Stratford; this miserable snake will not have me showing any weakness.

"Speak, you snake, and tell me what you know."

"You are so eloquent, your highness. Despite your bitchy, cold inflection, I will tell you what I have discovered. Let's get one thing straight, though, Stella. I don't fear you. You don't make me cower in my shoes like those other prissy assholes. You might be a cold killer, but I am one too."

He moves further into the room until he stands no more than two feet from me. I can see the golden flecks in his green eyes, anger, and refusal to bow at my feet prevalent in them. His ragged scar pulls across his skin with a determined smirk on his face. This one will be harder to manage. *It would be a blessing to Isabella if I had him murdered.*

"Then I will meet you in hell, Diego. We will both land there if you continue to pursue my Isabella. Now tell me what you know, or get the fuck out of my sight."

Shock momentarily crosses his face before he disguises it behind the mask he too wears. He watches me, the devious asshole. Is he wondering if my threats are idle? They won't be. I will protect Isabella from the world he would drag her into. My Isabella is pure light and I won't have his darkness taint her.

"The man who took Mia. Carter and I discovered who we believe he might be. James Hamilton."

His words make me take a staggered step back, one that I loathe because it gives up ground to this fiend. *James Hamilton.* That name brings nothing but revulsion across my skin. Mia's biological father, the scum of the earth that molested her as a child and beat my daughter-in-law bloody.

A memory of Mia calling me weeks ago to tell me that he was at her gate rises in my mind. I reassured her that she was safe. That I had it handled, and I thought I did. That piece of garbage has been under surveillance since that day. I sent men to give him a warning with their fists and at the end of a barrel of a gun to stay away from my granddaughter. I was just waiting for one wrong move so

I could send him back to that small cell and ensure he lived out the rest of his evil days trapped behind bars. *We should have killed him then. We should have had him murdered inside prison so he never had a chance at freedom.* My mind seethes, and a haze of red coats my vision.

It seems my warnings weren't enough and instead had the opposite effect. They made him angrier. Whereas when he showed up at the gate he was looking for a payout, he decided to take my Mia in order to punish me and Catherine. How did he get to her? How was he able to sidestep all of the provisions I had put in place? These questions run in vicious circles in my mind. I was ineffectual in protecting my granddaughter. I failed her. What good is power if it cannot be used to save the ones that you love?

"There's more, Stella. Jorge thinks your cameras here on the property might be compromised. That James somehow had been watching her for weeks before he took her. He was probably still keeping tabs on us here while he had her captive." Diego sighs and drags his hand through his thick dark hair. A look of exhaustion crossing his features.

I do have to begrudgingly acknowledge that he and his father have been actively helping to look for Mia since the very start, and without them we wouldn't have the information that we do. That doesn't mean I will allow him to be with Isabella in repayment, though. Fuck that shit.

"Stella, I'm confident that he was the one who captured Vincent and killed all his minions. I also have a hunch that Mia had something to do with the rage inflicted on Vincent's wounds before he died. I'm unsure if she killed him herself, but she must have helped end him."

His words speak nothing but the truth. I can feel it in their weight. It explains how he was able to get his hands on one of my heirs despite everything I put in place. Did he do it alone, or did someone else help him? That is the question. As for Mia killing Vincent Saint-Lambert, it doesn't bring me one moment of distress to know my granddaughter may have been capable of that type of brutality.

"What do you gain from telling me this, Mr. Cabano? Do you think I will repay you with my granddaughter?" I raise an eyebrow in his direction, my teeth clenching tightly with the need to scream.

"I never want what happened to Mia to occur to Issy. I will make sure nothing ever hurts her, Stella. Not you, not your enemies, nothing. She is the most valuable thing I own."

"You do not own her, you heathen!" I shout, my hand slamming out and connecting with his scarred cheek. His words of ownership make me lose my precious control. No man will own one of my granddaughters. They will be free from the taint of men trying to make them into possessions. The sound is loud in the air, skin hitting skin with a thunderous noise. He doesn't move back, doesn't even flinch. If it wasn't for the imprint of my fingers on his skin, you would never even know that I struck him.

"I will." He doesn't wait for a response from me before turning on his heels and storming from the room and leaving me standing there with my mouth gaping open and nothing but resentment filling the air.

Fuck! How many more of these deranged fuckers are going to fall in love with my granddaughters? Jaxon, my love, send me strength from wherever you are. I'm going to need it.

CHAPTER 19

Mia

"Was it hard?" I ask. Letting go? Not as hard as holding on to something that wasn't real." Lisa Schroeder

The sun is starting to go down, and the temperature is beginning to dip. My face feels the wind's chill as I bury it into the jacket's collar. James's scent wafts off the fabric, causing my painfully empty stomach to lurch in disgust. There is nothing left to throw up, though, and as much as I want to eat one of the granola bars I took, I know I wouldn't be able to keep it down. Better not to waste it. I don't know how long I will be lost in the wilderness.

Where before I was sweltering in this heavy puffer, now I am so glad for its warmth. Even if it has the monster's scent on it. I have no idea how far from the cabin I have managed to make it at this point. However far I've made it, it doesn't seem far away enough. I never want to see that wretched place of horrors again. *We will see it in our nightmares forever.* My mind warns.

The sun is starting to go down, and the temperature is beginning to dip. My face feels the wind's chill as I bury it into the jacket's collar. James' scent wafts off the fabric, causing my painfully empty stomach to lurch in disgust. There is nothing left to throw up, though, and as much as I want to eat one of the granola bars I took, I know I wouldn't be able to keep it down. Better not to waste it. I don't know how long I will be lost in the wilderness.

Where before I was sweltering in this heavy puffer, now I am so glad for its warmth. Even if it has the monster's scent on it. I have no idea how far from the cabin I have managed to make it at this point. However far I've made it, it doesn't seem far away enough. I never want to see that wretched place of horrors again. *We will see it in our nightmares forever.* My mind warns.

I have been walking steadily at a pace my injured body can handle through this densely forested area for what seems like hours. Tripping over thick exposed tree roots and sliding through slippery mud. I've been dragging a thick branch behind me to hide my tracks from those who would seek me, but my arm feels like it wants to fall off.

My only company is the sound of birds in the bulky trees and small wildlife creatures scurrying and trying to survive and make it to safety, just like I am. The fresh air is bittersweet. A welcome to my aching lungs, but it also brings with it a chill that is starting to drain what little energy I have left.

I need to get further away; there is a sense of urgency to run and hide flowing through my exhausted body. I don't know who was out there watching that video and might have come looking for me.

Whoever they were, they paid a hefty sum to ensure I was abused, which means they have resources at their disposal. Other fuckers who might want to trap and hurt the Stratford heir. *We need to find shelter. We are not going to make it if we don't.* My mind beseeches.

The sound of helicopters overhead has me seeking protection underneath a large eastern red cedar tree. I cling to the bark with anxiety as my heart rate picks up once again. My head tilts back to watch as they fly past, lower than I would expect, just above the tallest trees.

That's the second time I have seen them in the last few hours. They are definitely looking for something or someone. *Could it be one of the sickos that were watching out here looking for me? Maybe it's Stella?* How would Stella know where to look for me? No, it has to be one of the guys watching. I'm going to need to hide. I refuse to be captured again.

My hand slips into the jacket pocket and clenches around the bloody knife I used to slice off James' finger. No, if they try to capture me and it looks like I will not be able to make it out, then I will slice my own throat, and let myself bleed out. In no world would I allow myself to go through that hell again.

My beloved stepfather Jared and step-grandfather Jaxon will greet me with open arms in the next life and keep me safe until Stella, Issy, and my mom can join me. A tear slides down my face at the thought of not seeing any of them again. Would they be proud of how I saved myself, or furious that I put myself in harm's way to begin with, just to escape the pain that the kings caused me? I miss both of them so much. They are the only men in my life who never let me down or harmed me.

Thoughts of the kings make more tears slide down my face. *No, I can't break down right now.* I can't think of them and all the misery they have caused me. I was a fool to believe that any of them could have feelings for me. Look at how quickly they discarded me once they learned I was Amelia Hamilton. I swipe angrily at my face with the jacket sleeve and force myself to shut out any more thoughts of them. *Fuck them. They are next on my list to send to hell if I survive.*

I keep shuffling forward as the helicopters continue in the other direction. Nothing but thick trees and grassy hills greet me. I need to find somewhere to hide before the sun sets. Somewhere I can be safe from both types of animals that would be seeking me, *man and beast.*

I move another three hundred paces before I come upon a small creek, falling to my knees and slipping my hands into its icy waters. I take a deep drink of the refreshing liquid in my cupped hands until my stomach protests.

My eyes roam over the densely shrubbed area, looking for a place I can both hide and defend myself in, in case an animal thinks to make me its dinner. I know black bears, foxes, and bobcats are in these woods, and I don't mean to become anyone's tasty treat.

Up ahead, fifty feet from where I am perched on my knees, it looks like there is a deep crop of Mountain Sweet-pepperbush. I can hide in its deep depth and rest. My body is aching and exhausted, with various sore spots making every movement of my limbs excruciating.

The infection that is ravaging my body is causing me to both shiver and be slick with sweat in the jacket. I just need to rest for a little while. If I can just stop for a few hours, and let my body have a brief period of inactivity, then I can push harder and keep going.

I force myself to move forward until I am crawling underneath the thick leaves of the bush and pressing my body tightly to its thick bark. I gather as much loose debris around me as possible to disguise my body, the black jacket helping camouflage me against the dirt.

Once I'm huddled deep into the oversized jacket in the fetal position, I try to cover as much of my exposed skin as I can. I then grasp the knife tightly in my fist and close my eyes, hoping that the nightmares abate for now so I can get some rest. With a deep shuddering breath, I allow sleep to take me.

CHAPTER 20

Finn

"One man's remorse is another man's reminiscence." Ogden Nash

"**W**here the hell is she?" Mateo asks again with a panicked voice from my side as we drive through the densely wooded area. The light is starting to fade, and we still haven't found this cabin in the woods.

I'm trying hard not to show the girls and Mateo, that I too, am panicking. It's been hours since we saw that video, and there has been no sign of Mia yet. *She has to be out here. Please be out here and safe.*

"She made it out, Mateo...she's out here," Raegan repeats again, this time with a little less conviction while her grip on the seat belt tightens as we drive over bumps at rapid speed. Issy's frightened eyes meet mine in the rearview mirror. She's even paler than usual, her skin looking ghostly white and her blue eyes large in her pretty face.

The dark blue Land Rover racing further up ahead of me is being driven by Theo. The fucker insisted on driving and going with an insane Carter. Even though Carter clocked him one as they were leaving Mia's house. Theo just shrugged it off like it was nothing and got behind the wheel, and after a moment's hesitation, Carter slipped into the vehicle with him.

Keeping Carter from doing serious damage to Theo is becoming tedious and a full-time job. The only things that are stopping the two of them from killing each other right now are the need to find Mia and the testicular fortitude of that fucker Diego. *Yeah, fucking Diego.*

I never thought I would willingly be grateful to Diego, who got into the car with the two idiots. Even the thought feels like pure acidy shit in my stomach, but here I am, thanking whoever hears my damn prayers for him.

He has been able to stop Carter from completely losing it, calling him back from the depth of his insanity and getting him to focus on finding Mia. How he's doing it, I don't know, but Issy thinks it's because they are both insane. *Like calls to like, I guess.*

"We are going to have to get back on the road, the light is starting to fade too quickly, and I won't be able to see shit soon. I don't want to end up wrapping us around a tree." I utter, tightening my grip on the steering wheel.

Fuck, I want to keep looking, and if it was just me in the car, nothing would keep me from continuing forward in the dark, but I have the girls and Mateo in here with me. I can't risk them. *Mia would murder me herself if I hurt her sister or Raegan.*

Once again, the image of her face covered in blood as she promised death to those that watched her be abused crosses my mind and makes the hair on the nape of my neck stand on end. She was stunning in her violence. Her words chilled me right down to my very soul. I know that when we find her, she will unleash her wrath on us next, and I welcome it. She can do anything she wants to us as long as she's back and safe.

"What about them? Carter, Theo, and that snake Diego?' Raegan questions.

"I hope Diego ends up wrapped around a tree." I hear Issy mumble underneath her breath. I watch her roll her eyes and purse her lips through the rearview mirror.

Whatever Diego has done to Issy, he better watch himself. She may look like this perfect little doll, but she's as fierce and as vicious as my Mia. After all, Stella fucking Stratford raised the both of them.

Theo's car pulls to the right and pushes through a more wooded area before coming to a stop back close to the highway. He jumps out, and Carter, and Diego immediately exit the vehicle as well.

I watch with mounting frustration as we drive closer, as Carter once again gets up in Theo's face. He grabs onto his shirt and pushes him against the side of the car while Diego tries to drag him off of him. I pull in behind them, and Mateo and I are out of the car in a flash.

"WHAT THE FUCK, CARTER!" I yell as I approach the three of them.

"Carter, you fucker, you know he's right. We can't keep driving around in the woods looking for her. We are going to crash into a fucking tree. Be reasonable, asshole!" Diego wraps his arm around Carter's neck and forces him to relinquish his hold on Theo's throat.

"No, we are not stopping. My girl is out there! She's fucking hurt and scared! I need to find her!" He yells back, his face red with rage and his freaky pale blue eyes looking demonic in the fading light and shadows cast by all the trees.

"*WE* NEED TO FIND HER!" Theo yells back, pushing against Carter's hold.

"Naw, motherfucker. You're done with her. You're the reason all this shit happened. I will fucking end you before you ever get within ten feet of her." Carter steps back, pushing against Diego's hold on his neck until he releases him.

"You rotten scoundrels. You're over here arguing about who's going to rescue her? Are y'all dense? She doesn't need any of you fuckers. Were y'all not paying attention? She saved her damn self!" Raegan shouts as she approaches us with Issy in tow.

"I hope my sister guts all five of you fuckers. If she doesn't, I'm going to use my trust fund to make sure all of you are looking over your shoulders for the blade I will be sending your way for the rest of your miserable lives." Issy yells in frustration and with a look that is so "Mia" that it's frightening.

"All of you prissy rich pricks shut the fuck up! No one is saying we are stopping the search. We just need to be smart here. We are no good to Mia if one or more of us ends up wrapped around a tree." Diego runs his hands through his dark tresses while staring at Issy with longing.

"Fuck, Diego is right, and trust me, it feels like shit to even say those words." Mateo sighs, stepping in front of Theo and checking his throat and face. Theo's mouth is yet fucking again bleeding from another hit Carter managed to land.

"Thanks, *primo*. You're an ass, by the way." Diego grunts.

A phone rings in the car, and Theo rushes to grab it. He pulls the cell phone to his ear, not even bothering to utter hello. We all hold our breaths hoping for some news. He listens for a minute before pulling the phone away from his ear, his expression unreadable.

"Did they find something?" I question, hope rising in my chest. I know that Diego is in contact with his father's men that are searching on the ground, and that Clark is in constant contact with Theo, per Stella's instructions.

I was surprised when she even allowed us to come. Really I don't think she could have stopped us at this point. She would have had to shoot each one of us to keep us from looking for Mia.

"Nothing yet. The helicopters have to stop for the night, and the ground search is setting up a perimeter and camp up ahead. They will continue to search, but Clark wants us to head to the camp to be outfitted with night vision and weapons."

I meet each of my fellow kings' eyes, and I see the resolve in them to not stop looking for Mia. Nothing and no one will keep us from going out there and searching for her. Our queen is somewhere in this wilderness, and while she doesn't need a knight in shining armor to save her, she does need her kings by her side.

CHAPTER 21

Carter

"Hope is being able to see that there is light despite all of the darkness." Desmond Tutu

The minute that Clark outfits me with some high-grade night vision, tactical gear, and another gun. I'm walking away from the temporary makeshift camp of tents, personnel, ammunition, and my fellow kings, and heading at a brisk pace further into the woods. The need to find my girl is a burning fire in my veins. I know she's out here. I can feel it in my soul. *I'm coming, Mia; hold on, baby.*

My mind is still in turmoil from watching that video. Seeing what my girl has endured in captivity at the hands of a sadistic madman. A madman that she bludgeoned and took her righteous vengeance on. She was glorious in her rage, covered with his blood, her slim and battered body, standing defiant. The look of wrath on her face and the violence in her eyes, they called to me. *Cementing the fact that she is mine.*

Now I just need to find her, so I can wrap her in my arms and never fucking let her go. I will kill anyone that tries to take her from me, including fucking

Stella if I have to. Together, Mia and I will enact violence and retribution on all those fuckers that hid behind a screen and watched her torture.

Fast-approaching footsteps behind me have me ducking behind a tree, pulling the gun out of the holster strapped across my chest and releasing the safety. I raise it in my grip and shift out from behind a thick tree. "If you shoot me, fucker, I will end you." Diego's harsh voice echoes in the stillness of the night.

I roll my eyes and lower my weapon, clicking the safety before placing it back in the strap. Figures it would be this fucker that would come after me. *Would you rather it was Theo?* My mind questions. *Only if I get to put a bullet in his brain.*

"Why you following me, fucker? You need me to hold your hand going through the woods in case the big bad wolf comes for ya?"

A chuckle leaves his lips, and I can see his menacing smirk in a beam of moonlight through the trees. "I am the big bad wolf, asswipe. Nothing in these woods scares me, including your psychotic ass."

I nod my head and keep moving, not slowing my pace one bit further into the wooded area. If he wants to come with me and be another set of eyes trying to find my girl, I am not going to stop him.

He's probably right. He is one of the savage animals in these woods. If I'm unhinged and reckless, Diego is entirely without mercy. I see some of my own madness deep in his eyes. *It's why I secretly like the fucker, not that I would ever tell him that.*

We move silently for hours, dusk turning into deep night before the sky threatens to lighten again. It has to be four or five in the morning right now. I pull my phone out of my pants pocket and notice that it only has one reception bar, and my battery is almost halfway gone. Fuck, I should have charged it before we left camp. *Damn it! That was stupid and reckless of me. My two middle names, apparently.*

The biting cold has seeped into my bones as the forest closes in around us. We occasionally hear another group in the distance moving through the dense foliage, searching for Mia. They are focusing on the outskirts, closer to the road, but I know my girl. She would be smart and hide further in to ensure no one found her.

Images from the earlier video try to push to the forefront of my mind, but I force them away. I can't afford to lose it out here right now. I'm likely to start killing everyone in a blind rage. The only image I allow is the last moment before that video went black as her pretty eyes stared into the screen. Eyes filled with anger and madness, kindred spirits to mine.

Beautiful blue aquamarine stones filled with fire that I would give up my soul to see glancing back at me. I need to find her. To hold her in my arms and promise her that I will remain by her side until my last breath, if she will forgive my utter stupidity for trying to push her away.

"So, fucker, you know once we find her...you can't keep beating on Theo, right? Mia isn't going to allow that to go down. Fuck, she's likely to kill him herself, but she won't let you do it." Diego's voice calls out from the darkness behind me.

I can hear the laughter in his voice. It's been hours since we spoke a single word between us, both lost in our thoughts as we search for my missing queen. The companionable silence has brought me a measure of control, allowing me to focus and push the monster within back. For all his words, I know Diego enjoys watching me beat the fuck out of Theo. If there's one of us he detests more than the others, it's him.

A chuckle leaves my lips at his words. He's right, and I know it. Mia will hand me my own ass if she sees me going after Theo or after any of my fellow kings. She doesn't like others touching what is hers, and we are all hers one hundred percent. It might just be worth it to see my little warrior queen knock me down a couple of places. *Don't you dare get hard, fucker; now is not the time!* My mind admonishes.

Small rustling sounds coming from up ahead, past a small creek, grab my attention. I raise my hand to get Diego to stop and nod toward a thick grouping of bushes off to the side. It could be an animal coming at us. Bobcats and bears live in these woods. *Fuck, I don't have the energy to go toe to toe with a big black bear right now.*

From the corner of my eye, I watch as Diego slips around the tree directly behind the bush, silent like a ghost in his movements. *Fucker is slick. I'll give him that.* I move slowly, careful in my steps to remain quiet and not startle whatever is moving in front of me.

As I get within ten feet of the bush, a small red fox flies out with a high-pitched mewing sound and something dangling from its mouth. He stops his little furry body a few feet ahead of me, where his frightened gaze lands on me. He drops what is in his mouth and lets out a high-pitched screech that has all the hairs on my body standing on end. I move forward another couple of steps toward the little guy as I hear more rustling from the bushes. He panics and darts away, leaving whatever was in his mouth behind.

There's a bigger predator in that bush, and that little guy was scared for his life. I should be fucking wary too. I don't need my fucking throat ripped out, ending my life prematurely. I make my way quickly to where he was, just as Diego darts around the tree and motions with his finger for me to be silent. *What the fuck is that? Is that a granola bar?*

A large black shape crawls partially out of the bush, making grunting noises that have me jumping back. *Fuck, it's a bear!* I pull the gun from my strap and unlock the safety. Diego has his gun out, too, and points right at the shape. It's hard to see it clearly with all the shadows cast from the moon, but whatever it is, it doesn't seem as large as a full-grown bear. A cub, maybe? Shit, where there is a cub, there is an angry momma bear.

"*Motherfucker.*" The black shape hissed.

What the ever-loving fuck? Did that animal just speak? It crawls entirely out of underneath the bush and has my heart rate skyrocketing. A beam of moonlight hits it just as it lunges for me and attacks. I'm knocked backward by its momentum, and a snarling noise is loud in my face. Then I feel the sharp edge of a blade firmly pressed against my neck, digging in as drops of blood trickle down my skin.

Diego races behind whatever is holding me and presses his gun into its back. His eyes are vast, and his jaw tight with fury. "Remove the blade, cunt, or I'm putting a bullet in your back."

He yanks hard on the dark head of whoever is attacking me, and blonde hair shines in the moonlight before crazed ocean-blue eyes meet mine. *Mia! Holy fuck, it's Mia!* She's staring right through me like she doesn't see me. Angry growls are coming from her, and her teeth are bared in my direction.

If I wasn't so scared right now, I would be hard at the way she's holding me at knife point. Strength, determination, and a hint of madness radiate off of her in waves. I'm not sure her mind is even here with us. She's not seeing me standing here. She's reactive to a perceived predator. Someone trying to hurt her. *Fuck. I have to get through to her.* I need her to see it's me. That she's safe now. That I will never again let anyone or anything hurt her.

"Mia...baby...it's me." I drop the gun to the ground and try to lift my arm, but she presses the blade firmer into my skin, the sharp sting letting me know she's nicked me again.

"Mia. Mia, please, you are safe now. I'm going to take you back to Stella. Issy and Raegan are waiting for you. Please just put down the knife." Diego tries talking her down in soothing tones, but it's like she's not present in her mind. Like she's seeing something other than us right now. Is she seeing the fucker from the video?

"Blondie, it's me. Please, baby."

I watch as Diego shifts behind her, which causes her to push the blade further into my skin. Her body is locked up tight, and her breaths are coming out ragged and through her nose. Her eyes don't meet mine. They are sightless and dilated as Diego tries to pull her back by the oversized jacket.

"Listen, Mia, let me get you back home, okay? Then if you want to kill this prissy, disturbed fucker I will help you. I'll gladly help you murder all of your kings." Diego tries to coax her out of whatever living nightmare she's in. I'm not too impressed the fucker is offering to help kill me right now, but fuck, if it helps snap her out of it. I don't fucking care. I'll deal with his fucking ass later, with my fist.

A beam of moonlight cascades across her beautiful features. Her mouth, cheek, and chin are still covered in dried blood and dirt. She has bruises all over her face. Her left eye is swollen and black. Her nostril is caked in blood, and a cut right above her eyebrow looks terribly swollen and infected. *Fuck, that piece of shit did a number on her.* All these weeks, my girl has been living in hell. Being subjected to some of the worst crimes a man can inflict on a woman.

I try to raise my hand. The need to touch her skin, to convince my other senses that what I am seeing in front of me isn't an apparition, that it genuinely is my girl, overwhelms me. The minute I move, a feral growl leaves her lips, and the blade digs in further. *Jesus, she is going to slice my throat without even being aware of it.*

"Mia, fuck. You're slicing his neck open!"

CHAPTER 22

Mia

"Once you had put the pieces back together, even though you may look intact, you were never quite the same as you'd been before the fall." Jodi Picoult

"**M**ia...baby... it's me." The voice sounds familiar to my muddled brain, but fear is riding me hard, and there's a light pounding in my ears. My body is filled with *fight-or-flight* energy. The blood rushing through my veins makes me feel like my head will explode. I can feel sweat trickling down my back inside of this heavy jacket.

"Blondie, it's me. Please, baby."

"Listen, Mia, let me get you back home, okay? Then if you want to kill this prissy, disturbed fucker I will help you. I'll gladly help you murder all of your kings."

Lies! These voices are all lies; they are using them to try to trap me. They are not real. None of this is real. They can't be here.

My mind tried to call me back from the dark place it was resting in when that fucking rotten animal crawled underneath the bush and tried to steal all my food. The little fucker bit my hand in its eagerness to steal the granolas in my pocket while I was trying to sleep and keep warm.

"Mia, fuck. You're slicing his neck open!" The angry male voice behind me shouts close to my head before I feel his rough hands yanking on the back of the jacket. *NO! No one is going to hurt me again!* I will take all of them to hell with me before I allow myself to become a victim again. I don't think. I just react, slashing out at the male in front of me, turning quickly, and trying to stab the one behind me.

A sharp cry sounds in the air and fills me with satisfaction. *Good, I fucking hurt one of them.* The one behind me sidesteps my swing and releases his tight hold on me. I shift away from both of them, a red haze across my vision. All I see before me are male shadows. Ones that want to hurt me, to violate me and make me their prisoner. *No, kill them! Kill them all!* My mind begs.

"MIA! Wake up baby, please!" the one to the right yells. I don't take either of them out of my slightly blurred sight as I step back another couple of steps, preparing to turn and run. My only hope is to get back across the creek and to manage to hide in the denser part of the forest. I won't let them take me, not alive anyways.

"Fuck, Carter, she's going to run! She's not seeing us. She's only seeing her captor!" The shadow to the left yells. He moves slowly towards me with his hands raised in the air in front of him. *No, bitch, you are not getting those filthy hands on me. I will fucking kill you.* I lunge forward, slicing the knife in the air and screaming like a banshee. "I'LL KILL YOU!"

"Mia, fuck. No one is going to hurt you, blondie. Please, baby, put down the knife!" The one closer to me yells while trying to move back from the reach of the knife. A moonbeam lights a portion of his face and has me hesitating. He looks familiar. *It's a trick,* my mind screams. *Don't let your guard down. Kill them all!*

A spark of recognition is trying to make its way into the back of my mind, but I'm too frightened to attempt to decipher it. The other one moves forward slowly but without fear, and I bare my teeth at him, a vicious hissing sound leaving my throat. He's large, like the monsters in my living nightmares. I don't want him to touch me, to manage to corner me like an animal. They think they can hunt me. I will kill both of them and send them to meet the devil.

"Mia, it's Diego Cabano. It's Carter and Diego. You're safe. We are not going to hurt you."

Diego? Carter and Diego? Could it really be them, or is it a trick so that I let my guard down and they take me captive again? A snarl curls my lips, "Move into the light." *I take another step back, almost now at the outer edge of a crop of thick shadowed trees, as both shadow men move forward into a beam of moonlight.*

The silvery light crosses a broad, terrified face, eyes so light and wide they almost look white meet my gaze. Shock fills me as my eyes roam across a bleeding chiseled jaw, a Roman nose, and brown eyebrows furrowed in confusion. His hand raises slightly, showing me that he means me no harm. The light hits the rose tattoo on his hand and has my breath leaving me in a ragged gasp. *Carter.*

"Ca...rter." My voice fails me, sounding whispery to my ears. My mouth is so dry, and my tongue feels thick inside of it. Could it really be him, or is this a trick of my disturbed mind? *Am I even awake, or is this a nightmare?*

"Baby, it's me. It's me, Mia. Please don't run." His terrified eyes beg me not to bolt. My eyes drift over the male beside him, and I see compassion in Diego's usually miserable face. The jagged scar across the side of his face reassures me it's him. My whole body trembles before my legs refuse to hold me a moment longer, and I collapse to my knees on the forest floor.

Deep, ragged pants are making their way out of my mouth. I can't seem to catch my breath. My head spins for a moment, and the world is turned upside down. Both of them race forward toward me, my body flinches at their nearness, and I wrap my arms around myself, still holding tightly to the knife.

"Carter, stop!" Diego grabs Carter by the back of the shirt and yanks him back. The sound of material ripping loud in the silent forest. "What the fuck, asshole?" Carter breathes out anxiously.

The sound of his male voice in anger has a whimper escaping my lips, and me trying to make my body a smaller target. My mind wants to believe they are actually here and not a figment of my imagination. *Stop this shit right now. You are not some weak-ass bitch. Get the fuck up, Mia.*

The problem is I have dreamed over and over of one of them coming for me, rescuing me from the hell I found myself confined to. Every time I awoke, it was James there to abuse me, to bring me back to the horrific reality I was living in. *We killed him; he can't still be alive. We are free!* My mind tries to argue with me. Are we free? Will I ever be free after what I have endured, or will the nightmares of what occurred stalk me endlessly in my waking hours.

"Don't touch her yet. She's been traumatized." Diego utters cautiously.

I watch from below my lashes as Carter approaches me slowly, stopping three feet away and lowering himself to his knees. He eyes me with both a perplexed look and one of longing. His hand reaches out to touch me before he recoils it back, and his fists tighten above his thighs.

He is so beautiful in the moonlight. He doesn't even look real. *Don't all monsters look beautiful? Isn't that how they get you to let down your guard?* My mind whispers with caution.

It's when you get up close that you see their ugliness, the darkness that cakes their souls and mind. I am no different after all; I, too, am an ugly monster. Carter looks like a character out of one of those fantasy novels. A hero that comes to save his queen. Except this queen is beyond salvage, she is broken of mind, body, and spirit.

He tries to shift towards me, his movements restrained like he believes I'm a frightened animal. He's wrong, though. I am no longer fearful. I am willing to do whatever it takes to stay alive. They should be cautious of me. My emotions and mind are past the point of rational thought. All the tears, bruises, injuries, and horrors I have suffered have made sure of that.

"Listen to me, Mia. I love you. You are safe, babe. Nothing is going to hurt you. I will destroy anything that tries. You are mine, baby." His firm voice tries to reason with my mind.

I stare into his beautiful eyes, and outrage fills me. How fucking dare he tell me nothing is going to hurt me. *He hurt me. They hurt me.* They may not have hurt me the way James did, but they still caused damage. Now here he is, my would-be savior, on his goddamn knees, declaring he loves me and that I'm safe.

Fuck that load of shit. I saved myself, and I will continue to protect myself. I don't need a knight or king. All I have ever needed was a blade.

I scoff at his words; they are filled with deceit, just like they were all those weeks ago. Just like all those years ago when he hurt me over and over without remorse. My whole body and mind are whirling on an emotional upheaval right now.

"You're a liar, Carter. You don't hurt the ones you love. Only monsters do that. You're right, nothing's going to hurt me because I am stronger than those that have tried, and I will send anyone who tries mercilessly to hell." His words are grating on what's left of my nerves. False words from a false prophet. I don't trust a single syllable leaving his treacherous lips.

I stumble back to my feet, my limbs protesting in my weakened state. Diego moves forward to steady me as Carter remains on his knees with a look of shock and desolation across his features. "Don't touch me," I mutter through clenched teeth, trying to regain my composure.

He backs away, hands in the air before him. "Can I at least call for the helicopter, princess? Now that we have found you?" He eyes me questioningly with a smirk on his face, illuminated by the silver moonlight. I glare in his direction, a foul taste filling my mouth and my vision dimming. Is he really enjoying all this shit? *Psychotic motherfucker.*

"Yeah, asshole," I nod, giving him a combative glare, but just then, my head starts to spin, and my stomach churns. My vision goes in and out, and the world goes dark before I can utter another word.

I wake with an alarmed start; where the hell am I? Warm, strong arms are cradled around my body, holding me firmly against a muscled chest. We seem to be in motion. The loud sound of helicopter blades getting closer. I pull back from the hold, and the smell of lime, eucalyptus, and bergamot greet my senses.

Carter, my mind supplies. I try to push out of his grasp, but his arms tighten further, causing panic to start deep inside of me.

"I'm going to get you home, Mia. Please just let me get you back to Stella." He hums close to my ear. The feeling of his warm breath and the vibration of his deep tone has shivers racking my body and me burying deeper into the puffer jacket and his hold. *For just this moment, I'll only let him hold me until I can find the strength in my limbs to stand on my own.*

He passes me up to a waiting Diego, who holds me in the nestle of his arms as if I was made of fragile glass as Carter gets into the helicopter. "I'm so happy you're alive, princess," Diego mutters only loud enough for me to hear before he passes me back to Carter.

I want to protest that I don't need either of them to hold me. I don't want them to get comfortable touching me, but I am so weary. All of my bones hurt, my skin feels too tight, and my head is pounding along with the swishing of the helicopter blades. I just want to get back to my grandmother. I need to feel safe; there is nowhere safer than Stella's arms.

My heavy eyes close for what feels like a moment, but when I reopen them, I can feel that we are starting the descent back to land. Daylight has started to creep over the horizon, painting the sky in vivid pinks, blues, and purples. The smell of the ocean greets my nose, and I try to take a deep breath. My ribs and lungs immediately protest the action and cause a burning sensation to rush through my chest cavity. *Fuck that hurts.*

"We're almost there, Mia. We're already on the property." Carter's voice rumbles through his chest and into my back. The sensation, while not unpleasant, makes me acutely aware of how close he's holding me and how my body is pressed against his.

Once the aircraft has landed and the blades have slowed, Diego jumps down and rushes around the other side to help Carter with me. My temper bristles with being handed back and forth like a child. The minute Diego has me in his grip, I shove with all my might until I slide down his long body and my feet touch the ground. I stumble back a step but catch myself at the last minute just as Carter tries to grab hold of me.

"No!" I stammer out, unsure of myself. I know I'm being a raging lunatic right now. They are both just trying to help me, but their hands on me are causing the darkness to rise.

Both despair and anger are hitting me in waves. The anger I can't seem to control rushes through me, begging to be unleashed and allowed to set fire to the world around me. Despair because I know I am forever changed, and not for the better. The Mia I knew is gone, replaced by the battered one standing in the here and now. Right now, this Mia is more beast than human.

"MIA!" Raegan's voice shouts out from behind me, and I turn just in time for her to smash into me and wrap me tightly in her arms. At first, my mind and body protest the feeling of being touched, but then her scent and warmth fill me.

Tears are rivers streaming down her beautiful face. A face I have longed to see again. Her complexion is pale, her beautiful green eyes filled with untold fears, and her gorgeous hair a tangled mess. My arms wrap securely around her, and the feeling of safety fills me. Raegan is my home; my body, mind, and spirit recognize her as my safety.

Another pair of arms wrap around the both of us, and my eyes meet my sister's stunning blue ones filled with tears. "Mia, oh my god, I am so happy to see you!" Issy's voice wavers as she pulls us even tighter into her embrace until pain radiates through me and gasps leave my lips. 'Shit, too tight, I'm sorry!" She panics and releases her hold, and I immediately miss her comforting warmth.

They both pull back, and I take a step away from them, my limbs still shaky but feeling stronger in their presence. I look over Issy's shoulders, and Stella's arctic gaze meets mine. Tears are sliding down her porcelain skin. She somehow looks older, even though it's only been a few weeks since I saw her last. She opens her arms wide, and I don't hesitate to move into them. Her warm, snug embrace is everything that I have been craving since before James even took me. *Home. I am home.*

"You're home now, my love. Safe. I will never let anyone hurt you again. I swear on my life, Mia, I will find them all and remove every trace of them from this earth."

A Stratford never forgets or forgives. The world is about to learn that lesson as Stella sets fire to it. The knowledge brings me peace, one that I have spent weeks praying for to a God that all but abandoned me in that hell.

CHAPTER 23
Mia

"Sometimes life has a cruel sense of humor, giving you the thing you always wanted at the worst time possible." Lisa Kleypas, Sugar Daddy

As I'm ushered into the house, Raegan and Issy glued to my one side and Stella firmly attached to my other, I leave Carter and Diego behind. Tom stops me at the family room entrance off the back deck. His dark eyes roaming over me and assessing my condition in that methodical and composed way of his.

"Miss Mia, it is so good to have you back with us." I want to smile up at him but I can't. It's like my face can't hold the emotion. I'm drained of everything except pain and sorrow.

I hear movement of someone running towards our direction from the other side of the house. It only takes an extra second for my name to follow the sound of feet hitting the floor. "MIA!" Mateo's voice rings out in the air, as he moves quickly toward me. Without thinking my body immediately recoils against the possibility of his touch, a small moan escapes my lips. Before he has a chance to reach me, Issy throws herself between us. Her body is rigid like a feral dog, ready to lunge and rip his throat out. "Don't you fucking dare, asshole!"

"Mia, please." He says as he rushes to a halt. "I just want to make sure that you are okay." His voice is filled with so much pain that it lashes at my mind. I bite down hard on my tongue until my dry mouth is filled with the taste of blood.

I finally get a good look at him, and what greets my vision has me swallowing a painful lump in my throat. He tugs at his hair painfully as he shifts from one foot to the other, and his gaze keeps wandering from me back to the floor. *Shame.* That's what I see on his features. He can't meet my gaze. The fucking coward. *No, Mia, he's broken too, remember that!* My heart urges.

Mateo was barely back from Vincent's psychotic clutches before I was taken. He looked like a broken shell of himself then, a walking ghost, but now...oh my God. He somehow seems so much worse. His face is ashen and haggard; gone is the golden light of his skin. Dark shadows circle his eyes. His body is still so painfully slim, having lost so much weight in captivity that his clothes hang off him. It looks like he hasn't managed to put anything back on.

His eyes are filled with a world of pain, and I can see anxiety lingering just under the surface. Is he trapped in his mind too? A part of me wants to reach out and wrap my arms around him, offer him the comfort I can see he needs. Then the memory of when I tried to do just that, when he first returned with June, fills my mind.

How he dismissed me, not needing me to soothe his pain then because he had her. She was his support system while he was trapped. She calmed his ravaged spirit, not me. While I was alone, discarded, and unwanted. *He chose her.*

Now why is he here feigning concern for me? Is his guilt eating him from the inside out? Is that what this is about? Fuck him. I don't need his guilt or his pity. He can go back to her side. I will survive his loss, just like I survive everything else. Alone.

Fucking June! I want to be angry with her for taking him from me, but now having suffered what I have, I can't. My soul cries out in pain at the intimate horror we both share of being repeatedly violated by a man.

While I can empathize with Mateo and Theo for suffering a similar fate, June and I both know what it's like to be a woman in that type of hell. The lack of trust for any male will linger with me forever. I am eternally changed, as I am sure she is too. How can I begrudge her if she found peace with Mateo? I can't, so I have to let him go. He made his choice, and it wasn't me.

"I have nothing to say to you, Mateo. Stay away from me." My voice is small but firm.

I look away from him, allowing Stella to lead me further into the room where a medical team awaits to assess me. I can see them ready and waiting to cure the Stratford princess of what ails her. Do they have something that can put my shattered heart back together? How about something that can mend my broken soul?

Mary meets my gaze, and I see nothing but sympathy. The same compassion I saw when she told me of June's condition after Vincent's brutality. Am I now just a statistic too? *No fuck that; we are a survivor.* No other label will be applied to us.

A sound from the other end of the room rips my attention from Mary's compassionate gaze. Instead the next eyes I meet are dark chocolate brown. Their softness caresses across my skin, leaving tingles in their wake. *No, Mia! Be strong; he is a betrayer.* He has now betrayed you multiple times. His feelings for you are not valid; they are a charade.

Finn stands there, hands clenched at his sides. His large six-foot-three frame seems to have shrunken in on itself. His skin bunches around his eyes as his pained stare meets mine.

His wary expression tells me that he caught my words aimed at Mateo. He moves forward and then comes to an abrupt halt like he's forcing himself not to approach me or reach out and touch me. His mouth opens and closes, but no words leave his lips. Devastation reigns across his face. His gaze tells me everything I need to know about my own appearance. I must look like death.

No! We look like we just survived hell's painful clutches and are here to tell the story. Except there is no story to tell. I never want to relive what happened to me. Not in words, thoughts, or actions. That part of Mia Stratford was left in that cabin in the woods. This one will never be broken again.

A commotion behind me has me ripping out of Stella's tight grasp and pulling her behind me. A gasp leaves her lips, and I hear a scream from either Issy or Raegan. NO! Fear is racing through my veins, and my vision is clouding. My chest feels too tight, and I can't breathe, but I have to. I have to fight. *Someone is here to hurt us. Someone will hurt Stella. We need to protect her, protect Issy and Raegan too.*

A snarl leaves my lips, and I lunge forward, no longer remembering that we are safe and at home. My mind is seeing only the cabin, the wilderness, and the face of my abuser. I'm forcefully dragged backward and wrapped in thick muscular arms. Ones that hold me so tight that I can't even lift my arms, and my feet no longer touch the ground.

All I can do is thrash my head back and forth. I bang the back of my head into whoever is holding me as hard as I can. A hoarse cry sounds from behind me at the sound of impact, but the arms don't release me from their confining grip. The scent of Honeysuckle and smoke envelops my senses. I thrash against the embrace, the heat coming off the body making my skin crawl. "NO! NO!" I scream.

"Jesus, oh my God, Mia! It's alright, love!" My sister's voice tries to penetrate through the fog. Her high-pitched voice is loud even though my ears are ringing.

I try to control my breathing. I inhale in through my nose and out through my mouth, but it doesn't stop my heart from thudding rapidly in my chest. I repeatedly blink, trying to clear the haze from my eyes. *We are not back there, we are not back there,* becomes a mantra in my head.

"Issy, step the fuck away from her before she hurts you!" Diego's harsh voice sounds through the room.

Cool hands grasp my chin in a tight grasp and force my eyes to meet cold blue ones filled with emotion. "Mia, my darling, you are safe. We are all safe here. No one will hurt you." Stella's voice washes over me, and my body goes lax in the confining hold.

"Release her immediately, young man, and do not put your fucking hands on her again, or I will have them ripped off!"

The hold instantly disappears, and so does the heat at my back as Finn takes a few steps backward without a word. I stumble forward, but Stella's firm grip on my elbow steadies me. Sharp pain lances from the spot she touches, but I ignore it like I do all my other aches and pains. They have become as much a part of me as any other limb or organ. Without them, I would feel nothing but numbness.

My eyes search over Stella's shoulder for the disturbance that caused me to once again lose myself in darkness. It's not long before my eyes meet with husky blue ones. The look of shock on his face at my actions and my response to him entering the space causes him to stop short in the doorway, Diego's firm grip still on his shoulder, trying to pull him back.

"Mia, please don't run away from me. Tell me who did this to you." Carter's voice echoes through the silence in the room. It feels like everyone is holding their breath at his words. Everyone but me that is. I release the breath that threatens to strangle me.

"How fucking dare you, Carter Pemberton." Raegan gets in his face and pushes him back with both hands on his chest. "You fucking parasite. How dare you come in here and ask anything of her." She shoves him again until his back is firmly pressed against Diego's unwavering and immobile body. Carter never takes his eyes off me, even when Reagan uses all of her strength to shove him back out the door. "If Stella doesn't murder y'all, I will. Don't any of you worthless assholes touch her."

He doesn't seem to register what Reagan is saying to him, or he just doesn't care. It's like he forgets about her presence all together. His eyes still locked on me. He takes a rough step forward, one that catches Reagan off guard as she almost loses her balance. He reaches out instinctively to steady her, his eyes still watching my every breath. She slaps his arm away, the loud impact ringing out across the room, but that doesn't seem to phase him. He takes another two steps forward quickly and I recoil backwards without a second thought.

"Carter...stop!" Mateo utters.

"Stop, Carter, please!" Finn's voice rings out behind me.

"Carter, you're hurting her." The words sound through the air, and my heart literally feels like it stops. That deep, authoritative voice has me ripping my gaze away from Carter's and searching the room for the only man it could have come from.

I find him in a corner, off to the side, unseen when I first entered the family room. His face is a myriad of healing bruises, his beautiful blue eyes shadowed, his left eye looks like it is healing from a black eye and tinged in yellow-green.

For the briefest of moments, anger wells inside of me that someone has hit him. Someone has hurt my Theo. *Are you fucking lost, girl? That cunt is not ours. He made sure of that before we left. He is a worthless waste of human flesh. Whoever hit him should have done worse to him; it's what he deserves.* The thoughts race inside my head even as he cautiously takes one step towards me.

The cold mask he usually wears is replaced by one of fear and longing. He never shows his feelings willingly, but in this moment they are painted across his face. His pouty lips are open, and I watch as he bites down hard on the bottom one. Is he preventing himself from speaking? What, he has no nasty words to utter to me now? Of course not; now I am just as broken and tainted as he is.

His sparkling sapphire eyes flood with tears, and one after another, they quietly trickle down the side of his face, rolling over his chiseled unshaven cheek and meeting the corner of his mouth. I didn't know my heart could break further, that they were even pieces big enough to still shatter, but they do at the sight of proud, controlling, and demanding Theo Saint-Lambert's utter devastation. Why is he crying? Didn't he want to push me away? Didn't he want to destroy me? Mission accomplished. *There is nothing left of me now; I am barely breathing.*

"I'm so fucking sorry, Mia. You will never understand the depth of how very sorry I am."

I look away from him, my eyes glazed and unfocused. Once, I would have dreamed of hearing those words leave his sinful lips. I would have given anything to see him at my feet, apologetic, and begging for my forgiveness. I can't believe I bargained my future for this asshole. That I came back to this miserable town for him, for all of them. Needing satisfaction. Craving vengeance. The best revenge

I could have gotten on these four was to live a happy life far away from their tainted reach.

"Stella, you must know by now who did this to her. We need to make sure she's safe." I watch as Finn moves to stand before my grandmother, his shoulders raised and his face impassioned as he tries to implore Stella. Her eyes move past Finn and meet Diego's eyes. My heart rate rises. *No, fuck no!* I don't want anyone to know it was my biological father who did this to me. The shame that fills me with the realization that someone of my own blood hurt and raped me makes my whole body want to cave in on itself.

My eyes meet Stella's gaze, and I implore her silently not to tell them. Not divulge the true horror of my experience. I'm sure she has figured it out by now. I just don't think my mind can survive if they all look at me with disgust. *What the fuck are you talking about, Mia? Theo was abused by his own father too! You two now share an experience and bond.* My heart tries to reason with me, but self-loathing fills me.

I don't want to share anything with Theo Saint-Lambert. I don't want anything to do with his deceitful, destructive ass. He abandoned me. Discarded me like a dirty shoe. I was nothing to him at that moment. Now he's sorry? The only thing I am sorry for is that I didn't see the real him until it was too late, and I had already lost my heart. That organ is shriveled up now, so I no longer have to worry about it.

There's a long pause of silence that stretches from wall to wall of the room. Everyone's eyes are now on me, which is making my skin crawl. My eyes once again meet those beautiful blue stormy ones that I used to stupidly long for. My gaze travels down Theo's healing face, to his full and chapped lips and I watch as he opens his mouth to say something else.

"It's too late. I don't give a shit, Theo. Anything that I felt for any of you died in that cabin. That girl died up there. This one doesn't care what happens to you." I walk away towards Mary and follow her from the room with Raegan and Issy quickly on my heels. Tom and Clark quickly block the hallway behind us.

Behind me, I hear the fierce sound of a struggle, bodies hitting bodies as Carter shouts for me repeatedly, and the others stop him from following me. I don't care anymore, though. Let them kill each other. It will lessen the burden of me doing it when I heal.

A gunshot rings out, and the sound of bodies hitting the ground echoes down the corridor. I stop short, my body jumping in the air, and look back, seeing that Tom has his gun out and pointed at the kings. Stella's voice rings out clearly over the silence. "That was your one and only warning you demonic heathens. The next one of you to make a move towards my granddaughter will be met with a bullet between the eyes, and the rest of you will be expelled from the property. I will bar you from even getting a glance of her."

Silence greets her statement, and not a rustle of fabric is heard. I meet Raegan's eyes and watch as a bright smile crosses her face. She loves it when Stella is a raving bitch to them. I feel nothing, however, no sympathy or warmth. Just rage. The one emotion that lives within this new Mia.

The kings of Casbury will die at my hands, just like I died in that cabin with their cruel words in my ears. *I am wholly spent; there is nothing left of me now.*

CHAPTER 24
Carter

"Anger is like spitting at your own image in the mirror" Dr. P.S. Jagadeesh Kumar

I'm sitting in the family room with Diego, scrolling on my phone and trying to distract myself from my need to once again try to speak with Mia. It's been a few days since she's been back. Her words on the day she returned haunt my waking and sleeping thoughts. Not that I do much sleeping with Mia's screams ricocheting through the house. She's plagued with night terrors of what she endured at that fucking cabin in the woods.

Stella keeps punishing me for my attempts to get to Mia. Despite her threats to have me removed from the house, most of the time, she just has Tom and Clark lock me in my room under heavy guard. Fucking Diego even takes it upon himself to help her, the asshole.

Stella's an evil *fucking queen bitch*. As much as I like her, and I do, not that I would admit it right now, I hate that she's trying to prevent me from getting to my blondie. Doesn't she realize that my heart only beats for Mia? That she is my everything? *Yeah, fucker, that's why she hasn't had Tom or Clark shoot you yet.*

I would take it personally that Mia keeps rebuffing my attempts, but it's not only me she's refusing to communicate with. She can't stand being in the same space as my fellow kings, either. The look of contempt and revulsion any time one of us attempts to approach her is devastating.

I know we did her wrong. Fuck, I even realize we deserve to be punished harshly for the shit we did and said to her before she was captured, but I can't live without her. Without my blondie, even though the one that has returned to us is a battered ghost of the one I love, I won't survive. My sanity is barely holding. I need her to purge me of my darkness. Only in her arms, and I am not lost to my madness.

Mateo is basically a walking zombie, Finn is silently falling apart, and Theo, fuck, as much as I want to knock the guy out every time I see him, my heart aches for him too. He's a fucking mess, a shell of the once proud and strong Theo Saint-Lambert.

The fact that he continuously allows me to go at him and hurt him is starting to really grate on my nerves. A part of me wants him to fight back when I taunt and hit him. The need to get that fierce Theo to resurface partially egging me on.

Yet, he does nothing to stop the violence I reign down on him, and Mia watches from afar with an impassioned gaze. She no longer seems to care what happens to him or us, and that fucking terrifies me. What if we truly have lost her?

The only one that can stand my presence for even a limited time is fucking Diego. The silent fucker keeps me company while I slowly drown in my feelings for my girl. The fact that Issy is constantly glued to Mia's side probably has everything to do with his incessant need to continually keep me company. After all, Diego is such a great friend, fucking not.

A commotion by the front door has both Diego and me jumping to our feet, guns drawn, and rushing down the hallway. The first to enter my sightline is Stella, looking proud and menacing in one of her hunter green power suits. I swear the woman lives in them. It's like a uniform of armor that she puts on daily, Preparing herself to go to war against her enemies. *It just so happens that sometimes those enemies are my fellow kings and me.*

I keep wondering and dreading when she is going to force us to leave the property. I won't fucking go, she will have to shoot me, and even then, I'll still haunt the damn place. Nothing, not even the need to breathe, is going to keep me away from Mia Stratford. I will be her stalker and shadow for the rest of our godforsaken lives and in death.

Mia is off to the side, shoulders hunched and arms wrapped around her abdomen tightly. She makes sure that she keeps everyone in her sightline, with her back pressed against the wall. This new Mia is hypervigilant and wary of others. The result of her trauma, no doubt.

She is dressed in thick black, baggy sweatpants and an oversized black sweatshirt that comes all the way down to her knees. I might be wrong, but I'm pretty sure that shirt belongs to Finn, and I know those pants are mine. A sheepish smile crosses my lips at the realization that she doesn't want us near her, but she still seeks comfort from our things. I wish she would let me hold her.

Her face is still pale, the myriad of bruises and cuts healing and turning from purple to greenish-yellow. The swelling in her blackened eye has significantly reduced to the point she can now open it fully. Her beautiful dirty blonde hair is pulled back in a thick braid, offering me a tempting view of the sleek column of her neck. The one I long to kiss and rub my nose along, basking in her scent. The one that was covered in fucking fingerprints from that asshole.

She looks uncomfortable, surrounded by Clark, Tom, and a few others from the security team. Men, in general, make her jumpy now. Given what she's been through, I know it's normal; it just hurts me to see.

Her eyes meet mine before she pulls her gaze away and centers it on the wall. I hate when she does that. She won't fucking look at me. She won't let me speak to her or be near her. How am I supposed to get through to her? How am I supposed to make her feel safe when she resists my attempts? *Hey, asshole, I think that's the fucking point; she doesn't want your help.* The evil thought slides through my mind, but I immediately shut it down.

Where are they all going? Why are there so many guards with them? Can't they see she's uncomfortable? Don't they see she doesn't feel safe outside of the house?

Does Mia need to go see another doctor? I thought Issy said all the doctors would come to the house, so Mia felt safe. When they had to take her to get a CAT scan a few days ago, she reacted badly and had a mini meltdown at the hospital when the male technician tried to help her up off the table.

I thought for sure Clark was going to shoot my ass when I found out what happened. I lost my fucking mind seeing her pale, frightened gaze when she returned. Stella's fucking threats didn't work at that moment; my mind was lost watching my girl panic. I made it all the way into Mia's room. The tips of my fingers just barely grazed her face before Tom tasered the shit out of me and dragged me out of her room.

The small group starts to move toward the door, and I finally come to my senses and notice that they are all carrying weapons. Fear races through me, making the pit of my stomach tighten into a hard ball and sweat slide down my neck. *What the hell is going on here?* Are they taking her away somewhere? Is Stella finally complying with her threats to send Mia back to Manhattan and away from us? *FUCK NO!* I will fight every motherfucker in this house right now if they try to take her from me.

"What's going on here?" Diego voices the question before I can utter a word. My heart thuds loudly in my ears as I watch everyone in the room. I turn my gaze back to Diego and catch the look of suspicion across his malignant face too. He and I are very much in sync with our thoughts, something that has become a bit worrisome to the others. That means there are two unbalanced, psychotic fuckers under the same roof. I never thought I would say the guy was a friend. I'm not even sure I would go that far now; maybe a frenemy?

"None of your business, Diego Cabano." Stella sneers in his direction. She really hasn't warmed up to him, despite Manuel bringing us the information that helped us find Mia and Diego's endless searching for her. You would think the fucker scored some brownie points with grandma, but its like the opposite has happened.

My money is on the fact that she knows he's messing around with Issy. That fucker is going to get himself shot right under this roof and buried in a shallow grave. Stella doesn't fuck around; look at how many times she has had me tasered in just the last week. Not that it even matters. Issy is completely stonewalling his ass too. She won't speak to him or even look in his direction, and I can tell my new unhinged friend is about to explode from the tension.

"Really, Stella? After all my dad and I have done to help?" He questions with a raised eyebrow and a voice filled with sheer contempt. I want to pull him back. I want to call out, *"Hey buddy, just shut that fucking mouth of yours before she puts a bullet in your brain,"* but I can't; my focus is on the blondie trying her very best to be invisible.

The realization that Stella might actually be about to send Mia back to Manhattan and make good on her threats hits me so hard that I feel unsteady on my feet. No, she wouldn't do that to us, would she?

She's not that cold-hearted. She knows that we love her granddaughter, even that fucker, Theo. Who am I kidding? If it was possible, and it's not, to love Mia more than I do, I would bet my left nut, my favorite fucking nut by the way, that Theo would fall into that category. The guy went willingly into torture and his possible death to save her. It's the only fucking reason I haven't ended his miserable life.

"Stella, please. Please don't take her away from us...from me...I...please." I implore her, trying to show her how much I love her granddaughter with my eyes and how devastated I will be if she sends Mia back to Manhattan. "Please...I love her."

A deep sigh leaves Stella's lips, and I watch as Mia's shoulders stiffen at my words. She refuses to look in my direction, staring at a spot on the wall with vacant eyes, but I know she's hearing me. I just need to somehow get through to her.

A nod from Stella has Tom approaching Diego and me. His movements are careful and restrained. Tom doesn't like us very much anymore since the shit went down with Mia, and we tried to push her away. I wouldn't put it past the guy to want to put a bullet between all of our eyes. He definitely would like to see us gone and in Mia's rearview mirror. But he is shit out of luck. *I will never let her go.*

I watch as Diego's body goes rigid, and his hand moves closer to the gun he has on him at all times. Does he think Tom is going to try to hurt us? Is he going to try to stop me from following Mia wherever she is going? They will have to completely incapacitate me. There is nowhere on this earth that they can take my queen that I won't follow. *She is mine.*

"You need to leave this alone, boy," Tom utters gruffly. Though when I look at him, I actually see compassion in his eyes.

"No fuck that! She is mine. Wherever you are taking her, I'm going too. I need to stay with her." I try to push past Tom's large menacing form. "Please, Stella, don't do this. Don't take her away from me."

"Ugh, damn it, Carter Pemberton. No one is taking her away, at least not yet. We have captured one of the fuckers who were subscribing to that horrendous and malevolent site. She is going with us to seek her own vengeance." Stella yells in exasperation and annoyance. A look of complete frustration directed towards me as her eyebrows furrow and her lips settle in a straight furious line. *What the ever-loving fuck, like, has she lost her mind?*

"What? No! No, it's too soon. She doesn't need to get her hands dirty." I shove frantically past Tom and stand before Mia. "Baby, please don't do this. Let...let me do it. Let me dirty my hands for you. Please let me prove to you that I would do anything for you."

Mia's ocean-blue eyes lift and meet mine, and various emotions cross her beautiful features simultaneously. At first, I see anger, then disbelief, sadness, and finally acceptance as I release the breath I am holding. She tears her eyes away from my imploring ones and nods to Stella. Then she turns and walks out the door without a look back in anyone's direction. Clark immediately follows her out.

"I'm going too, then." Diego declares in a combative tone and with a snarl across his face. He doesn't wait for Stella's approval and shoves past a hulking Tom and follows Mia and Clark outside. *That motherfucker definitely has a deathwish, that and balls of steel.*

Stella approaches me, her pale hand reaching out and grabbing my chin. Her nails dig into the skin, causing a sting across my flesh, but I don't give her the satisfaction of reacting. I meet her arctic eyes, so cold and fearsome that they have a shiver of dread racing down my spine. She really is a scary-ass bitch. I can't wait to call her grandma too.

"Please, Stella, don't allow her to taint her soul any more than it already has been. Let me avenge her. Let me be the one to destroy her enemies, to send them back to hell painfully. She owns my heart. She is everything that is good in my life and my only reason for living."

A long moment passes between us, the silence in the entryway deafening. Stella tightens her grip on my face. Her eyes searching into my own, for what, I am not sure. Does she doubt the validity of my words, my affection for her granddaughter? I let her see everything, opening myself wide to her inspection.

I can't live without Mia. *How does one live without their heart?* It's Mia for me. It will always be only Mia. I have never loved anyone else, nor do I ever plan to. She is my everything. Her soul and mine are forever weaved together, and not even death will be able to untangle us. Stella releases her hold on my chin, and a deep resounding sigh leaves her lips.

"You truly love her, don't you, Carter?" Her frigid eyes seem to melt a bit, the ice thawing, compassion and curiosity streaking across her features.

Stella is still beautiful even at her age. Her features are classical and so similar to Issy's that I wonder if that's what she looked like at the same age. "You remind me very much of someone I loved deeply, Carter. If you love her, even half of how he loved me...." She doesn't finish her statement, sadly looking away and turning towards the door.

"Let's go, young man. You are about to play the role of executioner of my granddaughter's enemies. A role I have no doubt you will enjoy wholeheartedly."

CHAPTER 25

Carter

"I'd rather laugh with the sinners than cry with the saints."
Billy Joel

We walk into the warehouse, and a sense of foreboding and deja vu fills me. It's so similar to the setup that Vincent had. The one he used as a place to punish and force us to punish those that displeased him, that it makes sweat slide down my back. I committed my share of evil sins in that warehouse at the behest of that madman. How many will I execute now at the request of my queen?

My eyes trail over Mia's form in the short distance, surrounded by the security team and with Tom firmly at her side. A place that I should be standing in right now, but my little queen is refusing me the honors of. Stella moves up to her other side and takes her hand in her grasp. Envy fills me at her being able to touch my blondie, and I have to tamp it down.

The two of them together with their heads raised and shoulders back. The picture of two wrathful and powerful Stratford queens ready to rain down justice on those that attempted to harm their kingdom. And I am here to act as their willing executioner. The man that will destroy anyone that tries to hurt either of them.

We can hear the sound of harsh cries from up ahead as the cement walls of the corridor open up into a large, bright, windowless room. The walls and floor are all made of deep gray concrete. Large bright overhead lights hang down from various suspended naked bulbs. One of the only things in the room is a large white plastic folding table with multiple items scattered along the top of it.

Implements of torture, if I had to guess. The only other thing in the room beside us and the two guards who were already here, is the bleeding fucker that is hanging from a thick gray metal chain attached to the ceiling. The chain is biting into the meat of his flesh around his wrists, and it is clear that the skin is already torn and ragged from his attempts to free himself.

The beast inside of me wakes from his slumber at the sight. He craves blood and destruction. Anarchy and chaos are his names, and before me is a prize he can't wait to sink his claws into. He will get his taste of blood and flesh before this day is done.

The constrained fucker is naked except for a pair of white briefs that are stained and wet with piss, a puddle visible below him. He thrashes in his restraints, but it's useless. They pull his body taunt and force him to stand only on his tippy toes. His face is bloody and swollen. Someone must have already enjoyed taking their fists to him. A feeling of glee fills me with anticipation of the damage I am going to cause this fucker.

He not only watched hidden behind a screen like a deviant as my girl was abused, but he also paid for the privilege of having her tortured for his amusement. Even participated with his words urging that sick fuck to hurt her even more. He is going to suffer unspeakable horrors before I send him back to the devil and the hole where he crawled out of.

"And do not fear those who kill the body but cannot kill the soul. Rather fear him, who can destroy both soul and body in hell. Matthew 10:28 " My voice rings out loud and clear and has everyone in the room staring at me. Shock crosses Mia's face before she hides her thoughts once again behind that cold, indifferent mask she wears.

My eyes meet Diego's from across the space. I can see the same madness and need for blood in his eyes. Is he picturing Issy in Mia's place? The girl he loves but can't have? I have no doubt that if I were to falter in my actions, he would pick up a blade himself and make this creature regret his very existence. He is as bloodthirsty as I am. He, too, seeks destruction and pain to inflict on others.

What is more righteous than destroying a person who harmed the woman you love? This fucker hanging here might not have been the mastermind behind what happened to my Mia, but his actions and participation were to inflict damage on a Stratford, on Stella, and that can't go unpunished. My blondie loves and adores her grandmother; I will be their vengeance.

I have no intentions of faltering, though. I am going to take all the pent-up rage and fear from those weeks Mia was missing out on him. Then I will make him beg for mercy, one that I will not provide until my girl instructs me to end his life. Even then, I have no intention of sending him off in one piece.

"STELLA!" He thrashes, tears cascading down his swollen face. "You can't do this! This is madness! Release me!"

A snort leaves Stella's lips as she moves closer to the man. She cocks her head to the side as she observes him. You can see the vortex of fury within every line of her body. She wants to do damage to this piece of shit. She wants to end his life herself for hurting her granddaughter. Stella is vicious and a killer. Anyone who doesn't see that about her is blind.

"Madness, Jacob, was going after one of my heirs." She slaps him hard across his face with the palm of her hand, the sound loud in the silent room. Her fingers wrap around his throat, tightening until his face turns a shade of deep red. "Madness was thinking I wouldn't discover you were involved and that you could hide from me."

"I NEVER TOUCHED HER. I JUST WATCHED!!" He shouts in desperation as she releases her hold on his neck, and he gasps in a desperate breath.

"Did you hear that, Carter? He just watched as the love of your life was raped over and over. He didn't touch her, but his money did. His voice did, and so did his words. They all touched her."

A hurricane of molten rage flows through me. I step over to the table and grab a sharp serrated blade, holding it tightly in my grasp as I make my way over to the fucker, damning himself further with every word. I no longer see him clearly in front of me. That horrendous video plays again in my mind. The voices urging James to hurt her further are all I hear and see. I shake my head, clearing the fog that wants to take me and focusing my eyes on the piece of shit in front of me.

As more animalistic screams fill the air, ones that threaten to burst my fucking eardrums, I trail the blade down his collarbone and then stop at his chest. The first slash of the knife is quick and sharp across his chest, causing blood to trickle down from the wound. His screams get louder, if that is even fucking possible until his voice is so high-pitched that he would give *Mariah Carey* a run for her fucking money. They are beautiful music in my ears, and my beast craves to hear more of them.

I move closer until I reach his restrained wrists. "PLEASE! PLEASE!" His begging voice rings out in the silent air, but it brings with it nothing but satisfaction. He will find no mercy here.

I grab his left hand and slowly cut through the first two fingers, taking my time and ensuring he feels each one leaving his body. His pitiful screams rent the air, and he tries to swing his body from the chain to escape my grip on his wrist. The tight hold that the chains have on him prevents him from moving more than an inch or two in any direction. *Naw, motherfucker, you will suffer and not evade my justice.*

I keep cutting until his screams are blood-curdling, and I can hear shifting behind me. My eyes raise and meet Mia's, but she doesn't give her thoughts away. My hands and arms are covered in this fucker's blood, and the sensation is a slight balm to my soul. *More blood is needed. He hasn't suffered nearly enough yet*, my beast urges.

Once there is nothing left but bloody stumps on that hand, I start on the other, giving it the same treatment. He passes out momentarily, but Diego moves forward and pours ice-cold water down his head until he comes to with a startle and begins screaming again.

"Please! Please, I will give you anything you want. Take all of my fortune; please just stop." He begs.

"Did you listen when my granddaughter said please?" Stella's words are almost choked as she stalks forward and slashes her fingernails across his face leaving deep blood-filled gouges in her wake. "I will take everything you have anyway, Jacob. There will be nothing left to show you even existed when I am done."

I slam two of my fingers into his right eye. The feeling of meeting his eyeball with force is like sticking my fingers in thick Jello, and gouging it until the resistance in the socket gives way, and the eyeball crushes beneath my grip. He wails like a broken animal as blood pours from his eye socket.

"You watched my girl suffer; now I will take your eyes, motherfucker." I repeat my actions on the other eye until both his eyes hemorrhage, and he is rendered blind. His slippery blood coats my hands and runs down my forearms in rivulets of red. The sight makes my madness cheer inside of me, begging for more bloodshed.

I turn and meet Mia's gaze. Her eyes are steady, watching with interest as I punish the first of many fuckers that helped to hurt her. I don't see any fear or revulsion across her face. She welcomes my violence, needing it to cleanse her own soul from their harm. We are the same, my blondie and me. She is mine. It is why I will never let her go.

My hand grips the back of his neck, holding him firmly as I slam the blade's handle into his mouth, shattering his two front teeth with my enraged violence. I release my hold and grip his face, nodding to Diego, who approaches and somehow knows exactly what I need. *Kindred fucking spirit, that's what he is.*

He holds Jacob's face captive in one hand while forcing his mouth to open by slipping two of his fingers on either side of his lips and pulling until good old Jacob looks grotesque with his mouth gaping open. I grab a steady grip on his blood-soaked lips and slash the blade through his tongue, cutting it off and leaving a meaty, bloody stump behind. "Your mouth spewed evil words that caused my girl pain. You will never speak again."

Diego releases his hold on Jacob's mouth but grabs a fist full of his hair at the back of his neck. Forcing him to stop his thrashing and to remain conscious. Garbled screams fill the air as I slice the blade down his torso, causing the flesh to split like the skin of a peach and exposing the blood and guts below. The knife's edge meets the waistband of his underwear, and I slash through it until his shrimp dick is exposed. "Pathetic."

I spit in his face as I slash the sharp blade through his nut sack, wrenching them open and spilling their contents to the ground below him. I hear a few muffled coughs behind me, but I disregard them. I need to keep my focus solely on this piece of shit. His body stops moving, and he hangs limply in the restraints, passed out from the trauma but still breathing. That fills me with rancor and a need to do even more damage to him. How dare he try to escape the pain and suffering I am causing him when my queen wasn't offered the same mercy.

Her screams from the video enter my mind, the image of her lying on that sofa pretending to be unconscious while that monster touched her. The very thought makes my blood boil, and my hands start to shake. I have never felt such rage as I did at that moment. When I had to watch from behind a screen as Mia suffered, knowing my fury could do nothing to save her. That my own actions and that of my brothers were the catalysts for everything that happened to her. Nothing will ever be the same between any of us. We can never go back, but I can ensure that all the fuckers that hid behind that screen suffer tenfold. Naw, a hundredfold will still not be enough.

I slice his cock off and hear a few pained groans from the males in the room. One look from Stella and all of them are averting their eyes to the ground. My eyes meet Mia's from the small distance between us. I raise an eyebrow in her direction, dragging my blood-soaked hand through my hair and watching as her eyes follow the movement, and a hint of heat enters them. She likes watching me hurt this fucker. Is her need for vengeance through my hands turning her on? *God, I fucking hope so.* I would fuck her gladly in his blood if she allowed me to.

"End him, Carter."

I don't hesitate, sliding the blade through his throat and slashing it from one end to another. His thick warm blood sprays all over my face and neck, and I welcome the sensation of killing one of our enemies. Ending his miserable life won't change what happened to Mia, but it will be one less monster she has to worry about ever coming after her.

His body makes an awful choking and rattling noise as he attempts to take his last breath. I don't bother to spend another moment looking at the mess I happily created. One of many to come that I will destroy as she watches.

Instead, I move towards my queen and place myself in front of her. I try to get my own heavy breathing under control. I watch her as she stares at the prize of destruction behind me. Her tongue slips out, and she swipes it across her full bottom lip. Her cheeks have a slight pink tinge, and her eyes are bright like two ocean-colored gems in her face. Is that satisfaction I see that she makes no attempt to hide?

I can almost see the gears turning round and round in that pretty head of hers. She wants to be repulsed by my actions, by me standing before her covered in someone else's blood. The thing is, she's not. I know it, and so does she.

Just when I think she will take a step back and put some distance between us, her startling eyes meet mine, and have my breath trapped in my throat. *Fuck, I need to touch her, but I don't want to taint her with that fucker's blood.* Her hand tentatively reaches up toward my face, almost like she isn't even aware of its movement. I hold my breath waiting to see if she will touch me.

Her fingers trail through the mess of blood on my face, her soft touch making my heart thud painfully in my chest. I clench my hands tightly to prevent myself from touching her. I don't want her to pull away from me. I need her like I do air. I cannot live without either one.

"I will always protect you, blondie, with my very life. I never wanted to hurt you. I love you, Mia." Her hand freezes on my skin, and she quickly jerks it away as if my very touch has burned her. Her eyes flicker to mine, and I witness suppressed rage in their depths. She hates me; deep inside of her mind, heart, and soul, she hates me.

Will she never be able to forgive me? Will she not take me back even after I murder all her enemies? Will nothing I do ever make up for the damage I have done with my words and deeds? I can't live without her. I won't survive the madness that will take me in its clutches.

I raise my hand with the blade and point the end of it at my heart. "If you can't find it in you to forgive me, Mia, then please end my life now. I can't live without you,"

Her eyes trail to the blade, and her hand darts again, moving down my neck and over my chest until her fingers skate over the sharp edge. I watch with trepidation and rapt attention as her hand wraps around the handle of the blade and my fingers. Her grip tightens, and the sharp point pokes through my blood-soaked shirt. Fuck, is she really going to kill me? Is that what she truly wants? To end my fucking life or have me do it for her. The beast inside rages angrily; he wants his queen, his mate.

She leans forward, her sweet vanilla and jasmine scent reaching my nose and intoxicating my senses. "You don't get to end your life, Carter. I own it. It belongs to me."

She releases her hold, turns on her heels, and immediately walks out of the room with Stella, Clark, and Tom on her heels. I release the sharp breath that I was holding, and the sound is loud in the quiet room. The other guards shift forward and start the clean-up process, ignoring mine and Diego's presence.

Diego approaches me and takes the blade from my hands, throwing it across the room near the body. "I always knew you were a ruthless killer like me." He doesn't wait for my response before he, too, follows them out of the room.

Shit, she didn't kill me, and she just demanded my obedience. Why? Why didn't she kill me? Does she want me to suffer even more pain and anguish, knowing she may never forgive me? That I will never have her trust and heart again.

"I own it. It belongs to me." Her words cycle back through my mind. She owns me. Does that mean she will never let me go? Does she just want me so I can continue to be her executioner, or might there be even the smallest amount of hope there?

Fuck, her possessive declaration that I belong to her has my cock stiffening in my pants. I want to be owned by her. Everything in me wants to bow willingly at her feet. Shit, I am a psychopath, but on the bright side, I'm Mia's psychopath. Whatever her reasons, and for purposes I clearly don't understand, she still wants me. For now, that's enough. I will wear my queen down until she forgives me. *There is no way I am ever living without her.*

CHAPTER 26
Mateo

"Dread remorse when you are tempted to err, Miss Eyre; remorse is the poison of life." Charlotte Brontë, Jane Eyre

I t's been two weeks since Carter and Diego found Mia in the woods and brought her back to the house. Two painful and soul-destroying weeks since we all viewed that video. A video that turned my stomach and my world upside down, and took every last ounce of my strength to watch as the girl I fucking adore, the one who owns my heart, had to defend and save herself.

Alone.

Alone because of our actions and words. Our selfishness and need to protect her with deceitful words and deeds. The need that almost destroyed us all in the process. Will we ever recover? Will she ever be able to forgive us? Can we forgive ourselves? The sting of the cuts along my hip as they rub across the fabric of my pants assures me that I won't be forgiving myself anytime soon for my part in all of this mess.

The last couple of weeks have been filled with round-the-clock medical staff, security staff patrolling, and Mia ignoring us. She still won't let any of us near her. The minute we try, Raegan or Issy get right up in our faces. Raegan has declared an all-out war on all of us. Bludgeoning us every chance she gets, with Stella's approval.

Stella watches from a distance, not intervening but not asking us to leave. The knowledge that she could demand our removal from the property and that Mia would not intercede on our behalf causes me endless bouts of anxiety. There is a real possibility that Stella will bring Mia back to Manhattan now and take her far away from our reach. She would have every right based on our actions. The thought of being across the country from Mia has my body wired tightly and fear racing through me nonstop.

I'm sporting a busted lip and a throbbing eye from this morning's attempt to sit close to Mia in the family room. I just wanted a moment with her. To see her and touch her, but fuck did it backfire.

I move slowly, trying not to startle her. Her beautiful features are vacant, her blue eyes still, dull, and lifeless from the horrors she has survived. A feeling I can very well relate to as I live trapped in my own hell. I want to grab onto her so that both of us can escape together back into the light. The need is a drum beating in my heart, the restraint of doing precisely that is a deep ache inside of me.

Finn watches from across the room, his eyes centered on her. Whatever space Mia occupies when she is outside of her room is where he will be found. He stalks her like a shadow, standing as a silent sentry at a distance, watching and waiting for our girl to return to us. Is he dying a little bit inside, too, as each day passes and she seems to pull further into herself?

We can hear Carter out on the lush courtyard with Diego. His energy is too chaotic and charged around Mia. He unsettles her with his unrelenting attempts to reach her and earn her forgiveness or wrath, anything that shows that our girl is still inside the cocoon she has buried herself in.

The only time she seems to have any light inside those beautiful eyes is when she leaves the property with Stella to see justice served against those that harmed her. A shudder runs through my body at the image of Carter drenched in blood. His light eyes were crazed when he returned from their last venture off the property. He implored Stella to allow him to mete out justice against Mia's enemies; for some reason I cannot understand, she has allowed it.

I hesitantly manage to reach the other side of the three-seater leather sofa she's sitting on in the family room and sit my butt down softly. I don't move a single muscle, preparing myself for her to once again leave the room like she has every single time I have tried to sit next to her.

Her arms are wrapped securely around her knees, occupying as little room as possible. Making herself small and unseen. The total opposite of my Mia. This girl that has returned has lost that fire that once blazed inside of her. The one whose heat scorched us all. I need her back. I need my queen back. The one that would bloody me without a moment's hesitation when displeased. Is she still in there, trapped?

I hold my breath as my eyes collide with Finn's from across the room. Moments tick by, but she doesn't get up to leave like she has in the past two weeks. She seems to be only comfortable if Stella, Issy, or Raegan are with her. They are the only ones allowed to take up space in close proximity to her.

I clear my throat and see her body twitch from the corner of my eye, her arms tightening further around her legs and her forehead leaning against her raised knees. She tries to hide her face from our eyes. Does she not want us to read her thoughts? Her soft hair shimmers in the sunlight streaming through the windows, and I long to touch it. The memory of stroking it and feeling it moving through my fingers causing a sigh to leave my lips.

Finn's dark brown eyes move back and forth between us, watching and waiting. Is it destroying him, too, to see our once vibrant Mia so silent and still? She is breathing but barely here with us.

A few more minutes go by, tension riding thick in the air around us. I hold my breath as I once again shift slowly, moving closer across another seat cushion. I freeze, closing my eyes and waiting for her to rise, maybe even turning to me in violence for daring to be so close to her. Fuck, I would take it at this point. Any touch from her is welcome.

I open my eyes and stare at her, watching her shoulders rise and fall with each breath. She has finally started putting on some much-needed weight, even though she refuses to eat in our presence. I, too, have started eating again, finding my appetite again now that she is back home with us. Is this our home? My mind questions. Home is wherever Mia is.

I can imagine some of the thoughts that plague her. I have them too. The memories of what happened to me are ghosts that never leave me in peace. I hear her screams in the nighttime, and the desire to burst into her room and pull her in my arms is so fierce that I have to physically stop myself. The bloody lines that keep appearing with more frequency on my skin tell the tale of my restraint, or lack thereof, I guess.

All I wanted when I was found wandering in those woods with June was to feel the warmth of Mia's embrace. To have her arms wrapped tightly around me, reassuring me that the hell I survived was now over. Yet, I fucked it up royally when I finally did get to see her. I was an idiot, and now I am paying the fucking price. I need her, nonetheless. I want to offer comfort.

I hold my breath and reach out tentatively to trail a light finger down the hollow of her cheek. The bruises that were once there have faded, and the cuts are all on their way to healing. Her body jumps and then trembles at the feel of my touch, but she doesn't pull away. The need to wrap her in my arms is so fierce that I move closer. Feeling bolder, I let two fingers lightly trail over her soft skin, over her sharp cheekbones, and underneath the dark shadows under her eye and back down to her clenched jaw. She is so beautiful, my paradise. The woman I long to worship.

Her breath becomes sharp, leaving her in jagged pants. Finn stands straighter from his position on the wall, ready to save the queen before me, but she doesn't need saving. She needs reminding that she is a queen and powerful. A warrior queen.

I witness a spark in her blue eyes as they meet mine. Green clashing with blue. Mine trying to coax her back out from the hell she's confining herself to. Demanding that she remember the fierce will and power that lives inside of her. Trying desperately to force it to rise to the surface.

"Don't."

The word is uttered so softly that my mind immediately rejects it. This isn't my Mia! She's not this soft creature. She's violent and ruthless. Demanding and strong. I need her back. I need my Mia. Without her, I, too, cannot survive, and neither can the others.

We are all shells, filled with darkness, encased in an empty void, and waiting for our queen to breathe life back into us. I need her to call us all back from the brink of madness so that we can be as one again. So we can be hers, and she can be ours.

A small dark shape comes storming across the room from the direction of the kitchen so quickly that she's a blur before I feel the impact of her body as it slams into mine. Raegan lunges over the back of the sofa like a spider monkey. One of her hands yanks my shortened hair and pulls my neck back at an uncomfortable angle while the other slams into my mouth. Holy fucking shit!

My lip makes contact with my teeth, and the taste of blood fills my mouth as I jerk back from her banshee attack. "Fuck, Rae!" I fall on my ass off the sofa to the floor with her still tangled on top of me. I can't see shit with her curly hair in my face and her vicious little claws all over me.

"I warned you! You no good Spanish-speaking motherfucker, to stay away from my girl. I told you what I would do to your lying, worthless ass if you touched her!" She slams the palm of her hand into my eye socket, and pain radiates through my head. "Fuck, Finn, help!"

I hear a chuckle from across the room, but no movement happens as Raegan continues to rip out all my hair and slap me repeatedly with her hands. Damn it, I won't have any fucking hair left if she doesn't quit, and I doubt I look good fucking bald.

"YOU." slap. "DON'T." Slap. "TOUCH." Slap. "HER." slap.

I finally manage to pull away from her vicious grip, yanking out strands of my hair in the process, and slink away like a beaten animal across the room. Where I press my back against the wall, trying to slow my heart rate and my breathing. My eyes move across to watch as Raegan checks Mia over as if she was a small child and not a fucking queen. As if my touch hurt her.

Can't it? My mind questions. Didn't your touch and words cause damage already? You need to own that shit rather than just trying to move forward.

What the ever-loving fuck right now! She just gave me a massive beatdown; my head is still throbbing from the chunk of hair she pulled out, and now she's sitting there eating a stash of gummy bears and looking like a damn angel? Where the fuck did the gummy bears even come from? *RaeRae is fucking nuts.*

"Mia, please, mami. I would never hurt you." I implore from the safety of the distance between us.

Mia's eyes meet mine across the short space between us, which might as well be miles. She gives me a scathing look filled with contempt and anger. My words trigger her and cause rage to rise across her features. She doesn't attempt to hide it either; her blue eyes narrow in on me, and her brow furrows. The look of distaste on her face is a crushing blow to my soul.

I don't know what to do. The need to be with her, to reassure myself that she is alive and here with us, that she survived the evil done to her, is overwhelming. I didn't have a chance to even get past my own trauma. I put it all firmly on the back burner to deal with what happened to her. Now both hers and mine are mixing together to demolish what is left of my precarious sanity.

I'm pulled out of the memory of this morning as Theo shifts onto the counter stool next to me. He doesn't say a word, lost in his own thoughts and demons. He reaches for an apple crumble muffin on the clear glass serving dish between us. *Fuck, at least he's eating something.* The guy is wasting away, barely eating, not sleeping, and spending all his time down at that makeshift range Tom and Clark set up, firing bullets into targets. That's when he's not a ghost trailing through the halls, trying desperately to get glimpses of Mia.

Stella forbade him from being anywhere near Mia. Her threats to have him forcefully removed from the property or met with an unfortunate accident that would take his life ringing as a promise from the fierce queen. One she craves to fulfill. We all know it. We also understand why she hasn't yet. *Mia.*

His fear of losing Mia altogether has him obeying Stella's demands and biding his time. The question is, for how long? Theo won't allow Stella to keep threatening him and dictating terms. He needs control too severely to allow it for much longer. I see the cracks in his stern facade. He is fracturing before my eyes daily, and every moment threatens to bring us all crashing down when he finally unleashes all the pent-up rage that lives within him.

My thoughts return to this morning and how I realize I now have tremendous and painful insight into how Mia must have felt when I returned from Vincent's clutches. The memory of how I treated her. The way I behaved with June in her presence when she must have been distraught.

How she must have craved the need to reassure herself that I was fine, yet I pulled away and let another girl kiss me. Let someone else take her place for that moment in time and made her think I no longer wanted nor needed her. When that was the furthest thing from the truth. If what I am feeling now that she has returned is even a portion of what she felt, it's devastating, and soul crushing. *It destroys what little peace I have.*

My own memories of my recent trauma cause images to flash at the worst times. Day and night, scents, noises, and bodies too close to mine trigger me until I'm racing out of whatever space I'm in and cutting myself with my hidden blade in order to release some of the pent-up emotions. All of these demons are crippling both my mind and my soul. I want to find a way to help Mia and Theo, but the truth is I can barely help myself.

The queen of Manhattan, or as Carter likes to mumble under his breath, *"The fire and ice queen,"* laid down the law here at Mia's house that first day Mia returned. We are all once again confined to the property under strict military-style lockdown. While Stella cleans house, tracking down each and every one of those fuckers that helped hurt Mia, with my uncle Manuel serving as her vicious sword.

I long to participate in ending those fuckers' miserable lives like Carter is doing, and like Theo and Finn begged to be allowed to do. However, I know I am not strong enough to withstand another dark stain on my soul. One more, and I might genuinely lose what is left of me. *What is left that is worth saving, fucker? You're weak. Too weak to help yourself or anyone else.*

James' cabin was found filled with blood, but a body was not located. His truck was still parked in front of the house. We are unsure if someone managed to get to him and remove him or if he managed to get away himself.

My money's on the first one. I saw the condition that fucker was in on the screen. He wouldn't have gotten far without help. Which means someone out there is still looking to hurt my girl. Stella had the whole place burned to the ground and turned to ash so it could never be used for evil again. Theo, Finn, and I watched as Carter and Diego lit the damn match. We all needed to be there to rid the world of the place that held the evil that our girl endured.

The girl that won't look at me, won't let me speak to her so I can apologize, or even yell, and cuss me out. Fuck, at this point, I would willingly let her beat on me if she wanted to. She's physically here. Her malnourished body is getting stronger every day, but her mind...her mind is elsewhere.

I believed the screams we used to hear coming from Theo's room were the most frightening thing I could ever experience other than my own nightmares. *I was wrong, so very wrong.*

The screams and sobbing that we hear from Mia's suite while Raegan, Issy, and Stella try to comfort her, are tearing me apart, minute by minute, day by day, and I am not the only one. Theo hasn't slept more than a few hours in the last two weeks. The guy spends all night sitting with his back up against the wall opposite her door. He risks Stella's malignant wrath nightly, yet he won't stop. Can't stay away from her, just like the rest of us. He barely speaks or looks at anyone. I don't think he's showered in days. He's just broken, worse than when he returned from the hospital. He is an animal waiting to die; we all are.

Carter has had to be physically confined to his room on numerous occasions by the security team in the last couple of days at Stella's behest. He's losing his mind at the fact that Mia won't let him anywhere near her, despite Diego and him finding her.

To my knowledge, she hasn't said one word to him outside of that day when she arrived back at the estate. The only time he gets to be with her is when he plays an avenging executioner. I worry about what all of this is doing to his already nonsensical mind. When I questioned him about it, he brushed me off and refused to answer me. I can only imagine how gruesome it was and what he had to do.

The idiot also keeps picking fights with Theo, who won't defend himself, and it's starting to look like a damn MMA fight on a regular occurrence in here. Stella had him tasered this morning when he tried again to accost Theo. Clark was all too willing to do it. The fucker even grinned widely as Carter ended up on his knees.

The desire to go toe-to-toe with Clark was a fire in my blood. The need to hurt him was almost all-consuming. No one gets to fucking hurt one of my best friends, but I had to settle down and remember that Carter is an unstable psycho and deserves it. Even so, the next time Clark comes for him, he better prepare for the thrashing I'm going to give him, and Finn will most likely jump in too.

Then there's Finn, the one I share the closest bond with. He's nothing but a wraith walking these halls. He barely speaks, lost in his musings. The ones that no doubt call him a traitor for revealing that Mia was Amelia. Always following Mia from one room to the next, hoping, like the rest of us, to be able to speak to her. To beg her forgiveness and understanding. To urge her for mercy. *A mercy I am not sure she will provide.*

Finn slides onto the stool on Theo's opposite side with a deep sigh. "She doesn't seem to be getting better. Last night's screams were the worst so far, and I think I heard her breaking shit in her room." His voice wavers as his eyes meet mine, then Theo's.

"She was screaming my father's name. I'm almost positive that was what I was hearing from outside of her door." Theo replies gruffly.

"Vincent? Why the fuck would she be calling out his name?" Anger immediately fills me at the thought of the psychopath tormenting her in her dreams.

"I think she had something to do with how he was found on the side of the road," Theo utters matter-of-factly while taking another bite of the muffin. Like we are not sitting here discussing our girl causing massive torture to his demon fucker of a father.

"You know what, that would make a lot of sense. There was rage in the wounds inflicted. There was vicious intent behind each one. The fingers, the wound on his chest, the same as yours and Mat's. The fact that his dick was cut off and shoved down his throat before his throat was cut. Jesus!" Finn's throat bobs, and he pales, looking like he might get sick. "She did all that."

Theo nods and keeps eating, his eyes narrowed. I can almost see the wheels turning in that thick head of his. "We need to somehow reach her. Get her alone so that we can talk to her without Issy, Raegan, and Stella's hovering presences."

A snort leaves my lips at his words. "Are you insane? How the fuck are we going to manage to do that? Stella has this place on complete lockdown, and she won't hesitate to shoot any of us. My money is on her shooting Carter before the week is out."

"Why is my name moving across your cunt lips?" Carter shifts so quietly into the room that I didn't even hear him, and the hairs on the back of my neck stand on end. He's getting better at being silent when he wants to be. That knowledge makes Carter even more dangerous than he already was.

He comes closer and stands on the other side of the island, his lip curling and a snarl across his face as he meets Theo's eyes. "You know what! You two fuckers need to stop this shit!" I bellow, done with playing nice with each of these assholes. My nerves are shot, and them constantly at each other is just making everything worse.

I reach across and grab a fist full of Carter's hunter green t-shirt, pulling him flush against the island. "I get it, you insane fucker. You're mad at the choices he made. Ones, by the way, you went along with. We all did, Carter." His nostrils flare, and his fingers circle my wrist applying pressure, but I refuse to release my hold on him. He can go ahead and break my goddamn wrist, but this is getting fucking said, right the fuck now.

"We were all to blame, Carter, not just Theo. We all hurt her." Finn laments from his spot.

"He started this shit. Always demanding control. Thinking he knows best for all of us!" Carter replies through gritted teeth. His husky blue eyes are so cold, like chips of pure Alaskan ice.

"You're fucking right, Carter!" Theo pushes back from the counter and stands with fury etched across his features. His dark blue eyes blaze with a fire from within, and his shoulders bunch as he slams his palm against the counter in a loud thump. "Is that what you want to hear? That you are right? That I am the cause of all this misery?"

His hand drags down his tired face. "I was the cause, Carter. I have to live with that knowledge every fucking moment. Every second that I breathe, I know what I did caused what happened to her. I did that with my words and actions." We watch as his hands tremble as he clenches them on the counter surface.

"Everything that happened to her was my fault. Do you think I don't wish for death every moment? I can't fucking breathe, brother, knowing she was raped and beaten repeatedly because I forced us to push her away." He pulls a gun from the back of his pants and slides it across the marble surface until it's near Carter's hand. "Kill me, Carter, get it over with. Please."

I watch with sheer panic as Carter grabs the gun and clicks the safety off, pointing the barrel directly at Theo's head. "Oh, you want to die, fucker?" A menacing smirk crosses his features. "Naw, that would be too easy of an out for you. I'm not going to put a bullet in your head, Theo. If I do, you get to escape the horror of knowing you not only hurt our girl but helped destroy her."

He leans forward across the counter, his face approaching Theo's as he presses the gun against his temple. "You want to die, to absolve yourself of your part? Take the coward's way out, Theo. I'm not going to oblige you." He drops the gun on the counter in front of Theo and pulls back.

The breath that was trapped in my throat releases, and I grab for the gun at the same time Finn does. He gets to it first and clicks the safety back on, slipping it into the back of his pants. "No one is killing anyone. We are all guilty here. Carter, you can't keep going at him. He's your best friend and brother...and you are just as guilty as he is." Finn bites down on his bottom lip hard, aggravation across his features. "We are all guilty. We all claimed to love her but hurt her instead of protecting her."

"We need to fix this." I throw out with conviction. "You think getting her alone will help? I don't want to make shit worse. She's already so broken, Theo."

"Yes, I think if we can get her alone, her need for her vengeance will resurface. We can force her out of the darkness she's hiding in...like she did to me." He sighs and sits back down.

"How? How do we get her alone without one of the girls?" Finn inquires.

Carter leans both elbows on the counter in front of us, looking defeated. He meets each of our gazes, and for once since Mia went missing, I see calmness in his eyes. He even looks at Theo without menace. *Fuck, it's a start.* "Diego. Diego can get us off the grounds. His men are helping to patrol. He and I left the property yesterday without Stella realizing it."

"Where the fuck did you go?" Finn demands.

"To see my mom, but that's not important right now. Diego can get us out. We just need to get Mia alone long enough to get her out of the house."

"How?" Theo stares back at Carter, unflinching, and we watch as a mischievous smile crosses Carter's face. "I think I might know a way to make everyone have an extended naptime. I'm going to need to make some calls."

"Won't Stella fucking have us all murdered when she finds out what we have done?" I question with worry.

"No, bitch, she is going to enjoy shanking us herself." Carter lets out a cackle. I swear the guy is even more messed up than he was before all this went down. Hanging out with my *primo* is probably not good for him. Yeah, murdering people in cold blood probably isn't, either.

"You fuckers really believe that we can pull this off?" Finn sighs and runs his hands along the back of his neck.

"What choice do we have, Finn? Are you ready to let her go? Cause it's only a matter of time before Stella either removes us from this house or takes Mia back to Manhattan. Either way, we are going to lose access to her." Theo gets up and paces back and forth in front of the island while all three of us watch him get worked up. He hasn't regained his precious control yet, losing his temper more and more frequently. He hasn't knocked Carter on his ass yet, either, so there is still hope for him.

"Theo's right; if we don't do something, we lose her. If we do something, we might lose her regardless, but at least we know we tried, and there is still the chance she will hear us out." I rub my hands together, trying to alleviate some of the anxiety I'm feeling and the craving to go find a quiet place with my blade to release some of these emotions I have bottled up before I explode.

"I'm all in, fuckers; let's do this." Carter crows like a lunatic, and it pulls a smile on my face.

I guess we are about to steal our girl like a bunch of fucking thieves. Here's hoping none of us get shot in the process.

CHAPTER 27

Mia

"I sat with my anger long enough until she told me her real name was grief." C.S. Lewis.

"**G**randmother, what would you say if I wanted to return to Manhattan now, and have you set fire to this house?" The question leaves my lips as I meet my grandmother's cool gaze. She and I are alone together in the home office at her request.

I know she wants to talk to me about the guys. We can't keep holding them here against their will. Even though I doubt any of the fuckers will leave if given the choice. Raegan and Issy have filled me in on what happened when I went missing and the weeks that followed my disappearance.

Apparently, my maniacal and idiotic kings never meant to do anything other than to push me to return to Manhattan and the safety of the Stratford compound. Their actions all stemmed from their need to protect me from Vincent Saint-Lambert and his psychotic attempts to capture me.

They didn't give a shit that I was Amelia Hamilton or that I came back to Casbury to hurt them. Or so they say. It's hard to believe, to even make sense of all the shit they said and did to me in those final hours before I was taken by

James. I'm not sure if I entirely believe them. Issy and Raegan seemed somewhat convinced, but neither of them had the displeasure of experiencing the kings as malicious children as I did.

All of this could have been avoided if they just talked to me like rational human beings instead of animalistic cavemen, demanding my obedience. I am not sure if I would have returned to Manhattan at their behest had they made it instead of trying to hurt me. I could have avoided being captured by James.

James. That monster might still be out there, somewhere, alive. My body tightens painfully at the thought, and my heart rate accelerates. Images and traumatic memories try to force their way into the forefront of my brain, but I push them back with all my mental strength. I refuse to continue to fall apart every time I think of his name. *I'm a goddamn Stratford; no man will bring me to my knees.*

The mental strain is exhausting; fighting recollections and living nightmares day and night are taxing on what little strength I have gained back. Anytime I want to give up, to crawl into the fetal position or slice my own wrists, I think of Stella, my grandmother. Who has survived numerous attempts on her life and is still standing, still leading this family like the vengeful and resilient queen she is. I can't be any less ferocious. I am, after all, her heir. A Stratford right down to the very core of my soul. James couldn't take that from me, even though he tried.

The worst of the damage inflicted on my body has healed. A few cuts and bruises are still in the works of healing, but they are insignificant to my long-term health. I had to have my fingers re-broken and reset, and my wrist is in a cast. None of my ribs ended up being fractured, just severely bruised. I was lucky; the fucker could have punctured a lung. I might have died in that cabin or out in those woods had that been the case.

The infection in my vagina from his disgusting use of dirty toys, his fingers, and God knows what else has subsided with antibiotics. I was so relieved to find out the fucker hadn't given me an STD. The thought of him inside of me, raping me while I was unconscious, makes sweat break out across my body, and my mind want to retreat back into its safe dark hole. *No, no more memories, no more images.*

You would think that would be enough to give me nightmares, but my mind projects other horrors right along with those James inflicted on me. Images of the things I did in vengeance against Vincent Saint-Lambert. How I tortured him with my own hands before James ended his miserable life. Only Stella, Raegan, and Issy know of my actions. I couldn't successfully hide it from them. Whenever I close my eyes, I am accosted with the images of my deeds.

I would have thought each of them would have been horrified at my confession. That I cut off his fingers, broke his bones, stabbed him close to the heart and cut off his dick while he was still alive, and made him choke on it before James cut his malicious throat. Ending his miserable, evil life and freeing this earth from his demonic presence. Instead of horror, I witnessed unabashed and authentic pride across my grandmother's face and acceptance across Raegan and Issy's faces. *They don't think I am a monster, even if I do.*

"Mia, my darling. I think it is about time you returned to your home. This backward town has never been that." She shrugs nonchalantly, her eyes studying my face. What does she see when she looks at me? Does she see herself? A survivor, one that will not lay down and die? I hope that is what she sees rather than the pitiful creature I have allowed myself to become.

"As for setting the house on fire. My love, it will not stop the memories from returning from your time here with them, but if it is your heart's desire to see this whole town burn, this corrupted kingdom these so-called kings created. Then my darling, I will give you the match."

A smile graces my lips as I observe a look of glee across her face. She really would set this whole town ablaze if I requested it. There is nothing Stella Stratford wouldn't do to protect her own family. "I'll think about it. What did you want to speak to me about?"

"The kings. We need to discuss what happens to them and your future, with or without them, Mia." My chest constricts until it's almost impossible to take a deep breath. I knew this was coming. I just can't seem to make up my own mind.

The last two weeks since my return from captivity have been a rollercoaster of emotions. I wish the healing of my body would reflect the healing of my mind and soul or the constant pain my heart is in. The kings aren't making it any easier with their steady attempts to catch me alone or plead their cases and beg for my forgiveness. *Do I even want to forgive them?* Yes, my heart always answers.

Carter, that fool with his snarky personality, is wearing me down. He has become my executioner of death, a willing knight with a sharp sword, one who bows at my feet. That first day I permitted him to come with us to murder one of the men that watched me suffer wretchedly was only the beginning of more death at his hands. We have now captured three men, all of whom my willing king has bloodied to bring me my vengeance. A vengeance I should have taken myself but allowed him to enact in penance for his actions.

He begs for forgiveness for the injuries he inflicted against me with every slash of his blade. His stunning eyes plead for me to see into his heart, one that only seems to beat for me. His words of surrender to my will, have small cracks, ones he himself inflicted, healing.

I haven't spoken any words to him since that first day in that warehouse. There seems to be no need. He and I understand each other without the need for them. He sees into my scarred heart, enacts my rage, and then willingly surrenders at my feet, ready to be destroyed. Prepared for me to cut him open and watch him bleed. Do I want to watch him bleed out? If you had asked me that two weeks ago, the answer would have been a resounding yes; now, I wouldn't be so sure.

I have watched him take his rage out on Theo at the house daily. Using Theo's large body as a punching bag whenever they are in the same space. Carter regrets following Theo's lead. Where before they were inseparable, their loyalty to each other without reproach, now Carter can barely stand the sight of him. What does he see when he looks at Theo? Does he recognize the man that led him to his own destruction? That caused him to lose me?

I know I should stop Carter from continuing to hurt Theo. It's taxing on everyone's nerves, and Stella keeps punishing him for it. I just can't. Every wound he inflicts on him brings me a perverse pleasure and helps to bring me peace. Yes, my revenge and displeasure are being meted out by Carter's hands, but the point is it's still happening. I'm watching them all self-destruct from within. Pieces of the kings of Casbury breaking off until they too will be fragmented just like I am.

Theo, the ringleader, led them all to deceive me, to turn against me. My strong and powerful king is barely breathing now. I pulled him out of the darkness once, and how did he repay me? He pushed me away when he should have held me tighter. He should have stood by my side and realized I could handle anything this world threw at me. His worry for his father's attempts to capture me led me straight into another monster's hands. I have survived that monster, just like he survived his father. My body, like his, is intact, but my soul is crushed and weary. He should have realized that my fate and his were always predetermined. His attempts to save me failed and only led to more pain.

He prowls the hallways outside of my door nightly, trying to fight his own demons and begging for an opportunity to do battle with mine. I know he sits outside my door listening to me scream at the horrors I not only endured at James' hands but the ones I committed with my own hands on Vincent.

I only catch glimpses of him during the day as he hides around corners, always keeping a watchful eye, like a sleek panther observing its prey. He always seems to know where I am, despite my attempts to stay out of his presence. His dark midnight eyes call to me, begging me to let him back in. To allow him to wrap me in his arms and accept his sorrowful remorse.

Stella's threats to have him murdered or removed from the property if he approaches me have him staying at a distance, but I can tell Theo is only biding his time. He will come for me, my ruthless king, and when he does, I no longer know if I want to bloody him or fall into his arms.

Then there is Finn, my betrayer, and my silent sentry. The one who follows me from room to room, always watching and waiting. What is he waiting for? His own death at my hands? My rejection? Perhaps my forgiveness? It will be harder to provide it to him, more than the others. He and I have always had a connection, even when we were children. His betrayal cuts deeper into my soul, wounding me with an injury that refuses to heal. It festers and calls to the darkness inside of me that demands his destruction, even nevertheless my heart begs once again for leniency.

He is my constant shadow in every room I am in. He never approaches me, never even speaks to me. He just stands and observes, his dark ochre eyes attempting to reach me with their regret plain to witness. Does he see me, Mia Stratford, or the little girl that loved him, Amelia Hamilton? Does it eat him up inside to know that he backstabbed both of us? My heart wants to forgive him, but my mind insists he has not yet received his penance, that I have yet to take my restitution from him. *Revenge is a double-edged sword, Mia. Be careful that while you are stabbing him with it, you are not also cutting out your own heart.*

The last of the kings is my biggest weakness. I know it deep inside the caverns of my heart. Mateo is different from the other three. Don't get me wrong, he is equally vicious, but his heart is not as hardened. The sadness that has always wrapped itself around him, like a blanket of despair, is even worse now. My cinnamon roll of a king has suffered horrors that only another survivor of the same fate could truly understand.

My anger towards him at his betrayal of choosing June over me when he returned from Vincent's clutches is some days just a simmering heat. Other days it is still a blazing wildfire. Having experienced the true horrors of being subjected to that type of violence that he, Theo, and I were. Where someone takes from you without your consent and watches as it destroys you from the inside out. I want to be angry with him and a big part of me is, but the reality is, as painful as it was for me to experience his rejection, the other part of me is just glad he had someone to turn to. Someone to soothe his injured soul. Even if it was her and not me.

June was gone from the house before my return. I refused to ask Issy or Raegan what became of her. There is a real fear inside of my heart that he still wants her, that his depression is worsening at her loss. Is it her he craves? Does his heart call out for hers instead of mine? *No, bitch. Did you not see the beating he took from Rae this very morning just to be able to sit at your side for a mere moment?* It's you his heart calls to, and you know it. All you have to do is look into those beautiful green eyes to see the truth laid painfully bare there for you to see.

My heart and mind war with each other and what they want. Do I still want to be with the kings after everything that has happened? Does the information that Issy and Raegan relayed to me about the reasons behind their actions change anything?

Each of them is now as broken as I am. They are alive but shells of who they were. Destiny and fate, both fickle bitches have taken all five of us and ripped us apart, leaving sharp jagged edges that slice us and each other apart. Guilt breeds inside of me, spreading like a parasite into all the recesses of my heart and mind. Attempting to change my need for vengeance into sympathy and acceptance. How dare it.

Can I forgive them? Can I let them go? *They are fucking ours. Ours to destroy, ours to control.* My mind argues while my heart begs for mercy. Mercy, I'm not sure I want to bestow on any of them. *How much deeper will you let the blade slice you and them, Mia?*

The truth of the matter is that they have hurt me over and over. Doubt clouds my mind, causing it to resist what my heart desires and pleads for. I am not convinced that they are not the same horrible creatures that bullied me when I was younger. They will continuously hurt me if I allow it. *So bring them to their knees and keep them there. You are a Stratford queen.*

Stella watches me intently. "You are still in love with all four of them, yes? Is there one that you have stronger feelings for than the others?"

Am I in love with each of them? No, I can't be. How can I have fallen in love with the four men that hurt me? That deceived me? *Are you sure you are not denying it just to soothe your damaged pride, Mia?* Your need for revenge was years in the making, and you had all but abandoned it when you fell hard for the kings of Casbury before you left. Is it pain you are allowing to speak for you or genuine emotions? My mind is so confused. I know I care deeply for each of them despite what they have done to me. *Is that love, though?*

Even the very thought that I might actually have those feelings for them is ludicrous. It chafes me to admit that I may be in love, or at least was, equally with four different alpha assholes. Ones that make me certifiable on a good day. That all four of them hold a piece of my heart, even after bruising it terribly. But they shouldn't. If I were to forgive them, then I know there is no way I could choose one of them over the others. It would leave a gap of massive loss in its wake if I did. It's either all or none.

"I could never choose one over the others. I wouldn't use the word love, grandmother, but I have... strong feelings for each of them, despite all the shit they have put me through."

Stella's fierce eyes sear into me as if she can see right into my soul. Can she see the lies I try to tell myself? Are they indeed lies? I am not even sure of what I'm feeling anymore. *No, Stella can see all the bullshit I feed myself about my feelings for the kings of Casbury.* There is no hiding it from her. A deep sigh leaves my grandmother's lips, and the little lines around her stunning blue eyes crinkle. "Do you want to let them go, Mia?"

Her question causes my heart to pound painfully in my chest. My hands clench in my lap at the mere idea of not having them, of releasing them from my hold. *I will never let them go.* "No. I can't picture a life or future right now without them in it." My heart rejoices at my honesty while my mind begs me to reconsider. I want to take the words back.

"Isn't that the way of the heart, Mia? I would love to tell you that it will pass, that the love and affection will fade. But granddaughter, I have experienced this all-consuming love once with your grandfather, Jaxon. I can tell you with certainty that not even death will cause it to fade. You will hunger for them for the rest of your life."

Her words are filled with pain. I know she still feels the loss of Jaxon, even all these years later. I watch as her fingers run over the charms on her bracelet. She has never moved on, never even considered having another relationship with another man. When Issy and I teased her about it, she indicated, *she had already had the love of her life; anything else would pale by comparison.*

Do I want to end up like Stella, missing the loves of my life and alone? Seeking power and grandeur but never experiencing the touch of Theo's hands or the softly spoken words Mateo utters. What about the fierce loyalty and irrational possession that Carter demands or my deep soul connection with Finn? Are they my home, and without them, will I always be wandering without true shelter?

"You should know that I bribed each of them to leave you alone." She raises her manicured hand up to stop my objection.

"I dangled Theo's unrestricted fortune and inheritance before him. Mateo and Carter would have control of all of their family's interests and assets. Finn would receive his vast inheritance now. All they had to do was accept my terms." A smirk crosses her lips, and I see a twinkle in her eyes.

"To agree to never seeing you again, Mia. To stay at least a country's width from you at all times." She shakes her head as her lips break out into a small satisfied smile. *The devious little witch.* She gave them exactly what they craved. Something she is all too familiar with. *Power.* With their fortunes, they would have unlimited access to power.

I hold my bated breath waiting for her next words. My body feels antsy and restless, waiting for words that I know are going to crush me. They would never choose me when offered the prospect of all that power. They are the kings of Casbury, after all. The need for power runs through their veins. Seeds of resentment and anger once again start to sow inside of me and fill me with a chasm of sadness.

"Not a single one took me up on my offer. In fact, Carter very eloquently told me to go to hell." A spark of light shimmers behind her irises, and her eyebrows rise dramatically. "He, more than the others, reminds me of Jaxon. You will need to watch for him. He will self-destruct if you allow him to. He will also love you the hardest with a passion that will never settle and burn brighter than the sun, Mia."

"I released each of their funds regardless without telling them. Those vast fortunes belong to them, and they should have them, especially now. Seems young Theodore may have wealth to rival a Stratford with his mother's inheritance and his worthless father's assets." She snorts, and the sound is so out of place with my elegant, refined grandmother that it rips a chuckle from my lips.

My heart thuds painfully in my chest, the blood rushing in my veins making all my limbs feel heavy. None of them accepted her offer? Not one? How can this be? My mind is so muddled with confusion. They gave up the possibility of their fortunes for me, their future for me?

They couldn't have known that Stella would release them regardless. No, as far as they know, Stella is heartless. She would have left them penniless. *Yet they still chose me.* The block of ice around my heart begins to thaw with that knowledge and the understanding of the magnitude of their decisions. So they have gave up their fortunes, that doesn't mean they won't hurt you again, my heart snarks. *Shut the fuck up asshole,* my mind screams. *They gave up everything for you, without their fortunes, they are no longer the kings of Casbury.*

Hope. Hope is a sneaky bitch. She was there all along, waiting patiently while doubts voiced their displeasure loudly. She shines brighter now, a small ray of pure bright light, dispelling some of the shadows from my heart. Not one of them was willing to give me up? *Told you, bitch,* my heart does a little snide dance.

"So..." I don't even know what to say at this point. Why is Stella telling me all this? She has never hidden her displeasure or dislike of all of them. Even though I have my sneaky suspicion, she does genuinely like Carter. *Of course, she would like the most unbalanced fucker of the group.* I guess she is more like me than she knows. She raised me to get my vengeance on all of them for hurting me in my youth; now, she seems to be changing her tune. What has caused this massive change of heart?

Was it almost losing me? Did each of them show her true feelings in my absence? Is Stella telling me that I can have all four of them? That I don't have to choose, and she will allow it?

"What about your demand for me to marry to strengthen the Stratford empire?" I question, my fists clenched tightly in my lap as my nails bite deeply into the palms of my hands.

"I would say all four of those boys have legacies that will strengthen us for years to come. That is, if you choose to remain with one or with all of them. I will not hold your future hostage like mine was. You are not a prize, Mia. I should have never even made that bargain with you. I never had any intentions to proceed with it anyway. I just wanted you to be free of your past. To leave those four devils behind and make a fresh start for yourself. One where you were not burdened by their actions against you. However, it's a moot point, granddaughter, as I can see that you love those barbarians, even if you will not willingly admit it to yourself."

Her words cause my eyes to blur, tears wanting to crest, but I force them back down. "I...I don't understand, grandmother." I need to understand her intentions clearly. I want there to be no way that she can later backtrack on her intentions.

"Mia Stratford, you are my granddaughter and my heir. If you want to keep all four of those psychopaths and spend your life trying to control and manage them, I will not stop you; no one will stand in your way. You deserve whatever happiness you are able to obtain. Seek it, granddaughter, and hold tightly to it. One day it may be what you prize most."

OH MY GOD! Did she just not only give her permission for me to be in a relationship with all four of the kings of Casbury but encourage it? No, she's not encouraging it, shes just accepting it, but still how fucking progressive and frankly alarming of Stella. Do I even want a future with the kings of Casbury by my side? Can I trust them not to hurt me? They love you, and while they are fucking idiots with less than half a brain between the four of them, look at their actions since you have returned. Actions often speak louder than words. But what about their deliberate actions that have helped destroy me? That cannot be easily forgotten or forgiven. I am haunted everyday by the horrors I faced because each of them turned their backs on me.

Stella clearing her throat pulls me back from my unending thoughts. "Also, my darling, you should know that all four of them are scheming with that snake, Diego. They think that I don't know what is happening on this property every minute of the day. They plan to try to take you off the property so that they convince you of their intentions...bloody fools."

A giggle leaves my grandmother's lips, and it's such a shocking sound that it has one ripping from my own mouth. "I will allow it if that is your wish, granddaughter. You need to make a decision of where your mind and heart are, my darling. If it is your wish to allow them to play thief in the night with you, I won't hinder them, but I will keep the five of you protected and watched at all times. Of course, they don't need to know that. But they will be on borrowed time, Mia. I will not allow them to play with you like a cat does with a mouse."

My grandmother's threat makes a shiver slide down my back. The kings better be cautious of her. I learned about forgiveness from her, and she doesn't excel at it. No, she would rather focus on vengeance, like a true Stratford. So they are plotting to whisk me away? I'm not sure how I feel about that. Do they really have the balls to take Stella on? Do they think they can just demand my forgiveness by ripping me from my home? Where would they even take me? Probably one of their own homes, the idiots. A mix of emotions runs through me. I push those thoughts from my brain and nod my head at my grandmother, a silly smile I have never seen in all my years as her granddaughter crosses her face, taking years off her features.

"Diego, really?" I question with mirth. They are a bunch of reckless idiots if they think Stella doesn't know every move Diego is making.

"I will deal with him shortly for thinking he could manipulate both of my granddaughters. I might send your sister off to a place where the malignant snake can't reach her. For her own safety and sanity."

Shock once again rushes through me, and my eyes widen with alarm. "You knew?"

A haughty look of disapproval crosses her aged features. Stella is still beautiful, even with the years mapped across her skin. They are road maps to her suffering and struggle, and one day I hope to say that I conquered as much as she has in my lifetime.

An unladylike cackle leaves her lips, making her sound more like an evil witch than a reigning queen. "Give me some credit, Mia. I know every move you and your sister make. If I allow you to make your own mistakes, it's so that you experience life outside of this bubble I want to wrap you in. You need to learn and handle challenges yourselves. I will not always be here to save you."

Just then, there is a knock on the door, and before we can even acknowledge it, Carter is walking into the room with a tray of cookies, pastries, and cups of tea upon it. *He looks a lot tastier than the treats do... OH MY GOD!* Where did that thought come from? *No, Mia, he is the enemy!* My mind screeches, but a part of my heart admires him anyway.

"Beautiful Stratford queens." He nods, with that charming smile of his painted across his features. The one that reaches all the way to his stunning blue-gray eyes. "I had some pastries and treats delivered from that bistro the girls like. I hoped you ladies might want some."

He watches expectantly as we look over the tray. My eyes meet Stella's, and I watch, enthralled, as my grandmother tries desperately to hide her smile. She winks at me, while composing herself and then turns to glare at Carter, a hint of humor behind her eyes.

"How lovely, Carter. I think I will indulge this one time, young man. After all, it's not every day a handsome fool brings a queen an offering." She reaches forward and takes a cookie and one of the teas. Carter watches her intently as she takes a bite. A look of satisfaction crosses his features once she takes a few sips of her tea.

Oh, Carter, you indeed are a fool. This must have something to do with them taking me off the property. He truly is an idiot if he thinks he can hide his intentions. Look at the pleased look on his face. He is practically giddy, the scheming fucker. He doesn't even know how to wear a mask like Theo, Stella, or I do.

Yet, despite all the shit he has put me through, for some unexplained reason I feel my heart skip a beat just once. *That weak bitch.*

The truth is I am as much to blame as they are. I shouldn't have reacted the way I did to their hurtful and disrespectful actions. Behavior that was out of character for me, running scared away from a fight. No, I should have stayed here and brought all four of them to their knees. Like I first intended to do when I returned to Casbury. My cowardice was as much to blame as their malicious words for James having the opportunity to get his hands on me.

I grab a cookie and take a large bite, the buttery flavor melting in my mouth and a groan leaving my lips. His beautiful husky eyes meet mine, and a small smile crosses his lips. "Thank you," I utter the first words I have said to him since the warehouse. I watch how my words slide over him, a field of emotions crossing his handsome features. Pain and grief momentarily make their way across his face and shadow his eyes. All of a sudden the desire to reach out and let my fingers slide down his face soar through me, but I hold back. It is a desire I never thought I would feel again. At least not for these four so-called kings.

"I would do anything for you, Mia. There is nothing you could want or need that I wouldn't provide." His throat bobs, and his lips tighten as if he is trying to stop further words from escaping his pouty lips. Fuck, those pouty lips do things to me, even now, when that should be the furthest thing from my mind.

I let my eyes trail over his toned fit body. He looks like he's put on even more muscle than when he was playing football. His arms bulge from below the sleeves of his red T-shirt, all that beautiful art across his skin and trailing up the thick expanse of his chest and peeking over the collar of his shirt and along his neck. I know that he and Diego have been working out for hours daily. Their bromance both intrigues and amuses me.

An inkling of appreciation at his male form starts deep in my core, the feeling initially shocking. After everything I have been through, I didn't think I would ever be able to feel that sensation again. The mere thought of any kind of intimacy has made me nauseous since I was found. I don't want anyone touching me; the feeling suffocates me, even with the girls sometimes. Right now, nonetheless, my body and mind are wavering in their desire to push him away, and a tiny ember of desire tries to light. *Hello, where is Mia Stratford, and what the fuck have you done with her?* My mind snarks, trying to recapture my righteous indignation.

Carter is a more alluring treat than anything on that tray, and I find that I am curious to see what he and his fellow kings have in store for me. I wonder which of their houses they are going to bring me to. Although I am not sure I can completely forgive them, some part of me recognizes that I am no longer filled with the consuming rage I was in when I entered this room. Speaking with

Stella has forced me to process some of my thoughts that I refused to entertain. One thing is for sure, I will not let them see me bend so easily. I hope they like spending lots of time on their fucking knees. I plan to make it their permanent home, right at my feet.

CHAPTER 28

Theo

"Find a place inside where there's joy, and the joy will burn out the pain." Joseph Campbell

I can't believe Carter and Diego's idiotic plan to put sleeping agents in cookies and tea fucking worked. The first smile in weeks breaks across my face as I carry a sleeping Issy to the sofa while watching Mateo do the same with Raegan. *The little banshee looks like an angel when she's not beating on us.*

Shit, these two are going to be spitting mad when they wake from their little naps and realize that we have taken off with Mia. A shudder runs through me at the thought of the violence that Raegan will put us through when we return. The little *she-devil,* who knew that personality lingered behind that quiet girl facade.

You're worried about Raegan? You should be concerned about what Stella will do to all of you, including Diego. As far as we know, she has personally killed three people and probably had countless others murdered. What do you think she will do with the four of you once she wakes and realizes you absconded with her granddaughter and heir? The one that just returned from brutal captivity at the hands of a psycho. Well fuck, here's hoping this all works out to plan and Mia still has feelings for us. Otherwise, we just signed our own death warrants.

"Are we all good in here?" Finn strolls into the room, looking lighter and filled with confidence. A look I haven't seen in weeks, maybe even months, since all this shit started. The fucker got tasked with carrying Stella up to her room. We actually had to pull straws. None of us were willing to volunteer to be the one to handle her in case she wasn't a hundred percent down for the count. Can you imagine what she would do to us if she wasn't knocked the fuck out? My balls throb painfully and want to run and hide at just the thought of how Stella would cut them off and serve them to me.

"Yup, the queen of Manhattan is down for the count." A wolfish grin crosses his lips.

"Carter and Diego have Mia?" The question raises my hackles. At first, I was worried about the two of them collecting Mia and taking her down to the hidden vehicle on the eastern side of the property. I wouldn't put it past him to run away with her, and Diego to facilitate his getaway. The only thing that stopped me from refusing it be them was the need to repair shit with Carter.

Mateo and Finn are correct. We can't continue on like this. We have never been at odds with each other in all our years of friendship. He is my brother, part of my heart, and my right-hand man. He wants Mia just as much as we do. He also knows she won't only choose him. She's made herself very clear from the beginning, it's all of us or none of us. I have to believe that he wants her too badly to try to fuck me over.

As for Diego, my gaze makes contact with the beautiful pale princess on the sofa. Her raven hair trails down her back in thick waves and over stunning doll-like features. She looks like *Snow White* asleep, awaiting her prince. A chuckle crawls up my throat when I think of Diego as her prince. More like the fucking villain. I know where his head and heart are at. It's plain to see if you're paying attention. He's in love with her. He doesn't want my Mia. He has another Stratford princess in his devious sights.

Finn nods with a look of glee across his round high cheekbones. His brown eyes sparkle in the light streaming through the window. Hell, he looks almost back to himself; there is still a shadow there, cast by his regret, I am sure. The guilt of telling us about Amelia Hamilton.

I've made peace with the knowledge that Mia is Amelia. The recollection disturbed me for a moment before I realized that karma really is a bitch. How else do you explain that the four of us fell madly and irrationally in love with the same girl we bullied years ago?

How about the fact that all four of us who have alpha tendencies are willing to share her just to have even a small piece of her. Better yet, how she is one hundred percent the only female that has ever brought all of us to our unwilling knees.

The reminder of why we bullied her in the first place is a solid weight around my chest. What I did to her years ago was to save her, or at least that is how I rationalized it in my pubescent mind. I wanted to keep her and Catherine safe from my father's clutches.

Did I go about it the right way? *Fuck no! I went about it the Theo Saint-Lambert way, destructive and damaging.* Did I rope my fellow kings in to do my bidding with my need to lead them and also keep them safe? *Yeah, I fucking did, to mine and their detriment.*

Was I the stupid, irrational asshole that did the exact same thing years later to the same girl? The one I know I love and would burn the whole world down for. *Yup, that's me, fucking supreme idiot. All hail my massive stupidity.* All of this has taught me that I need to rein in my control tendencies and that maybe, I shouldn't be leading anyone, not even myself. I don't make rational choices when I feel backed into a corner, and I tend to lead my fellow kings down a path of soul-shattering destruction.

"Let's fucking go already!" Mateo bounces on the balls of his feet with excitement. It's so good to see some life in him. I was worried that his depression had deepened and that he was once again having panic attacks. After everything he just went through at the hands of my demon father, it wouldn't be unwarranted.

"Plane is loaded with everything we will need and already on the tarmac waiting for us. I'm not sure how Diego and Carter were able to pull all of this

off, but I can't wait to be far away from Casbury with our girl all to ourselves."
My voice comes out gruff with emotion.

Yeah, Mia will have nowhere to run once she awakens from her slumber. The
sedative in the pastries and tea should hold her over for a little while. We also have
a couple of syringes at the ready to keep her under for the duration of our flight
to a place no one is going to be looking for us. *Baffin Bay, Nunavut* in Canada.
A place with just under fourteen thousand inhabitants and deep in the Arctic
north. The only other inhabitants I'm expecting to see for however long it takes
to convince Mia to take us back are polar bears, whales, and Arctic wolves, and
they can't have my girl.

It's precisely the place we need to confine our warrior queen and give us time
to plead for mercy and win her back. Will Stella most likely kill each of us when
she eventually finds us? *Hopefully not.* I will gladly take any punishment, other
than giving up Mia, that Stella deems to inflict if it means I get my queen back.

Will Mia likely maim each of us when she wakes and discovers what we have
done? Probably, but it will be worth it if it ignites that spark back in her dull,
lifeless eyes. She is not herself, and I don't expect her to be after what she just
endured, but if it's in my power to pull her back from the darkness like she did
to me, I will gladly suffer her wrath.

We make it down to the running Land Rover and a waiting Carter and Diego.
I quickly check the back and see that Mia is lying across the back seats, still out
and waiting unknowingly for our departure.

"Are we good?" I inquire, my eyes sliding from Diego to Carter. They both
nod back at me, and then I watch with humor as they do some complicated
handshake shit, and Carter moves to the back left passenger seat as Mateo opens
the right side door. *Who knew that Carter and Diego were going to be thick as
thieves?*

They both carefully lift Mia in tandem and lay her across their laps. Making
sure that she's strapped to the seat by the belt and their arms are holding her
tightly. "Fucker...thank you for this. You know Stella is going to hunt you down
for helping us, right?"

An evil look crosses his face, and his devious smirk has the scar across his golden skin, pulling up tightly and giving him a dark, deranged look.

"She can try. I plan to make her work for it." He gives me his fist and meets my eyes. I fist-bump him and nod, moving to the driver's side door just as Finn gets in the front passenger seat.

An amused thought enters my mind. If Diego ends up with Issy permanently, we will all be practically related. Who knew we would end up with the snake as basically a brother-in-law? I wonder if I will ever see Diego alive again? *If Stella finds him, it's highly unlikely.*

I put the car in drive as Mateo lowers the window and calls out to Diego. "*Gracias, primo.* Run far and fast before Stella wakes. I would hate for there to be one less Cabano in this world."

Fucking hell, it's freezing out here! Why is it so freaking cold in May? It's only fifteen degrees Fahrenheit out here. Like shit, this is Spring in the great north? "Holy shit, we are going to freeze our balls off out here!" Carter moans as we make our way off the private plane that apparently he now owns.

It took us just under five hours to fly from North Carolina to Nunavit and the trip is not even done yet. We have hours before we can rest, and I'm already exhausted. All I want to do is wrap my arms around Mia and go to sleep. *Do you want to wake up with a blade at your throat?* My mind chuckles with glee. *Maybe.* It might be worth it just to see her looking at me.

Carter, the fucker, neglected to tell us when we were making all the arrangements that he had a friendly chat with his mom. One that resulted in her having a gun firmly placed between her lips as she agreed to go into a very early and completely secluded retirement far away from Carter, and his brother, Foster. As Carter put it so elegantly, if she didn't, she would be joining Mack in hell, where Carter sent him. I guess the fucker really has no qualms about ending both his parent's lives.

"Good thing we have no intentions of leaving the cabin." Mateo groans as his whole body shivers despite the heavy jacket he has on. I wrap my arms more firmly around a blanket burrito Mia and bring her closer to my chest. She's so small and slight, having lost so much of her weight in captivity that she barely weighs anything.

She started to awaken on the plane while we were in the air, but Finn gave her another dosage of the sedative. If the plane crew believed anything was strange about four wealthy male fuckers carrying a clearly unconscious female onto a plane, none of them opened their mouths. *Who are we kidding? They used to work for Mack and my dad. They have probably seen worse.*

"You have got to be kidding me, Carter!" Finn's voice sounds aghast as he makes it down off the plane. We are greeted by nothing but miles and miles of white snow, ice, and sizable rugged snow-capped mountains. The sight is stunning and like nothing I have ever seen before. It looks like something out of a fantasy novel like *A Song of Ice and Fire.* We are definitely in the great North. Shit, I just hope it's far away and desolate enough to keep Stella from finding us until we have won back our girl.

"All aboard, boys, we gotta get moving. Daylight is burning!" The loud voice sounds ominous in the vast cold space. We are greeted by the burly Inuk ship captain, who will be taking us all the way to the cabin on the arctic tundra. The one that Carter also now owns. *Killing Mack has come in real handy.*

The captain is nestled in his oversized colorful parka with beautiful thick gray fur along the hood. I climb onto the small ice boat with Mia still in my arms. The captain looks like he wants to say something but then stares back at the private plane and all the items the crew, Carter, Finn, and Mateo, are unloading and shuts his mouth. He leads the way to the only cabin on the boat with a cot, and I place Mia down, covering her with the fur blankets he provides.

"She alright?" He questions with concern. His face is sharp and angular, and his presence is commanding - the type that demands respect and undivided attention. "I don't want to be involved in kidnapping no ladies, ya hear."

I give him a severe look, my eyes hard and my body ready for a fight. *Fuck, I'll throw this guy right off his own ship if he tries to take Mia from me.* "She will be once we get her to the safety of the cabin. She's not being kidnapped. We just need to force her to rest. She's been through something traumatic." *Tread carefully*, my mind warms. *Keep your dominant, condescending shit down to a minimum. You are in reach of what you want now. Time alone with Mia.*

He sizes me up but must hear some truth to my words. He nods, mumbling in a foreign language under his breath, and leaves the room to help load all of our additional provisions on the boat.

We had non-perishable food, firewood, and weapons sent ahead to the small fifteen hundred square foot solar-powered and gas-generated cabin. It's going to be tight with all five of us in there. We will probably all want to kill each other after the first or second day, but I don't give a shit as long as I have Mia.

Soon we are underway on the beautifully clean and crisp bay waters, as large sheets of ice pass us. The captain, whose name is River Toestoo, points out Greenland in the distance and whales frolicking in the waters up ahead. We don't see another human or building in sight for the three-hour ride to the cabin.

Once we pull up to the small frozen dock, River and his one worker help us unload all of the provisions we brought with us. He hands me an old fashioned radio transmitter. "You know how to use that, boy? Your fancy cell phones won't work out this far. No towers."

I take the item as Carter brings out Mia from the small boat cabin and walks across the dock without a look back. "Thank you for transporting us. The agreement is for you to return with more provisions in a week at double the rate we paid you."

"Yes. I'll bring more provisions with me, but you all take care now. There are wild animals like polar bears and wolves out here. Eh, just so you know, If you get sick or hurt, there's no hospital for almost a day's journey."

Fuck we truly are in the middle of nowhere. I hope this plan works and doesn't end up biting us in the ass. I don't know what's more dangerous right now. The polar bears and wolves or Mia when she wakes up and realizes we have kidnapped her and taken her to the Arctic to hide her from Stella.

My money is on Mia being the most dangerous thing we are about to experience out here.

CHAPTER 29
Mia

"We are so busy teaching girls to be likeable that we often forget to teach them, as we do boys, that they should be respected." Soraya Chemaly, Rage Becomes Her: The Power of Women's Anger

M y head feels groggy, and my mouth is filled with gross cotton. There are so many heavy blankets on top of me that I'm starting to feel suffocated, and my skin is clammy and hot. I open my gritty eyes, and panic seizes me immediately. The sight of yellow-toned wood walls paralyzes me. *No! No, I can't be back in the cabin with James. Wake up! Wake up*, I beg my brain.

I scramble from underneath the oppressive weight and stumble onto a thick wool green and blue abstract patterned area rug next to the massive rustic wood bed that could sleep four people. My eyes dart around, trying to figure out where I am and how I got here. *It's not the same cabin. My mind screams. Look around, smell the air. It's not the same.*

I can hear rumbling noises outside of the room. The wood door is slightly ajar, and it seems to lock only from the inside. *We are not locked in*; my mind tries to reason with me. I try to calm my harsh breathing as I get my wits together. *Where the fuck am I, and how did I get here?* My last memory was of Carter bringing Stella and me pastries and tea after we had our discussion about the guys. Stella warned me that they were planning shit with Diego. *Could this be them?*

I felt so tired as I sat there reminiscing with my grandmother about my stepfather, Jared. I must have closed my eyes, and now I'm awake and have no idea where I am or how I got here. *Where the ever-loving fuck am I?*

I stare around the room, noticing all the rich tapestry and thick window coverings. There's indigenous art framed on the pale logged walls. The massive bed is covered in thick animal furs and colorful wool blankets. A roaring fire across the small room gives off delicious heat and beckons me closer.

I run my hand across the soft pelt of the nearest blanket. *No, this is not the same cabin.* Wherever I am, this place is not the one that haunts my nightmares. It is also clearly not one of the guys' houses. Anger soars through me. I glance down at myself and see that I'm wearing thick wool socks, the same joggers I was wearing earlier, and a thick fleece sweater. There is a chill in the air, but the fire casts stunning rays of reds, oranges, and blues. The sounds of the crackling logs are soothing to my frazzled nerves. Hell, if I wasn't so frightened, this would be a paradise to me.

I make my way to the only window in the room, pulling back the heavy weighted dark navy blue curtains. My breath catches in my throat at the sight outside of the thick paned glass. Nothing but massive expanses of pristine white snow greets me. It looks like there might even be some snow-covered mountains in the far distance. *Holy shit, where the hell am I? This is definitely not North Carolina.*

A male laugh catches my ears from outside the door, and I move cautiously in that direction. *Fuck, I need a weapon.* I'm hoping it's the guys out there, but I'm not willing to go out there unarmed. *Who are we kidding?* We need a weapon to bludgeon those fools for somehow taking me, wherever I am.

I search around the room, but there really isn't much in the small space. Grabbing the small metal table lamp on the round wood side table next to the bed. I quickly remove the shade and tightly wrap the cord around it, holding it firmly in my fist. Once I'm confident that I have a firm grip on it, I sneak out of the door and force my body to move slowly and flush against the wall across from the room's entrance.

The hallway is short, with just two more closed doors to the left and opens up to one large room. Large windows allow fading natural light into the space. It has to be close to nighttime, yet the sun looks like it is still above the horizon with its pink, orange, and yellow tones. Was I out fewer hours than I thought? Have I just been out for an hour or two? How is that fucking possible? It was midmorning when Carter approached Stella and me with the cookies.

I look around, my eyes feeling too large in my head and a bowling ball of fear stuffed in the pit of my stomach. The walls in the large open-concept room are all the same honey-colored wood logs from the bedroom. A massive warm fire greets my eyes in an enormous stone fireplace that takes up a whole wall across the room. Two small ochre leather sofas draped with colorful printed blankets fill the space surrounding the fire, a brown, green, and red pattern accent chair sits off to the side, and a rustic round wood coffee table that looks like it's been flayed from a giant tree trunk finishes off the seating area. More indigenous art graces the walls, brightening the space with its vivid colors.

A dark head pops up above the back of the sofa, causing my breath to get trapped in my throat. I don't hesitate to rush for it with my arm raised and ready to attack. Just as I am about to crack their skull open. A large forearm circles my waist and yanks me back forcefully and off my feet, and I miss my intended target. I end up hitting their shoulder with the base of the lamp instead.

"WHAT THE FUCK!" An angry shout rings out over the space as I fight the fierce hold pulling me into a hard male chest. The dark head in front of me turns around, and I glimpse Mateo's frightened green eyes as he stands up and moves away from the sofa.

I fight the hold keeping me trapped, and it suddenly releases me and steps away from me, forcing me to take a stumbling step closer to the sofa. I turn sharply on my feet, and find Finn behind me with a concerned look across his face. His mink brown eyes are alarmed and large, and his eyebrows are practically at his hairline.

"What the fuck? What the fuck is right! Where the hell am I?" I screech, my voice getting louder with every word uttered. I can hear my blood rushing in my ears, and my head is starting to spin. I stumble forward and grasp the back of the sofa to steady myself. Mateo takes another step back, a look of fear across his elfen features. Naw, Mia, don't fall for the cute innocent puppy dog look he can pull off. This is some seriously deranged shit happening right here.

"Mia...I...we...ah shit." Carter's voice catches my attention across the room. There is both amusement and fear in his jewel-like eyes as he glances the length of my body and lands on the lamp base, still clutched in my grip. The look I give him back is scathing and definitely conveys a "*fuck around and find out, fucker*" vibe. If he makes the slightest move towards me, he's the next one I'm swinging at.

"You're in the Canadian Arctic north. Baffin Bay, to be exact." The deep voice accosts my sense, coming up from behind where Finn and I are standing. I swing in his direction, the lamp clutched firmly in my sweaty grasp and ready to strike. Two pools of dark blue meet my gaze, unflinching and completely unrepentant. *Jesus fucking Christ.* He looks like some warring, king warlord right now. So confident, so much like the king he was when I first returned to Casbury.

The embers of rage begin to stir within me, called to life by his unremorseful tone. Ultimately, I knew they were planning to take me, the bloody heathens. Stella's warning was issued thankfully in time, so I wasn't the bearer of this incredulous surprise. "What do you mean I'm in the Canadian Arctic north? Have you all lost your mind?" I whirl around to give each of them a deadly stare. My chest is so tight. I can feel myself getting more and more worked up. "Do you fools know what Stella will do to you?"

"Killer, please...we needed to be able to talk to you alone. With...without Stella, Rae, and Issy constantly surrounding you." Finn's throat bobs up and down, and I watch as his pink tongue peeks out and moistens his plump bottom lip. *Nope, I refuse to be even the slightest bit tempted, fuck him and his sexy lips.*

"So you drugged me, like fucking lunatics, stole me from my home, and brought me to another country?" I raise both my hands in exasperation. The weight of the lamp is still a comfort in my hand. How do they not realize that this shit sounds crazy? Are they all really this nonsensical?

"*Mami*, could you please put down the weapon?" Mateo's bright olive-green eyes meet mine. Before his glare meets Carter's across the room. "I thought you removed anything she could use as a weapon, asswipe?"

"It's a fucking lamp, asshole, the only source of light in the goddamn room!" Carter yells back with agitation. He takes a step towards me, his hands raised and his face flushed. "Mia, babe, please."

He gives me puppy dog eyes, and for a brief moment, it almost sways me. I almost lower the weapon in my hand. My body suddenly and desperately wanting to be wrapped in his arms, even though the thought of one of them touching me has made my stomach turn upside down for weeks. But then I remember the look on his face when he tried to force me to my knees. The awful harsh things he said to me when he divulged that he knew I was Amelia Hamilton, and my spine goes ramrod straight.

Fuck him, fuck all of them right now. Anger flows through me, replacing any forgiveness or hope I had in my home office with Stella. Do they want to pretend like that didn't happen? That they didn't make me fall for each of them, only to abuse me and discard me like trash. I no longer care if they believed it was the only way to keep me safe. They caused me so much anguish and heartache, not to mention everything that happened to me with James because of their actions. *Hey Mia, don't forget you bear some responsibility, too. No one told you to run.* The bitch that lives in my head reminds me.

"We are sorry that we drugged you. We are, however, not sorry that we took you from the house, Mia. You refused to speak with any of us or be present in the same room with us. How else were we to reach you?" Theo moves closer and reaches out for the lamp. His grip tightens as he tries to yank it from my hand, but I refuse to relent my hold on it. Theo forgets himself, I don't obey him, and I'm not afraid of him.

"Did it ever cross any of your egotistical, toxic male minds that maybe I have nothing to say to any of you?" I inquire incredulously while raising my chin and meeting each of their eyes, mine blaring with a fire lit from within. I want them to see my anger, my disdain for each of them, so that they understand that forgiveness will not be so readily given. No, I plan to make them beg and crawl. To bow at my unrelenting knees, and then maybe, just maybe, I will forgive them.

"That I might want nothing more to do with any of you?"

"Blondie, you are lying to yourself and deluded if you think we would ever allow you to discard us so easily. I don't give the slightest fuck that you're mad." Carter takes giant steps toward me, his eyes blaring as he releases a low menacing chuckle that sends chills down my spine. He's a predator moving, a wolf ready to take down his prey. *Me.*

"In fact, be mad all you want. You are fucking mine, Mia. You belong to me, to us. You don't get to walk away from this. Not while you're still breathing, and even then, I will track your violent ass into the next life."

He lunges for me at the same time Theo rips the lamp base from my hands. Carter gets his arms wrapped tightly around my abdomen, and we both start to fall back. He rolls at the last minute to take the brunt of the impact and cushions me tightly against his heaving chest.

One of his hands tangles in my hair at the back of my neck, holding my head tightly and forcing my face closer to his. My chest is tight, my breaths harsh, and I'm having difficulty getting enough air. The impact jarred my ribs, which are still bruised, and my wrist in the cast. His grip on my hair is relentless, bringing my lips closer to his as a cry escapes me.

"You are mine, blondie. I will never let you go." His mouth closes the gap between us, and his firm lips meet mine in a brutal kiss that is all force and no finesse. His tongue pushes against my sealed lips, demanding entry. When I refuse him, he yanks hard on my hair until a pained moan leaves my mouth, and he takes full advantage and plunders deep.

His mouth tastes like orange juice as his tongue tangles with mine. A harsh groan leaves his lips as his other hand pulls my body closer until I can feel every ridge of his pressed up against mine. The kiss is scorching, bringing with it illicit heat and the need for more. My fingers rise to his face and trail along his high cheekbone, over the new stubble growth, and down over his jaw.

When they finally make contact with the skin of his neck, I let them skate across it until they are cradling the long, strong column. Wrapping them tightly, I apply pressure before sinking my sharp nails into his skin and cutting off his airway with my grip.

My eyes glare into his, so close that I see all the different flecks of gray inside his pupils. His tongue slips out of my mouth, and his lips pull back from mine. His breath caught in his throat, moving below my firm grip. I tighten further until color rises up his neck and across his cheeks. His eyes grow more expansive with the understanding that I'm not playing with him. *Oh, Carter, you never fucking learn.*

I slide my knee in between both of his legs and raise it as hard as I can into his nuts. A pained cry tries to leave his lips, but my grip prevents it from being more than a muffled sound. I hear groans of pain all around us as the others no doubt clutch themselves in pained sympathy. *Lunatics, the fucking lot of them.*

"I am not yours. I am not theirs. I belong to only myself, Carter Pemberton, and the next time you forget that, I will make sure you breathe your last fucking breath."

I jump up and move as far away from him as I can. Putting much-needed distance between all four of them and me. Carter continues to lay there, grasping his nuts with a look of agony across his features. *God, that felt good.* The rest of them watch me warily from the small distance the room allows.

"Return me to my home immediately, you fucking imbeciles," I demand with my chin raised and my hands squeezed into tight fists at my side. The need to bloody all of them, to let my rage out and maim them, is riding me hard.

"We can't, your highness. We are all trapped here for the next few days until the captain returns to replenish our food. There is nothing but snow and ice for hundreds of miles, Mia. We are as far from civilization as we could get you." Theo's words have a chilling effect on me.

No. No, I didn't hear him correctly. There is no way they have trapped me in a confined space with them, and they think I will be at their mercy. They have another thing coming if they think I will just roll over like some dog, forgive them their abuse, and allow them back into my heart. I will have my vengeance. My soul demands its atonement. *We love them*, my heart utters, begging me not to fight what we desperately want. *Them.*

"Give me your phone. I will have my grandmother send someone to retrieve me." I hold out my hand towards Theo. He ignores my limb with a haughty, annoyed look. *Fuck, I want to slap that look right off his face, maybe wrap my hands around his neck and squeeze as tight as I can.*

Finn places his cell phone in my palm. His dark soulful eyes trying desperately to meet mine and convey the need for my understanding. He wants me to understand that he betrayed me once again; I *got it.* That he's sorry his actions put me in irreparable harm, *I got that too.* He's looking for my forgiveness; *I'm not sure yet if he's worthy.*

"It won't work, Killer. We are too far out in the wilderness. There is no reception."

I press buttons on his phone, keeping one eye on the menaces in front of me as I try to connect, but nothing happens. *Fuck, there are no bars.* These psychos really did take me out to the middle of nowhere. I can't be trapped here for another week alone with them.

"You miserable fucks, you have trapped me here like an animal caged against my will."

"Exactly, Mia, you're picking up the situation quickly. We are all trapped here together. We will not release you, and no help is coming. Stella has no idea where you are. You had better get comfortable, your highness. We have no intention of letting you go. Not now, not ever, Mia. You belong to us." Theo yells, his face flushing with a pink tinge and the vein on his neck throbbing.

"Do you fuckers not understand what you have done! YOU KIDNAPPED ME AFTER I WAS KIDNAPPED BY A MADMAN!"

I can't breathe with how angry I am right now. My blood pressure must be through the roof because my body feels like it's an inferno, and I'm starting to feel light-headed. "You thought it was okay to take a recent kidnapping victim to another cold, dark cabin and lock her away from her friends and family just mere weeks after...." I can't finish my sentence, I don't need them to see me as weak and what those memories of James' cabin do to me. "Are all of you stupid?"

There's a long silent pause as I see my words register on their faces. "Mia....Fuck, we are such fucking dumbasses. What the hell were we thinking?" Finn drags his hands down his face with shame. I can't even handle the stupid devastated looks on all their faces. They really are completely deranged fuckers. In what world was this the right move? How did they think bringing me here would help them earn my forgiveness?

I need to get the fuck out of here right now. I storm to the cabin's front door as all four pairs of eyes watch me with fear. I'm so angry right now that my mind is a cyclone of thoughts. The primary thought is calling me an idiot for having any feelings for these fools. I forcefully open the door, and it smashes into the wall next to me. Cold air hits my skin, which feels like a blessing on my overheated flesh. I don't hesitate walking out the door and instantly regretting it as my socks get soaked with the snow. Nope, I don't fucking care. I need to get away from them. I keep moving forward another sixty feet before I hear feet thundering behind me.

I look over my shoulder to see Mateo running towards me. He grabs me by the back of my waist, lifting me off my feet. "Mia, what the fuck! You can't just go running off like that. You don't even have a jacket or shoes on, my little *reina*. This isn't Casbury or the woods!" Cold shivers rack my body at his words, and I return to myself as my feet ache and go painfully numb. I fight his hold, trying to release myself, but his arms become two bands of steel around me, tightening and holding me to his heaving chest. Fuck, I don't care; at this point, I would rather freeze to death than be their hostage. *No, you don't bitch; you're just mad. Simmer down, and make them regret their reckless decisions.*

"Listen to me, Mia. We are fucking idiots. I don't even know how I let this happen. We weren't thinking logically, but you need to come inside. You can have the room you woke up in all to yourself. No one will hurt you, and you don't have to talk to us if you don't want to, I promise."

His words have me going lax in his hold, and he senses my resolve crumbling. Fuck, it's so cold out here. My hands are starting to go numb, too, and I tuck them underneath my armpits in an attempt to keep my fingers from falling off. Mateo changes his hold on me until he carries me bridal style in his arms and turns back for the cabin. I spy the other three outside waiting to see if I will return to the cabin kicking and screaming. "*Mami*, while you don't have to talk to us, you should know we are not leaving here until we work through this shit together." He tenderly presses his lips to the side of my head, but I'm not having it. I pull as far away from his embrace as I can while still remaining in his arms.

"Blondie, please talk to us. We are so fucking sorry."

The minute we pass the other three lunatics, and I'm inside of the cabin, I shove out of Mateo's hold and walk across the room, back towards the bedroom I came out of. When I'm inside, I slam the door in their faces and engage the lock, leaning my forehead against the door's surface.

How could they be so clueless?

CHAPTER 30
Carter

"There is no refuge from memory and remorse in this world. The spirits of our foolish deeds haunt us, with or without repentance." Gilbert Parker

"*L*et's go, fucker!" *Theo screams back at me as he races for his bike. I'm frozen to the spot, my heart pounding in my ears. I can hear her little screams from a distance behind the tree we tied her to.*

Theo rides off, a crying Mateo right behind him. The fucker needs to toughen the hell up, or he will never be able to survive the world we live in. The one where real monsters walk the streets in fancy ass suits and pretend to be good guys. Guys like my dad and Theo's.

My eyes meet Finn's, and I see the fury in their depth. He wants to punch Theo and me, maybe even Mateo, even though the ass did little to help. Finn doesn't like it when we go after Amelia. They used to be best friends when he lived on that side of the tracks. Fuck, I don't like it either. It never feels good to hear her cry. Yeah, she's annoying and mouthy. She thinks she's smarter and better than us. Which is a laugh cause she's dirt poor and has nothing, literally.

Still, her nothing is better than my everything. Her mom doesn't beat on her or say hateful things to her like my parents do. I would trade lives with her in a second, even with all our bullying and her being poor. Her world doesn't really make sense to me, Theo, and Mateo. None of us have winning parents. Ours are neglectful, abusive pieces of shit. At eleven and twelve, all three of us understand that. Finn's stepdad and mom are a huge step up from our parents, but even they aren't like Amelia's mom.

"We can't leave her there, Carter! She could die; someone could come around and hurt her. You guys are messed up!" His fists rise with his agitation. "Why do y'all keep picking on her? She doesn't deserve it!" He shoves me hard until I'm forced to take a few steps back.

My anger starts boiling over inside me, like a thick heat that rises across my skin. The thought of violence is comforting for me. I understand violence and pain. I hate when I get all up in my feelings, and my head is a mess.

Finn and I are evenly matched, even if he's an inch or two taller than me right now, and his shoulders are broader. I could take him. I know it. Nothing stops me once I let my monster out of his cage. Even Theo is afraid of me at that point, and that fucker isn't frightened of anything.

"You really don't want to be starting shit with me right now, Finn," I demand, my fists tightening at my side. I like the fucker, he's been our friend for almost a year since he started at Casbury Prep, but I won't hesitate to knock him on his ass. "Back down."

"Fuck you, Carter. I'm done with you guys hurting Amelia. If that's what being y'all friends means, I would rather be alone." He steps forward towards where we both can hear her thrashing against the tree. Her sharp cries, little daggers accosting my skin.

"Theo's dad and mine hurt women and girls." I blurt out. He turns sharply on the spot and stares at me with wide mocha eyes.

I watch as he swallows painfully. I think he has an idea of what I am talking about. There are rumors all around town about Theo's dad and the dungeon he has down in his basement. Unfortunately for Theo, they ain't made-up stories.

That's his tragic reality; his dad is a monster. Mine, of course, has to be his faithful companion. We are both damned with our wretched, psychotic parentage.

"Okay...what does that have to do with...Amelia?" *He questions with a furrowed brow. Finn is always the most serious of us. It's like he's continuously afraid to make a wrong move or say the wrong thing in case we don't want to be friends with him anymore. He shouldn't want to be friends with us. We are all damaged goods.*

"Her mom. Theo's dad and mine want to do bad shit to her. Amelia, too."

His hand runs across his forehead, the sweat glistening in the bright sunlight.

"Like, sexual shit?" *He questions with a nervous look, his eyes darting back to the tree.*

"Yeah, and...and worse. They...they are monsters, Finn." *It hurts and embarrasses me to have to admit that. Who wants to admit their dad is a monster to someone else? Fuck, I know Finn has seen all the bruises and cuts I'm constantly sporting. I think he knows it was my dad that broke my arm a couple of months ago in one of his fits of rage.*

"Amelia is just a little girl; why would they do that? You sure you're not making this shit up?" *His arms wrap around his chest as a look of panic crosses his face, and his dark brown eyes meet mine a little wider than before. The anger that was there is now gone, replaced with a look of fear. One I am all too familiar with. The same fear lives inside of me day and night.*

"They won't care that she's a little girl, Finn. They enjoy hurting females, hearing them scream."

"What's this have to do with you bullying Amelia?" *A confused but tentative look crosses his high rounded cheekbones. His dark, tight curls glisten with sweat as he rubs his hand through his hair, his broad shoulders up by his ears. Finn's going to be a big boy sometime soon, then maybe even I won't be able to take him. Naw, fuck that. Size doesn't matter. Crazy is all that matters, and we have that in abundance, my mind snickers.*

"We are trying to keep her and her mom from getting close to Vincent. Theo thinks we might be able to get them to leave town if we bully Amelia enough." *Fuck, so far, it hasn't really worked, and even I am starting to doubt Theo's plans.*

"Why not just tell them? Why bother doing all this mean shit?"

Hell, I have had the same recollection over and over in the last couple of months. Mateo has all but begged us to, especially with the wicked ass shit we have done to Amelia.

Locking her in that gardener's shed almost broke me. The guys don't know, but I spent the whole night sitting outside of it in one of the trees listening to her cry. Making sure that no one came to hurt her in the dark. That I was the only monster out there. The only thing that stopped me from letting her out was the image of what Vincent and my dad did to a girl a few years older than us a week before that. We found that girl bloody and beaten, tied down in Vincent's dungeon.

Theo was beside himself when we found her. Shit, even I had to throw up as we released her and got her out of there. She was so weak and broken. They had whipped her until her flesh was peeling from her back in places.

The sore ribs and bruises Theo is still sporting were the punishment and consequence dealt out by Vincent for our actions. When I asked Theo if he regretted helping her escape, he said, "he would do it again. Fuck his dad."

The thought of them doing that to Amelia, or her mom, is what kept me from releasing her. We need them to leave Casbury. To get the fuck away from here and the sick monsters that live within this town's city limits.

"Theo doesn't think they would leave. That they wouldn't believe us cause we are just kids. He thinks if we bully Amelia enough, her mom will take her out of this town, and they can be safe from my dad and his."

"Why do you always do what Theo says? He ain't God, you know? This sounds stupid. We should just tell them."

I pull my phone out and flip to the picture I took of the girl, the one I use to remind me what my dad and Vincent are capable of. I throw the phone at Finn, and it hits him in the chest before he raises it and stares at it.

"They whipped her, raped...her and...beat... her bloody. She could barely walk when we got her out. She's only a few years older than Amelia, Finn." I shake my head to try to dispel some of the images from my mind. "Theo is sporting a broken rib and bruises all over his chest and back as punishment for getting her out. His dad is insane, Finn."

Finn looks green. Little trickles of sweat are sliding down from his hairline and streaked across his face, dripping onto his pale yellow shirt. "Holy shit." He whispers as he hands me back the phone, his eyes staring forward at the tree Amelia is struggling and confined to. We can just see the back of her little head thrashing and her dark hair moving from this side of the tree.

"We need to force her out of town."

His eyes meet mine, and a spark of anger is back in their depths. "I think Theo's plan sucks; y'all are crazy. You need to stop following him around like a soldier, Carter. He's not always right. He's not right about this. There are better ways of handling shit than violence."

I wake with a start, a slimy feeling of regret coating all of my limbs. The dream makes me momentarily forget where I am. My eyes clear, and I see Mateo's fucking hairy, long toes are in my face. *Fucking gross, man.*

I swear I am going to break each one off if he doesn't move them. I shove him hard, and a gruff leaves his lips as he tries to shift on the small uncomfortable sofa that we are sharing. *Fuck this shit, my neck is spasming, and it's frigid in here.* I push away from the couch, none too gently if Mateo's mumbled cry is any evidence, and stand. Stretching my arms wide and trying to crack my sore neck.

My eyes slide across Finn's long body, which is draped across the other sofa, his brows furrowed even in sleep. The memory of the dream, trying to rise. *Yup, I was right.* That little boy ended up with a big six-foot-three massive body packed with muscle. *I could still take him, nonetheless*; a chuckle leaves my lips at the thought.

My eyes track across the room until they find Theo on the honey-toned hardwood floor, his back pressed against the wood-logged wall, his arms wrapped around his bent knees. He has a thick indigenous geometrical print blanket draped around him to keep him warm. How the fuck he continuously sleeps like that boggles my mind. *Fuck him, though.* I'm all out of sympathy where he is concerned. I move over to the pile of wood and throw another log on the simmering fire.

In retrospect, it might not have been the wisest thing for me to buy a one-bedroom cabin in the middle of nowhere with only one bed. Where there is zero chance of me getting another one shipped asap. The cabin has a small room at the back that is supposed to be an office den or something. Right now, it has a small wooden desk and a lone chair. It could make for an extra bedroom if we had a mattress.

Shit, I would even take some sleeping bags on the floor right now. The only reason I didn't take my ass to sleep in there is the lack of heat. We have very limited firewood to hold us until the captain returns with provisions. Theo, *the dick*, pointed out that if we started going through it too quickly, we would have to trek up to those mountains in the distance and cut some trees down.

The temperature when we arrived yesterday was "freeze your nuts off" cold, and I don't feel like having to trek that distance, fighting snow and ice and dragging some trees back. Hence, Mateo's fucking rotten feet in my face all night.

We are going to have to come up with some other plan if Mia isn't going to let us into the massive bed I ordered. The one that should fit five adults comfortably, but that she sleeps in alone. Presumptuous of me, yes, I fucking know, but a fucker has to dream, doesn't he?

I still can't believe we managed to pull this off in just under thirty-six hours. That I now own my dad's plane and this little slice of solitude paradise and that my girl is here with us, even unwillingly. When Theo suggested that we get her out of the house and alone, it was like my whole body lit up. The need to talk to her without interruptions, without her being able to put Rae or Issy in our way as obstacles, was too much of a carrot to dangle in front of me.

Shit certainly didn't go to plan if you look at her reaction when she awoke from the sedative we gave her. Shit, my nuts are still aching from her knee. She was so livid with all of us, her eyes were bright blue, and there was a red flush across her face. She had never looked more beautiful to me. Beautiful because, for that moment in time, she was alive again. It was a glimpse of my blondie and the fire that lives inside of her.

Walking over to the window, the sun is only starting to rise over the mountains. Deep shades of purple and pink are starting to crest on the night skies. My eyes follow the shadows in the distance, nothing but the shimmer of the snow and ice meeting my gaze. A sigh leaves my lips as I drag my hands down my face.

"She will eventually forgive us. She has to."

Theo's deep, raspy voice has me jumping out of my skin and a yelp escaping me. The fucker has always been able to move silently, like a sinister ghost. A byproduct of being raised as Vincent Saint-Lambert's son, no doubt. When your father is the devil, you learn to stay unseen and unheard so as to not bring his wrath your way. "Maybe we made a mistake. This could make shit worse."

"I refuse to believe that, just like I refuse to give her up." He stares out at the horizon as his shoulder lifts in a half-shrug. "She will forgive us, or we will live here in captivity with her until she does, or all of us die."

The way he says it is so matter of factly. Like it doesn't really matter which way things end up swinging sends shivers down my spine. I want Mia too, but I don't want to hurt her further. She needs to choose us willingly. While I'm not on board with keeping her a permanent hostage, I also know I can never give her up. My thoughts are a contradictory mess, one immediately rolling into the other. Does that make me a psychopath? *Probably.* Am I in good company with the rest of the kings? *A hundred percent.*

I turn and make my way back through the room and towards the closed bedroom door. My head leans against its silent surface. The one my violent queen is sealed behind after Theo's declaration last night, and she ran out into the freezing cold in nothing but a pair of damn socks. When Mateo finally convinced her to return and carried her inside. The minute she was on her feet she rushed back out of the room and down the hall, filled with indignation and unwilling to spend another moment in our presence, to my dismay.

We heard the door slam and firmly lock before furniture was dragged across the floor. My bet is on the wood dresser being up against the door now. My blondie decided to lock us out and took no chances with us forcing the door in to get to her. It seems we are in for an upwards battle to regain her heart. *Did you really think it would be so easy? You hurt her, deceived her, and treated her like you did when you were children.*

Fuck! I know! I drag my hands through my hair as I lean my head against the solid wood door of the bedroom. How do I make this right if she won't let me in?

"She's been in there all day, Theo. She hasn't eaten shit. This was a bad idea." I sigh once again, staring wistfully at the locked, solid wood door. The one that holds my heart's desire and my obsession behind it. Mia has been holed up in the room since late evening yesterday. She has refused to come out to eat or even open the door so we could at least provide her a tray of food. My girl is incredibly stubborn, and right now, she has dug in deep.

Her anger at us is warranted though. I acknowledge that, but the need to hold her, talk to her, or even see her beautiful features is like a thick rope around my neck. One that is slowly tightening and making it harder to breathe with every moment we are apart. She's right behind that door and no more than thirty feet away from me, but it might as well be miles.

The only way I know my girl is still in there is because of the nightmares she's having. *Fucking alone, without me there to wake her or comfort her.* We heard her screams in the middle of the night. Sounds that seemed ripped from her very soul.

They caused further scars to appear on my heart, knowing I had a hand in causing them. I wanted to break down the door, pull her into my arms, hold her tight, and promise that nothing and no one would ever hurt her again. The only thing stopping me was all three of the other kings holding me back and telling me if I charged in there like some unhinged asshole, I was likely to cause further damage, and Mia would probably maim me.

"She will have to eventually cave and come out. The only washroom is in the hallway, and she's got to be starving and needs to pee. As much as she's

angry with us, she knows she can't stay in there for a whole week." Finn's reply
does nothing to soothe my rattled nerves. Mateo's incessant pacing isn't helping,
either. I wonder if Mia will come out to save him if I put his head through a wall.
I shrug to myself; it *might be worth a try.*

"Do you think Stella is looking for us? Do you think she might have murdered
my cousin by now?" Mateo walks past me again, and I just can't take it. The
monster inside of me is pacing like a caged tiger, demanding to be set free so he
can reclaim his mate. I'm close to the breaking point. I need her to forgive me. I
need her to come out here and scream or beat my ass. Something, anything right
now, other than silence.

I grab him by the scruff of the neck and slam him into the wall. He lets out
a yelped cry and immediately starts pushing back against my hold. "What the
fuck are you doing, you psychotic bastard?" He yells loudly.

"Carter, WHAT THE FUCK!" Theo bellows from the sofa, getting up and
heading towards me with rage on his features. I release my hold on Mateo and
turn just in time to meet Theo's fist as it lands hard against my jaw with a punch
so filled with fury that it has my head snapping on my neck and makes me
stumble back.

The taste of blood in my mouth is a match taking this fire simmering from
within me and making it an inferno. *Hell, fucking yes!* Now we are talking! After
weeks of this fucker just taking my punishment repeatedly, the real Theo has
finally decided to make an appearance. *I'm all here for it.*

I can only think of two ways to rid myself of this miserable energy inside of
me. One is with my cock buried to the hilt inside of Mia's tight pussy while I
wrap my hands around her slim neck, and I feed her one of my brother's cocks.
The other is throwing down with Theo, Finn, and even Mateo. At this point, I
am so rallied up that I will take on all three of these assholes at the same time.

"Come on, you weak, broken motherfucker! Don't hold back. I'm not going
to break like you!" I scream and dodge his next swing, charging him and grappling around his middle. He takes a few steps back with me, holding tight to his
abdomen before Finn tries to pull me away.

I release Theo and swing as hard as I can at Finn, clocking him right in the nose. The sound of his harsh pained cry is loud in the large room. Blood starts pouring from one of his nostrils, and the sight fills me with even more excitement. *Yes, fucking, please!*

"Carter, you crazy bastard! I think you just broke my nose." Finn slides his hand under his gushing nose, stares at the blood, and a look of menace crosses his features before his long arm, corded with muscle, is returning the favor and knocking me in the nose. *Ow, fuck that hurts!*

"You want to play, fucker! You need someone to put you in the ground? You have come to the right place, shithead. I have been dying to beat your ass for weeks!" He swings wide again and lands a punch to my ear that has it ringing like the *Notre Dame* cathedral bells.

"Come on, Finn. You can do better than that!" I charge him, and we go crashing together into the sofa as Mateo grabs onto my hair and yanks it like a little bitch.

"Stop this shit, Carter!" He yowls and then slams the palm of his hand in my eye. Pain sparks and radiates from the socket as I reach back with my elbow and slam it into his ribs. A pained grunt leaves him as Finn tries to get his arm wrapped around my neck in a chokehold. *Fuck no, I'm not going to be subdued.* I push against his hold, slamming my fist repeatedly against the side of his chest until he releases me.

"Carter, fucking stop, asshole! You're breaking shit!' Mateo yells.

I push off the sofa, slamming my bent legs into Mateo and shoving him harshly backward until he's sliding across the floor, the movement causing his breath to leave him in a long, pained exhale. "You son of a bitch!" He cries as he gets back to his feet.

"Hey, Finn, your momma is real nice, boy. She looked even nicer wrapped around my cock!" I shout with menace, trying to entice him into further mayhem and violence. *I know, I know, I'm a jackass.*

The minute I am back on my two feet, Theo is coming at me again. His muscled arm flies forward and gets me in the right cheek before I throw out a kick that lands in his stomach. He bends forward, trying to catch his breath as

Finn grabs me from behind and slams an elbow into my back, driving me down to my knees. *Now that's what I'm talking about!*

"Imma fucking kill you, Carter. I warned you to keep my momma out of your filthy mouth." He slams another elbow down hard in the middle of my back, and my knees buckle, forcing me to the ground.

"No worries, bro, it was my cock that was in her mouth." He lands another hard elbow, this time on my lower back. Fuck, pretty sure the fucker got a kidney. Mateo is around the sofa in a flash, wrapping his arms around my neck and trying to choke me out with a vicious groan.

"WHAT IN THE EVER-LOVING FUCK ARE YOU MANIACS DO-ING?" Mia screams from the room's doorway. A look of vicious wrath across her features.

CHAPTER 31

Mia

"I mean, maybe I am crazy. I mean, maybe. But if this is all there is, then I don't want to be sane." Neil Gaiman, Neverwhere

I'm lying here on the thick, soft rug in front of the fire, trying to figure out how I will get back to Casbury now that these savages have kidnapped me and brought me to the middle of nowhere. A frozen paradise that sits right outside of my confinement, taunting me with its inescapability. I'm over my original moment of surprise; now I am just angry. How dare they think that keeping me locked up in forced proximity was the right way to go about trying to fix shit.

I swear the four of them don't have one brain cell to rub between them. *Fucking men and their caveman tendencies.* What do they think will happen here? That I am going to fall willingly at their entitled, misguided feet? A snort leaves my lips at just the possibility. I'm going to guess that Theo, the controlling fucker was the mastermind behind this shit. He never learns, and neither do they, following his disastrous and misguided lead.

A grin crosses my lips as I remember that they don't know about the embedded tracker chip Stella insisted that Issy and I get implanted when I returned from captivity. I slide my fingers over my arm, unable to feel the bump just below the surface of my skin with all the warm clothes I have on, but I know it's there. A little bit of my anger fizzles at the reminder. Stella will always find me. It will only be a matter of time before my grandmother shows up.

These fuckers think they are so slick, drugging us all and stealing me from under Stella's nose. Like she didn't already know they were planning something. I can't wait to see what she does to them when she finally arrives here to collect me. She said they would be on borrowed time. This might all be worth it, just to watch all four of them tremble in her presence while she makes them beg for their lives. And they will beg at her feet or mine. One way or the other, the kings of Casbury are about to learn how to bow at a queen's feet.

Loud shouts and then the sound of shit crashing outside the room has me jumping to my feet and racing for the door without any thoughts of my own self-preservation. I can't fucking believe I let Mateo talk me into even coming back inside. *What, freezing to death would have been the answer?*

What the hell am I doing? Why am I running to get to them like some reckless imbecile? They are probably out there killing each other. Masculine hormones and toxicity at its finest. *We should wait here until they have done enough damage to one another, then force our way out of here. There was a gun on the counter yesterday. We should hold the fuckers hostage,* my mind snickers.

"Carter, you crazy bastard! I think you just broke my nose." I hear Finn's angry shout through the wooden door and then the sound of more stuff breaking. Mateo is yelling sharply, the tone sounding agitated and nearing panic. The sound speeds up my heart rate and makes my hands clammy. *Jesus fucking Christ, what are they doing out there?* More sounds of pained grunts, anguished cries, and shit hitting walls has me quickly shoving the sturdy wood dresser out of the way and racing out of the room. My pep talk to myself immediately forgotten.

"WHAT IN THE EVER-LOVING FUCK ARE YOU MANIACS DOING?" I shout, my heart racing in my chest, the sound thundering in my ears with a whoosh. My sock-covered feet slide on the hardwood, and I have to brace myself on the corner of the wall to keep from falling in my haste to get in here.

I'm shocked at the scene before me. All four of them are grappling with each other in a tangle of long limbs. Mateo, Finn, and Carter are bleeding. Theo has a bruise already sprouting on his face. One of the sofas is upended, and two of the wooden kitchen chairs are smashed on the ground. My eyes quickly spy the forgotten gun on the kitchen counter. *Reckless fucking idiots, they really think I'm no threat to them.*

Focus Mia! All four of them freeze at my shout, suspended in time, with comical looks on their faces. Mateo has a fistful of Carter's hair in his tight grip. Finn's arm is wrapped securely around Carter's throat from behind, who is a shade of puce. Theo is trying desperately to hold down Carter's legs, so he can't kick out. *Carter.* Why am I not surprised that he is the cause of all this reckless behavior. *Why would you be? When there is mayhem afoot, it is always Carter's doing.*

"Babe…" He tries to call out, his gray-blue eyes begging for assistance, but Finn's grip tightens on his neck. It's comical that he thinks I would help him. I'll help put a bullet in his deranged brain if he wants. *Liar!*

"Have all four of you lost your damn minds?" I question disapprovingly, my eyebrow raised, my eyes narrowed, and my arms wrapped around my middle. A smirk threatens to cross my lips at the priceless look of guilt on all of their faces. I swear I am dealing with four naughty kids instead of mostly grown men. *Sexy, almost grown men.*

Finn, Theo, and Carter drop their holds, but I think Mateo has forgotten that he has a chunk of Carter's hair still in his hands. He shifts forward towards me, causing Carter to let out a cry. "FUCK, MAT!" Mateo pays him no mind, his eyes solely focused on me. Their rich green depth, trying its best to see right into my soul. *God, he is pretty; should any man be that pretty to look at?*

"*Hola mami*, how are you feeling? Can I get you something to drink? Eat?" He rubs his hands together with anxiousness. A silly grin graces his handsome face with that flirty look that I have missed. "Carter and Theo's heads on a platter?" I take a step towards him before I catch myself. *Naw, don't give in to his Latin lover charm. Stay strong bitch!* My mind scolds me.

My eyes roam over all of his features. I loved Mateo's long hair and how thick and wavy it was. How it felt running through my fingers while he kissed and caressed me. The way it cradled his high cheekbones and made him look like he was an elf from *Lord of the Rings*. My own sexy *Legolas*. His shortened locks look cute and somehow make him older and more mature, or maybe that was his experience at the hands of Vincent. Little lines of sorrow bracket those beautiful eyes, divulging to me that he is no longer the same, that his trauma has changed him. I now understand that sentiment with an intimacy I wish I didn't have.

The reminder of that psycho Vincent has my body locking up tight. Just his name wanting to trigger memories of that day in James' cabin. The day I finally took my vengeance on one of the men that wronged me. James would follow, and now it's the kings' turn. *They, too, will learn that a Stratford never forgets.*

"I don't need anything that you're offering, Mateo." I give each of them a spiteful, cold glare. "I don't want or need anything from any of you except for you to return me to my home. The one you bloody savages stole me from."

Theo stands up from his bent position, straightening his back and shoulders with his head held high. Those midnight blue eyes intense and trying to burn a hole through me. To see right into my very soul. *What will he find there now?* An unremorseful killer? A woman that is now walking around with a tarnished soul. Destruction, chaos, and malignant energy? The desire for more bloodshed?

I am no longer the same Mia, just like he is no longer the same Theo. Our experiences have changed us, reshaped us, and not for the better. We are both utterly damaged, and I don't think we will ever heal from the desecration of our souls.

He's lost a lot of weight, never really putting it back since his release from the hospital. His cheekbones and jaw are more pronounced now, and even though I can see the shadow of unmistakable muscle in his chest under his tight gray Henley. He looks like he has lost some muscle mass too. Did his lack of appetite stem from his betrayal and my capture, I wonder? *He hasn't suffered near enough!* The vengeful banshee in my head yells. None of them have.

I roll my eyes at all of them, wholly disgusted with all their antics, and I shift to move back toward the room I spent the night in, feeling foolish for even coming out here. Who the fuck cares if they are beating each other bloody? I sure as fuck shouldn't.

"Mia, I am sincerely sorry. This was stupid and reckless. I know full well what you have just been through...I should have given your feelings more thought." Theo's voice trembles as the words leave his lips. His dark blue eyes shine with despair and honesty.

"I'm sorry too, blondie. I don't ever want to hurt you. You're my heart." Carter tries to give me his puppy dog eyes, but I roll my eyes at his antics.

"You know how I feel, my *reina*. I would sooner stab my own heart than hurt yours. I'm sorry, *mami*, for our recklessness." The sadness on Mateo's face has a lump forming in my throat. I shrug it off. Their words are just that, words. They gave no thought to their actions.

I don't give them any response to their apologies. I'm feeling incredibly self-conscious and foolish for even coming out here in a panic like I did. These kings play on my emotions nonstop. I turn on my feet to return to the safety of the room, and Finn steps forward in a flash, reaching out, grabbing my arm, and pulling me, stumbling into his tight embrace.

My whole body feels like it hits a brick wall as my chest and thighs make contact with his muscular body. His arms wrap around me and pull me into a tight hug, and his lips press against the top of my head. His scent of honeysuckle and smoke overwhelms my senses, and I let my body melt into the heat of his frame for a moment. "No, Finn, Let me go. I don't give a shit that all of you are sorry. I don't want anything to do with any of you." I push against his restraining grip.

"I am sorry, Mia. So sorry that you can't even imagine how it guts me to see you hurting." He tightens his hold on me; heat radiates off of him in waves against me. My eyes meet dark pools of melted chocolate. In their depths, I see remorse, but I also see longing.

"Too fucking bad, Killer. I need you, and I have zero intentions of ever letting you go again." His mouth descends to mine with a ruthlessness that leaves me utterly breathless. His other hand grips my lower back in a tight hold, preventing me from being able to escape him.

Finn's warm lips crash on mine and roam over my own, demanding and seeking. His tongue peeks out and tries to slip between my clenched teeth, but I refuse its entry. His grip tightens on my neck as firm and relentless fingers dig into my skin, forcing a sharp cry from my lips that he takes full advantage of to plunder my mouth. His tongue pursuing mine in an intimate dance.

I try to pull back in his sure grasp, but his fingers tighten further, forcing my body to mold to his. For a moment, panic fills me. His touch is violent, demanding, and possessive, and a haze tries to take my mind. That panic tries to induce my mind to slip into the dark memories of someone else's hands on me. But I am called back from its clutches by the smell of Honeysuckle and smoke. The sensation of soft meeting hard as I try to fight his hold has a cyclone of emotions running through me at his touch. I feel myself softening, craving the demand of his touch. *We need to stop this, be strong, bitch!*

His warm tongue slowly strokes mine and then skims over the roof of my mouth. A moan leaves his lips and vibrates into my mouth. The sensation causing a whimper to be trapped in my throat. *No, Mia, pull fucking back. Stop this madness!* My mind yells, but I feel weak to obey it. Just one more moment and I will, I reassure it.

Finn's broad chest rubs against my breasts as his breathing picks up. I can feel his hard, thick cock pressed against my stomach. The sensation causes an electrical current to sizzle across my flesh and goosebumps to explode all over my body. My traitorous core starts to weep for him, dampening my panties in response to his mouth and the aggressive nature of his control. *Weak ass bitch, come on! Resist!*

A heated body presses firmly against my ass, and a muscular chest presses rigidly against my back as the scent of citrus awakens my senses and tells me that it's Mateo leaning into me. His strong fingers feather along my neck, down my collarbone, and skate down my shoulder, leaving tendrils of heat in his wake.

We are in trouble here, bitch! Two-on-one is not fucking fair! Come on, willpower, you can show up any fucking time now.

Mateo's heated breath advances over my skin making shivers race down my spine before his lips trail over the column of my neck with mere wisps of contact. Forcing me to have to whimper into Finn's mouth at the sensation of the caresses. Finn applies pressure inducing my head to bend to the side to give Mateo easier access. The sensation of both their mouths on me at the same time is overwhelming all of my senses. I try to fight their embraces, but my attempt at resistance is weak at best.

"You belong to us, *mami*, just like we belong to you. There is no point in fighting it. You will never be free of us."

His words slide over my skin as Finn pulls back, creating space between our two bodies, and places soft kisses across my lips, nose, and cheek. Mateo's fingers trail down the right side of my rib cage, those long fingers dancing over my covered skin as Finn drags his own fingers up the other side. Both of them reach the hem of my shirt and slide their large hands underneath, skittering over my pebbled flesh and meeting the soft, round globes of my braless breasts. My nipples are hard and standing at attention, just waiting for their touch. *Hello, Mia! Are you for fucking real right now? WHAT ARE YOU DOING?*

"Fuck, Killer." Finn moans into my jaw as his fingers reach and caress my nipple before pulling it and pinching it with his deft fingers. The sensation forcing a moan to leave my lips before Mateo imitates Finn's caress, and the two of them are priming me to explode. My core feels needy and throbs, the sensation of being empty causing me to squirm in their hold. *Bitch, are you really getting hot and bothered right now? RIGHT FUCKING NOW! With these traitors' hands on you? The ones who hurt you?*

"Fuck, that's hot." A moaned groan sounds from across the room, from Carter's mouth. The realization that he and Theo are just watching us makes more illicit heat lick over my skin.

Mateo's fingers slide down my chest, over my stomach, and into the band of the sweatpants and underwear I'm wearing. The pads of his fingers stroke over my wet pussy lips before thrumming my hard little bundle of nerves. The sensation causes my body to betray me and undulate in his hold.

A moan leaves my lips as Mateo sucks deeply on the flesh of my neck, simultaneously as Finn bites on my lower lip. Mateo slips a finger, followed by another, inside my tight hole while Finn pulls and pinches my pulsing nipple. The sensation of both touches sending me ratcheting closer to the edge. *Fuck, that feels so good, so right.* I need to stop this; I need to get myself under some control.

"Nooo..." I try to utter the word, but it leaves my lips in a pitiful whimper.

"Yes, *mami*. This is what you need. You need us to reclaim our queen. You want us, don't try to act like you don't. Give in to us. Let us make you feel so good." Mateo thrusts his fingers in time with his words, and I have to brace myself as I widen my stance to keep my legs from going under me. His palm rubs deliciously against my clit as his thick fingers move through my wetness and cause my core to tighten until I'm so close to coming that I can feel it ready to crest over me. A spiral of sensations causes my core to tighten in anticipation.

"No...stop." I moan as my body follows the movement of Mateo's fingers, trying desperately to meet the strokes and force his fingers deeper inside of me. Little mewling and panting sounds are leaving my lips, and I can't seem to stop them.

Finn pulls back and lifts my shirt, yanking the whole thing off my body until I'm standing exposed from the waist up to everyone in the room. The cool air hits my skin and is a balm on my overheated flesh. His face leans forward, and takes my right nipple into the heat of his mouth and sucks deep while he rolls the other one between his strong fingers as Mateo continues to fingerbang me. Fuck, it's almost too much; the need to explode is just out of reach but hurtling toward me.

My pussy is drenched and spasming, little shockwaves hitting me in a rolling motion and cascading over my skin. The sensation causing my breath to hitch. My wetness is sliding out of me, coating Mateo's fingers, my pussy lips, and even the sides of my thighs. The sound of his fingers sliding in and out of me, loud and obscene, in the air around us.

I'm so close that my legs are trembling, my breathing is becoming harsh, and my vision is starting to see bright spots. Mateo's other hand wraps around my neck, his fingers tightening as he bites down on my shoulder, and my body explodes like a bomb detonating with the hit of pain.

"Fuck!" The scream leaves my mouth and sounds like the call of a wild animal before my breathing is restrained by Mateo's fingers. My half-closed eyes look over Finn's shoulder and spy Carter, not six feet from us, stroking his long, rigid, pierced cock, drops of precum escaping from his slit. His blue-gray eyes are heated and hungry. The look on his face unmistakably one of a predator, that of a wolf, ready to consume his prey. *Me.*

"You're so beautiful when you shatter, Mia." Finn's voice in my ear is thick with need. His hand releases my nipple as he bends down and yanks down my pants, forcing me to step out of them while Mateo continues to stroke me through aftershocks of bliss. "I need a taste, Killer."

Two tortured groans leave the mouths of the males watching their friends bring me to the edge of madness. Observing me not putting a stop to this wanton behavior and allowing it to escalate, as Mateo and Finn bring my body back to life and to the edge of ecstasy.

"Finn...Mateo...fuck. No." The words leave my lips with no conviction, and they both disregard them. *Great attempt there, bitch. That was so convincing.* The snide bitch inside of my head fake claps.

Finn lowers himself to his knees in front of me, his lips leaving small open-mouthed kisses along the edge of my stomach, over my hip, and down my pelvis until they meet the soft wet skin of my pussy lips. His slippery, long tongue slides out and licks down my slit before sucking one of my folds into his mouth. My hand reaches out without my consent and digs into his thick dark hair, pulling him closer as waves of euphoria continue to cycle through my body. *I need this.*

Carter moves forward, his cock still clenched in his tight fist. His eyes are deep ice chips, the pupils dilated and a flush of pink across his cheeks. He leans over Finn's kneeling body as Mateo sucks deep on my neck, leaving nothing but marks in his wake. Carter's warm lips meet mine in a demanding kiss, one that immediately tries to consume me.

Finn's lips release my folds as he uses his hands to part my pussy lips, opening me up for his survey. "Fucking gorgeous, what a pretty cunt."

A moan leaves Finn's lips as he licks over my hard, throbbing nub with his tongue before he sucks on it sharply. Carter takes that opportunity to plunge his tongue deep into my mouth, as Mateo pulls and twists my right nipple. All the sensations at the same time are causing my body to overload.

Another orgasm threatens to barrel down on me. I'm so wet that I can feel it coating Finn's face as he groans into my pussy with Mateo's masterful fingers still deep inside of me. My whole body is strung tight, the hairs on my arms standing on end, and a humming sensation soothing over my limbs. I can hear my blood rushing through my veins, the sound thunderous in my ears.

Mateo quickens his thrusts, inserting another finger until the feeling of being full and stretched is almost overwhelming as he plunges deeper. Finn's teeth graze my needy clit as Carter sucks on my tongue, and I explode once again. The orgasm crests in a sensation of light and heat that has me barely able to stand. Different sets of hands hold me as the waves of pleasure keep rolling through me as gushes of my wetness escape me into Finn's greedy mouth.

"Fuck, that's beautiful." Theo's voice is filled with emotion, but I can't open my eyes to more than slits to look at him. Finn's greedy tongue laps at all my folds and slips inside my tight hole as Mateo pulls his fingers from inside of me and strokes my puckered hole with his soaked digits.

"*Mami*, you are going to take me in this hole while Finn fucks your needy pussy. We are going to fill you up and stretch you out baby, so you know whose cocks you belong to. You're going to be my good girl, Mia, and let Carter fuck that pretty mouth. While Theo watches us fill you full of our cocks and cum."

A whimper escapes my mouth and is quickly swallowed by Carter's. Finn pulls away from my core, and I feel Mateo wrap his arms around my waist and lift me off my feet like I weigh nothing at all. Carter breaks the kiss, his breaths coming in deep pants, and he steps back while Finn rises from his knees, my arousal slick across his pink lips and chin.

Movement from the corner of my eye has me witnessing Theo righting the sofa back into place as he steps back and gives Mateo room to move with me in his hold. My self-preservation returns for a moment, and I try to shove out of Mateo's hold. He releases me, but Finn has me wrapped in his arms before I can even take a step or two away. "No, Mia. Enough of this shit. You belong to us, and we belong to you. Don't fight this between us."

"Fuck you, Finn." I try to catch my breath and calm my heart rate. My hands clench into tight fists, the desire to knock him right in the face filling me. Don't they realize by now that I hate to be controlled. *Do you, though? When it comes to their cocks, you enjoy being their willing slut.* The snide voice inside my head disparages me.

"Oh baby, I plan to fuck you in every one of your holes before we are done, including that vicious mouth that belongs to me." He pushes me backward, and I land on a naked Mateo, his warm flesh meeting my exposed one. His arms become bands of steel around my waist as his cock nudges between my asscheeks, and he keeps me pinned against his chest.

"Let me show you how much I need and miss you, *mami.* Let me deep inside of you. I want to come home, baby." Mateo whispers into my ear, and my whole body squirms with the sensations running through me. Carter moves to the side of the sofa, grabbing my jaw in his tight grip. His features are stern, with a no-nonsense look that will not be denied.

It's incredibly hot watching him take control and be forceful with me. More moisture seeps from my core until I feel it trickling down my crack and landing on Mateo's hard cock head. Heat strikes between my parted thighs, and I have to bite down on my lip until I can taste rich copper to prevent the moan that wants to escape me.

"Open, blondie." His grip tightens painfully until I comply, and his thick, pierced cock head is slipping through my lips. His salty taste hits my tongue and makes my eyes want to roll back into my head. *Weak ass bitch, one taste of cock, and you're a goner for them.* A moan crawls up the back of my throat and vibrates along Carter's length making his cock throb in my mouth.

"Killer, look at how that pretty pussy glistens for our cocks." Finn's groan is a deep rumble in his chest as he watches me take Carter in my mouth with desire evident across his features. My heart races in my chest as our eyes meet, and he holds my gaze.

I want him. Fuck, I want them all. Despite everything that they have done to me. All the heartache, pain, and suffering I have endured at their miserable, egotistical hands. I want to get past my last horrific experience of sex. I don't want my body to always remember hate and abuse at the hands of a man.

I never thought I would be able to feel this type of desire again after everything I have endured. I thought I was forever broken, but they are bringing me back to life, healing that part of me that James tried to take from me by force. I need this, just this one time, so I can help repair all my shattered pieces. So I can experience one more moment of bliss with all of them. *Then I will let them go.*

Mateo's cock nudges my back entrance, the blunt tip just barely breaching the tight ring of tissue. He hasn't prepped me enough back there, even though my arousal is slipping down my body and coating my puckered hole. He slides his thick cock head through my wetness, over and over, before starting to push in. A slight burning sensation has me swallowing more of Carter's cock as my body tries to push Mateo back out, but he won't be dissuaded. "That's it, my perfect little *reina*, relax baby, let my cock inside of his paradise."

Carter threads his hand through my hair, pulling on the strands and forcing my eyes up to his husky ones. "You were made to take all of our cocks, Mia. Let us into that sinful body, baby." He thrusts deeper until he's hitting the back of my throat, and I gag on his cock. My mouth is filling with saliva, and it is spilling down the corner of my lips and down my chin.

Carter's words have me groaning along his long veiny length. I can feel his piercing hitting the back of my throat each time he pushes forward, making me swallow more of him until my airway is filled with only his thick cock.

Mateo thrusts forward and seats himself deep inside of my ass, the sensation of being stretched around his long cock causing a tear to slide from the corner of my eye and down my face. Finn moves closer, catching my tear with his thumb before bringing it to his mouth and sucking it off his digit. "Every part of you tastes like ambrosia, Mia."

He leans forward, running his fingers through my wet slit before inserting one of his digits inside of my core and thrusting slowly. Making me crave the feeling of being used by all of them, to have all of me filled with their cocks.

Carter chooses that moment to thrust harshly down my throat, forcing me to choke down on his cock as it makes its way into the tight confines of my throat and blocks my airway. He holds still, giving me no opportunity to fight his hold with a grip on my hair as Finn and Mateo each take hold of one of my hands.

It's too much! All of it is too much for my body to take; the tornado of sensations is making my head spin. Harsh sounds of breathing, moans, and the sound of me gagging mix in the air of the room. My chest rises and falls in an erratic rhythm inside of my chest. The tempo, a drum beating wildly that I hear in my ears. I'm going to explode again, and this time there will be nothing left of me.

Mateo thrusts inside me, forcing me to take his whole length again and again. My pussy clenches around Finn's finger at the same time. "Fuck, she's so tight when you fuck her ass; she's strangling my finger. I need my cock deep inside of her, Mat."

No, I won't be able to take more; my nerves are already on fire. Every part of me is now a wildfire, uncontrollable and ready to decimate my very soul. I try to garble the word no, but it's lost with Carter's thick cock being forced down my throat.

"It's alright, my perfect little slut; they are going to fill you up and make you feel so good with their cocks." Carter coos to me, forcing my eyes to meet his heated ones. I watch as he licks his lips, a look of possession in his depths as he pulls his dick back out until just the tip is brushing my lips. He slides his pierced crown across my mouth, coating my bottom lip and my cheek. Before he slaps it on my chin, covering me in my saliva and his precum. "These lips were made for sucking my cock, Mia. Look how they glisten and pout for me. You are mine, my little cock whore."

Mateo's thrusts slow and become shallow as I feel Finn's crown at my entrance. His hands grab my legs underneath my knees and force my legs wide apart, draping them over Mateo's waiting forearms. His hard tip runs through my slit, lubricating himself in my juices before bumping my clit. "You're soaked, baby. This pussy is about to stretch so nicely for my cock."

Carter's hard dick slips once again through my lips, and he forces it into the soft flesh on the inside of my cheek until it causes my mouth to stretch grotesquely. "Look at my blondie, about to have all her tight holes filled with her kings' cocks." He slams back into the back of my throat, and tears roll down my face with the treatment. The cry that wants to leave my mouth is silenced by his cock as I try desperately to get air in through my nose.

"Suck Mia, taste what belongs to you." Carter's fingers trail down my face, spreading the wetness of my tears. "You're so pretty when you cry, Mia, but only when those tears are for us."

"Fuck so tight, *mami*, your ass is strangling my cock." Mateo groans near my ear. Heat races through my body as I try to close my legs, but his grip tightens on them, keeping me wide open for his fellow king.

Finn's engorged crown slips inside of my tight hole, and his thumb rubs circles on my needy clit, before pinching it. My body starts to ramp up again with all the stimulation, and my hands reach out, sliding my fingernails down Mateo's exposed arms and trying to claw at Finn's chest. "Relax, Killer, let me fuck this plump, pink pussy."

Carter's fingers encircle my throat as he pulls out until just the tip is still inside my mouth. His piercing pressed against the roof of my mouth. I try to cough to release the choking feeling in my throat, but it seems to egg him on, and he slams back into my throat until my nose is pressed against the hard muscle of his warm pelvis. I panic and start clawing at all of them, but they don't seem to care about my struggle for air. "Blondie, I am going to cum so deep down this little throat. You're going to be feeling me for days when you swallow."

His fingers dig so deep into my throat that I know I will be sporting a hand necklace come the morning. His other hand reaches out, and his palm slaps my exposed breasts, first on the right and then on the left. The sting of heat and pain makes my nipples harden further until they ache. I try to let out a scream, but his cock traps the sound in my throat. Rivers of tears and saliva run down my face as he pounds the back of my throat without mercy.

He's completely lost to his own pleasure and using me to get to his release. All three of them are. I should be panicking, my mind is telling me to panic, but my body is lost in the euphoria of each of their dominating and possessive touches. For this brief moment, they own me; I am theirs.

"What a pretty, messy girl you are taking cock. Look at all those crystal tears. Are they all for me, Blondie?"

Finn slips inside my pussy slowly, one agonizing inch at a time. My channel tries to stretch to accommodate his thick girth. The feeling of fullness has a hint of sweet pain accompanying it as he finally bottoms out inside me, as Mateo continues delivering shallow thrusts to my ass. I'm so deliciously full; every part of me vibrates with energy as all three of them use my body for their pleasure. *Dirty whore, look at you allowing yourself to be used by all three of them.*

"I'm not gonna last, fuckers. She's squeezing me like a vise." Mateo grits out as he picks up the pace and thrusts rapidly inside of my ass. The sound of skin slapping, grunts, and moans are loud in the space. I can hear how wet I am every time Finn goes balls deep inside of me, his thrusts matching Mateo's. Fire licks across my limbs, rising up my spine and breaking out across my skin. My fingers and toes tingle with the energy that has my body stretching and tightening like a string on a guitar. Until finally, like a Fourth of July fireworks display, my body shatters.

My orgasm is the catalyst for theirs. First, Mateo cums harshly in my ass, grinding deep and holding me too tight. His mouth presses against the damp skin of my back, and an animalistic groan leaves his lips. Carter grunts and forces his cock as deep as it will go down my throat before I feel the spurts of his cum emptying inside of me. There's so much thick cum, and his cock is lodged so tightly down my tight throat that I can't stop rivulets from escaping down the side of my gaping mouth as I drag air through my nose and try not to lose consciousness.

Finn picks up speed, holding me tight by my hips and slamming over and over inside me. Each deep, harsh thrust pushes me back along Mateo's semi-hard length. I can feel cum trickling out of my ass and wetting my butt cheeks. Carter pulls out of my mouth, his hand automatically going to my lips as I try to take a deep breath. "Naw, Mia, you need to swallow every drop. Then I want you to be a good girl and lick me clean."

Sweat is trickling down all of our bodies. Finn grunts as he watches where our bodies are connected, his dark brown eyes riveted to the spot as he bites down on his full lip. "You feel so good, Killer. So tight with both of us inside of you. Look at how beautiful you are, filled with all our cum."

Heat surges through my middle, coiling in my stomach and making my heart slam in my ribs as he forces his hard cock inside of me and it hits that sensitive spot that has me seeing stars. Fuck! Mateo holds me wide open for him like a meal before a king. "Take it, Killer, show me you belong to me. Cum on my cock." My pussy spasms with aftershocks, and I cry out from the overstimulation. As Mateo rubs his middle finger over my clit. "No more...please," I beg. "I...I can't."

Finn thrusts twice more, and then he's filling my swollen pussy with his cum. I can feel it pulsing deep inside of me as he slams one last time, hitting the end of me. "Fuck, you're mine, Mia." He grunts as his forehead meets mine, and all our breathing is loud in the air around us.

Carter's grip on my neck forces my face back in his direction, his cock bobbing before my lips, still hard. The slit and head are coated in cum as drops escape and trickle down his length. "Lick, baby, lick me clean, my little cum whore."

My tongue slides out as I lick all the cum from his slit, lashing his piercing and then the mushroom head of his crown. I slide my tongue down the raised vein on the side of his proud cock until I meet the root of him, licking and sucking first one ball and then the other before releasing them with a pop and starting up the other side. When there isn't a drop of cum left, I pull back and stare into his eyes, which are filled with satisfaction.

"Baby, you have one more cock to take. Theo is going to fuck you in all of your holes that are now filled with cum. He's going to baptize you in his release, so you are fully reclaimed. You'll take it all like a perfect little slut. Like our perfect fucking queen."

CHAPTER 32

Theo

"To burn with desire and keep quiet about it is the greatest punishment we can bring on ourselves." Federico García Lorca, Blood Wedding and Yerma

Her fierce ocean-blue eyes meet mine from across the short space at Carter's words. Is that desire or hatred that I see in their depths? She looks boneless and completely ravished now as she lies on top of Mateo after allowing Carter, Finn, and Mateo to manhandle her and have their way with her body.

I watch as Finn pulls out of her core, his cock still hard. Once with Mia will never be enough for any of us. Our bodies crave hers like a powerful narcotic. An addiction that all four of us willingly succumbed to and hope to never be cured of. The air is thick with the scent of lust, twisted emotions, and hedonistic depravity. It calls to me with its cloying scent, urging me to shed my restraint, loosen my control and take what is before me. Take possession of my girl, burying my sins deep in her core with my cock, and beseech for her forgiveness and mercy. She will be the saint I pray to for the rest of my life.

Her gaping pussy trickles with Finn's cum, the milky river making my hard cock throb with anticipation of joining where it's escaping from. I pull off my shirt and undo my pants, letting my cock spring forward from its restrained confines. My eyes lock on hers, and I watch her reaction to me. I don't want to scare her, but the need within me is a wild animal demanding to be let loose from his cage.

The tip of my cock weeps beads of cum for my queen. Mateo lifts her gently until his cock releases from inside of her and causes a whimper to leave her lips. *Fuck, we should be heedful of overdoing it.* Her body is still healing; she just came from a traumatic experience. *One I am all too familiar with. She, after all, was the one to pull me out of the deep recess of darkness that I was languishing in.* I want and need to do the same for her. I need to call her back to the land of the living so she can breathe again and forgive my sins against her.

As much as I want to restrain myself from taking my turn reclaiming her sinful body, knowing full well that I should. *I can't; I need her.* I need to be deep inside of her until there is no her or I; there is only us. She will always be my beginning and my end.

I move toward her as her eyes watch me intently, they glance down at my hard cock, and her tongue wets her bottom lip. She's still in that semi-drunken state from her release, her body sated and her mind blissed out. She looks ravished and beautiful, her golden skin tinged with pink. Her nipples are two hard points on her round full breasts, and her swollen pink pussy taunts me with my heart's desire to be firmly inside of her.

Fuck, the things I want to do to her holes. The way I want to consume all of her until there is nothing left and she is mine. I can't, however, she would never allow herself to be just mine. If I want my vicious little queen, I will have to share her. A prospect that no longer causes me any discomfort.

She was always ours; we just didn't know it until she came back into our world with the intention of destroying us. She's completed her mission; we can no longer live without her.

Her features are trying to disguise her thoughts from me, but I have always been able to pick up on Mia's cues. She's not sure if she wants me to touch her.

While she may be vexed with the others, most of her fury is actually directed at me. *As it should be.* I was the imbecile that convinced the other three to go along with discarding and pushing her away in an attempt to keep her safe, not once, but twice. A plan that had disastrous consequences.

"No." She tries to pull away from Mateo's hold, but he immediately pulls her back. Carter's fingers wrap around her throat from the side. I watch, mesmerized, as he tightens his grip, causing the color to rise in her cheeks. "Yes. You will let him fuck you raw and fill you with cum, Mia, or I will choke you out with my cock. You belong to him."

"I...belong...to...myself." She gasps out through Carter's harsh hold. Ever the defiant little queen. She thrashes in Mateo's hold, even though both Mateo and Carter's grip tighten on her sinful body.

"While that is true, Mia, you do belong to yourself. You also belong to each of us, and I will have you, my little queen. You can choose to fight me or not, choose to punish me, but one way or the other, I will reclaim what is mine."

In my heart, I am hoping that she will relent and let me claim her. Let me seek my forgiveness with my body and show her how much she means to me. I won't be dissuaded, though. I know she is on a precipice, one that if she pulls back too far, she will forever be out of our reach. I can't allow that to happen. Mia and I have always had a strong fiery bond since she returned. She will always fight me, and I will always hold onto her a little tighter.

My hand reaches out, and my fingers dig into her beautiful thick, dirty blonde waves. "You are mine, Mia. You will always be mine." Her eyes meet mine, and I see a fire relit within them, one I have craved to witness for weeks as she moved around, lost and broken, within the confines of her home. I guess she has decided to fight. The knowledge doesn't deter me one bit. She can be angry all she wants. Rage against me and my need for control, but no matter what happens in this lifetime, she is mine. It's time I reminded her of that fact.

"I hate you, Theo Saint-Lambert."

Her words are daggers in my heart, yet there is no strength behind them. She's saying them because she feels the need to. She wants to hurt me like I hurt her. She can hurt me all she wants; she will still be fucking mine.

My lips meet hers in a harsh kiss that is all teeth and force as Carter, and Mateo keep her immobile. I bite down on her bottom lip until she opens for me, and I can plunder the warmth of her mouth. The first lick has her taste reintroducing itself to my senses. I can taste Carter's salty cum along with her own heady flavor. Even knowing he has just fucked her mouth like a goddamn savage, something that would have previously deterred me, has no effect now. Nothing will stop me from having her.

A deep groan leaves my lips at the very thought of all her holes tasting like my brothers. I'm a hedonistic kinky deviant, and so are they. I've come to grips with the fact that I not only enjoy causing my girl pain during sex, get off on depriving her of breath and bloodying her, but get immense sexual gratification from sharing her with my brothers. I find it incredibly sexy when she is filled with their cum, and I get to reclaim her after.

I pull back from her lips, my forefinger trailing along their soft surface as her tongue peeks out and licks the tip. My cock bounces against my stomach with the warm touch of her wet tongue, and I can feel drops of precum sliding down its surface. "Don't bother fighting, baby, you have been captured by your kings, and we plan to ravish you over and over in the most barbaric ways. You are my queen, Mia, but I am your king."

I lean forward, lick her lips, then down her chin, and slowly trail my tongue until I meet Carter's tight fingers still wrapped around her throat. His eyes meet mine as he releases their confinement, but he doesn't remove them entirely from the column of her neck. I continue down the path of her soft skin until I reach the round globe of her breast, pressing my lips to the delicate skin before enveloping her hard nipple in my mouth and lashing it. A moan leaves her lips that she tries to swallow, and her body flushes with goosebumps.

She tries to reach forward to push me away, Carter and Mateo loosening their grip on her at my nod. I want her to have the ability to hurt me. The little hellcat doesn't disappoint me or make me wait. Her fingernails claw at my bare chest and neck; the sting feels so good that a moan escapes me. Her touching me, even if it's in anger after all these weeks, is a balm to my miserable, destitute soul. "Finn, Carter, hold one of her arms and legs. Open her up for me." I instruct, and my fellow kings heed my request, opening Mia up and restraining her so I can have my wicked way with her uninhibited.

In the back of my mind, warning bells are sounding that this might be taking it too far. It was only a couple of weeks ago that she escaped James' clutches after being raped by that psychopath. She needs to know we would never hurt her. She needs to be reclaimed by us so she can see how we worship her body, heart, and soul. The look on her face of anticipation and desire tells me I'm right despite my reservations. She wants to be owned by me and my fellow kings. She craves our touch just as much as we desire hers.

"Don't, Theo. I don't want you..." Her voice trails off as her words are uttered without any verity.

"Are you trying to convince yourself or me, your highness, cause this pretty pussy is throbbing for my cock. She craves a ruthless pounding." I raise an amused eyebrow, and a devious smirk crosses my face at her look of indignation. *Oh, Mia, how much I fucking want and need you. You will never understand, not even when I open all the chasms of my heart and soul for you and lay them at your feet.*

"Release me now, you fucking devils. I'm going to murder all four of you!" She continues to thrash as all three of my brothers restrain her. Forcing her body to go pliant and await my ministrations. Mia wants me to fuck her in anger so she can convince herself to keep emotions out of the interaction. She wants to push me until I lose my precarious control and take her hard and fast, but I won't be prodded into doing her bidding.

I suck in her nipple again, this time letting my teeth lightly graze it, and her back bows against Mateo's chest, her breathing picks up and the vein in her neck throbs. A chuckle leaves my mouth at her reaction. My girl loves her hits of pain. My fingers trail down her stomach until they reach their prized destination of her core. Her pussy lips are swollen from Finn's cock pounding and Mateo's fingerbanging. I trail them through the mess Finn left behind and slip two inside of her as she immediately tightens down on my digits.

I release her nipple, and my mouth follows my finger's path, bringing me to my knees before her. My digits and gaze meet her swollen bundle of nerves as I lash it with my tongue and my fingers thrust inside of her drenched pussy. She's so warm, wet, and tight, even after Finn just wrecked her cunt with his huge cock.

Fuck, I wonder if two of us took her pussy at the same time while one of us took her ass, would her body strangle all our dicks before sending us to heaven filled with bliss? The image of all four of us using all her holes at the exact same time, filling her body with pleasure and cum, almost has me cumming right in front of her without her even touching my cock. That is, for fucking sure, something we are attempting in the future when she's not so livid with us.

"What a good little slut my queen is. Theo's gonna make you feel so good, baby." Carter moans as he restrains her arm and leg, keeping her wide open for me, as pearls of cum drip from his hard-pierced cock. He, more than the others, enjoys sharing Mia's pussy. It's a massive turn-on for him, one that he never tries to disguise.

I lick down her slit, tasting the heady combination of her sinful musky taste and the salty-sour taste of Finn's cum. My tongue meets my thrusting fingers, and I force it inside her tight hole, stretching her further as a whimpered cry fills the air. My eyes rise below my lashes, and I watch as Mateo pulls on her nipples, one at a time, elongating the tips and twisting them mercilessly. She's not evening fighting their hold anymore; in fact, the fuckers are barely restraining her. She's lost to what I am doing to her and enjoying the feel of my mouth on her.

"Fuck, holy shit! Fuck!" The words are tumbling from her lips as she is racked with the desire we are creating in unison inside of her cunt. Carter trails his fingers up and down the column of her neck, occasionally tightening them and then releasing them as she tries to suck in air.

I remove my soaked fingers, letting them stroke between her pussy lips up to her clit, massaging it in tight circles as my tongue plunges inside of her core, and I get a mouthful of her juices and Finn's cum. I pull back slightly and watch as she closes her eyes, her lips parted. "Open your mouth wide, baby. I want you to taste the combination of Finn, you, and me." I slip my tongue back inside of her, lashing, licking, and thrusting, and pull back out, my face leaning closer to hers. She opens her lips but keeps her eyes sealed. She can try to fight all she wants, but she is ours. I spit in her mouth and watch as she swallows and licks her lips. *Fuck, that's sexy.*

My cock is throbbing and refuses to be denied any further. Mateo leans further back, angling her body on top of his, and I plunge my hard cock into her cunt in one go, reaching the end of her as a scream leaves her lips. One that has my balls tightening and threatening to paint cum inside of her warm cunt before I even had a chance to fully enjoy her.

"Too much, fuck, too much!" She moans as her body clenches around my cock. I rub her clit as I wait for her body to adjust to my hard thick cock and thrust, pulling all the way out to the tip and thrusting back in again. "Fuck, fuck, fuck." She chants as my thrusts increase in speed. Mateo slips a finger below her body and inserts it inside of her puckered hole, fucking her in unison with my strokes. "Oh my god, yes, fuck!" Her cries are music to my ears.

My orgasm is racing up my spine in electrifying tingles that have the combination of goosebumps and beads of sweat breaking out all over my skin. I lean forward and take her red pouty lips, slipping my tongue into her mouth and mimicking what my cock is doing to her pussy. She meets me stroke for stroke with her own tongue. *Jesus, this woman is going to wreck what's left of my soul.*

"Fuck, Mia, look at you baby, what a dirty, slutty little whore you are cumming on Theo's big dick. Look at how Theo's cock is coated in your juices and Finn's cum." Carter's groaned words aren't fucking helping my cock's desperate need to release. *Motherfucker and his filthy erotic mouth.*

I need her to come before I find my own release. My fingers stroke her clit as Mateo's digit in her clenched ass picks up speed. Carter's hand makes its way back around Mia's neck, and he squeezes tightly until her breath hitches in her throat, just as Finn leans over me and forces his tongue inside of her mouth. Holy fuck, all of us on her is insanely hot. She must think so, too; she comes with a harsh breath, squeezing my cock like a damn python.

"Fuck, Mia, I love when you are filled with our cum, baby. Look how beautiful you are when filled with a cock. Look how your pussy swallows Theo's thick monster." Carter groans next to her face.

His words and her pussy's grip on my cock have me plunging over the edge and streams of cum leaving me and coating her womb. I trail my fingers across her lower stomach, feeling the imprint of my hard cock inside of her. One day soon, I'm going to put a baby inside of her so she will never be able to escape me. No matter where she goes, she will have a piece of me with her.

I pull out and stand, my throbbing cock still hard and ready to go again. Her juices, mine, and Finn's cum coats my cock. I rub my tip across her lips, covering them like lipgloss and making them shiny. "Suck baby, suck all that goodness off my cock."

Her mouth opens, and I slip inside as her lips close over me, and she hollows her cheeks sucking me hard and deep as I push to the back of her throat. Tremors rack my body as my cock is encased in the warm heat of her mouth. I hit the back of her throat, and she gags. Carter's punishing grip on the column of her throat loosens so she can get more of me down. I fuck her throat in deep thrusts until, once again, hot streams of cum shoot out of me and down her throat.

I can feel Mateo and Finn's hands moving between our bodies, and from the moans vibrating along my shaft, they both are finger fucking her holes again. Her whole body tightens; I feel her deep shudder, and then she releases a cry around my cock, tears cascading down the sides of her face as she cums and then goes slack.

I pull back, letting my cock bob between us, the tip smearing my release across her lips and cheek. Cum dribbles out of her mouth, coating her lips and chin, and mixes with her hot tears to trail down to her chest. I run my fingers through the mess, feeling like a goddamn king.

"Please..." The word is spoken in a pleading tone. She's no doubt sore after taking all of us and cumming repeatedly. Fuck, I will never get past the sounds she makes and the way her body looks as she reaches her climax. There will never be a more beautiful sight than Mia, filled with rapture.

I grab her chin in my hand, tightening my fingers until she is forced to meet my gaze with her tired eyes. "No more, Mia. I am sorry, so very sorry I hurt you. That we hurt you. I will spend my life making it up to you. You are mine. Ours. We will never let you go."

CHAPTER 33
Mia

"In general, pride is at the bottom of all great mistakes."
John Ruskin

H is words should bring me peace and satisfaction. Yet they don't; instead, they fill me with a fiery rage, one that threatens to have me seeing red. *I'm his... THEIRS?* No, they are fucking MINE. *Oh he's sorry?* Great, I'm glad that he's realized that he fucked up. That his actions were wrong and caused me so much heartache, pain, and trauma. Does he think another simple apology and a fantastic round of sex with all of them will fix everything? Of course he does; he's a man. *Fucking delusional assholes.* My pussy thanks them for the effort, though.

No, my heart and soul are yearning for their retribution. I came to Casbury to seek vengeance on the kings of Casbury, and that is precisely what I should have done instead of falling in love with the four of them. Of all the mistakes I have made since leaving Manhattan, that is the one that has helped destroy the most significant piece of me. They have hurt me over and over while professing words of grandeur and love to me, and only now that they have each used me for their own satisfaction, they are sorry? *You liked it*, my treacherous brain whispers to me.

How many times did each of them declare that I was theirs only to throw me away like garbage? Did they do it with good intentions? *So they say!* But what happens the next time they have *good intentions*? How much more of a beating can my heart take? A round of sex doesn't make those fundamental issues go away. *No, I must now draw a line in the sand and force myself to stick by it.* If I allow them to, they will continue to destroy me until there is nothing left. They aren't sorry. They are just upset they couldn't get their dicks wet when I wasn't there. They didn't bring me here to beg for my forgiveness. They aren't in love with me. They just like sharing me and feeling in control of a queen.

They can't live without me, they say, *well too fucking bad*. I'm not sure that my heart and soul will survive them going back on their thoughts and feelings again. No, I need to do what I should have done from the very beginning. I need to look out for Mia Stratford. I should have never allowed them to make me weak.

A Stratford is never weak. They want me back? I will see them bow at my feet. No more of this demanding that I acquiesce to them and trying to coerce me with their cocks. *I am a goddamn fucking queen, and they are my subjects.*

I pull with all my remaining strength against their holds and push Theo away, rising to my feet unsteadily and putting distance between their bodies and mine. Various parts of my body are on fire, and I am still feeling the remaining waves of too many orgasms and the ghost of their touches. I can feel cum dribbling down the inside of my thigh from my pussy and from my puckered hole, not to mention the fact that it's smeared on my chest and face. *Animals.* The sensation both repulses me and makes me clench my core. *These fuckers made a fucking mess of me.* Marking me like four primal beasts.

I need space to think. I can't breathe when they are so close to me. My self-preservation seems to disappear whenever they touch me. *Fuck, my pussy is aching, assholes.* I need to make sure that they understand that I won't back down just because they were each inside of me. I don't belong to them anymore now than when I first walked into this room and was greeted by the sight of them fighting each other like overbearing barbarians. *Liar,* my mind muses.

The anger racing through my veins is twofold. First, it's directed at them for using me and not caring about their impact or the damage that has been done because of them and at their very own hands. Anger for them acting like everything could be swept under the rug with a highly enjoyable round of sex. Secondly, at myself for ultimately having allowed said round of sex. I need to get the fuck out of this cabin and away from this ice prison before I lose my willpower and my anger softens toward them.

I take careful steps back toward the kitchen, the gun that is still sitting unattended on the counter catches my eye once again. A tinge of excitement fills me at the prospect of teaching them a lesson. *Fools,* they really thought that I would just be dick drunk and allow them to consume me. To turn me into some feeble-willed female that will follow where they lead and forgive them with their pretty, meaningless words.

I have no desire to be that woman; they should have known better. They underestimate me at every turn. I move slowly to prevent them from realizing my destination while keeping them in my sightline. Fuck, four naked kings are definitely a temptation. *Stay strong, Mia.* Their cocks might be glorious, but that will never be enough. They don't truly know me. They don't know my heart or what I've been through. They just know how their bodies fit with mine. *Oh they fit so well.*

They all are sporting various looks across their handsome faces. Theo's face is serious, his dark blue eyes trying to plead with me to see the so-called sincerity behind them. He's also trying to see inside my mind, to understand what my next move is, ever the conniving fucking strategist of the group.

Carter's husky eyes slide all over my body, and I can still see heat blooming within their depths. Fuck, he's ready to take me again; I can feel it. I'm just a piece of meat to him. If I make one move to indicate I'm interested, he will be on me so fast. Fucking *Energizer Bunny.*

Finn has a look of restraint across his face, almost like he can read my thoughts and knows where my mind is leading me. He will be the first to try to restrain me. I can see it in the readiness of his limbs. He's waiting to pounce on me like a lion playing with his food. Well fuck you, Finn, you don't know me anymore, and I sure as shit don't know you, you fuckin' traitor.

Mateo looks exhausted, confused, and annoyed at my retreating figure. His green eyes beg me not to run from them. They implore me to wrap my arms around him and tell him that everything is going to be okay. Except it's fucking not, and I can't. He may be the most sensitive one of the group but he has also hurt me without a second thought. He can't be trusted, just like the rest. I start turning my head away when something catches my eye. What the fuck is that all over his stomach and thighs? *Are those cuts?* I don't have time or energy to think about what I am seeing. I'll leave it for another day. *Or I won't because I shouldn't even care.*

I know what I must do. I stalk forward the last three feet and grab the gun off the counter, holding it in my tight grip and releasing the safety as I point it in their direction. All four of them take steps toward me but come to a dead halt at the gun locked and loaded, ready to shoot them.

A cold calculating mask slides over my features. The Mia from within, who refuses to be taken for granted and is a survivor rises to the surface. The one that is a cold-ass bitch, with little to no regrets at her righteous anger.

"WHAT THE FUCK, MIA!" Finn shouts, and they all shift forward another foot. *What the fuck is right, asshole!* I point the gun at his chest and wait for him to realize that I'm not fucking playing around here.

"Baby put the gun down!" Carter yells, anger radiating across his all-American boy-next-door features.

"Mia, you're not going to shoot any of us; put the fucking gun down before someone gets hurt," Theo demands in his haughty voice. *Fuck him.* I will a hundred percent shoot one of them if they keep moving toward me. My days of compassion for any of them are over. It's time to remind these four who the fuck I am.

I point the gun just over Theo's shoulder and pull the trigger. The shot echoes loudly as it embeds into the wood-logged wall, and I watch with satisfaction as they all duck to the ground. Carter throws himself behind the back of the sofa and drags a panicked Mateo with him. "I will shoot all of you fuckers. You underestimate my level of hate for all of you right now."

"Mia! Please, *mami*, don't do this!" Mateo begs from Carter's side.

Finn takes the opportunity to try to slide toward me, but I point the gun two feet in front of him and fire. "FUCK MIA!"

"I'm not playing, Finn. The next one of you that tries to make a move toward me is going to be getting a bullet to his body. By all means, fuck around and find out if I will make good on my intent to cause you four fuckers real damage."

"Babe, please!" Carter begs from the back of the sofa, peeking over the top, so I can just see the top of his dirty blond head and his light eyes. I allow the most sinister look I can produce to cross my face. The look that was present through all of my planning to garner my vengeance on the kings of Casbury for their sins.

"Jesus, fuck. She's going to shoot us!" He whimpers. "Blondie, please remember you love me!" A snort escapes me at his words. He will be lucky if I don't shoot him first, the demented bastard.

"Mia, what are you doing? This is insane! You don't want to hurt us. We love you. I love you." Theo takes a step forward, his arms clenched at his sides and his eyes vigilant and prominent in his face. It's almost comical how we are all pretty much naked, and I am now holding them at gunpoint. Except it's really not, it's fucking devastating that all of this shit has led us here.

I hold my ground but point the barrel of the gun directly at Theo's chest. "You wanted control and power, Theo Saint-Lambert? I hope it keeps you warm at night when I am gone. Your choices have consequences. It's about time you learned that lesson, one I hope you never have to repeat. You are not a God. Your time as one of my kings has ended. In fact, the time of all of you being at my side has ended. This is over between us."

Outrage crosses his chiseled features, the look on his face letting me see my words are making an impact like the bullets in this gun. He can deny it all he wants, but he had to know a reckoning was coming. Anger is flowing through me, overshadowing any feelings I may have had for these fuckers. They should have known that in no world would I just allow them back into my life after all the damage they caused. This is now over. It has to be. For my sanity and maybe theirs. There are no more kings or queens of Casbury, no kingdom to return to, and no Mia and her kings.

A loud sound outside of the cabin has all of us whirling toward the large window that shows a rapidly darkening sky. Finn shifts closer and stares out, his body large, tight, and rigid. I watch him while still keeping Theo in my sightline. I don't trust him; he would take a bullet if he thought it would allow him to control me. *Let's see if he survives one to the fucking heart.*

If I'm not mistaken, that's my rescue out of this ice prison. Perfect fucking timing, grandmother! "Fucking hell, Theo. It's helicopters, closing in fast."

The sound of multiple helicopters can be heard landing outside of the cabin. I lower the gun and quickly pull a blanket off the back of the only accent chair in the space. Wrapping my body tightly in the fabric as the guys' attention focuses back on me, and I see a look of disbelief on Carter's face. Theo's looking a little pale right now. Does he understand what is about to happen?

"How?" Theo questions. His eyes widen, and his mouth sets in a hard line. He has a little twitch happening right below his right eye. You can see anger rolling through him like a fierce tidal wave. But it stands no comparison to my own. His body looks like it grows more menacing, if possible, his shoulders seem to widen and his body lengthens to its full height. *I'm not scared of you, fucker.*

"She had a tracker chip embedded under my skin after I returned. She knew what you were up to before you even tried to take me off the property. None of you are as smart or as devious as you think."

"Blondie, fuck. Why? Don't you know I love you? You are mine, and you can't fucking leave me!" Carter snarls from his position now in front of the sofa. Shit, I didn't even see him move. *Pay fucking attention, Mia, or he will trap you.*

"Killer, please. Please don't do this. Don't walk away from us."

I advance closer to Finn, my eyes blazing with furious emotion as it coils around my body like a venomous snake, wrapping me tightly in its poison. A poison that threatens to take me to my veritable knees, but I am a Stratford, and I can't allow that to happen.

I tip my head up to meet his chocolate brown eyes, the ones that, as an innocent child, I loved looking into. As a woman, I craved the heated emotion I saw in them. That is until he once again showed me who he truly is deep inside. A liar, a backstabber, and no friend of mine.

I grab onto his jaw, letting my nails sink into the skin and forcing a hitch of his breath in his chest. I loathe him and all that he has done to me repeatedly. How his betrayal stings deeper than the others. I want him to see that loathing in my eyes so he understands the damage he has caused.

"You walked away from me first, Finn, all those years ago. I wasn't good enough then for you. You betrayed me back then, and you did it once again when you had the opportunity to stand at my side. You took their side; you will always take their side." I sniff, forcing myself to hold back the emotions that are trying to overrun my senses. "You are a Judas, Finn, and no friend or love of mine."

The front door slams open, and Clark stands there, pointing a rifle toward us. I can see Tom outside the door and more men circling the house, all dressed in full tactical gear as if they were prepared for a war. The kings stand frozen, shock across their faces at the violent intrusion. What did they honestly think was going to happen here? They idiotically believed that they could win against a Stratford? It's pitful how fucking stupid they can be when ruled by their emotions. *Hey Mia, not twenty minutes ago, you were letting all four of those fuckers dick you down, so pot meet kettle, bitch.*

"Miss Mia, it's time to return to the safety of your home and your grandmother." Theo moves forward, and Clark points the gun right at his head.

"I wouldn't, boy. You have caused more than enough trouble. I might like you, but that won't stop me from putting a bullet in that skull of yours if you try anything. That goes for all of you. Mrs. Stratford has instructed us to shoot you if you try to stop Mia from leaving here."

Shoot-to-kill orders? Stella must have woken up cranky when whatever they gave us wore off. She doesn't sound like she's sympathetic to them anymore. Oh well, they don't deserve her mercy anyway. If she doesn't shoot them, there is a massive chance that I might.

I search for my shoes but don't find them. A pair of large warm, looking snow boots sits next to the door. I slip them on, they're way too big, but they will have to do. Right now, my priority is to get the fuck out of here and away from the kings of Casbury. I approach the door, and Mateo's voice calls out, sounding utterly shattered.

"Mia, please! *Mami,* take me with you. Please don't leave me behind. I...I can't live without you!"

I turn back in his direction and get my first real glimpse of his long slim body that is riddled with so many fresh cuts, all done in neat little lines across his stomach, hips, and thighs. What the fuck has he been doing to himself? Is he cutting himself because of his anxiety, because I was missing? Is some part of what he is saying true? Does he care more than the rest ever have? I almost waver; the desire to wrap my arms around him and soothe his obvious distress rides me hard, but I force myself to remain where I am. I know he struggles with his mental health, and after everything that he experienced at Vincent's hands, it is probably much worse than it was before. Yet I must remember that he rebuked me when I tried to take care of and comfort him. No, he didn't just rebuke me, he utterly embarrassed me in my own home in his choosing of someone else. His regrets are his own, and I will not absolve him of them.

"What happened to June, Mateo?" I question with a raised eyebrow and a lifted chin. My one hand clutches tightly to the gun still in my grip, while the other holds onto the blanket in a death grip, using it as a shield between us.

"She's gone." His voice comes out small, desolate, and solemn. Is that regret I hear? Fuck him; I am no one's second choice.

"Well then, I guess you lost us both, then, didn't you." I don't hesitate again to move toward the door, giving the kings my back.

"This isn't over, Mia! It will never be over between us! You are mine!" Theo shouts.

I pause for a moment, my feet stalling on the door's threshold. The cold air meets my face and helps to clear my head. Maybe once I would have desired to hear those exact words ripped from his chest. They would have brought me immense satisfaction. Now all they bring me is pain.

There is nothing left of *us* now. No kings and Mia. No, Mia and Theo. There isn't even anything left of Amelia Hamilton. I am hollowed out from the inside, all my fragmented pieces having turned to dust. I move toward the running helicopter that is waiting to transport me back to the safety of my grandmother and to my lonely new beginning. Tom ushers me quickly inside, and I force myself not to look back, but I hear a commotion at the door before a couple of shots ring out. *Don't look, Mia, don't look.* My mind begs me.

The helicopter is up in the air, within moments of me sitting inside of it, with an agitated Tom piling more heavy blankets on top of me. My glance back down at the ground shows me the other helicopter with Clark and more of my grandmother's men lifting off and following us in our wake.

Four semi-naked figures stand against the harsh glare of sparkling white snow. Looking smaller and smaller as we make our way further away from them. My heart tightens painfully in my chest as I tear my gaze away from them and stare at the mountains of ice around me. Like them, I, too, will be frozen, formidable, and utterly removed from my emotions. It's time I took my place at my grandmother's side and became an ice queen in waiting.

There is nothing left for me here now.

CHAPTER 34

Finn

"There is no person so severely punished, as those who subject themselves to the whip of their own remorse." Lucius Annaeus Seneca

I t took us almost twelve days to get back to Casbury. Stella, the witch, had paid Captain Toestoo not to come and get us as planned when the first week was out. In fact, Carter had to promise to buy his damn boat off of him and order him three new snowmobiles before the fucker would relent and come and retrieve us. We were down to rations by then. Theo and I had to travel over two miles trudging through frozen tundra to cut down some trees for firewood and bring it back just so we could stay warm. I couldn't wait to get the fuck out of that frozen desolate land.

The time in confined captivity with the guys did not go well, as you can imagine. Carter pretty much lost his shit the minute Mia got on the helicopter. In fact, Clark had to shoot at him to prevent him from trying to get on his helicopter and following Mia. I wonder if the fucker actually missed on purpose or not? My bet is on not.

We finally had to admit defeat after she was a mere blimp in the night sky. We returned to the cabin's interior, resigning ourselves to the fact that she left all four of us behind without even a look back. It caused devastation in all of us. I thought my heart had felt real pain when I lost her the first time when we were kids, then when she was taken, but in reality, it is nothing like the vision of her walking away from me willingly. Her truthful words spoken with the intent of hurting me is like acid in my veins. She's right to call me a betrayer. *I am.* I will have to live with that destructive and painful knowledge for the rest of my life.

The minute we got inside and I got a good look at an abandoned Mateo, I lost my shit again. He didn't even attempt to hide what he had done to himself, so lost in his grief at being left behind and at Mia's sharp barb about June. The fucker has been self-harming to cope with his anxiety and depression. I think the only reason that Theo and Carter didn't end up taking their frustrations out on each other is because we had Mateo to focus on to ensure the fucker didn't hurt himself further.

Forty-seven cuts. That's how many lines Mateo has drawn on his skin since Mia was taken. Some were in the process of healing, others more recent and still prone to bleeding, and some already healed and scarred on his golden skin. He confessed that it was either self-harm with the shaving blade to try to get some relief from his emotions or he was going to throw himself into the ocean and end his life. Just the thought that he could have done that, that he felt the need to go that far has a permanent chill down my spine. It's also a reminder of Mia's impact on our lives and how we will never be the same without her.

If he was struggling before, now that Mia is genuinely gone and ended things with us, he is beside himself. He had barely spoken to us and had refused to eat for the miserable, inconceivable days we spent waiting for a return to civilization. I had to force food and water down his throat while Theo and Carter held him down. It was beyond fucked up.

He spent the majority of the time waiting, sleeping, and wrapped in a thick blanket on the floor near the fire in the room Mia had occupied. All the light has gone out in his green eyes; all that remains now are shadows. Will he try to end his life if we can't get Mia to forgive us? Only time will tell, but I am determined to make that an impossibility with my vigilance.

Now that we are back in Casbury, our first and only destination is Mia's house. We need to desperately try to convince her to give each of us another chance. One that I am absolutely not hopeful that she will indulge us with. When she left us, her actions and words seemed final and resounding. They did so much damage with their apathy. It not only bruised the beating organ inside my chest, it smashed pieces off of it when the girl I love acted like I meant nothing to her. I should crawl into a deep dark hole and let myself die at her lack of feelings toward me.

Fuck that, though. I am a motherfucking king of Casbury, and she is my queen. I will never give up on her. She wants to punish me; let her. I will bow willingly at her feet for the rest of my life, as long as I can choke her with my cock and keep her with me. Mia underestimates the lengths that I will go to have her. The kings of Casbury will stop at nothing to reclaim our queen.

When we reach her gate, it's closed to us. *Of course, it is!* Did we really think she would give us access to her? I watch as Tom walks toward us with a cold, calculating look and stops on the other side of the thick iron gate. His gaze assesses each of us before giving us a dismissive look. A look that makes my blood pressure skyrocket, as it relays vividly that he doesn't think we are a threat. Fuck him; I'm a massive threat to him or anyone else that tries to keep Mia from me. If he would just open this gate, he would find out firsthand from my fist.

"Tom, let us in; we need to talk to her," I demand, trying to control my raging temper. My shoulders are stiff and heavy, like a herd of elephants are just sitting on them. My neck is in a stiff knot, and I can feel a muscle twitching in my jaw.

"No can do, Finn. You and your merry men are now barred from the property per Mrs. Stratford and Mia's orders. In fact, all your belongings have been sent off to your parent's house, Finn." Although the fucker doesn't actually grin at his words of dejection, there is a look of satisfaction in his eyes. The need to put my massive fist to his jaw is a living, breathing desire within me. I'll knock that smugness right off his aged face when I make him eat his teeth.

"I demand to speak to Mia, Tom. She can't just avoid us. She's fucking ours." Theo rattles the bars of the gate, his face growing tight and his features murderous. He's getting closer and closer to losing his precious control. The one he prides himself of. Who am I kidding? We all are. Except maybe Carter; that fool never had any, to begin with. This situation has become tedious and unbearable for all four of us.

"Tom, is she alright? Please, I just need to know that she is okay. Can you just tell her that I care about her? Can you bring her here so I can see that she is okay?" Mateo begs. The sound and tone of his voice are so fractured and painful that it has my own chest tightening. *Jesus, fuck, he is falling completely apart.*

Carter, the fucker is making me really nervous. He keeps pacing back and forth like a caged lion behind us. Stopping and staring up at the gate, mumbling shit to himself and then pacing again. That unstable idiot is up to something. His mental state is way past crazy at this point. I fear for everyone's safety around us. The gun at my back is a reassuring shape in case I have to shoot him to stop him from doing something reckless.

It also doesn't help that his brother from another mother, Diego, the snake, has disappeared and is not answering his phone for him. Poor Carter; he seems to be losing everyone he loves. Will all this shit push him over the edge that he straddles daily? Will I have to shoot one of my best friends to keep him from hurting himself or others?

"You can demand whatever you want, Saint-Lambert; it means shit. The fact of the matter is you boys got yourselves into this mess all by yourselves. If you're angry, look in the mirror, you spoiled shits. Leave that girl alone. You've done enough damage to her over the years." He turns his back on us and walks back up the driveway, motioning to the guard at the gate to activate the electric fence.

Smart fucker, he must know that Carter is a breath away from scaling it to get to Mia. Fuck, I'm not even sure the high voltage will be that much of a deterrent to the crazy fuck.

"THIS IS NOT OVER, TOM! SHE BELONGS TO ME! I WILL NEVER LET HER GO!" Carter shouts at the gate, rage across all his features as his gray-blue eyes burn with an interior fire.

"What do we do now? She won't even let us through the gates." Mateo's weary voice sounds from behind me. I turn to watch him lean back against my Caddy with his arms tightly wrapped around himself. His head is lowered, his eyes trained on the ground before him. He looks pale again, fuck. If Mia could just see his state, maybe she would at least forgive him. She's always understood his mental health issues. Right now, I am so worried that he's going to do something that there will be no return from.

"We don't give up. This is Mia pissed off at us. She has a right to be angry but not to leave us." Theo runs his fingers through his hair in agitation as he paces back and forth in front of me.

"What if she never lets us back into her life? I...I won't survive watching her from afar, Theo." Mateo sighs with a deep shudder.

"She will never be free of us. Never. I will follow her to the end of the world if I have to. I will tie her stubborn, reckless ass up and fuck her raw until she can't fucking breathe. She is mine, and no one gets to take her from me, not even herself." Theo gets in the car, the rest of us follow suit, and we head to my parents' house to devise a strategy to get our girl back.

Fuck, I hope it's not one that gets us all killed. *Is she worth dying for?* My mind questions. Yes. She's also worth living for.

CHAPTER 35

Mia

"Even in the grave, all is not lost." Edgar Allan Poe

"**G**irl, are you sure about this?" Raegan asks me for the fourth time as she gets into the passenger seat of my Range.

Honestly, her questioning is valid. It's also fucking annoying. No, I'm not sure about anything right now. My chest is aching, I can't freaking sleep, and my heart calls out for four useless fuckers that have only continuously hurt me. But I can't say that shit out loud to anyone. It would be weak and would guarantee to have my grandmother strong-arm me into leaving right this second for Manhattan, and I still have shit to do here in Casbury.

"Rae, I can't hide in my castle anymore. I need to return to Casbury Prep to put things in order before I head back to Manhattan. Once those maggots know I have left and there is no one controlling them anymore, it will revert to chaos. Plus, I want to say goodbye to Jessie, Evan, and Spencer in person."

It's been two weeks since I returned to Casbury from Canada. Two fricken weeks since I left the kings behind on that frozen plain and ran for the safety of my home and grandmother. Time filled with turmoil, pain, indecision, and acceptance. If I am honest with myself, I left the largest part of my heart behind with them.

I returned to my house only to find an irate Stella, Raegan, and our security detail present, my sister having "*apparently*" returned to New York during the chaos. Except the sly little fox never made it there, and conveniently Diego Cabano is also missing. I should be relieved that Stella is now occupied hunting the two of them down before they make her a great-grandmother. At least her focus isn't on watching my heart rupture and my resolve trying to pick itself up from the trampled dirt.

"What about the kings? You know, the minute they hear you are at the school, they are gonna make an appearance to try to get to you. They are not going to stop, girl. They haven't even stopped coming to the gate day after day, even with Tom's threats to shoot them." A devious smirk crosses her lips at the thought of Tom shooting the kings. I even found her trying to bribe him with chocolate brownies to shoot Carter in the leg. I roll my eyes at her antics, bless her, she at least keeps me from crying.

"Those hounds won't let you go so easily. They are going to keep trying till the cows come home. They believe to their very core that you belong to them." She stares at me with her striking green eyes and stunning mane of loose curly hair surrounding her face. She is so beautiful, inside and out. She is a diamond amongst nothing but harsh pieces of coal. No one has brought me more joy and peace than this girl right here. *My ride or die forever.* The one that will always have my back and be a warrior at my side. My sister and grandmother are a very close second.

Raegan may not be my blood sister, but she will always be the sister of my heart. She helped nurse me back to life after I came back from James' clutches, and she has been my rock since I returned from the frozen north and the kings' kidnapping attempt. An attempt she was furious about and threatened to murder all of them for. I have no doubt that if Raegan gets her vicious little hands on any of them, they are going to be feeling some severe pain.

I love her and am so glad and honored that she has decided to take the next step and come with me to Manhattan. This is the last week at Casbury Prep;

graduation is literally in four days. All of us are technically graduating, regardless of our attendance, even the fucking kings, Stella's last gift to them. Stella Stratford demanded it in her queen voice, and I am sure the school principal bowed at her feet, just like everyone else. The power she wields is intoxicating and alarming all at the same time.

My decision to return to Manhattan after this week wasn't made lightly. I came to Casbury with a purpose and a plan, neither of which I really managed to accomplish. Falling in love with the tormentors of my past certainly wasn't one of them. *Jeeze, you fucking think?* The snide bitch in my head cackles.

Yet despite everything that has happened. All the pain, misery, and new scars on my soul, I wouldn't have changed a thing. Well, that's technically not true. I would have changed what happened with James, *fuck him. I hope he's rotting somewhere.* I just need to move on from the kings. To put some much-needed distance between us and focus on healing my mind and heart. *You'll never get over them,* my heart whispers. *We can try,* my mind retaliates.

The look on all four of their faces as I left them naked in that cabin after they fucked my brains out will haunt me for all of my days. Their demands that I return to them and stay with them run rampant in my head, day and night. I almost lost myself to them once, I won't allow myself to fall again.

They would consume and spit me back out when they are done with me. *They love us.* Do they? I am not sure that any of them even understand what that entails. They are all so broken inside, and so am I. All our various scars are open and bleeding. The large gaping holes are so intermixed that we can no longer determine who is actually bleeding out from all the wounds.

I am Mia Stratford; that name means something. I am an heir to a fortune and an empire. The granddaughter of a queen and a badass bitch. I forgot that along the way, saving these kings of Casbury. I felt too much for each of them, fell too quickly at their demands and feet, and they took too many parts of me until I didn't recognize myself. It's time I remedied that and found myself again.

"I will not be dissuaded, Rae. What was between all of us is over. Their demands will fall on deaf ears. They will be forced to realize that I don't want nor do I need them."

"Bless your heart, girl." I take my eyes off the driveway in front of us to stare at her. I catch a look in her eye, one of genuine care but another hint of something else. She doesn't fully believe that I will stick to what I am saying. Before I can tell her that she's wrong, that little hint in her eye changes quickly to that of humor. "You know that Carter tried to scale the back fence just last night, right? Heavens to Betsy! Thomas, one of the guards, was reporting it to Clark this morning, and I heard all about it. It took four of them to take him down. Not sure how you're going to manage to tell that shit for brains you're not interested. He's got gumption and the persistence of a blood tick; I'll give the fucker that."

Great! I, in fact, did not know about his most recent attempt to get to me. "Shit, it's only a matter of time before Stella tells the guards to shoot him." My lips twitch, but I refuse to laugh. It's funny, but it's also serious. He needs to stop before he gets himself seriously hurt. *Why do I care? Let him get hurt. Serves him right.*

A snort leaves her lips as she sits back, and I drive us down my long driveway and through my fortified gate with Tom, my faithful bodyguard, right behind me in his vehicle.

A slight apprehension fills me at leaving the safety of my home. This is yet another reason that I need to go back. I can't live like this, fearful of my own shadow. Afraid someone is going to take me and hurt me at every turn. Yes, James might still be out there, and there are enemies behind every corner. I still need to be able to live, though. I need to regain my strength so I can be the badass bitch Stella has raised Issy and me to be. Cowering behind my high gate will not help me.

"Okay, Mia, whatever you say. Just know, girl, that I will a hundred percent smack them around if they try to retake you. I swear it from my hand to Jesus. Also, Tom gave me a blade." She wiggles her defined eyebrows like a cartoon character, pulls out a small sheathed blade, and waves it around. "I can't wait to stab Carter with it when he gets on my nerves!" She cackles like an evil old witch, and it pulls a giggle from my throat.

Lovefool by Twocolors starts playing through the radio, and Raegan lets out a huge belly laugh. "Might be your song, girlie." I try to ignore her as the song lyrics wash over me and cause my chest to tighten. She might be right, and that makes everything even more painful to bear.

All too soon, we are pulling into the school's parking lot, and I watch as all eyes turn in our direction. *Deja vu much?* Why again did I need to return to this parasite environment? Shit, this already sucks, and I haven't even stepped foot inside the building.

Freedom, yes, we were going to regain our freedom. Are you sure that's it, or is it the possibility of seeing four specific, obnoxious assholes in the flesh and sparring with them so that you feel alive? Nope, definitely the first option. I park and then sit in the car for a moment, steadying my breath, and forcing my thoughts to clear and focus on what needs to happen next. *Be strong bitch! Head held high. You are a motherfucking reigning queen.*

"You know you don't have to do this, girl. We can just head to Manhattan early. I don't care about any of these people, Mia."

I close my eyes and lean my head back for a moment. I can do this. I was strong once; I came here prepared to do battle with not only the kings but with all these maggots. I have to stop living in the past and allowing my trauma to dictate my future. I refuse to be held hostage by it. I open my eyes and stare out the passenger window. I tell myself I am not looking for any of their vehicles, and I almost manage to convince myself that it's true.

Tom's car pulls into the parking spot behind mine, and he stares at me through the window. His thoughts are clearly on display. He doesn't like this one bit. He would have rather I not return to Casbury, never mind my decree that he not follow me inside or intervene if the kings make an appearance. I need to fight my own battles so that I can regain my strength. Otherwise, I will always be broken and looking over my shoulder.

A large body moves in our direction and stands at my driver's door. His goofy grin and joyful, bright blue eyes greet me. *Jessie.* Why couldn't I have fallen in love with him? My life would have been easier and happier if I had. I open my door, and before I even have a chance to do more than step out of my seat, I am crushed in his tight, teddy bear embrace and pulled right off my feet.

Fuck, I had forgotten what a big boy Jessie is. All that packed-on muscle is now pressed firmly against every inch of me. I should feel attracted to him, I was once upon a time, when I first came here, but now everything is muted and dull. He doesn't bring out the same sensations that they do. *We have to forget them, move on, and re-find ourselves.*

"Fuck, Mia, I am so happy to see you." His scent envelops me, and I allow myself to melt into his tight embrace for a moment. It soothes my injured soul to know he truly cares about me. His lips place a delicate kiss on the top of my head, brushing my hair back with such a soft caress that a small smile tries to peek across my lips. He shifts me back on my feet but doesn't release his hold on me, almost like he fears I might disappear again if he does. I crane my neck and see a look of genuine happiness across his chiseled features.

"Shit on a cracker, boy. Have you gotten even larger?" Raegan calls from the other side of the vehicle.

Jessie gives her a smile filled with sunshine. "Hey Rae, girl, it is so nice to see you too! Evan is going to be beside himself when he gets a look at you." He waggles his adorable eyebrows in Raegan's direction, who scowls at his statement.

Hmm, maybe Rae is no longer into Evan cause she's missing some rich, entitled blond asshole who up and left her behind when he took his ass back to Manhattan without a fucking word. I will fix Raven with a blade in his gut when I return to the East Coast for hurting my girl.

We move away from the SUV, heading towards the courtyard stairs. Jessie's arm wrapped snugly around my shoulder, its heavy weight somehow comforting. For a brief moment, my mind blares at me. *It's the wrong arm, attached to the wrong body, touching us.* I disregard it; I need to stop thinking about them. There is no future there, only pain waiting to befall me.

I can see Spencer waving down at me from the top of the stairs, a shy look across his features. I wave back, and it brings a bit of joy to my soul to see him not hiding and here to greet me. I always liked the guy, even when he couldn't stand up for me. I get it; not everyone has a Stella Stratford behind them like I do.

However, the feeling of so many different pairs of eyes on me makes my skin crawl. All of the student body is congregated in the front courtyard, watching and waiting for whatever happens next. These maggots seek drama, only content when bad shit is happening. Have they come to welcome back their queen? Somehow I doubt most of them are happy to see me. Quite a few meet my eyes and nod or smile; others hold my gaze and don't look away. Suspicion immediately rises within me at their actions.

The loud screech of tires echoes in the parking lot as a black Cadillac races across the asphalt and stops suddenly, the smell of burning rubber permeating the warm air around us. They don't even attempt to park in a regulated spot, just leaving the car haphazardly in the way of other vehicles. Doors open and close quickly, and then there they are, standing in all their malicious glory. *The kings of Casbury.* My heart jumps painfully in my chest at seeing them before me.

Carter is the first to stroll forward, anger and destruction evident across his features. His eyes zeroed in on Jessie's arm wrapped around me. I watch with amusement as his body goes rigid, and his fists clench as Jessie angles his large body slightly in front of me. Putting himself as a human shield between me and the kings. *Jessie has grown brave.*

"You better fucking move that arm away from my girl before I tear it off your body, asshole." Carter snarls.

"Listen to me, you psychotic, reckless bastard. She's not yours. You need to leave her the fuck alone, Carter. You four have caused her enough pain." Just then, a few of the other football players move forward, standing with Jessie along the steps and apparently backing him up against the kings. *Oh my, how the tables have turned since we have been away.*

"What the fuck is this?" Finn steps up and observes all the scowling faces staring menacingly back at him. "Y'all think you're doing what exactly?" He folds his thick arms across his dark green T-shirt, his chocolate brown eyes filled with venom as his tall, stocky body stands ready to lunge forward and attack Jessie and the other guys.

My mouth waters at the way he looks, filled with rage. *He is one fine-looking man, delicious, really.* It's just too bad he was never concerned with loyalty to me. It could have been him by my side. *Fucking traitor.* I look away from him, unwilling to risk him being able to read my thoughts.

"You four need to go. You're no longer welcome here." Evan steps up with his arms crossed and an angry glare directed at the kings. More bodies step up and stand united with Jessie, all of them blocking the kings' access to Raegan and me. Well, shit, look at my little army. I almost want to laugh out loud, except inside, I'm really crying. What's left of my heart is trudging through nothing but piles and piles of ash.

"Have you fuckers lost your damn minds? We are your motherfucking kings, asswipes!" Carter yells with conviction. His angry eyes try to meet mine, but I avoid his gaze. I can feel Theo's sharp glare searing a hole into my head, but I don't give him what he wants. *Acknowledgment, attention, my fucking soul.*

"There are no kings here anymore, fucker. That is ancient folklore. This school has one queen, and she doesn't share her power with anyone." Jessie replies as he wraps me more firmly in his arms. I watch the vein in Carter's neck throb quickly. His face is filled with rage, his husky eyes crazed. He's a moment away from taking all of them on, regardless of the odds being stacked against him.

"Careful, Mia, instigating a bloodbath upon your return would not be a smart move." Theo's voice rings out with a clear threat. I hear a few people mumbling with the fear that he can still instill.

A curly-haired fairy flies down the steps, and before anyone can stop her, a loud crack sounds in the air. "You are a cancer, Carter Pemberton. All four of you are a poison waiting to destroy everything you touch. Stay away from my girl, or I promise you, my face will be the last you see before you take your last breath."

She doesn't wait for a reply as she moves back to my side and grabs onto my arm. Carter stands there gawking at her, silent for once, his cheek red with the imprint of her palm. No one moves, stunned at Raegan's actions and waiting for the events to escalate more. "Mia," Theo calls my name, and I finally meet his gaze.

Dark midnight blue eyes meet mine like sparkling sapphires glowing in a night sky. He has dark purple shadows under his eyes, letting me know he's not sleeping any more than I am. More than a day's worth of dark stubble graces his high cheekbones, and his full red lips are in a tight straight line. He's wearing a dark red Henley that accentuates his large, broad chest, arms, and trim waist; dark blue jeans encase his long, strong legs and are finished off with a pair of white Jordans. *He looks sinful.*

Anger and displeasure are evident in every inch of his body. My chest tightens painfully, the desire to run my hands over his face and hair and smooth the angry lines across his features, tries to pull me in that direction, but I hold firm, keeping my feet frozen to the step I'm occupying. Sweat beads and trickles down my back, inside of my shirt, and I clench my fists until my nails sting the skin of my palm. The only signs of my unease. "Think very carefully about what you are doing, my little, wicked queen. You know very well who you belong to, and this game you are playing is dangerous."

An evil smirk graces my lips as I move around Jessie's body and meet Theo's stare head-on. Jessie, who apparently has a death wish, places his hand around the curve of my waist. I don't fight the hold; instead, I allow my fingers to trail along Jessie's arm. Theo's eyes are riveted to every move I make, the anger in them egging me on.

I will have to have a discussion after this with my little football player, slash new knight in shining armor, that has apparently found his backbone, about his actions and whether he understands the consequences of them. Is this an act of support, a declaration of possession, or a jab at the kings to incite them? I won't be a yo-yo between any of them.

"You're right, Saint-Lambert. I do know who I belong to, and it's not any of you. It's my fucking self. Don't threaten me, Theo. Stronger and more malicious demons than you have tried to end me, and I am still right fucking here. Standing. Breathing. Ready to take on all comers. But you know your part in that already, don't you?"

"Don't do this, *mami*, please," Mateo begs. His olive green eyes are too large in a face filled with sorrow. My elf king, he looks even worse than Theo does. His face looks gaunt, his lips dry and bleeding from the grip his teeth have on them. The white fitted top he wears is loose on his frame, and his shoulders look like they are caving in on himself.

He looks like a fragment of my once proud Mateo. Have I done that to him? Am I the reason he looks like that, that he is suffering? Maybe they are not the only poison here; perhaps I am as much a poison as they are. The image of all those lines cut into his skin pops into my mind and has my breath stalling in my throat.

NO! I need to get away from them. I need to breathe, and I can't when they are in front of me. *We are weak.* Raegan threads her fingers through mine, tightening her hold and pulling me back from my morose thoughts. "Let's go, Mia. There is nothing worth seeing out here."

Jessie wraps his whole arm around me, turning us away from the kings and escorting me and Raegan up the stairs. A quick look back shows me the rest of the football players closing ranks on the stairs, blocking the path to me, and shutting the kings out so they can't follow me. *Small mercies, I guess.* It looks like I now have a willing army.

"Watch your back, Jessie. I'm coming for you, motherfucker!" Carter yells loudly.

I'm going to need all the strength and help I can get, to survive through this week intact. I will persevere, though, I am Mia fucking Stratford, and no one is bringing me to my knees again.

CHAPTER 36
Carter

"Suffering whispers, shouts, and screams the story no one wants to remember: we are not in control, and we are all going to die." K.J. Ramsey, This Too Shall Last: Finding Grace When Suffering Lingers

"I'm going to kill that fucking weasel! I'm going to murder all of them and throw their bloated fucking bodies in pieces into the damn ocean for the sharks to eat!" I run both my hands through my hair in agitation. I can feel a fucking tic starting in my jaw, the twitching causing my blood pressure to rise even higher. "Naw, fuck that! I am going to mount their traitorous heads on pikes outside the gates of my house as a warning to others!"

I pace back and forth in the front courtyard of Casbury Prep, my eyes seeing nothing but a red haze and the monster that lives inside of me, begging to be released from his confines to seek retribution and destruction on those that would try to keep my blondie from me. My beast rages that some other man's hands have been on her, that someone else had the sheer audacity to touch her. He needs to fucking die a painful death. SHE'S FUCKING MINE!

"Carter, you need to calm down. We can't do anything reckless. We have to be smart about how we play this." Finn sighs from the top of the hood of his car. I turn my furious gaze on him. How the fuck is he just sitting there calmly while our girl is inside with that fucker's hands touching her. I need to rip Jessie's fucking head painfully off his shoulders; that will teach him to covet something that is mine.

"Reckless? The fucker just threatened everyone here with a painful death right after she walked into the school with that asswipe, Jessie. I think we are past the point of recklessness. We will be lucky if he's not arrested by the end of the day." Theo groans loudly from his position on the bottom step.

I'm going to break every one of Jessie's fingers one by one, then shatter his wrist and dislocate his elbow and shoulder before I flay every single piece of skin that made contact with my girl. I will take a blade to his fucking tongue and cut that malicious organ out before I make him choke on it for talking to us the way he did. Then I'm going to poke out his fucking eyes for even looking at her. *MY FUCKING GIRL!* She is mine. He doesn't get to defend her or touch her. She belongs to me.

Mia will watch me do it all; I'll fucking make sure of it so that when I serve him broken, bloody, and beaten at her feet, she knows she allowed it to happen. Sanctioned him to touch her without a word of reproach and with that look of rage on her face. My fucking girl, the one that wants to see me lose my ever-fucking mind. She permitted him to wrap his arm around her, touching places that are mine on her body. *All of her is mine.*

She won't go unscathed without punishment for her actions. My anger is a living thing, and it demands satisfaction with my cock choking off her fucking airway. Even when she begs for mercy, and she will beg in that wrathful voice of hers, I won't give her any. I'll fuck each of her holes brutally over and over again until she passes the fuck out, and even then, I won't stop. Not until she has my fucking name branded across her beautiful skin so everyone can see my ownership of her. I pick up a nearby garbage can and launch it at the front lawn of the courtyard. It does nothing to soothe my heated rage. Nothing will except reclaiming her. "FUCK!"

My gaze lands on Mateo sitting on the ground. I don't think he has said a single word since she left us out here like discarded trash. His knees are raised, and his head is bent low between them. I can see his chest rapidly moving up and down. Is he crying? Fuck! Is he having a panic attack right now? My heart thunders in my chest, and fear races down my spine. The lines cut across his body make me nervous. While I rage outwardly, expressing myself with violence on others and any object that I encounter. Mateo does internal damage to himself. Of the two of us, the way he handles pain is much scarier.

"Jesus, Mateo! Fuck. Breathe buddy! Please!" Finn calls. "Mat, I need you to take some deep breaths, alright? Let's remember to do what the therapist taught us, okay? We are going to look for five things we can see" I kneel down and rub his shoulders, trying to force him to lift his head and take deep breaths with me. He finally raises his head and looks around. "Okay, now, four things you can touch." His eyes search around us, and I see some of the tightness on his face easing. We sit there for a while until I hear him mimicking my deep inhale and exhale.

"You're doing great, Mat; now, three things you can hear." Mateo's shoulders drop from around his ears, and he unclenches his jaw. I feel his body coming down from the racing panic. I also recognize that it's helping my own anger to slowly deflate. "Two things you can smell, Mat." I watch as he closes his eyes, and his chest rises and falls with less strain. "Now, one thing you can taste, Mateo."

"Does Mia's pussy count? Cause I swear I can still taste it." A chuckle leaves my lips at his response. "Yeah, it counts."

Fuck that was an excellent idea of Finn's to take Mateo to that therapist the day after we returned from Canada. I'm glad that he insisted all of us attend a session with him so that we could understand how to help Mateo when he's in this state. After his chilling words in the cabin about wanting to end his life, I am more determined now to make sure he never has the chance.

"Mat, we need you to try to stay calm. I know it's not easy right now with all the shit that is going on. The doc said the meds would work. You need to take them." Theo sits next to him on the ground, his eyes watching Mateo intently. He, too, looks like shit. *Fuck, all of us do.*

How can one fucking woman have this kind of power over us? One pretty dirty blonde with beautiful eyes and a body made for my most sinful, erotic dreams. One I can't seem to stay away from and have zero self-preservation against. If you told me a year ago that this would be my life. The life that is falling fucking completely and devastatingly apart because I fell in love with a chick. I would have pointed you in the direction of the nearest psychiatric hospital and laughed in your face. No one woman was worth any of that stress except, as it turns out, Mia is. She is the exception to every fucking rule.

Here I now sit out in the courtyard of a school I no longer rule, with my three best friends, who are as devastated as I am. Having just survived numerous attempts on our lives and sanities by fucking satan and his spawn. While the girl all four of us are in love with and are willing to share is inside, dismissing us, and allowing another motherfucker to touch her.

"You know what will make you feel better, Matty?" Mateo's green eyes rise to mine, and I see the desperation in them. He's lost, shattered on the inside, and the one person that can bring him peace is acting like an irrational bitch right now. *Lies! You know she is justified. You just don't like her tactics, asshole. You four deserve everything you're getting and so much more!* The snide voice in my head cackles.

Naw, my queen is playing fucking games with what's left of our minds. Does she not know that I have literally nothing left to lose? The only things in my world I care about are her, my fellow kings, yeah, even Theo the fucker, and my baby brother. The rest means nothing to me. She's also forgotten that I live for chaos and mayhem. *Maybe it's time I reminded her.*

"W...what?" He takes a deep breath, and I see genuine curiosity in his eyes. My boy here needs a way to channel that inner turmoil. An outlet, if you will, one that bleeds. An evil grin crosses my face. I'm about to give him a target.

"Beating the living fuck out of that smug bastard, Jessie. That will make you feel a hundred percent better." I waggle my thick eyebrows at him and finally see a smirk cross his elfen features. I'd tease him about being so pretty right now, but I doubt he's in the mood to spar with me. *Naw, I want all his anger directed at Jessie.*

"He's right. I hate to fuckin' admit it, 'cause Carter should never be right...but knocking that fucker down to the ground and making him bleed will make all of us feel better." Finn gets up from his sprawled-out position on top of the car and gives Mateo his hand, tugging him from the ground before doing the same for Theo and me.

"What do you suggest?" Theo questions, for once taking a backseat to Finn. I'm honestly surprised that the fucker is not already scheming and forcing us to follow along. Maybe Mia's words back at the cabin had a significant impact on him, or perhaps that control freak that lives inside of him is just biding his time.

"Jessie wants to play at being a white knight? We are about to storm the fucking castle. I'm not giving up my kingship or my girl to that asshole, and anyone else that gets in my way will end up as collateral damage. I have nothing to lose if Mia is truly gone." Finn drags his hands down his face and across his neck, his head cocked to the side, and his tone clipped.

"Fuck yes! Let's go in there and wreak mayhem!" I shout, already moving up the steps and cracking my knuckles.

"What about Tom?" Mateo asks with concern. I look back and stare at the man glaring at us through the windshield of his car. He watched the whole scene go down. Mia dismissing us, that fucker touching her, and even Rae's violent actions, which by the fucking way, my face is still stinging from. Little hellion packs a wallop in that hand of hers. All the while, he never even got out of the car. I raise both my hands and give him a middle finger salute so that he can clearly see what I think about him. "Fuck Tom. He can eat my dick."

"Where the fuck are you going, you unhinged fucker?" Theo bellows from behind me.

"To reclaim my blondie and teach her a fucking lesson about who she belongs to." I hear their footsteps racing up the stairs behind me. Classes started an hour ago, while the four of us stayed outside licking our veritable wounds like beaten dogs. Fuck that; I am no one's bitch. I'm done holding back. There is no threat, not even from Mia herself, that will prevent me from getting to her.

I lose the guys in the hallway, taking the necessary turns to get where I am going. I have been stuck in purgatory, my heaven out of reach and hell refusing me entry. A genuine smile crosses my face at the anticipation of the fight Mia is going to put up. She's anger and wrath personified, and I am a moth to her flame. I couldn't stay away from her even if I wanted to, and I fucking don't.

I head towards Mia's second-period class, *American Civil History*. If my memory serves me right, and of course, it fucking does when it's about my girl. She always makes a pitstop in the girls' washroom before heading to that class. It's about time I had a word with my wrathful queen one-on-one behind a locked door where she has no way to escape me and no one to save her.

I slip into the empty washroom and wait behind the door. Yeah, yeah, I know. I'm a creepy motherfucker, but only for my girl. I hear the bell signal the end of the first period, and I hope to fuck; I'm not wrong, and she sticks to her habits. Rae's not in that class with her, so here's hoping I don't have to deal with that banshee at the same time.

Rae is getting brazen, attacking me nonstop. The only thing preventing me from teaching her a lesson is the knowledge that Mia will one hundred percent shank my ass if I do. It might be worth it just to see her eyes light up when she hurts me. Fuck, and now my cock is getting hard at the thought of Mia beating on me.

I hear noises out in the hallway; the classrooms have allowed their captives to escape. The loud sounds of laughing and locker doors opening and closing reach my straining ears. What the fuck am I going to do if another girl besides Mia comes in here first? *Deal with that shit as it happens; no one is keeping us away from our girl.*

The door slides open, and a brunette with glasses perched on her nose walks inside the bathroom. She doesn't notice me behind the door until she is almost at one of the stalls. She must spy me out of the corner of her eye 'cause a sharp gasp leaves her lips. I grab her and push her firmly up against the wall next to the door, my forearm digging into her neck. Her breath leaves her lips in a panicked squeak. Pretty sure her name is Sandra, Sandy, fuck it, it's something that starts with an "S." I think she might have even sucked my cock once after a football game last year before my little queen arrived and tore my world apart.

It doesn't matter who she is. If she screams right now, she will alert Mia to my presence, and I can't have that. I need to get Mia alone. "If you make one single fucking noise, I will end you. Do you understand me? Nod if you comprehend me." Her lips tremble, but she tries nods her dark head, her brown eyes filling with tears that slide down her face.

The sound of the door reopening has my concentration moving away from the frightened girl and back to the door. I push my weight against her, forcing her to take small breaths as her air becomes trapped in her throat and give her a warning glare to shut the fuck up. A dark blonde head greets my gaze as she moves into the small room. Her eyes meet the frightened girl's standing against the wall before quickly turning towards me and stepping back.

"What the fuck, Carter! Are you deranged?" She screeches and crosses her arms against her chest. Forcing her delectable breasts to push together and her creamy skin to be seen between the parted side of her shirt. *Those are my fucking breasts. MINE.*

"Hey, blondie. Miss me?" I question with a smirk and push the door closed firmly. My back presses against it as I drag the girl with me, my hand now loosely wrapped around her neck. I can feel her heart beating rapidly in her pulse against my fingers. The sensation should repulse me with how frightened she is. Instead, it brings me satisfaction. She's just a scared little bird. Fear is an aphrodisiac to someone like me; it calls to my darkness like a siren.

"Please! Please let me go." The girl cries, tears and snot running down her face. So weak, not like my queen standing there with rage in her ocean-blue eyes, ready to decimate me. She is perfect for me, made for me. I will never get enough of her, and I will never let her go.

"Carter, let her go. This is fucked up even for you." Mia seethes.

I nod towards the door, opening it slightly but not entirely releasing my hold on her. The cowering girl tries to move forward, but I tighten my fingers, leaning my head close to her ear. Sobs rip from her throat as tears cascade down her face. "What's your name?"

"Cindy." She mumbles with a choked sob. Fuck, I wasn't even close on the name. It's a good thing my manwhore days are over.

"Cindy, you will leave here and walk right out of the school and head home. You will not tell anyone what is happening in here. If you do, you and your family are my next visit. Do you understand me?" I lean in and press my head next to hers so she feels my warm breath on her skin. The poor girl looks like she's about to faint, and a little tinge of remorse tries to rise within me for probably scarring her for life. "Go."

The minute she's gone, I lock the door behind her. I pull my hidden gun from the waistband of the back of my pants and turn all of my attention to my vicious queen, who is still standing there looking unimpressed and unafraid. I point the gun in her direction and shift closer, awareness and caution racing through my senses. "Is that really necessary, Carter? We both know you are not going to shoot me?" She questions with narrowed eyes and a clenched jaw.

She stands there so nonchalantly like she's not the person who holds my whole world and heart in the palm of her hands. As if she didn't implode it when she first returned to Casbury months ago and didn't crush the remaining embers when she left me in that fucking cabin in the snow and ice.

"I wouldn't be so sure, blondie. You have a way of releasing my insanity with your impetuous behavior. In fact, you make the monster inside of me rattle the bars of his cage, demanding freedom. Be careful, Mia. I may just let him out."

A chuckle leaves her pouty red lips. The ones I crave to suck and bite. Fuck, she really is the most beautiful woman I have ever seen. Standing there with her dirty blonde hair loose and sliding down her back in thick waves. My fingers crave to run through it and wrap the long strands around my wrist. Her ocean-blue eyes blaze like gemstones filled with fire. The school uniform that looks ordinary on other girls makes her look like a naughty representation of every man's fantasies. She's mine, though; they can't fucking have her.

"What do you want, Carter? We have nothing left to say to each other."

"I beg to differ, Mia. We have lots to discuss, like how you willingly let another man put his hands on you." I stalk towards her, the beast inside of me moving through me and demanding we restrain her, confine her to us. I watch as she leans against the counter, ankles crossed, bare legs on display, and a haughty tilt to her head. Fucking hell, I need to fuck that superiority and defiance right out of her.

"I don't answer to you, Carter. I never did. If I want someone else's hands on me, that's none of your fucking concern."

A blast of fiery rage rises up my spine, and my grip on the gun tightens until my fingers are white and my body is filled with tension. My hand reaches out and grasps her neck harshly, my fingers squeezing and jerking her forward. I stare down at her and let her see the wrath that flows within me, the monster I cage that wants his freedom to wreak havoc on everyone and everything in its path. "Careful little queen, your words and actions have consequences. I would hate to force you to stop breathing."

CHAPTER 37

Mia

"I felt like an animal, and animals don't know sin, do they?"
Jess C. Scott, Wicked Lovely

His fingers are harsh on my neck, forcing my body to tilt forward. A small gasp leaves my lips before I seal them tight. I can't believe this lunatic was holding a girl at gunpoint in the washroom to get to me. *Why are you surprised? It's Carter, after all.*

"Carter, release me now," I demand as I clench my molars and strain in his hold. His gaze is predatory when it meets mine. Those gorgeous husky eyes are so pale and light, yet darkness and madness lie in their depths. A thrill slides up my spine with the knowledge that he is insane. That part of him has always called to my own insanity.

"Never, Mia. I will never release you; not even in death will you be free of me. You know that, don't you blondie, yet you keep fighting me. Well no more." His mouth crashes down on mine. Thick, firm lips meeting and overtaking my soft ones as our teeth clash together. He bites down hard on the corner of my bottom lip, and I can taste blood in my mouth.

The taste causes my core to clench painfully and feel its emptiness. *He could fix that for us with that big pierced dick of his; my* mind reminds me of the part of him that always brings me so much pleasure. His tongue forces its way into mine, brushing and tangling with mine until there is no oxygen left, and I strain in his tight hold. A gasp tries to leave my lips but is immediately swallowed by his.

His fingers dig into the nape of my neck, forcing me closer and refusing to release their hold on me as my body is crushed against his. My breasts meet his hard chest, my stomach, his swollen erection, and my thighs, his muscular legs. They force me backward until I am trapped between his body and the counter. I try to rip my mouth from his, managing to pull my lips away as he trails his warm tongue down the side of my face to my jaw. Where he bites down on the flesh before moving to the space below my ear. The sharp sting causes shivers and goosebumps to break across my heated flesh at his touch. More, *I need more.* No, I should be resisting, not playing into his hands.

His scent envelopes every breath I take; the smell of lime, eucalyptus, and bergamot, which has continued to muddy my mind, confusing me and making me doubt my resolve, now also brings me rage. I push back against his embrace, letting my nails sink into the skin of his neck and exposed arms. A pained moan leaves his lips before he bites down hard on my neck, his teeth breaking the surface and a hit of pain radiating from the spot. His grip on my neck tightens, forcing my head to pull away from his as I try to bite him back.

"Let me go, you fucker!"

His predatory gaze meets mine as I dig my nails in deeper, marring the beautiful tattooed artwork on his neck and arms. The vibrant colors, lines, and details are a masterpiece across the canvas of his skin. A tinge of sadness rises within me at the thought of ruining such perfection.

Rather than following my request, his hand, still holding the gun, slides up the fabric of my short kilt, the cold metal of the weapon, and his warm knuckles skating slowly across the skin of my thigh and rising towards my core. "Don't, Carter." The words leave my lips in a harsh tone even though my traitorous core tightens in anticipation of his touch.

"You let him touch you, Mia. Touch what belongs to me. Did he get to feel this perfect cunt, my little slut? Hmm, did he touch your soft skin? The skin that belongs to me? Did he get to feel how wet you are? How this cunt weeps for its owner. For fucking me?" Every word is punctuated by the barrel of the gun and his fingers moving higher across my pebbled skin until it is pressed right up against my soaked mound. My wetness escaping me and drenching my panties and the tip of the weapon. "You enjoy provoking me, blondie, relish watching me lose what little of my sanity remains."

A malicious smirk crosses my face, and I leave my self-preservation at the gates of hell, knowing I'm about to egg him on and push him further into his unrelenting madness with no thought for my own safety. That's the thing about Carter; he calls to me in a way the others don't. He makes me crave the violence and damage that only he can provide me. Every part of me wants him, even if I try to deny it.

"Yes, I let him slip his fingers inside my pussy before class. Let him fuck my tight hole with them, and then I watched him lick them clean so he could get a taste of my pussy."

"Mia, I will fucking kill him and then you before I join you in hell. Don't fucking lie to me." He grits between clenched teeth. I can see him losing control of the beast he tries to contain within himself. The one that begs to be let loose to wreak havoc on all those in its path. The beast I crave to see and provoke to take me by force. "I'm not even sorry, Carter; he fucked me so good." I let my words brush across his lips. The ones clenched tight in displeasure.

His hand wraps tightly around my neck, forcing my breath to stutter. I bite down hard on my lip, causing more blood to trickle into my mouth as he pushes the gun barrel into my opening. Forcing my panties to go with it until both are sliding into my hole. The menacing scent in the air and drifting off of Carter in waves elicits a myriad of emotions to break across my skin, lust, hate, fear, and anticipation for his complete loss of control war with each other and cause a thrill to soar through my body. "This pussy is mine. You are my whore, Mia. Mine. If someone other than my brothers have claimed it, I will burn this whole fucking world down around us."

His grip tightens even further until white spots are starting to appear before my vision. I can't get a drop of air through to my lungs with his confining hold. His eyes blaze into mine; madness and rage reside there at the thought of someone else inside of me. Another man claiming what he deems his. Am I his? No, my mind screams, while my body screams yes. My pussy spasms against the invasion of the metal and fabric in my hole. *Fuck it's not enough. I need more.*

He pulls back, the barrel moving away from my core, and a whimper tries to leave my lips, but there's no air left. My eyes lower to slits; he's going to make me pass out. His hold is too tight; I can't breathe. The sound of ripping material is loud in the small confines of the bathroom. Then the cold metal meets my swollen pussy lips and slips through my folds. I can feel my wetness coating it as he bumps it against my clit over and over until tingles are racing up the back of my neck and heat is flooding my body. "You have a death wish, blondie, one I'm willing to grant you. We can both go meet the devil together."

He slips the end of the gun into my tight hole, and I feel my flesh envelop it before my pussy spasms and tightens its grip on the cold object. "Look at how your needy pussy swallows my gun, Mia. How fucking wet you are, my little whore queen. How this tight little hole needs to be filled." He moves the gun in shallow strokes inside my core, the sound of wetness loud in the air.

My chest is burning, the lack of air making my head sway and dizziness assault me. Just when I'm about to pass out from his brutal hold, he loosens his fingers allowing air to rush back in and a shuddered gasp to leave my lips as my lungs fill with much-needed oxygen.

I can feel my wetness coating my inner thighs, my nipples pebble painfully in my bra, and electricity shoots across my skin. The erotic sensation of danger has me so close to cumming that I can taste it. If I could just touch myself, touch my needy clit, or get a hit of pain, I would detonate.

I release my hold on his arm and slip it down to my waist; Carter's eyes don't follow the movement. His eyes are frozen on mine, determination, anger, and heat visible in their depths. His breathing is ragged as his powerful chest moves up and down in the confines of his shirt.

I reach into the pocket of my skirt and slowly pull out the blade I keep hidden there. Opening it and tightening my grasp on its handle before raising it quickly to his throat. I press the sharp knife against his skin, and his Adam's apple rises and falls against the metal. A drop of blood immediately wells on the surface of his golden tattooed skin.

"Do it, blondie." He presses the gun firmly inside of me, breaching my hole in a sharp thrust until I can feel his clasped fingers around the trigger guard and grip, making contact with my heated flesh. The sensation of both the warming metal and his skin causing my core to spasm. The feel of its thickness inside of me and the danger it imposes, forcing my breath to wheeze out of my chest. "In no world will you escape me, not in this lifetime or the next. You belong to me, Mia. You are my queen, my whore. You will always be mine."

I watch, mesmerized, as a trickle of blood slowly makes its way down his neck and into the collar of his dark gray t-shirt. The red path it leaves tempts my lips to follow its lead. My grip on his neck loosens, and I run the tips of my fingers through the blood. "I will end your life, Carter Pemberton, and bathe in your fucking blood if you do not release me."

I re-press the blade firmly against his golden skin, and the trickles increase until rivulets of blood are meeting my fingers. Rather than any fear appearing in his features, all I see on his maniacal face is arousal. He's turned on at the prospect of me killing him. He craves my violence as much as I do his. He's right; at this very moment I do belong to him, just as much as he belongs to me. *We are twin flames of madness.*

"Then we can die together." *You still fucking hate him,* my brain screams but it doesn't change anything. His lips descend on mine in a harsh kiss that has oxygen evaporating in my throat and my hold on the blade slipping. His thrusts increase in speed and force as he fucks me with his gun. My tongue meets his as it lashes and tangles with mine. Moans and whimpers leave us both before there is no more oxygen, and we have to pull apart in order to breathe.

His breath is labored as he struggles to catch it. "Get on the counter, Mia. I want my cunt back, and I mean to reclaim it." My tongue dips out of my mouth at his words, my core clenching tight at his request. I should be trying to push him away; this is madness. I need to put distance between me and the kings, not allow them to make me a needy whore. Not again. *Shut the fuck up bitch; he's about to make it feel like heaven.*

He pulls the gun from inside of me, and I immediately feel its loss, and the sensation of being empty is almost devastating. Carter's hand from around my neck slips to my chest, and he pushes me backward. The gun meets the counter next to me with no care, as his hand is gripping my waist, lifting me until my ass is meeting the counter, and he's flipping up my skirt. I need to stop him; this shouldn't go any further. I'm still angry at him. At them all. My mind races, and my chest tightens at the sinful look of arousal on his face. He's staring at my pussy, like it's his greatest desire, a man starved for riches, ones only my pussy hold. More moisture coats my pussy lips and seeps out of me as saliva pools in my mouth at how entranced he is by the sight of my cunt.

In mere seconds his forefinger and middle finger slip through my drenched folds, rubbing on my throbbing, swollen clit before reaching my tight empty hole. They slip inside with a deep thrust that has a moan wrenching from my lips. His thumb strums my bundle of nerves before circling it and applying pressure.

Waves of ecstasy fill me repeatedly, making my temperature rise and sweat trickle down my back and dampen my hairline. My eyes close at the sensations he's causing inside of me. Waves of euphoria are ready to crash over me and to bring me a soul-trapping orgasm. They slam into me over and over until my pussy is tightening around his fingers. Every limb in my body is on fire, my body tensing in anticipation of falling into a deep abyss of pleasure.

"This pussy is mine. Look at what a good girl you are clamping down on my fingers. This is what you need, isn't it, my little slut? You need me to make you cum over and over. You're a greedy little cum whore aren't you, Mia?" His words bring me to the edge, but yet I can't cross over it. The release is right there, so close that I can taste it. I need more, though. I need his violence along with his dirty words. He pants as he thrusts deeper, curling his fingers and hitting the spot inside of me that has my breath strangling my throat. I need to push him over the edge. I need him to lose control.

"He...he made...made...me...cum...too!" The words are ripped from me, and I watch as Carter loses complete control. His hand grips my breast in a painful hold, squeezing the globe in his hand before he rips open my shirt and tears the front of my bralette. His mouth lands on my nipple and bites down hard, his teeth leaving an imprint and breaking the skin. The sting is sharp and painful, just the perfect hit of pain I craved. His fingers trail up my chest and grasp my neck in a bruising grip until there is no doubt he wants to murder me.

His mouth moves over to my other breast giving it the same treatment, and pain rips through me at the feeling of his teeth biting down on me. "Fuck!" The word tries to escape my lips, but his hold tightens on my neck until it comes out garbled and wispy. Bite after bite makes its way across my skin until I think nothing will be left of my chest that isn't sporting his teethmarks. His fingers pick up speed while his thumb is pressed firmly on my clit which has me detonating around them with a muffled cry.

The orgasm hits me like a tsunami crashing over me and forcing my body to clench tight and thrust into his hold. My hips undulate on his digits until I can feel my juices coating all of his hand. Wave after wave of pure energy hits me, making my body sing and feel alive. His lips meet my collarbone as I'm shattering, his tongue lashing out before he bites down on my fevered skin. My head feels heavy, the lack of oxygen and my orgasm making it fall backward. My vision blurs until darkness threatens to take me. The waves don't stop coming, my core clenching and spasming against his relentless fingers, still thrusting with powerful strokes into my core.

"You lying, little slut. I'll stop you from fucking breathing, Mia. I will end you as I rip apart this perfect little cunt. This pink swollen pussy is mine. You are mine."

"Ca...Carter..." I try to get his name out, the blade slipping from my hands completely and hitting the counter. My limbs feel weak, the loss of oxygen making them heavy as I try to grasp his forearm and tear it away from my neck. I've pushed him too far; his beast is in control of him now. He's going to end my life without realizing it. It will be too late when he finally realizes what he has done. My grip on his arm goes slack, and my head lolls to the side on my neck, completely boneless as darkness bleeds in. I feel my heart rate slowing down completely. Even the sound of blood rushing in my ears dims until there are no other sounds, nothing but the uneven thud of my heart. My eyes close, my long lashes meeting my cheeks as I lose sight of Carter, and oblivion beckons. A shudder races through my body as his grip tightens, crushing my throat before releasing.

The air rushing back inside of my mouth, throat, and lungs is painful. He releases his merciless grip on my throat, tears his fingers from inside of my pussy, and before I can utter a single word, his thick, pierced cock is thrusting inside of me in a vicious stroke that has my body pushing backward. The back of my head slams on the mirror behind me. I take huge gasps of air, trying to get my breathing to slow down, to fill my lungs and control the panic that is seizing me. Carter rams his cock inside of me like a ruthless maniac with a punishing rhythm, demanding my surrender, fucking me like an animal, punishing me for my words. Forcing me to agree to his demands for ownership.

"Mine. Mine. Mine." Each word releases in the air in a growl punctuated by a deep thrust in my core, hitting the end of me and bringing both pleasure and pain. He sounds like a vicious animal, with snarls vibrating from his chest. "My girl. My queen. My whore." His grip on either side of my hips is punishing. His thrusts are powerful and ripping tears from my eyes. I feel them sliding down my cheeks as moan after moan escapes my lips.

I can feel another orgasm cresting, like a waterfall of tingles, emotions, and sensations sliding down my body. Forcing my nipples to pucker and harden painfully and shivers to rack my body. My core pulses as Carter continues to pummel me with harsh thrusts that have skin slamming into skin. The sound is so loud in the air that it drowns out the sharp sound of our breathing. "Mine. This cunt is mine."

He groans as his thumb presses down on my clit before pinching it between two of his fingers. His eyes lift from the view of his cock punishing my pussy and meet mine. They're at half mast, a crazed look across his features. A pink tinge is flushed on his high chiseled cheekbones, his swollen red lips begging to be sucked.

"Carter...oh my...fucking...God!" The words leave me as he picks up speed, thrusting in me so hard that my teeth rattle. The sting of his flesh hitting mine continuously is a delicious sensation and helps to push me toward rapture.

"I'm not your God, Mia. I. AM. YOUR. EVERYTHING!" He shouts as he empties himself inside of me, cumming hard and painting my womb with his essence. His breath staggers in his chest and his body leans into mine, depleted. His forehead lands on my chest, and his lips nestle on the upper part of my breasts. His breathing is so harsh that the sound is both terrifying and electrifying.

Deep in my wrathful heart, it pleases me how completely undone he is at the feel of my body. My body spasms, and the orgasm threatens to crest just as he rips his pierced cock from my core. A cry of devastation rips from my lips at the feel of his piercing trailing against my throbbing walls and trying to escape me. "No!'

He staggers back, his rigid cock bobbing between us, covered in my arousal and his. Blue-gray eyes meet mine and hold my gaze. I can feel his cum slipping from inside of me, and the sensation of loss fills me. "No, my little devious slut. You don't get to come again unless you tell me the truth. Did you let Jessie touch my pussy?"

I want to deny him his demand. I want to plunge the fucking blade I had into his throat at his words. He seeks to control me. *Fuck him! I'll give myself a fucking orgasm. I don't need him.* I trail my fingers through the mess he made of my pussy, his creamy cum, coating my fingers as I slip two inside of me and use my thumb on my throbbing clit. I fuck myself hard and fast with my digits, coasting the orgasm right back to the edge as I push myself over it, pulling on my right nipple with my other hand until a moan leaves my mouth. All the while, Carter stands transfixed, watching as I cum with his cum still dripping from inside of me.

"Holy. Fuck." His words leave him in a sharp moan as his cock bobs and beads of cum slip from his pierced tip and trail down his veiny long length. My mouth waters at the need to have him in my mouth, but I restrain myself. He will never learn that he does not own me if I give in to my baser needs.

When I'm nothing but a mess of shudders, cum, and aftershocks, I meet his heated gaze. "You want the truth, Carter?" I question with a raised eyebrow, my lungs still staggering for air. My heart rate is pounding in my chest, and I can feel heat everywhere on my skin. "Bow down to me and please your queen."

He doesn't hesitate, falling to his knees before me, grasping both my thighs, and pushing my legs wider until I'm stretched open and gapping for his intense gaze. His tongue slips out of his delectable mouth, and he licks my folds, a deep moan leaving his chest. His tongue lashes across my overstimulated clit, and it throbs in both pain and joy.

Carter licks every inch of me, licking and sucking my folds deeply into his hot mouth, cleaning me with his tongue before fucking my tight hole. His fingers open me wide for his feasting, animalistic groans and grunts leave his lips as whimpers leave mine. His thumb slips through our combined cum and then makes its way to my puckered hole as he continues to eat me like a man who has served twenty years in prison and has been finally given his freedom.

"Mmm Mia, you taste so fucking good. You and me together is my favorite fucking dish." His words rumble into my pussy, causing wisps of heat to race along my skin.

He thrusts his thumb inside my back hole just as a shockwave of sensation fills me, and a petite orgasm has me coating his face in my release. "Fuck, so good. Soak my face, baby." He mumbles into my wet folds. A hum escapes his throat, making my toes curl in my shoes. Fuck, Carter will be the death of me figuratively and literally one day; of that, I have zero doubt.

When I can't take anymore, and my core is screaming for a reprieve, I dig my fingers into his hair and pull him back away from me. He moans with the pain of my grip and the loss of my pussy. Licking his lips like he still can't get enough. His beautiful eyes are fully dilated, looking like an addict after a hit. A man addicted to my pussy and my taste. The thought brings me so much pleasure that I have to try to swallow the pleased sigh that wants to escape my lips.

"No more...sore." The words leave me in raspy mumbles as I try to catch my breath and slow my heart.

I slip off the counter, my body groaning as the blood rushes back into my legs, and I momentarily sway. Carter reaches out to steady me, but I swat his hands away. He tries to rise from his knees, but I grasp onto a fist full of his hair and hold him in place. "No, stay there on your knees in subjugation, Carter. Where you belong."

I release my hold, pick up my blade from the ground and walk toward the door. "Mia, did you let him touch you?" Carter questions with alarm in his voice. I turn the lock and open the door, staring back at him over my shoulder. I want to inflict more pain on him. On all of them, really, but I also don't want Jessie to die. Carter is unhinged on a good day, and I wouldn't put the insane fucker to actually shoot poor Jessie.

My eyes meet his, ocean-blue meeting turbulent gray-blue. "No, I didn't, but I will if you don't leave me alone, Carter. What we had is over. I've had my fill." I don't wait for his reply as I walk out the door. Leaving my underwear and pieces of my heart with one of the kings of Casbury on the bathroom floor. I hear the sound of the mirror shattering as a ferocious growl sounds in the hallway.

CHAPTER 38
Mateo

"In a mad world, only the mad are sane." Akira Kurosawa

Finn, Theo, and I lose track of Carter almost immediately upon entering the school. The maniacal bastard takes off like a bolt of lightning is firing up his ass. "Ah fuck, we lost him. That can't be good." A lamenting sigh leaves Finn as we stand in the middle of the hallway, trying to figure out what direction Carter went in.

"Let's hope he doesn't kill anyone with that gun of his. I don't want to have to visit him behind bars." Theo chuckles in amusement. How he thinks that's funny, I have no idea. Carter might actually kill someone.

I honestly hold no hope that Carter isn't off-creating massive amounts of fuckery. The guy is unhinged at best, certifiably insane at worst, and a serial killer in the making most days. As much as I want to find Carter so we can put a leash on him. My desire to locate that fucker that had his arms around my *reina* is stronger. Anger is giving me something to focus on and something to live for. If I don't zone into this anger, then who knows how long I would be stuck on those school stairs trying to catch my breath.

"Let's go." I nod towards the football change rooms. It's just before second period, and the noise in the hallway is deafening as students race from one place to the other. That is until they see us prowling through the halls, then everyone comes to a standstill and watches us. Some hold their breaths and look away, while others meet our gazes with defiance. Naw, that just won't do. None of these worthless people get to defy us. They are feeling brave. They shouldn't. We have nothing left to lose. I have nothing to lose. I have already lost my heart.

I slam my fist into the first fucker that curls his lip at me. His head hits the metal locker behind him with a loud thud, and he goes down like a ton of bricks. A thrill runs through my body. It feels good to feel any other emotion than sadness and panic. One of his buddies, another football player, heads in my direction, but he meets a similar fate at Finn's hands. He falls and takes two of his buddies down with him like he is a bowling pin. *Fuck, yes! This is exactly what I need.*

Theo lifts a fucker by the scuff of the neck until he's dangling above the ground. "Listen here, you cockroaches. That was an interesting display of courage out there. I almost want to applaud you fuckers."

He shakes the asshole in his grip and sends him flying down the hall, knocking three girls down that are frozen, watching the spectacle before us. They fall in a tangle of limbs, screeches, and fear. "Unfortunately for all of you, you wasted your time. The next one to try to stop us or thinks they have some sort of power over us will end up meeting his or her maker."

Gasps ring out across the hallway as people stand, shocked at his blatant threat. They all know that Theo doesn't just make threats; he makes promises and carries them out like the ruthless tyrant that he is. His words are gospel here. Somehow in our absence, they became brave, and they had forgotten that. It's time for the little mice to run; the big cats are back.

"WE ARE YOUR MOTHERFUCKING KINGS!" I shout, incensed by their disobedient and reckless behavior. I try desperately to regain my composure, but I can't. I am too far gone with rage. *Beats anxiety and depression, doesn't it?* The anger that fills my body is like a pot boiling over and needing to expel its contents. It will burn everything in its path on its way to vengeance. I need an outlet, and these fuckers are putting themselves heedlessly and without thought in my path. "Your betrayal will not be disregarded or, for that matter, go unpunished."

"The fact that y'all thought you could so easily dismiss us shows how very stupid you are. Run, you fucking maggots, slither away and hide before we teach each and every one of you about the wrath of your kings." Finn shouts and punches a locker, denting the door and merely missing Thomas Brantford by an inch or two, who proceeds to duck and run for his life. *Smartest fucker in this hallway right now.*

They all scatter like the vermin they are, heading in different directions and cowering before our might. It's not enough, though. Energy storms through my veins. The promise of more violence breathes life into me, forcing my anxiety and desperation back to where they can be contained. "I want Jessie. That fucker is going to pay with his blood for touching her."

I march off down the hallway towards the football change rooms in hopes of catching a glimpse of him. Students and teachers cower in open classrooms awaiting, I am sure, further destruction. As much as I want them all trembling at my feet, at our feet, they will have to wait. My wrath craves the sight of Jessie's blood, and nothing else will do right now.

I don't have to wait long. The fucker presents himself to us at the end of the next hallway. Standing tall, powerful, alone, and more importantly, without fucking fear. A part of me respects the fact that he didn't try to hide. That he doesn't try to use Mia as a shield, either. He knows we are coming for him, and he stands there, ready to meet his maker. He is so sure in his actions and convictions that he no longer fears the kings of Casbury. *That just won't do.* There is only one person that should never fear the kings of Casbury, and that is because she belongs to us.

"Ready to meet your maker, fucker?" Finn questions with mirth as he steps forward. It takes a hell of a lot to make Finn lose his cool. The guy is usually filled with a steel will that's only rivaled by Theo's, but he's lost his grip on it right now. If his mind is anything like mine, he's replaying this fucker's hands on Mia, and it's eating him up inside. Just like it's doing to me and probably

Theo. We are lucky we found Jessie before Carter ended his life with a bullet. Jessie should be thanking whoever he prays to for small mercies.

"You should let her go, Finn. You keep hurting her constantly. All of you do." Jessie's sobering stare is filled with contempt and meets each of us as his body goes rigid, preparing for the retribution he knows is coming his way. Nevertheless, he doesn't back down, the fucker.

His words sow seeds of resentment inside of me, deep inside the emptiness that is hollow since Mia left me behind in that cabin once again. Since she uttered June's name and made me understand that my destruction was self-inflicted and she was merely the blade cutting me deeper.

"Regardless if you are right or not, Jessie, the fact remains that you put yourself between us and our girl. She's ours, not yours." Theo replies in a clipped tone, his face back to that cold mask where you can no longer read his emotions. The one that has always sent chills down my back because it means he's shutting off his feelings and his humanity.

"Someone has to protect her from you. You four are parasites that destroy and infect everything you touch. I know what you did to her back when you were kids, Raegan filled me in. I also know about what that psycho did to her because you fuckers pushed her out of her own house with your senseless words and actions. You will continue to hurt her until nothing is left of her."

His words are bullets hitting me repeatedly, causing pain to bloom throughout my body. *You pushed her out of her own house with your senseless words and actions.* It repeats over and over in my mind. I was the last one to see her, the straw that broke the camel's back.

His words hold truth, a truth I don't want to acknowledge or entertain, but I have no choice. Even if it feels like a dagger is piercing my heart. Will we continue to hurt her? We all love Mia; we can't live without her, but that truth doesn't take away from the truth behind his words.

If you genuinely love her, why wouldn't you let her go? The thought skates through my mind, and I can't escape it. I never want to cause Mia any pain. Will we continue to hurt her? Will things never settle down between the five of us so that we can be happy? I desperately want her to be happy, for all of us to have some peace from all the trauma and demons that constantly attack us.

"That person isn't you. She doesn't need protection from us. She belongs to us, with us. We are hers, just like she is ours." Finn replies in a gruff tone. Is he, too, thinking over Jessie's words? Is he hearing their validity?

"You, out of all of them, should let her go, Finn. How much more are you willing to hurt her? You have betrayed her trust repeatedly for these fuckers. She loved you then and allowed you back in, only for you to hurt her again."

I watch as Finn flinches from the impact of Jessie's words. His throat bobs up and down, Jessie's words hitting him deep, where they can do the most damage. His anger and resolve seem to melt, sorrow and pain taking their place. "I love her, Jessie. I loved her then. I love her even more now. There is nothing without her. I let her go once, and it was the biggest mistake of my life. I will never let her go again." A deep sadness clouds Finn's features, his hands clench at his side, and his shoulders lift in sorrow.

"Even if she hates you? Even if you end up destroying the very girl you claim to love? That's fucking selfish and self-serving, not love." Jessie inclines his head, his nostrils flaring and his mouth set in a deep line.

"I will spend the rest of my days at her feet begging for forgiveness for my callousness, betrayal, deeds, and words. I know that I am not worthy of her, that I will never be worthy of her. I also know that no one will love her more than we do. I would give up my life for her completely."

Jessie's head bobs up and down, and his stance goes less rigid. His eyes meet each of ours, and his hands unclench, some of the anger retreating from his features. "She loves you fuckers, has from the moment you brought that crazy fool, Carter, to her house. Why I don't know, considering you psychos keep hurting her."

He shakes his head, his eyes filled with regret and loss. His whole body deflates, and it's like all the anger is sucked right out of him, and only despair remains. The realization hits me then, he loves her too, probably has since the moment she walked through Casbury's doors, but he had to compete with us. He lost before he could even be an active participant. She was always meant to be ours. Our futures were tied together by strings of fate from the moment her mom attended Theo's mom's funeral. *He never stood a chance.*

"We didn't mean to hurt her; we just wanted to protect her from Vincent. We were trying to save her." I run my hands through my shortened locks and pull on the strands. My own anger has evaporated within me and in its place the anxiety and pain are seeping back in. My arms wrap themselves tightly around my chest, trying to keep together the shards of my shattering heart. How much more can I take? The reality is I don't deserve her, but I can't live without her either.

My mouth opens again and words just spill out like a river. I don't have a chance to even think them through before they are tumbling away from me. "Fuck, you have no idea how much each of us loves that girl. Theo crawled out of hell for her. A hell he sacrificed himself to, to protect her from his father. He wouldn't be here today without her - without her putting herself in harm's way to bring him back from the darkness that overtook him and his mind. She is the only one that has ever cracked his tough, all too put-together, and always in control facade. Carter's madness is contained by only her; she holds his blackened soul in the palm of her dainty and vicious hands. She settles the monsters of his past and his existence without love. A truth that he has spent his life running from, always hiding behind his fists and temper. Finn has never been the same since she left when she was a child. He lost a piece of himself then and now. He has never been able to forgive himself. His entire being has been searching for that friend and for that love he once had in the palm of his hand. It is his biggest regret that continues to haunt his every nightmare."

My breath leaves me in quickened pants, my chest rising and falling with all the emotions spiraling through me. My feelings threaten to overwhelm me, to rob me of the morsel of sanity that remains within me, one that becomes smaller by the hour, without Mia's forgiveness.

"She is the only one who has ever fully understood me. She has never shown fear or judgment at the demons that plague every waking moment in my mind. She brings me peace. She persuades the panic to stay away. With my hand intertwined in hers, I feel invincible. I feel seen. I barely survived; she was my only motivation to live through all the shit that I endured. Mia is the only fucking thing keeping me from ending this miserable existence. Without her, living is not worth shit. I can't breathe without her.' "

A noise behind us has each of us whirling on our feet and staring at the sight that has my breath catching in my throat. Mia stands behind us; how long she's been there before deciding to make her presence known, I don't know. My guess would be long enough to hear not only Jessie's words about her loving us but also my reply.

Her cheeks are flushed with a red tinge, her lips are swollen and bleeding, and her hair is a disheveled mess. The front of her shirt is tied together in a tight bow, exposing her creamy soft skin to our eyes. She looks completely ravished. Like an animal attacked her and tried to fuck her to death. *Carter*. The fucker must have found her first.

A dark cloud of envy fills me at the sight before me. Did he get to have her? Touch her? Did she willingly allow him to touch her, or did the fucker take from her while she bloodied him? I look behind her, but there's no sight of Carter anywhere. I wonder if he's lying in a pool of his own blood right now? I wouldn't put it past Mia to retaliate in violence. After all, she is our violent and wrathful queen. Insistent on bringing each of us to our fucking knees and forcing us to bow at her unrelenting feet.

What she doesn't realize is that I would willingly give up my life to be able to spend it at her feet. It doesn't make me weak. It makes me strong to know how much value this woman before me has. How much she means to me and how I could not survive the loss of her.

"Mia," Theo calls out her name, and the word seems ripped from his very soul. His eyes light with a fire from within at her presence. It's like looking in a mirror. I know that my body and soul have the same response to her.

Her blue eyes roam across all of us, various emotions making themselves visible across her stunning features. Jesus, she really is beautiful; every time I see her, it's like a punch to the stomach. Her beauty guts me. Mia narrows her attention on me and I may be mistaken, but I see a hint of tears pool in her beautiful eyes. She takes a step in my direction before catching herself and stopping. My heart races in my chest at her action. She's not as indifferent as she pretends to be. A beacon of hope lights in my chest, and with it, the realization that there really will never be a me without her.

She cocks her head to the side, her eyes burning holes into mine as her eyebrows furrow, and I watch in suspense as she clenches and unclenches her hands. All too quickly I see her emotions turn to anger. My breath catches in my throat at what I know is coming. "You speak of love, but you four demand ownership. You profess love, yet each one of you threw me away, harshly, I might add, without a moment's hesitation." She raises her hand to stop the objections trying to leave all three of our mouths.

"You can't live without me, Mateo? How convenient now that you don't have June to hold on to." She turns her blazing gaze towards Finn, meeting his without reservation. "You regret your actions, Finn? Yet you betrayed me again rather than confronting me with the truth you found out." She inhales a deep shuddering breath, then turns her attention to Theo. "As for you, you're always the mastermind behind all the plots, aren't you, Theo? You enjoy hurting me but then claim you love me. You tear me to pieces and then try to pull me closer. Fuck you, Theo."

She takes a step back, her hands squeeze into fists, her nostrils flare, and her eyes flash. "Carter is the most psychotic out of all of you, but he's honest to a fault. He knows he fucked up; he hasn't tried to make excuses. He immediately offered to pay his penance, offering himself as a pound of flesh for my wrath. It's why I let him beat the fuck out of you, Theo, day in and day out."

"Mia...please," Finn calls out.

"Mercy will not be given, Finn. Mercy must be earned." She turns on her heels and walks away from us. Her kilt swishes with her unhurried steps. Keeping our gazes locked on her until she's out of sight.

"FUCK!" Theo rages and punches the wall, causing the sheetrock to buckle and a giant fist-sized hole to appear.

"I wish you luck, fuckers. It doesn't sound like she is going to take any of you back. And while I know that she doesn't want me in that way and still loves all four of you. I won't feel the slightest bit of guilt watching you fuckers suffer." Jessie's eyes crinkle at the corners, and a smug look crosses his broad face.

I take a giant step forward and my fist flies before I can restrain it. It makes contact with Jessie's nose in a loud crunch that echoes off the hallway walls. I pull back at the sharp sting across my knuckles and the skin that has torn open. It feels so good that I want to hit him again, and I move to swing once more, but Finn restrains my hand in his tight fist, shaking his head in the negative.

Theo's already walking down the hall in the same direction Mia went without a backward look. I turn and grin back at Jessie, who is trying to stop the gush of blood from his nose. "No hard feelings, motherfucker. Let that be a reminder not to touch her next time." Finn and I follow a rigid Theo down the hallway and leave Jessie behind in our wake.

We have four days until school is out to convince Mia that we are worthy of her. We suspect Stella will force her back to Manhattan right after graduation. That means there isn't a fucking moment to spare in our plan of attack to persuade Mia to allow us to remain at her side.

CHAPTER 39
Mia

"The fears we don't face becomes our LIMITS." *Robin Sharma*

I'm sitting in class after the disturbing fucking scene in the hallway with the kings and Jessie. All four of the kings have decided they are now in this class with me despite the teachers' protestations, all of which fell on deaf ears when she tried to get them to leave. She gave up trying after Theo treated her to a menacing stare. I watched as she gulped down her next words and took a few steps away. She immediately backed down. Look at that; even when we try to strip them of power, they still seem to have some. *Fucking kings of Casbury.*

The sensation of crawling ants across my skin is starting to play havoc with my nerves. I can feel various pairs of eyes on me. I know all four of the kings are silently watching me intently. Unfortunately, it's not only their gazes I feel. Everyone is holding their collective breaths to see what happens next between the kings and me. If I am being honest, I'm restraining mine too. I'm filled with anxiety, anger, and confusion about what to do.

My heart pleads for me to stop this madness. Mateo's words have made an impact on the broken organ inside of me. They did what they intended to do, trying to fill all the fragmented pieces of my heart and glue them back together. My mind, however, is refusing to relent. She's a stubborn bitch and wants the vengeance she was denied, and nothing short of them bleeding and broken before her will soothe her.

My phone vibrates on the table, and with a look at the teacher from below my lashes, I discreetly turn it over and bring it closer to my body to disguise my perusal of it. I'm not afraid of the teacher; let's be clear. I just don't feel like being a disruptive and rude cunt to her. No, I hold that pleasure solely for the kings of Casbury.

Controlling Fucker

You are mine. This will never be over. Not when you are lying in your grave & I am rotting right next to you. You will never be able to leave me. I will chase you through this life & all the others.

My gaze rises and meets dark blue eyes so filled with emotion that it forces me to swallow the painful lump in my throat. Theo's eyes are no longer showing signs of sorrow or asking for my forgiveness. They are unrelenting, cold, and demanding that I give up this fight and give him my surrender. *Well, fuck him.* I have no intention of surrendering to him or anyone else. I let him see all of the anger inside of me. All the memories of the words and intimacy that we shared that he destroyed with his cruel words and indifference. How he reopened old wounds that were festering with poison that is now flowing through my veins once again.

He doesn't look away or break the stare as both of us war with each other from a short distance without words. His sinful lips thin, and the corner rises with promises of debauchery. I watch from my seat as he crosses his thick muscled arms across his chest with the look of a villain biding his time until he gets what he wants. I slowly lick my lips, a smirk pulling across them, and give him a much-needed taste of his own medicine. The fucker is temptation, but I know I am his weakness. His eyes immediately heat, the blue becoming darker and more sinister, forcing me to clench my core from the heat sizzling between us.

My phone is still in my hand, and it vibrates once again, catching my attention and breaking the connection. I roll my eyes. Is this one of the other fuckers, also sending me their demands? They really need to get some new material. All the demanding and constant claiming that I am theirs lacks originality. I get it; they have caveman tendencies. They want to beat on their chests like giant gorillas, so I acknowledge their masculinity and their alphahole personalities. They are also massive fucking drama queens.

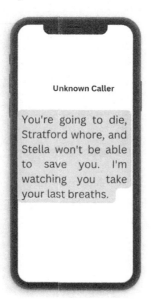

The phone slips from my hand and clatters on the desk as a gasp leaves my lips. The sound of my heart beating rapidly is loud in my ears and drowning out all the other sounds around me. My vision blurs until I can barely focus. I feel like I am leaving my body, and the sensation of falling fills me, causing shivers to race through all of my limbs. The hair on the back of my neck and arms stands on end. *I can't breathe. I can't fucking breathe!* He's coming for me. *James.* He didn't die, and he's watching me, threatening me.

I come back to myself with a hard tug at the feeling of someone's fingers digging into my shoulder. Fear causes me to react rather than center myself on where I am, and I lash out with my elbow until it connects with someone's hard abdomen. "Fuck, Killer." The grunted words bring me back to the here and now and pull me out of the dark void I was starting to free-fall into.

"Mia, baby, look at me. Breathe, baby." Theo's words call to me as I try to focus on the sight in front of me, where he's crouched in front of the desk and grasping my hand tightly, his fingers entwined with mine. When did he grab my hand? When did they leave their seats? Fuck. I try to swallow the painful lump logged in my throat.

"What the fuck just happened? Is she ok?" Mateo questions from my other side, but I can't seem to turn my head to look in his direction. My eyes are locked on Theo's, on the demand within their depths to return to him. To the look of violence within their deep blue sea that promises he will drown everything around us with his rage.

A tattooed hand reaches in front of me and grasps the abandoned phone from the desk. My body watches everything as if from a distance. Theo's hand tightens on mine as my fingers tremble in his grasp. "You're safe, Mia. I will never let you go. Nothing will harm you. We will protect you." His words allow me to release the breath that is strangling me, and the ache that has formed in my chest lessens but doesn't dissipate. I believe him, deep inside of me I know he will protect me with his very life, even though he knows that I am still enraged at him and his actions.

"What the fuck? Who the fuck sent this to you?" Carter demands with fierce anger and a raised voice. My eyes break Theo's connection, and I stare up at Carter. His hand is clenched around my phone. Dark gray-blue eyes flash with the impending winter storm that wants to crest, destroy, and wreak havoc on everything in its path. A red flush is making its way up the thick column of his neck, and his jaw is clenched tightly.

"I will execute terrible vengeance against them to punish them for what they have done. And when I have inflicted my revenge, they will know that I am the Lord." The bible verse appears in my mind as I watch Carter's beast move behind his eyes. Jesus, he looks like an avenging angel right now.

He turns the phone and shows it to the others, and I see Mateo's panic as he turns and looks around the room. Finn's eyes immediately travel to the nearest window as he closes rank tighter around me, putting his body as a shield between me and whatever may threaten me. It's then that I realize that there is complete silence in the room around us. Everyone is watching and waiting for something to happen. My reaction to the text message on my phone has gotten everyone's attention, probably because my four cavemen instantly reacted to my panic. I can't do this, I won't allow myself to be entertainment for these maggots.

I need to get the fuck out of this room now and try to get myself under control before I lose my mind. "Mat, run out and grab Tom, right fucking now from the car," Theo instructs as his grip on my hand tightens, until he's crushing my fingers without realizing it, and he forces my body to rise from my seat. Finn grabs my other elbow, and the two of them usher me between their large bodies out of the room, with Carter menacingly staring down everyone around us. Just daring anyone to open their mouths or try to stop them from taking me from the room.

"No, Mateo...don't" My voice comes out weak and breathless, but it halts him in his tracks.

I finally come to my senses when we step into the hall and realize I am permitting myself to be manhandled by them. I rip myself out of their holds and take a step back and away from them. *Get it together, bitch!* My mind screams at me, but the words from the text are replaying in my head continuously. *"You're going to die, Stratford whore."*

Tears slide down my face without my permission, and a bowling ball of dread hits the pit of my stomach. *"I'm watching you take your last breaths."* The image of that cabin of horrors in the woods enters my mind. The black metal ring on the wood floor that had me trapped and confined like an animal flashes before my eyes. I can almost feel the sensation of the thick metal chain around my leg and wrist and the ghost of evil hands along my skin. He's going to drag me back there and rape me again and again, use me up like I'm nothing. Chain me like an animal at a zoo while others watch me perform despicable acts.

I need to get out of here! James is watching me; he is going to try to recapture me, and this time he will kill me. *No! Fuck No!* I will end his miserable demonic life. I refuse to be this weak,

sniveling bitch. The girl that still lives inside of me, the survivor, screams with enraged passion.

Remember what we did to the sadistic demon Vincent? We weren't afraid then; we were filled with wrath. You saved yourself; you beat him once. He will never be able to hurt us again. We will do so much worse to him than we have already done. He wants to try again; we will send him back to the bottomless pit of hell he crawled out of.

"Go get Raegan. I think she's going into shock." Finn calls out before I see Mateo running down the hallway. It's like my mind is here, but it's also locked in a state of unrelenting fear, one that wants to siphon the life out of me.

"Mia! Mia, look at me, baby. I promise you no one will hurt you. I will murder everyone around us before I let anyone hurt you ever again." Carter's hand reaches out, his fingers wiping the unending tears from my face. My eyes raise and meet his, and it breaks the spell that has me captive. I shake my head, trying to force the ghosts from my past back into my nightmares and not let them bring me to my knees in my present.

My eyes look around us, and I notice various students standing in the doorways of classrooms. Curiosity, surprise, and even boredom are displayed in their features. Finn grabs the phone right out of one fucker's hands who's obviously recording me and throws it at a wall, shattering with the impact. *Fucking great. I am giving them all a show.* If that psycho really is watching, I'm sure I am bringing him nothing but joy right now as I self-destruct before his eyes.

Carter grabs onto my wrist and drags me further down the hall and away from the prying ears of all the gawkers. Finn becomes a malicious, menacing shadow at my back, blocking their view of me and staring them all down with murderous intent.

"Mia, do you think that was actually from James? That there is a possibility that he is still alive?" Theo's words have me pulling away from Carter's touch and meeting his angry glare. I shut my eyes and take a deep, grounding breath, and then another. In and out, the air flows in my chest until the trembling in my body subsides, and I feel more in control of myself.

"Yes. No. Fuck, I don't know if he died. I was too panicked to check. The need to get away from that cabin was riding me. I was scared that one of the fuckers watching was going to come for me next." It's the first time that I have spoken to the kings about what happened to me. I refused to recount the details of what occurred in that cabin to anyone other than Stella. Even Issy and Raegan only know bits and pieces. I couldn't force myself to relive that horror more than once through my words.

"Could this be someone other than James? Fuck, his body was never found. Someone must have helped him escape. This could be them and not him, or it could be him and them trying to scare you." Finn's aggravated voice sounds harsh to my ears.

"It doesn't matter who it is. If he comes for my girl, he's fucking dead. They are all fucking dead." Carter pulls the gun from his lower back and holds it with determination in his hands. Our fellow students scatter with fear at seeing him with the weapon. *Smart fuckers.*

"Mia, look at me," Theo demands in his deep voice. "Why didn't you want Mateo to run and get Tom?"

I take another deep breath and step back, putting some space between mine and the kings' bodies that are completely enveloping my personal bubble. I can't breathe when they are so close. My heart and mind war over allowing them even closer, giving up all of my own sanity to feel their arms close around me. As much as I would love to feel the safety of their arms holding me tight right now,

I can't permit that to happen. I need to stand on my own two feet and fight my own battles.

"Today was the first day I left the estate without an army at my back. My first day of freedom and normal nineteen-year-old behavior since this shit with all of you started. I will not allow anyone to take that from me and make me a prisoner once more. I am no one's hostage." My hands fist at my side, and I grind my molars, frustration and fury filling me. "If you tell Tom, Stella will know instantly, and I will be locked behind my gates forever. A princess in a locked tower in fear of the monsters around her."

Understanding crosses Theo's features. He knows my words are true. Stella will see this as the threat it is, and her first inclination will be to lock me away from anyone who would attempt to hurt me. She would be justified, too, based on what has already occurred. I just can't allow that to happen. I can't be a prisoner, not of her good intentions, not of anyone. I need to feel safe again, and the only way to do that is to fight my own monsters.

"I don't want, nor do I need an army at my back, Theo. I refuse to cower and wait for this monster to have the opportunity to hurt me years down the line while I look over my shoulder with constant fear. I will not allow that to happen to me."

"My little queen, you may not need or want an army at your back, but you have one nonetheless. You have four kings that will set this world into a fiery blaze to protect you. No one will take you from us. I promise you that we will protect what is ours."

CHAPTER 40

Theo

"The need for control always comes from someone that has lost it." Shannon L. Alder

I watch as my words hit their intended target, Mia's heart. She is so fierce and determined to stand on her own two feet. To fight back against the monsters that seek to harm her. While I admire that determination, strength, and self-reliance, it also irritates my soul. The need to protect her is always a brutal, tightened fist around my heart. Even when she needs protection from me and my own insanity.

I want to drag her kicking and screaming into the safety of her estate, where I know Stella will protect her with the might of the Stratford empire. At the same time, I want to grab her and my brothers and run away to hide in some corner of the world where no monsters will ever be able to get to her. *Well, at least no other monsters aside from us.*

The knowledge that I can't do either makes me want to lose my mind and kill anyone who breathes too close to my queen. For once in my miserable life, I am going to try not to be the controlling, demanding fucker that I always am.

I will let Mia dictate what she wants to happen next while firmly placing myself between her and any danger coming our way.

"What do you want to do, Mia?" The question feels like acid leaving my lips.

Her tear-stained face turns back in my direction, and at its sight, it has sorrow filling me. I never want to see her cry again, at least not tears that are not due to happiness or ones of rapture when we make her cum. I'm determined to make that my life's mission. Her head cocks to the side, almost like she's reading my mind and understanding how I am relinquishing my control to her. Giving her my power. I let a little corner of my lip rise and see a flicker of interest in her eyes.

"What have you fucking monsters done to her?" Raegan comes running down the corridor with a frightened Mateo right on her heels.

Mia grabs onto Raegan with both hands around her biceps and stops her from attacking us. Jesus, she didn't even wait to get an answer. She just immediately gravitates towards violence against us now. I think too much of Mia's penchant for violence has rubbed off on little Rae-Rae. "Nothing, it wasn't them. Show her the phone, Carter."

Carter takes a step back from Raegan, who is trembling with suppressed rage, and hands her the phone. He keeps his eyes on her the whole time, like a zoo keeper that knows the minute he turns his back, the lioness will attack him. His grip on the gun is forgotten and stressing me the fuck out. I don't want him to accidentally shoot one of us. "Carter, put the fucking gun away before the school administration calls the cops." He looks at me with shock, like he forgot he was holding it. Fuck my life; this guy is causing a million gray fucking hairs to sprout on my head.

"Who sent this, Mia? Was it James? We need to call Stella." Raegan starts pressing buttons on the phone, and I know she is one second away from alerting the vicious Manhattan queen of what is happening here. I grab the phone from her hands and pocket it.

"What the fuck are you doing, Theo?" Raegan's eyes flash with violence before she moves forward in my direction, dragging Mia with her.

"Rae, listen to me. We can't call Stella, girl. She will have me shipped out and locked up in Manhattan so quickly that it will make your head spin. I...I can't, Rae. I can't be a prisoner. Not anymore" Mia releases Raegan's arms and drags her hands through her beautiful thick hair.

"Mia...this is insane. You need Stella to protect you."

"We will protect our girl," Finn announces with an assurance that makes my eyebrows raise in his direction. He meets my gaze, and I see nothing but determination and belief in his words.

"Protect her? Who the fuck is going to protect her from you? You psychopath?" Raegan questions with frustration. "Don't you fuckers be using this as an opportunity to get back in with her, ya hear. I'm watching y'all."

"What do you want to do, Mia?" I repeat my question again, trying to get us back on track. Right now, we are not the threat to Mia. Someone out there sent her that message. They know she has left the estate, so they are watching and biding their time to get her.

I'm uncomfortable being out in the open with Mia while she's a sitting duck for someone's malignant attention. I watch as Carter's eyes trail across the hallway, and then so do Finn's. They are both aware that a threat could come to her in the form of a bullet from any of these classrooms. We need to get the fuck out of here.

I grab Mia's hand and drag her into the empty classroom on the left; and the others follow behind us. Immediately Finn goes over to the windows and pulls all of the blinds down, shutting out any daylight and prying eyes.

Mia looks at each of us, meeting our gazes and taking a deep shuddering breath. Her color is finally coming back. She went deathly pale when she received that message. Her paleness and her eyes were the first things that alerted me that something was wrong before she even dropped the phone on the desk.

"I want to lure them out." Her words have the impact of an atomic bomb going off.

"Fuck no, blondie."

"*Mami,* have you lost your mind?"

"No fucking way, killer."

"Girl, no, absolutely fucking no."

I don't say anything, just meet her intense, fierce eyes and see the resolution in them. She's not asking; she's not even demanding. She's telling us what is going to happen. My fierce little queen will not cower. She refuses to wait for this sicko's timeline to come at her when she's unprepared. She wants to lure him out so she can fight back and finally be free. I don't for a second like this idea; the risks are too high. I can also see in the sternness of her jaw and the way she's squaring her shoulders that she doesn't give a flying fuck what my opinion is.

"How?" I question and watch as her shoulders lose some of their stiffness. She's ready for me to fight her on what she wants to do. As much as I want to, in fact, the dominant alpha inside of me demands that I do. I keep myself from uttering the words that will shatter this moment of a ceasefire between us.

"He's watching me, trying to freak me out, so I run. This could be James, but I'm betting it's not him alone. Someone else is involved. Someone with power and money that used James' need for revenge for their own purposes. I was suspicious about the fact that James managed all he did alone. The surveillance on us at my house, killing Vincent's men, and capturing Vincent." She waits for my response to her words. Does she think I haven't heard her crying his name in the night filled with terror?

"Go on." My voice shows no emotion. Even though I desperately want to grab, kiss, and reassure her that whatever she did to my father was a blessing. She ended the evil that had infected all of us, and with it, she brought a measure of peace to my heart and soul. I no longer fear that devil's grasp coming for me. My queen vanquished him.

"I think whoever is after me is doing it not only as a way to punish and hurt me, but they are trying to hurt Stella. In fact, I'm positive that's the case based on that message. This is about me being a Stratford. James was fresh out of prison, he had the anger and hatred but not the resources to pull off what he did."

"Stella has a lot of enemies, killer. How do we figure out who is trying to hurt her through you?"

"That's the beauty of it, Finn. All I have to do is place myself in their grasp, and they will come out of hiding to get me, revealing themselves to us."

"No, girl. This is crazy. Mia, they could get to you, retake you, or even kill you." Raegan's face is filled with fear. I can see that the images of Mia when she returned to us, are running through her mind. I know because they are running through mine as well. She was so broken and terrorized when she arrived at the house. I can't risk that happening again. I also can't deny her. If I do, she will put herself at risk without us having her back.

"Mia, please, my *reina*, be reasonable. There has to be another way."

Except she's right, and I hate to fucking admit it. Everything in me wants to reject this suggestion, but I can't. The temptation of her right out in the open will be too much for this fucker to deny. He wants to get to her, wants to hurt her. If his ultimate goal is to punish Stella Stratford, what better way than to kill her beloved granddaughter and heir?

"How?" The minute the word leaves my lips, Finn's hand grabs my neck forcefully and tightens. "Have you lost your fucking mind, Theo? She could get hurt. She could fucking die. There is no more following your idiotic plans, fucker."

Mia's hand reaches over and wraps around Finn's tight fist, which is clenching my airway so tightly that I'm moments away from passing out. "You're not following his plans, Finn. You will be following mine."

Finn releases my neck, and blessed air flows through the abused organ, forcing me to bend forward and cough. Motherfucker would have choked me completely out with how incensed he is.

"Do you trust me?" Mia questions, forcing each of our gazes to meet each other and then hers. Do I trust her? I trust her with everything I am, with my beating heart and my tarnished soul. It doesn't mean I won't still do whatever is necessary to protect my queen.

I'm her fucking king; that's my job. To stand at her side, ride into battle, and destroy all of our enemies.

CHAPTER 41

Mia

"The things you let go will someday teach you how to fly."
Jenim Dibie

Have you ever had one of those moments of utter certainty and surrealism? I'm having one of those right now as I tell the kings of Casbury and Raegan my plans to lure James and whoever is helping him out of hiding. The fact that Theo, the control freak, is not arguing with me has surprise and shock racing through my body.

I can see that he wants to. It's right there on the tip of his tongue to try to exert control over me, but he is restraining himself. Right now, fucking Finn is acting like a rabid dog and choking him out. I wrap my hand tightly around his wrist. Letting my nails sink deeply into his flesh and forcing him to focus on me and release his dangerous grip on Theo. It doesn't escape me that the other two didn't attempt to stop him from attacking Theo or that they made no attempt to force him to release him. *Fucking idiots.*

"Do you trust me?" The question leaves my lips with the certainty that all of them will answer no. It both shocks and brings me unlimited joy when none of them actually provide that answer. "With my life killer." Finn is the first to reply with such confidence that it fills me with heat. I tear my gaze away from Theo's and meet his.

"Do you trust me with mine?"

"Mia...this is dangerous; so many things could go wrong." Poor Raegan is beside herself. She can see she will be outnumbered in her protests by the kings. As much as they want to argue with me, I think each of them realizes that this is the crossroad between us. If they try to force me back to Stella's protection, they will lose me forever. If they follow me and help me in my plans to take down my enemy, there is still hope that I can heal from their betrayal and that things can be put right between us. We can't ever go back to those peaceful days before Mateo was taken. Those fleeting moments in time when all five of us were safe, together, and happy in each other's company. But maybe, just maybe, we can build new moments.

Right now, at this very moment is when I realize how much I actually care for each of them. How much I desire that they stand with me in my fight and help me in my act of vengeance. I not only need their support, I want it. I am still in love with all four of them. I know that now without a doubt. Every piece of me, even the fractured, dark and angry pieces, crave them. They are Helios, the sun god, and I am desperate to warm myself in their light. I cannot live without them any more than they can live without me. We were meant to be united by the strings of fate. The five of us, individual threads, that will form a strong rope. We are made stronger together. The pain they inflicted on me truly just made me stronger.

I no longer seek to burn them with my vengeance. No, they are no longer the monsters in my story. While the harm they committed was life-changing and forced me to morph from Amelia Hamilton to Mia Stratford, it wasn't life-ending. In fact, they gave me a new life and a new purpose.

James and this monster hidden behind shadows, have had a profound effect on my life. He has caused nothing but devastation to my body, heart, and battered and weary soul. They are the monsters that will haunt my living dreams for the rest of my life if I don't stop them. The need for satisfaction and revenge is a call to war in my veins. I will have it, and no one will take it from me.

The kings can either stand with me, support me in my fight to rid myself and the world of the evil that has tainted me with its touch, or they can move aside and live in my past. I will not make any further allowances for them. There will be no more chances. They wanted my mercy. This is how they redeem themselves in my eyes. I know if they don't take this last olive branch between us, my heart will shrivel up and die inside the cavity of my chest.

I take a deep breath, one that I have to force down through the tightness in my chest. *Please, pick me. Love me enough to do what I need.* I place my hand out in front of Theo and wait. His midnight blue eyes meet mine, and I watch as his jaw tenses as he grinds his teeth. Then with a grunt, he pulls my phone from his pocket and places it in my hand. The desire to hug him fills me, but I restrain myself. *Get it together bitch. We are a badass queen, remember?*

Unknown Caller

You're going to die, Stratford whore, and Stella won't be able to save you. I'm watching you take your last breaths.

I'm not afraid of you fucker. You will die at my hands. I'm a fucking Stratford. We don't forgive or forget.

CHAPTER 42

Carter

"When you're the only sane person, you look like the only insane person." Criss Jami, Diotima, Battery, Electric Personality

I don't like this fucking plan, not one fucking bit. Everything inside of me is telling me to grab Mia and run. It's a living, breathing desire in my body, one that has all of my body tensing as I watch my girl from a distance with my gun ready to end whoever this fucker is.

I can't see each of my brothers, but I know they, too, are hidden and have their eyes closely watching Mia. We couldn't convince Raegan to stand down and hide. She's out there on the courtyard grass sitting with my little blondie, pretending not to be concerned at the prospect of a fucker coming to kill her best friend.

The plan is relatively simple when you think about it. Not that it doesn't have my hackles up and my body threatening to explode with hives. Mia sent that text message to the unknown caller taunting him to come and get her. Then my little psycho queen went back to class like nothing had happened, going through the motions of an ordinary day, betting on the fact that the assholes won't be able to help themselves. We know they are in the area based on the message she received. We are betting that James and whoever is by his side, are so filled with anger that they won't enact a huge plan to take her away again, and will instead jump on any opportunity to make her pay.

In the meantime, Finn, Mateo, and Raegan stayed by her side like loyal warriors while Theo and I went out to meet a contact of mine. That contact supplied us with an arsenal of weapons to protect our girl. Did Tom think it was suspicious that Theo and I left the school grounds with nothing in our hands and returned with a black backpack each? If he did, the fucker didn't say anything when I once again blessed him with my two middle fingers. He sat in his vehicle, staring us down with that cold, killer look of his. Should I be worried that one day Tom is going to come for me? *Maybe. I plan to make him work for it, though.*

It's almost the end of the lunch period, and so far, the only thing we have seen approaching Mia was a gray squirrel that tried to steal a fry from the takeaway container on her lap. She's sitting with her sexy legs outstretched in front of her, all that gorgeous skin on display in the sunshine. A smirk crosses my lips at the knowledge that she's pantiless cause I ripped them off and had my cum dripping out of her a couple of hours ago. *Focus fucker, you can't get distracted with daydreams of Mia's pussy. There will be plenty of time for the real thing once she's safe.* My mind chastises me.

I'm ready to leave my hiding spot and call it quits on this stupid plan when I see Raegan get up from her spot next to Mia and walk back toward the doors leading into the school to throw out their trash containers. Suddenly from the very corner of my eye, I see a large shadow moving behind one of the bushes closest to her. Before I can even warn my brothers, a large burly man with dark hair and a white bandage across one of his eyes is grabbing Raegan from behind and wrapping his forearm around her neck, forcing her body close to his as he holds a blade to her stomach.

Raegan releases a screech that catches Mia's attention, and Mia jumps up to her feet. A scream leaving her lips as she starts to move towards Raegan and the fucker holding her at knifepoint. "Hello Amelia, did you miss your daddy, girlie? You've been a real naughty little bitch. I think you need to be punished." I watch as his words cause Mia to falter. He must have said some of those words to her before because her body is suddenly frozen, and her face is going pale. Her beautiful eyes are too wide in her face, and her chest is rising and falling too quickly. Shit, she's about to have a panic attack. I recognize them now that I have seen Mateo have them so many times. I want to charge out there and save Raegan and pull my girl to safety. To put a fucking bullet in the middle of this fuckers eyes, but I promised Mia I would stay hidden until the second fucker appears. I hate this stupid fucking plan.

Move, baby, please. Come on Mia, pull out of whatever nightmare you're trapped in. *Fight baby.* I beg with everything I have, silently praying that she emerges from the horror her mind is seeing. Raegan lets out a deafening scream and fights James' harsh grip. It has Mia shaking her head and her eyes refocusing on the sight in front of her. I let out the tight breath that I was holding and steady my grip on the gun in my hands, pointing it directly at James's head.

"Release her, you disgusting fucker!" Mia screams, her hands clenched at her side.

"Is that any way to talk to your daddy, Amelia? What an ill-mannered whore you are. I can't wait to pound that tight pussy of yours into a bloody mess and make you remember your manners." His words have rage filling every part of my body as a red haze makes itself present across my sightline. The waves of anger I felt before don't compare to the overwhelming and all-encompassing need to destroy this monster before me. I'm going to enjoy killing him. This fucker is not going to get a quick death. I will tear him apart, one organ at a time, until nothing is left of him. Then I'll make sure to scatter him to the four corners of the fucking earth so no one will ever find a trace of him again.

"Big words for a pedophile with one eye, James. It's obvious YOU didn't learn your lesson, but you will. This time I will make sure I take your other eye and finish cutting off the little shrimp you call a dick before I end your fucking life." She takes a few more steps forward, but in the time of a single blink a dark shape jumps out from behind the Sassafras tree beside her.

It's a fucking man, probably in his mid-sixties, dressed all in black with a black baseball cap on his head. He moves quickly and silently behind Mia, creeping up on her before she detects his presence. Before I can pop out of my hiding spot in the tree thirty feet away, he's on her and has a gun pressed against the middle of her back. NO!

My heart races as I jump down from the tree I was perched in and race towards her. Theo, Mateo, and Finn also rush from their hiding spots in the nearby bushes and run forward with guns drawn.

"I'll fucking shoot her if you don't all put down your weapons," the new addition announces as we all stop around them with our own guns drawn. A brawny laugh leaves James' mouth as he presses the blade into Raegan's stomach, and we see the telltale sign of blood appear on her white Oxford button-down shirt. "Mia, save yourself," Raegan shouts before James' grip around her neck traps her breath and words in her throat. "I'm going to enjoy watching you die, Amelia."

"Rae!" Mia tries to take a step forward, but the man yanks her back by the hair and forces her to remain pressed against his gun.

"I will fucking kill her. Lower your weapons and throw them toward me, or I will shoot her."

Theo's eyes connect with mine before he throws his weapon toward the man holding my girl hostage. I watch as Mateo and Finn do the same, but I hesitate taking another two steps forward. "I'm not fucking with you, Carter Pemberton. I will shoot Mia if you do not comply." His voice rings out loudly and with anger. He tightens his grip on her hair, forcing her neck and back to arch painfully in his hold.

The fact that this fucker knows my name pisses me off. He has obviously been watching us for a while. I hesitate for another moment, even as I watch him pushing the gun into the middle of her back, and her cries of pain find my ears. *This is complete fucking bullshit!* Who is this fucker? I need a name so I know who I am going to hunt down and murder for causing my girl pain.

"Carter, drop the fucking weapon," Theo yells at me with desperation and fear clearly evident in his tone.

Fucking hell. I knew shit was going to go wrong. I tried to tell them that we needed to fucking get additional eyes in the bushes to protect Mia. I even offered to go look for that cunt Jessie to help us, but I was outvoted. Mia didn't want to put anyone else in danger. One of us should have stayed in the bushes, stayed hidden so we had another card to play, but we didn't think this through properly. Not that any of us would have had an easy time staying hidden with our girl in danger.

Now look, some fucking insane asshole has her once again in his clutches and is threatening to shoot her, while her psychotic bio dad is holding Rae-Rae hostage. Why the fuck does no one ever listen to me? *Cause you're a psycho too,* my mind supplies the answer as I throw my fucking weapon toward the man whose death I am going to enjoy causing for having his hands on my girl.

No one fucking touches my girl!

CHAPTER 43

Finn

"Scared is what you're feeling. Brave is what you're doing."
Emma Donoghue, Room

Come fucking on, Carter, just do it, you reckless bastard. If I could walk over and slap him upside the damn head right now for his insolence, I would. Does he not see that he is risking both Mia and Raegan with his behavior?

I warned Theo and Mia that we wouldn't be able to control him. Did either of them fucking listen to me? *Nope.* Even Mateo reassured me that Carter wouldn't risk harming Mia. Yet here I am, watching him play chicken with a fucker holding a gun to our girl. I swear to fucking God, if she gets hurt because of him, I am going to put a fucking bullet in the back of his head.

"Carter, drop the fucking weapon," Theo yells from twenty feet away from me, and after a moment, the reckless idiot throws the gun down on the ground, but not before taking a few more steps forward. What the fuck is he doing right now? Another pained cry leaves Mia's lips as the guy almost has her neck snapping with his vicious hold.

From the corner of my eye, I watch as Mateo takes another few sneaky steps forward while the guy in black holding Mia at gunpoint is distracted by Carter's antics. I'm still the closest one to them, my eyes locked on the gun he has forced on her back. Who is this piece of shit? He looks like someone's grandfather. Why does he want to hurt Mia?

It fucking kills me to admit, but we should have listened to Carter when he suggested we ask Jessie and a few of the football players to help us keep watch from the bushes. Who the fuck knew the one time the disturbed fucker made a suggestion that actually made sense, we would disregard it. I know Mia didn't want to involve more innocent people in this mess, but how the fuck are we going to save her now? We should have told Tom, even if he chose to drag her ass away kicking and screaming, at least she would be safe.

"Who are you? Why are you doing this?" Mia screams.

A baleful laugh leaves his lips, and I watch as he loosens his grip a bit on her hair. My chest is on fire with fury, watching the pained look cross her features as she tries to turn in his tight grip and get a look at him. "Who am I? What a good question, little Stratford whore. I'm vengeance forty years too late. I am the man your disgusting family took everything from. Your grandparents and great grandparents took my love, my wealth, even my good name, and left me to rebuild everything from scratch. I am patient and wrath personified, and you will be my greatest revenge on Stella Stratford."

"Don't forget you promised me another taste of my girlie before you end her life. I want to see the fear in her eyes as I choke her with my cock." James cackles from his position.

Sick motherfucker, I am going to rip his innards out through his nose. I take a step forward, but it recatches the attention of the psycho holding the gun on Mia. "I wouldn't do that, Finn. I would hate to end this all too soon with your pretty Stratford princess' brain splattered on the ground around us."

"Release Raegan, and I will go with you. You can take me and murder me, just don't hurt her." Mia begs. Fear skates down my back at her offering herself in return for Raegan's safety. *No! Fuck no!* I want to yell out, I want to demand that this fucker take me in her place, but I know he won't accept. He wants a

Stratford to hurt, and the only one present is Mia. I watch with devastation and fear from my spot as his body goes rigid and his face flushes with anger.

"I don't want to murder you, Mia Stratford. I want to take you and your worthless life apart one piece at a time. I want you to suffer at my hands like I suffered at your grandparents'. I want you to feel panic and rage as I destroy your whole world as Jaxon did to me. Force you to still breathe and go on without hope after everything you love is taken from you. I want your cunt of a grandmother to know this is all her doing and that I am the one repaying her for her sins."

His arm swings away from Mia's back, and he fires toward Carter. "I want to take your love away, so you die inside." A scream leaves Mia's lips as she tries to jerk from his hold. The bullet misses Carter completely, but the distraction allows Mateo and me to rush forward. Mateo is almost on him when he presses the barrel of the gun into Mia's neck.

"You fuckers move again, and I will put a bullet in her pretty head."

"I'm going to kill you slowly, motherfucker. You should try to run now." Carter spews with venom.

We can hear a commotion coming from inside the cafeteria; students, having heard the shot, are now running for their lives inside the school. We can see them from the glass windows that face out into the vast green lawned courtyard. Jessie comes to the glass door leading out and tries to get my attention, but I nod my head no for him to remain inside. Hopefully, Tom heard the gunshot too, from his position in the car at the front of the school. If not, at least all the kids running from the building will alert him that something is wrong, and he will come running to find Mia. He better hurry the fuck up. I feel like we are running out of time here to save the girls.

Theo tries to get my attention with small hand motions near his waist. At first, I have no idea what the fucker is trying to tell me. Then he slightly nods, the action almost imperceivable if you're not paying attention, bringing my attention back to Raegan. My eyes can't fucking believe what they are seeing. Somehow little Raegan had a small blade hidden somewhere on her body. I'm going to bet she was wearing it strapped to her thigh like Mia is prone to do.

James hasn't noticed her slow, methodical movements yet, and the guy with the gun isn't looking their way. He's distracted with us.

I try to get both their attention on me so they don't realize what's going on with Raegan, and maybe Mateo or Theo have an opportunity to jump the asshole with the gun. "You're just some slimy old fucker with a grudge, aren't ya? What happened, old man, Stella hand you your ass?" An evil chuckle leaves my lips.

"Did the queen of Manhattan destroy your pitiful kingdom, dick? I'm sure it was well deserved. What, you couldn't take her on yourself because you're a weak fuck, so you had her granddaughter kidnapped and raped by a monster as some sign of strength?" I shout all the words with violent rage behind them, taking a step forward and then another. I'm not more than ten feet from my girl now, and I can see the fear in her ocean-blue eyes. I can also see the anger in the light blue eyes of the fucker before me. Light blonde strands of hair peek out from beneath the cap he is wearing, and you can see freckles across his lined face.

"Shut the fuck up, Finn." He yells, the color rising on his face. Look at that; I must have hit a sore spot with my words.

"You're a nobody. Just some pitiful old man holding a gun to a girl with more strength than you will ever possess. Pathetic. Whatever Stella did to you clearly wasn't enough. You deserved more."

"SHUT UP!"

A cry sounds to the side, and I glimpse Raegan with the blade slashing at James' arm. He lets out a massive roar as he releases his hold on her and tries to rip the knife from her hand, and she falls to the ground, scrambling away from him. Carter runs forward and pulls her back behind him, grabbing one of the guns from the ground and pointing it at James.

The distraction is all that Theo needs to slam his large muscled body into the guy holding Mia hostage. The force and momentum behind his attack has the guy releasing his tight hold on Mia and staggering backward, but not before a shot rings out in the air. I rush forward and dive for Mia, wrapping her in my arms and cradling her body as we hit the ground hard, and she is underneath me. A searing, burning pain rips through my shoulder, and a groan leaves my lips.

More shots ring out, and then chaos breaks out all around us. Raegan is screaming and crawling towards Mia and me on her hands and knees. I lift my head and see Carter straddling James and repeatedly slamming the butt of the gun on his face with destructive blows. Angry growls leave his lips, and his body is tight with rage and violence.

I turn my head and spy Theo fighting with the guy with the gun; he's throwing punches but also taking them. Mateo runs across the grass and picks up one of the discarded guns, rushing back toward Theo and pointing the gun at the man in black. "STOP, OR I'LL SHOOT!" He shouts.

"Finn, fuck, you're bleeding. Finn, are you okay? Can you release me?" Mia begs from below me as she pushes against my chest. All of my weight is pressed down on her and crushing her. I look down to see her blonde hair covered in blood. Holy fuck, did she get hit? I raise myself on my elbow, and pain races down my back. A grunt leaves my lips as Mia tries to escape from below my heavy weight. "You're bleeding. Are you hit, Killer?"

"It's not my blood Finn; it's yours." She screams as her hand presses firmly down on my shoulder. FUCK. THAT HURTS!

Theo and Mateo get my attention again as the guy stops fighting, and Theo forces him down to his knees by kicking the back of his legs out. Mateo comes forward and presses the gun against his forehead. "Give me one fucking reason why I shouldn't blow your fucking brains out right now."

"NO, MATEO!" Mia screams as she finally scrambles from below me and races in Mateo and Finn's direction.

"Jesus, Finn, we need to stop the bleeding." Raegan firmly presses her hand against my shoulder as I try to stand back up.

"Fuck, Rae, we have to stop Carter." I groan as I force myself back to my feet, pain radiates down my arm and chest, and for a moment, my vision sways, but Raegan takes a hold of my waist and pulls me toward an insane and blood-soaked Carter. He's still smashing the butt of the gun continually in James' face which now looks like bloody raw meat. The fucker is unconscious and sprawled out on the lawn below Carter.

"Carter, fucking stop! It's done!" I yell and shove him as hard as I can off of James. He stumbles to the side and turns his husky eyes on me, filled with madness in their depth. He turns back, tries to straddle James again, and swings his fist before I grab him by the back of the shirt and pull him off James. The sound of material tearing combines with the sounds of our heavy breaths.

"He has to die." He growls, his words are uttered between clenched teeth.

"He's not yours to kill, Carter. That pleasure belongs to Mia." Raegan helps me drag him back another foot.

Just then, we hear the sound of lots of footsteps moving toward us.

"Clear."

"Clear."

Fuck, thank God, the Stratford cavalry has shown up.

CHAPTER 44

Mia

"Above all, be the heroine of your life, not the victim." Nora Ephron

"Clear."

"Clear."

"She's over here!"

Male voices surround us and have me turning in a panic, thinking more assailants are heading in our direction. My eyes meet Theo's frightened, cold blue ones as Mateo continues to hold his gun at the guy's head, who is now down on his knees.

There is a darkness in Mateo's glare that makes my blood run cold. His lips are curled in anger, and his nostrils flare. His whole body is wrapped with tension; you can see it in every line of his frame. The arm holding the gun vibrates with his tight grip. He wants to hurt this man. He wants to end his life for trying to kill me. A part of me wants him to pull the trigger. To finish this all once and for all. Yet the part of me that yearns for vengeance demands her reckoning. She doesn't want him to take away her need for satisfaction, for the blood of her enemies.

"Mateo Cabano! If you pull that goddamn trigger, I will put a bullet in your head next!" Stella's enraged voice thunders all around us and has the very air freezing in my lungs at her harsh words and tone. An immediate sense of relief fills my body, the sound of my grandmother's voice a balm to the fears that claw at my insides.

My head swings around to see my grandmother rapidly crossing the grassy lawn surrounded by her security team and flanked by Clark and Tom. The latter breaks rank and runs up to me with furious eyes and multiple weapons strapped to his chest.

"Miss Mia, we will be having words about your reckless behavior...again." Relief floods my body, and I don't hesitate to throw myself into Tom's arms. Which surprises the hell out of him and forces him to have to take a step back. I've never been so happy to see his stern face etched with displeasure and disapproval more in my life. "I'm so happy to see you, Tom!"

He pats my back, clearly uncomfortable with my hold, but I don't give a shit. "My *reina*, could you please release Tom? Theo is over here looking a bit enraged and like a caveman about to lose his shit." Mateo calls from his position to the side of us, still pressing the gun into the guy's head.

My grandmother stops before me, a furious look across her features. *Shit.* She is incensed and probably unreasonable right now. I'll be lucky if she doesn't drag me away and lock me up somewhere forever at this point. Her cold blue eyes assess me for injuries and hone in on the blood splattered against my skin and hair. "Tom, get a medic; she's bleeding!"

Stella's face goes so pale she could pass for a ghost. Little lines of strain etch her mouth and eyes, causing her to look older than she is. Her hair is falling out of her chignon, and her clothes are disorderly. Stella kind of looks a mess. I'm not sure why that thought makes me smile, but it does. I reach out and place my hand against my grandmother's upper chest, feeling her heartbeat thundering through her skin and into my palm. She's terrified, fuck. "I'm alright, grandmother. I promise I'm not hurt."

She grabs onto my chin with her cold, trembling hand and holds it firmly, staring into my eyes, probably thinking I'm suffering from blood loss at my loopy smile. "It's not mine; it's Finn's. He took a bullet meant for me." I see immediate relief apparent in her eyes at my words.

"Did he now?" She questions with a raised eyebrow. I can't read her thoughts; her cold mask is in place. Despite her unruly appearance, she is still the same frightening queen. The one I both love and fear right now because she will wreak havoc and destruction on us all for our reckless actions.

Stella stares over her shoulder at Finn, who is still holding onto an insane-looking Carter. Carter is soaked in so much of James' blood that his skin and clothes are painted red. His dark blonde hair barely shows any of its rich colors; the strands now changed to crimson with the sanguine fluid. He looks like a Viking warrior enthralled by the spoils of war and relishing in the destruction of his enemy. All the fucker is missing is a sword or an axe in his hands, and the image would be complete.

I should be terrified and disgusted at the sight of him, but I'm not. My body heats at the look of my king, wrathful, filled with merciless rage on my behalf. He really would destroy anyone who hurts me. The world will tremble before his mighty steps as he rains fire in his wake. He is *Arawn* personified, come to earth to be revered. I almost want to bow at his feet, praise my would-be god, but I am queen, and I don't bow to anyone.

James lies on the grass in front of them, unmoving. *Is he fucking dead?* The anger that lives inside of me hopes not. I want to seek my own vengeance on him. I demand retribution, and I will not be denied. Blood is trickling down Finn's arm and chest, coating his shirt and making it stick to him. He looks a little ashen as his eyes meet mine from the short distance; relief and pain cross his beautiful features. "Get him a medic!" Stella roars and breaks the spell between us.

A man runs towards Finn with a medical bag strapped to his chest. I watch as Finn releases his hold on Carter and allows the medic to cut the shirt off of his body. A groan leaves his lips as the guy prods the injury, and I see his body sway. There is so much blood across his ochre skin that it creates a gruesome abstract piece of art across his chest. Jesus fuck, I should have paid closer attention; that looks like a lot of blood.

"FUCK, RAE!" Carter's shout rips mine and Stella's attention back in his and Raegan's direction. It looks like he was trying to kick James's prone body, and Raegan has pinched him hard to stop him. "What in the Sam Hill, Carter Pemberton! Don't you try to hit that devil again!"

Stella lets out a chuckle at Raegan and Carter's antics as Clark walks over and checks James for a pulse in his neck. His eyes meet Stella's, and I watch as he nods in the affirmative. The fucker is still breathing. Relief fills me that I will still have my revenge on that demon. I don't doubt that Stella will ensure I get my retribution before this day is done. I plan to send James to meet Vincent and Carter's dad in hell. The three of them, I am sure, will have lots in common.

Stella's gaze returns to the man in front of us. The one Mateo is still holding at gunpoint while Theo stands sentinel behind him. I have no doubt that if the fucker tries to run, tries anything at all, Theo will beat him bloody. His face is a mask of discontent; his chest rises quickly with his exhales. Theo looks like a Roman gladiator in the Coliseum, seeking destruction in the arena, one that will kill everyone around him to survive. He doesn't possess Carter's blood lust, but don't be fooled by his controlled rage; it is just as deadly.

"Ajax Pickering. You sniveling, cowardly piece of shit. I should have let my Jaxon murder you years ago." The wrath in Stella's voice is frightening, and I can see its effect on not only this Ajax fucker in front of her but also on Mateo, Theo, and even Carter, who has walked over with deranged glee on his face. *This motherfucker really does enjoy mayhem, doesn't he?*

"Ajax, huh? Sounds like the name of a small dick fuck to me." Carter cackles with manic amusement. I can't stop myself from rolling my eyes; he can be such a ridiculous dweeb. The idiot can't read a room to save his life. My grandmother turns her vicious eyes on him before slapping him hard on the back of the head with her hand. "Shut up, Carter."

"Stella, you know you love me. I'm going to be your favorite grandson." He grins back at her, his straight teeth appearing shockingly white against all the red mess marrying his skin.

Stella lets out a huff of agitation, but I notice she doesn't dispute his charge. *Fucking hell, he really is her favorite.* Really? Out of all four of them, she has to love the crazy one the most?

"Give me the gun, Mateo." She moves forward to his side and reaches her hand to take the weapon he has centered on Ajax's head.

"You're going to shoot me, Stella? Here in cold blood? In front of all these children? I always knew you were a psychotic cunt." Theo slams his fist hard into the back of Ajax's head at the venom spewing from his mouth.

"I spared you years ago, Ajax. After you almost killed the love of my life. This is how you repay my moment of mercy? You come after my granddaughter. Align yourself with a madman to rape and abuse her?"

"Mercy? You think that was mercy, Stella? You, Jaxon, and that cunt mother of yours destroyed my whole life, tore it to pieces leaving nothing behind but ashes. I loved you once, you were my world, but you chose him despite Jaxon forcing you down that aisle. You still fucking chose him when I would have loved you forever. You watched silently as he blew up my whole world, taking my family's legacy from me. Ruining my name so I would be an outcast. I have spent over thirty years in hell because of you! You're nothing but Jaxon's dirty whore."

Stella's hand strikes out with the gun, slamming it into Ajax's face. The crunch of his nose, as it meets the barrel of the weapon, sounds loud in the sudden silence around us. Everyone has just stopped moving, a hush falling over us as we watch what is happening between Stella and the fucker on his knees before her.

"You should have suffered more. You tried to take me from him, and I was not yours to take. You seek vengeance on my kin for my husband's righteous actions. I was swayed once, Ajax, in light of our past. That small mercy I granted you has come back to haunt me. I shall be the tool of vengeance now. My eyes will be the last you see in this world." Stella pulls the trigger. The sound is so loud that it has birds squalling into the air from the trees surrounding the grassy area. A ringing starts in my ears, and I have to shake my head to try to clear it.

Ajax's body falls backward onto Theo's body, a huge part of his skull gone. Blood and brain matter have exploded everywhere and landed on all of us in close proximity. Theo takes a few steps back, blood, skull fragments, and gore covering his chest and face. Ajax's body slides off of him and hits the grass with a heavy thud. A frightened gasp leaving Raegan's mouth pulls me from my frozen state, and my eyes turn to my grandmother.

Her face is splattered with blood, and her blue eyes shine with madness as she still holds the gun in her tight grip. Stella's glare never leaves the sight of Ajax's body before her, but a trembling begins to settle around her. Her shoulders rise and fall rapidly and then shake, her lips tighten, and tears start to trail from the corner of her eyes and down her face, where they make grotesque lines through all the blood. Carter reaches forward, removes the gun from her fingers, and she allows him to take it before turning her gaze on me.

Her eyes are filled with so much pain that it makes my breath stutter in my chest. "I'm so sorry, Mia. I am so incredibly sorry, child, that this lunatic went after you in order to seek vengeance on me and your grandfather." She sniffs and swipes at the tears, causing them to smear along her high cheekbones. "I should have let Jaxon kill him years ago like he demanded. If I had, he wouldn't have been able to come after you. It was a moment of weakness, sparing Ajax's life because of our complicated past."

I move forward and wrap my arms tightly around my grandmother's waist, holding her in my embrace as tears continue to fall down her face and her body is wracked with sobs. Her arms wrap around mine, and we clutch each other tightly. Each lost in our own suffering but also unified in our love for each other.

Her head leans against mine, her scent of vanilla and jasmine filling my senses and bringing me a sense of home. "You must never show weakness, Mia. You must be stronger than I am. My moment of mercy almost cost you your life." She pulls back from me and holds on to both of my shoulders as her intense gaze meets mine. "Promise me, Mia, that you will end the life of anyone who seeks to harm you and those you love without mercy."

CHAPTER 45

Theo

"Don't be afraid of your fears. They're not there to scare you. They're there to let you know that something is worth it." C. JoyBell C.

After what happened in the courtyard of Casbury Prep yesterday, I think we are all still walking around in a bit of a daze. After Stella shot that fucking piece of shit Ajax, she ordered Clark to dispose of the body and that James be taken. Where I don't know, but I wish I did.

My need to be alone with that vile creature who hurt my girl, and break every single bone in his body, is a restless energy within me. It's taking all the control I possess not to demand Stella let me have time alone with him. Not that I think she will listen to a word that leaves my lips. Let's face it, she's not my biggest fan.

I'm not the only one who is suffering from their need to inflict violence on James. Carter is walking around with manic energy, his body still wired from yesterday and his lack of satisfaction from the preceding events. He is once again pacing in front of me, mumbling to himself, and it's starting to give me a damn headache. All of us are once again back in Mia's house.

Stella tried to stop us from coming with Mia back to the estate, but it just led to further violence, as my brothers and I would not be denied. Carter took two of her guards down, much to everyone's fucking surprise, and Mateo almost ended up with a bullet in his back before she called a halt to the madness and begrudgingly allowed us to come with them. Here's hoping Stella doesn't have us all murdered here. *Who am I kidding? She would kill us herself, not order it.*

Mia, however, never said a fucking word in our defense. She didn't demand her grandmother allow us to accompany her back to her home. She just watched the anarchy happen before her with a look of reflection across her beautiful face. Was she in shock at the sight of her grandmother killing that fucker in cold blood before her eyes? I wonder what is going through my little queen's mind right now?

I'm not going to lie and say that Stella killing that man in cold blood, right there in the open, with no repentance wasn't chilling. *It fucking was.* It caused a shiver of unease to skate down my back. *She really is a killer.* I need to watch mine and the guys' backs for her blade.

Finn groans from his place on the sofa in the entertainment room. The fucker's arm is in a dark blue sling strapped across his chest. He was so freaking lucky that the bullet was a clean in-and-out shot and didn't do any real damage. He will always have a scar, though. I guess he and Mateo are now twins.

Rae-Rae was in here earlier, teasing Finn about it. "Y'all are so dramatic; it's a flesh wound. Now get up, you good-for-nothing rascals." Even though she jested with him and was kinda mean, she had a new look of respect in her eyes for him. She even shoved some chocolate oatmeal cookies she had made in his hands before slapping Carter upside the head for trying to steal one.

Before she left the room, she pulled me aside. Her bright green eyes narrowed on me, a fierce look presented on her features. "I don't know that I like y'all with my girl. I still think some of your kinky fuckery is insane. Y'all need Jesus. I'm not going to try to stop you, though. I know you love her, despite all of y'all being demons." She grabbed the front of my shirt in a tight fist and pulled me down close to her face. "If any of y'all hurt her again, though, just know that what Stella did to that Ajax guy is gonna look like a divine blessing, ya feel me.

I'll let you think on that, Theo Saint-Lambert." Then she patted my head like you do with a dog and sauntered away. *Fuck, Rae is starting to really scare me too. All the women in this house are frightening.*

The door to the room opens, and Mia walks in looking beautiful in a pair of fitted gray workout shorts and a loose black Casbury Prep sweatshirt that hangs off her shoulder. My eyes narrow on the shirt; pretty sure that's my fucking shirt. The one I gave her to wear that disastrous day I took her to my house so many months ago. She closes the door firmly, leans her back against it, and her eyes move over each of us. All of our gazes are transfixed on her.

"We have to talk." She crosses her arms across her chest and moves further into the room, and like the lovesick fool I am, my eyes watch her every movement and appraise her stunning features.

"Whatcha wanna talk about, blondie?" Carter moves forward and tries to reach for her, but she evades his grasp.

"I need you four to tell me the truth...even if it's going to hurt me." A feeling of unease races across my body, and I recoil. The look on her face is so serious, demanding even. I try to regain my composure, squaring my shoulders, keeping my face neutral, and meeting her questioning look. "What do you want to know?"

Her eyes roam between the four of us, the mask she knows how to wear so well, firmly in place. "Why did all four of you bully me all those years ago? I barely knew the three of you, yet you made it your mission to make my life as miserable as possible. Why did you hate me so much?" Her blue-green eyes narrow, and I see pain and disgust in her features before she hides her emotions.

"Ah, shit. I knew this was coming. It was only a matter of fucking time." Carter trails his hands through his thick hair and moves to stand in front of her. His head turns to me, and his eyes meet mine. I nod my head at him and let my mask slip away, showing him my despair and grief. We need and love her, we have to be honest now, or we will lose her forever.

He and I have always been able to communicate without words, so I know he's seeing what I am projecting. A sigh leaves his lips as he closes his eyes and falls to his knees in front of her. "We never hated you. It was never about that. In fact, blondie, it was the opposite for me; I envied you."

"Envied me? What did I have that you didn't have, Carter?"

"Love, Mia. You had love. Your mom loved you unconditionally."

An incredulous look crosses her face at his words, and her eyebrows furrow in a deep "V." "It's true. We never hated you. This all started years ago, Mia. When my mom died. Your mom came to her funeral. I guess she was a friend of my mom's at some point. She looked so sad when she saw my mom; she even brought her a flower." The memory of that day wants to wash over me, but I fight its hold.

"She was the only other person in the room who was genuinely there for my mom and was sad for the world's loss of her brightness... but your mom got my dad and Mack's attention. We overheard my dad say he was going to pursue your mom so she could be one of his playthings tied up in his dungeon to be used by him and his friends. Mateo's dad commented about you and asked if my dad would play at being your stepdad." Anger tries to rise within me at the memory of the look of sick pleasure on my dad's face at the question.

"Vincent said that they would hurt you if you looked anything like your mom and...make us hurt you... so that you learned how to be an obedient sex slave. We were ten, Mia."

"You were just a kid, and yet they were talking about raping you, abusing you, and forcing us to hurt you." Carter breaks into my story, the words sliding from his lips filled with rancor and agitation.

Her eyes widen with shock, and a shudder makes her body sway. Carter wraps his hands around her waist and leans his head against her stomach. "We couldn't let that happen, babe. We couldn't let them get their sick hands on you or your mom."

"We devised a plan to try to force your mom to take you out of Casbury. We wanted to get the two of you the hell away from here and our dads. I didn't know then that my dad was involved with Mack and Vincent's schemes. That he trafficked women for them." Mateo grabs onto his hair and pulls, his green eyes haunted and his face getting paler by the minute.

"A plan that you came up with, Theo?" Mia questions as she pulls away from Carter's tight grasp and puts some distance between them. Fuck is she already pulling away? Does she not believe that we never hated her? Even then, as kids, we felt the need to protect her. Sure, we went about it the wrong way, but there was always this pull between us and her.

"I wanted to protect you and your mom, Mia. I already knew by then what a monster my dad was. I saw it first hand. He hurt my mom for years, even when she was sick and dying with cancer. He let his friends hurt her too. When she finally died, it was a fucking blessing. She was finally free of him.. I wasn't. I didn't want that to happen to either of you." I give her a sobering stare and drop the mask I wear, allowing her to see into the darkness that taints my soul.

I am the son of a monster who let his cancer-stricken wife be passed around and sexually abused by his friends. "I couldn't save her, Mia. Her screams and tears were a constant companion in my nightmares for years. I couldn't save her from those monsters. I couldn't even defend myself. I blamed her for leaving me behind... even though she had already suffered unimaginable horrors at his hands. She stayed in that house all that time for me. To protect me in any way she could from my father. She knew that he would never let her take me and leave. She paid the price for standing up to him and I... I couldn't save her."

"The bullying was a way to force Catherine to see us as a danger to you, Mia. The hope was that she would pull you out of school and maybe move elsewhere, where a bunch of rich delinquent fucks couldn't keep tormenting you." Finn interjects.

"Why didn't any of you just approach my mom?" Her question is valid. We have struggled with the knowledge that we put her through all that pain, torment, and suffering, and had we just used half a fucking brain cell between us and talked to her mom, all of that could have been avoided. Catherine was already frightened of my dad; maybe she would have taken us seriously.

"We didn't think she would believe a bunch of rich kids." Carter acknowledges with a bent head, staring at the ground. "But that's what we were. We were just kids. We made a terrible, stupid mistake. We didn't think about the consequences, only the result we wanted, which was for you to leave for safety...where none of us could."

"And you, Finn? Why go along with it? Why not tell me what was going on? I was your best friend for longer than they were. You crushed me when you turned on me."

A huge sigh leaves his lips. "You have no idea how much I have always regretted going along with them. You're right; you were my best friend. It wasn't because I stopped wanting to be your friend or cause I chose them over you. I was stuck, Mia. My life was upside down. I was in a new world with new kids and a dad. I had never had a dad before. He had expectations, and I didn't want to disappoint him. My mom put so much pressure on me to fit in. To leave that old life behind because she didn't want a reminder of it. When they started to bully you, I fought them every time afterward. I didn't want them to hurt you. I just didn't know what to do. But none of that is an excuse. You have every right to still hate me for what I did. I do."

"Mia, do you remember when we tied you to a tree?" Carter questions.

I watch as her hands tighten into fists and anger crosses her face. Oh yeah, she remembers, alright. That was such a fucked up thing that we did to her. All of it was fucked up and dangerous. So many things could have gone wrong. *So many things did go wrong,* my mind seethes.

"Yeah, I remember fucker. I remember being so scared that I peed myself and had to sit for hours like that in my own urine. That ants and other bugs crawled all over me, biting my arms, legs and face, but I couldn't fight them off because my hands were restrained. Then finally, when that homeless man untied me, I worried he was gonna hurt me too, 'cause he looked at me funny. I had to run all the way home with tears trailing down my face. So yes, I fucking remember! I had nightmares for weeks about bugs!" She yells. The sound of her voice breaking with the horrors we inflicted on her makes my own heart pound painfully in my chest.

"Finn tried to break ties with us when we did that to you. He was done. He didn't fully understand why we were hurting you. He tried to fight me so he could release you, but I showed him pictures of a sixteen-year-old girl that

Theo and I rescued from Vincent and Mack's clutches. They had beaten her so bloody, Mia, that she couldn't even stand. Multiple men had raped her over and over for hours while they kept her tied down so she couldn't fight back. The pictures showed the state she was in once we got her out of there. I used them to remind me daily of why I was hurting you, why I needed you desperately to leave town so you didn't end up like her."

"I didn't fight them anymore after that, Mia. I didn't participate either, but those pictures, they haunted me. I kept seeing your face instead of hers. Every time you cried, I saw those pictures in my mind. I convinced myself that we were doing the right thing. That the guys were right, and it was the only way to keep you and your momma from falling into Vincent's clutches. I'm so sorry, Mia. I have to live with the knowledge that I was a coward and didn't protect you for the rest of my life."

Tears are sliding down Mia's face, first one, then another, until they are crystal rivers making their way over her high cheekbones and falling off her chin to disappear into the thick sweatshirt. The need to wrap her in my arms as she shatters before us at the confession of our sins urges me forward. I take a few steps in her direction until I am by her side. She doesn't stop me from reaching out to her. My thumbs wipe at the tears. "We tried to protect you. We wanted to protect you. We felt the need to protect you, but we went about it the wrong way. We loved you even then. We just didn't know it. I don't know how to make it up to you, Mia, but I swear I will spend my whole life trying to."

"You had better, Theo Saint-Lambert." She rises on her toes and crashes her lips into mine, taking me momentarily by surprise. My mouth opens under her tongue, prodding at my lips, and I surrender myself to her. Letting her consume me. I was always hers.

CHAPTER 46

Mia

"Your memory feels like home to me. So whenever my mind wanders, it always finds its way back to you." Ranata Suzuki

As their confessions leave their lips and they acknowledge and take responsibility for the hell they put me through, I feel my battered and weary heart lightening. Their words don't absolve them of the crimes they committed against me, but somehow now, hearing their reasoning behind doing it lessens the pain and brutality of the memories. It allows my soul and heart to begin the process of healing and forgiving them.

I had already decided yesterday that if they stood by me, I would dissolve my plans to continue to seek retribution against them. Not only did they stand with me, they fought for me. Each of them putting their very lives on the line for me. Finn even took a bullet that was meant to end my life. *If that doesn't speak of love, I don't know what the fuck does.*

While complete forgiveness for their actions will not be readily given. I, too, have work to do to process all my trauma. I also made mistakes. I returned to

Casbury with nothing but hate and revenge in my heart. The desire to destroy their lives and implode their world was my only priority. Then I discovered that there were depths and layers to these four kings of Casbury. My bruised heart sparked around them, and as much as I tried to deny the need and want of them in my heart, mind, and soul. It refused to die or stay dormant.

My vengeance was what I came here seeking. That need to hurt them as they did me caused poison to run through my veins. A poison that the kings siphoned from me inch by inch with each other's words, deeds, and actions. Where hate wanted to drown me in the misery of my past, love found me and created a new path. Will things ever be healed entirely between the kings of Casbury and myself? *I don't honestly know.* I will never forget my past experiences; they helped shape me into who I am today. The kings will also not be able to erase that they were the monsters in my nightmares, but together I'm hopeful we can move past it.

I no longer want to live trapped in my past, filled with righteous anger. I want to move into the light with the four men that I know I love and can't live without and that love me back with a fierce passion that is stunning in its brilliance. The time to sit and wallow in my regrets and theirs is over. This corrupted kingdom has been set fire to, and nothing will extinguish the flames. I plan to rise from its ashes like a phoenix and create my new world.

My heart will always belong to the four kings of Casbury, my tormentors, my demons, my sinners, and, more importantly, my loves. They are the future I seek, and I am done stopping myself from having it.

My lips meet Theo's in a clash of teeth, lips, tongues intertwining, and throaty groans. His muscular arms wrap around my waist and pull me closer until my body is pressed against him, and I can feel every inch of him. His cock thickens and lengthens, pressed against my stomach, and tendrils of fire rise within my core. I rub myself against him like a cat in heat, looking for friction against my needy core and pebbled nipples. A hard body greets me from behind, and the scent of lime, bergamot, and eucalyptus overwhelms my senses. *Carter.*

Carter's hand threads through my hair from behind, pulling on my strands and loosening them from their confinement of my messy bun. A pair of warm lips meet the back of my neck and cause shivers to race through my body. Theo releases his arms from around my waist, and one of his hands trails up underneath the sweatshirt that I am wearing. His strong fingers glide across the skin of my ribs, causing tingles to race up my abdomen, as his digits greet the side of my bare breast. An animalistic groan leaves his lips and vibrates into my mouth, causing my core to weep.

Two different hands slide up the back of the sweatshirt and roam the skin of my back, kneading my flesh and pulling senseless whimpers from my lips. Theo pulls back from the kiss; his dark blue eyes meet mine as he steps back, lifts the sweatshirt's hem, and rips it off my body. Warm fingers meet the waistband of my tight shorts and pull them down with my panties until I stand naked and exposed before my kings.

"Fuck, look at that pretty pussy." The groan comes from beside us, and I look over and meet Mateo's heated gaze. He's stroking his cock over the fabric of his track pants, and a pink blush is tinged across his high elfen cheeks. His striking green eyes are filled with passion as they meet mine, and his sinful pouty lips quirk up in a devious smirk.

Theo's hands slide up my abdomen and palm both my breasts in his large hands, massaging them, tightening and pulling both my nipples between his thick fingers. A gasp leaves my lips as he pinches them hard. My head falls to the side from all the intense sensations, exposing the column of my neck. Carter takes full advantage, suckling and trailing his lips down to where my shoulder and neck meet. He sucks deeply, grazes his teeth, and then bites down on my skin until a cry escapes me and bolts of pleasure race down my spine. *Fuck that feels so good.*

Warm hands press against my asscheeks, grasping and pulling them apart, then releasing them. A thick finger slips between my crack and slides down to rub against my puckered hole. "Are you getting wet for us, baby? Does this pussy and ass ache to be filled?"

I feel Carter lowering himself behind me, and my core squeezes tightly in anticipation. One of Theo's hands leaves my breast and snakes back up my chest until it wraps around my neck. His fingers tighten as his mouth crashes against mine, forcing my breathing to become stunted.

A loud slap sounds through the air before I feel the sting and heat on my asscheek. Another slap lands immediately over the same spot with force, and I scream into Theo's mouth. He greedily swallows the sound, and growls meeting my lips in return. My body is forced to tilt forward by Carter's hands yanking me back by the waist.

My asscheeks are pried open, and I feel a wet tongue pushing against my back entrance. I squirm in their dual hold, and Carter's hands on my fleshy globes tighten. Theo's merciless fingers tighten on my neck as he pulls back from my lips and kisses my jaw, cheek, eye, and forehead. The kisses are so tender and soft that a sigh tries to leave my lips, but his tight grip on my throat traps it.

"We love you, Mia Stratford. Remember that 'cause we are about to fuck you hard and mean like we don't." His words are punctuated by the further tightening of his fingers just as Carter's tongue slips inside of my back hole and has me trying to fight against his hold. My breathing is becoming shallow and erratic, and my vision is spotting. I'm fighting to stay conscious as waves of pleasure rise within me. Theo's mouth meets my hardened nipple, and he sucks deeply before grazing his teeth on the very tip, causing my whole body to tense at the sweet sensation of pain.

The erotic thrill of his mouth on my nipple while Carter fucks my ass with his tongue and being deprived of air has an orgasm barreling forward and lightning racing across my skin. Just when I am about to fall over the peak and explode, both their mouths leave my body. *NO!* I struggle in Theo's tight grip, and he loosens his fingers until I can drag a morsel of air through my tight throat.

"Oh no, my little queen, you don't get to come yet. You need to please your kings first." Theo's throaty demanding words are breathed along my flesh and have goosebumps rising along my skin.

Carter gets up from the ground behind me, skating the tips of his fingers along the skin of my ass, up the middle of my back, and along the back of my neck before he threads his fingers through my hair. He captures the strands in a tight ponytail, yanking hard so my neck bends backward. "You're going to get on your knees like our good little slut and swallow each of our cocks, Mia. We are going to fuck that tight throat of yours and fill you with our cum." *Jesus, fuck me, that's hot.* His words have my pussy flooding with more wetness.

He pulls me out of Theo's hold and yanks me stumbling towards Mateo, who has pulled off his pants and is sitting on the oversized theater recliner like a king on a throne with just his shirt on and with his hard veiny cock standing at attention. "Get down on your knees, Mia, and worship your king."

Carter yanks on my hair until I fall to my knees between Mateo's spread thighs and take his cock in my hands, stroking it and rubbing my thumb across the swollen wet head. I hear the sound of clothes being removed behind me as Carter and Theo strip down. The desire to watch them get naked fills me, and I turn my head to watch, but Carter pushes me forward by my hair until my lips graze Mateo's tip. I open my mouth wide, taking him inside the warm, wet heat of my mouth. I lash the crown with my tongue, licking and sucking the bulbous end and sliding my tongue along his slit. Carter's merciless grip on my hair pushes me further down Mateo's cock until it's deep in my throat, and I am gagging and choking on it. The sound of my struggle is loud in the air around us, as are the harsh breaths from the males in the room.

"Mat, grasp her fucking hair and force her to swallow your cock while I fuck her pretty pussy." He releases his strangling hold on my hair, and in the next instance, Mateo grasps the strands, using his grip to move my head up and down on his cock at the rhythm and speed that he demands.

"Fuck, so good, *mami*, just like that, choke on it."

The sound of a zipper releasing and a moan greets my ears. I try to pull back to catch a glimpse, but Mateo pushes my head down until his long cock is down my throat so far that I feel like I can't breathe. My hands frantically slap against his upper thighs in panic. He disregards my struggle and holds me tight as he groans and then releases me. I frenziedly pull up and try to catch my breath. Saliva is pooling in my mouth and slipping out with each hard thrust. Just as I'm about to pop off Mateo's dick, Carter grabs me around the waist and forces my ass up into the air, and delivers a hard slap to my right asscheek. He pushes his hard thickness against my pussy lips and coats himself in my wetness, which flows from my core and wets my thighs.

He plunges in without warning, thrusting deeply, and a heavy groan leaves his lips. A scream gets trapped in my throat as Mateo forces me back down his cock until my nose almost reaches his pelvis. Carter begins a punishing tempo of hard thrusts, his piercing dragging along the interior walls of my pussy and forcing my upper thighs to smack into the front of the leather recliner over and over.

"You're such a good girl, taking it from each end, baby. Do you feel how you're soaked for us? Your pussy juice is dripping down my cock and wetting my balls, Mia." He thrusts hard and deep, hitting the end of me and stilling. *FUCK! Too deep!* The sting of pain mixed with arousal has my heart pounding erratically in my chest.

Mateo shudders below me, and a ragged moan leaves his lips as he cums down my throat. I gag on his cock, cum spilling around his thick length and coating my chin. "Thank you, mami, you're such a good little cum slut."

Carter pulls my head off Mateo's cock, and his cock pulls out from inside of my pussy. He stands up, my hair still fisted in his hands and pushes his pierced dick in between my lips. "Suck baby, lick every drop of your wetness off my cock. Taste how fucking delicious you are." I hollow my cheeks and suck deep and hard on his cock. Tasting the combination of me, Mateo's cum, and Carter's cock on my tongue. My thighs clench tightly as my core throbs with emptiness.

Carter pulls back and pops out of my mouth, and I take a deep, shuddering breath. My chest rises and falls with short pants. I'm not getting enough air inside my heaving lungs, and my chest feels too tight. He drags me to the next chair by his grip on my strands, the one holding Finn.

Tears trail down my cheeks at the tight hold on my hair, yet I refuse to beg him to release me. I meet Finn's melted chocolate brown eyes and see nothing but passion in their depths. He has lifted up his shirt displaying his tight abs, gorgeous smooth coppery ochre skin, and his adonis belt that makes me want to both swoon and lick it with my tongue.

Fuck, he is beautiful. He bites down on his thick pink bottom lip as I lean forward and lick his abs. Sliding my tongue along the rugged ridges and following the lines of his muscles down across his pelvis, and continuing with following his happy trail to where his cock is proudly standing erect between the open halves of his jeans.

I let my tongue trail across his base, licking up one side, across the thick deep purple head, and back down the other side. I lick him like an ice cream cone, wrapping my tongue around his cock, transitioning back and forth between sucking just the crown and licking his girthy length. Carter pushes me forward again, forcing my ass into the air, and slides back inside of my pussy, fucking me with brutal thrusts that drive my chin into Finn's warm flesh.

"Suck me deep, killer. Swallow me down your tight throat, like my sweet dirty whore." I take his thick length deep into my mouth and swallow his dick until his tip meets the back of my throat. I gag, pull back to the crown and suck on the head, and then take him back down to the back of my throat. I hollow my cheeks and start a grueling rhythm of licking, sucking, and gagging. His thumb grazes my cheek and the corner of my mouth in a soft, tender caress. Saliva coats his thumb, and he rubs it along my skin as his body tightens. "Fuck, Mia!"

His abs clench, and he cums down my throat with a breathy grunt that has my nipples painfully hardening and my pussy seizing on Carter's long cock that is thrusting into my body with powerful strokes. The sound of skin hitting skin, wetness, and my muffled whimpers are seemingly too loud in the space around us. His balls hit my pussy lips each time he meets the end of me and make them tingle with a sting. Finn slides from my mouth as his cum dribbles down the side of my cheek.

If I could just touch my clit I would explode; my body is locked so tight. I slide my hand down my side with the intention of rubbing my bundle of nerves, but Mateo, now out of his seat and next to me, grabs that hand and yanks it above my head while Finn grabs my other arm and does the same. "Naughty queen, were you going to make yourself cum, killer?"

"Please..." The moan leaves my lips in desperation of the need to cum.

"Fuck, I'm going to cum. Mia, open your mouth wide for me, baby!" Carter rips from my body, and I release a cry at the loss of his fullness as he stands up, pulling my upper body away from Finn before he pushes his cock through my lips and floods my mouth with his cum.

I swallow what I can, but there's too much of the creamy thick substance. One of his hands rises to my face, and his fingers pinch my nose, forcing my mouth to open wide and for me to choke on his length and his cum. "That's it, baby. Look at my messy girl. Do we taste good, Mia? You look good guzzling cum, don't you, baby?"

He releases his hold, and I pull back, choking and needing air. My senses are overwhelmed with being deprived of my orgasm once again. My clit and pussy are a throbbing mess, and I can hear my blood rushing in my veins. I need to fucking cum so badly that it's almost painful.

Theo slides in front of me, his fingers trailing through the mess of three men's cum on my chest, neck, and chin. He pushes his fingers into my mouth, and my tongue lashes them, cleaning off the residue and nipping at his skin.

"Baby, I need you so badly to swallow my cock, but I want your other holes filled with my brothers too. You're going to be my perfect whore queen, and let us take all your holes, stretching you wide till you gape for us, aren't you, Mia?"

Fuck, his words are so sexually stimulating; they make every part of my body hum with need. I can feel my own wetness embarrassingly sliding like a river from my pussy, coating my upper thighs and trickling downward. I want to take them all, let them fill me up until I'm painfully full and bursting with them.

A tinge of fear races across my mind with the promise of pain from being stuffed so full of their cocks. Theo must see the desire within the depths of my mind displayed on my features. "I promise, baby, we are going to make it feel so good for you while we use all your holes."

"Mat, slide her up on your lap and slip inside her ass." Theo's words have a whimper leaving my lips. Carter helps me climb up on the seat Mateo is sitting in and turns me around until my back is flush with Mateo's chest. Mateo's hard length rocks against my pussy lips, coating itself in my wetness. "Fuck, one of you prime her ass with your fingers and suck her pussy. I don't want to hurt her." Carter demands with a lust filled voice.

Theo steps forward and falls to his knees between Mateo's spread legs. Mateo slides his hands underneath each of my knees and opens me up like an offering for a waiting Theo. I'm a gift for a king, one to be used for his pleasure.

Theo's fingers slide through my wetness, rubbing circles over my clit with his thumb as two of his fingers rub against my puckered hole, and slip inside with a scissoring motion, stretching me and fucking me with the digits. A garbled cry leaves my lips as the orgasm once again rises within me.

I lean my head back against Mateo's shoulder, closing my eyes to half-mast as electricity flows through my veins, up my spine in a live current that threatens to stop my breath. Carter gets up on the chair next to us and wraps his hand around my neck as his mouth descends on my hard nipples, sucking deep and tightening his hold. I'm so close to cumming that my whole body tenses, and my hands clench.

Theo pulls out his fingers and stops the movement of his thumb, and Carter pulls back from my breast. *No, what the fuck! Not again!* I want to scream in frustration and pain at once again being denied my release. Mateo lifts me up in his arms until I'm hovering above the tip of his cock. "Put me inside you, *mami.*" He moans into my ear, and I feel the pull of his command as I reach down and position him at my back hole. His tip pushes through the ring of muscles and my wetness and sinks inside of me. The sensation sends bolts of pleasure soaring down my spine, and wetness squirts from my cunt. "Good girl."

He bounces me on his cock for a few deep strokes, filling my ass and stretching me. I grind down and roll my hips, wanting to regain some control over my own body and ride his dick fast and hard. My body feels like it's filled with a fire from within. I bounce and ride his dick hard, my breaths becoming labored and sweat trickling down my skin as the other three watch with rapt attention. "Fuck, so good. Her ass is so tight." Mateo groans next to my ear.

"Mat, stop her for a sec; let Finn and me slip inside her pussy. We are going to stuff her tight hole with our big, thick cocks." Mateo stops my movement, and a whine leaves my lips.

"First, she cums, or it's going to hurt her." Theo spits on my hole and plunges three fingers back inside my pussy, hooking them upwards and finding my G Spot as Mateo regains his pumping rhythm into my ass. Theo's fingers rub over and over against the spot, and he leans forward and sucks my needy clit, and I shatter with a scream.

The orgasm that had been denied repeatedly rips through my body with pain and fire and forces me to bow my back and push down hard on Mateo's cock as my core clenches around Theo's digits. Carter and Finn pinch my nipples, prolonging my return to earth from euphoria with the hit of pain, causing another minor orgasm to cascade through me.

I feel like I've died and gone to fucking heaven. Pure bliss races through my body and makes even my toes curl. My mouth goes slack, and my eyes see prisms of light. I watch from my daze as Theo moves back and Carter bends to his knees in front of me, his thick, pierced cock in his grip before he plunges it into my spasming cunt. He thrusts with hard grunts, sweat beading on his forehead and chest. I long to slide my tongue along the beautiful colorful artwork along his chest and neck and trace the designs, but all my limbs feel heavy.

He and Mateo thrust in unison for a few strokes before they stop, and Carter pulls back, allowing Finn to slip in front of him without pulling out. A giggle wants to leave my chest at the fact that Finn's ass is now in Carter's face, but my breath is stolen from me as Finn's cock pushes against my tight opening, already filled with Carter's cock and a sharp pain and burn fills my pussy before he breaches the hole and both of them are inside of me.

"NO, OH MY GOD, NO!" I scream. The sensation of being overfilled and impossibly stretched threatening to have me lose my mind. "Fuck, it hurts; pull out!" I beg and try to push against Finn's chest. A sound of pain leaves his lips as I hit the sling on his arm.

Theo climbs up on the recliner next to us and looms over me with his cock firmly grasped as it approaches my face. "No, no more, too full." His hand wraps around my tender and bruised throat, and he pins me back against Mateo's chest as Mateo grasps both my hands and threads his fingers through mine, preventing me from pushing them away.

The look in Theo's eyes as they meet mine is dark and addictive and has me stopping my attempts to release my body from all of their cocks. My pussy and ass throb and spasm, the pain merging with the pleasure and pushing me closer to another release. "Your holes are ours, Mia. You can take all of us. You will take all of us into that sinful body of yours. Your kings demand it." He pushes his cock against my lips, coating them in his precum before slapping my chin with its length.

Carter, Finn, and Mateo all thrust into my holes. Finn and Carter find a tempo where they move together inside of my cunt, and Mateo thrusts forward as they pull back. It's insanely hot to know that I am stuffed full of them. My pussy feels swollen, raw, and achy. At the same time, desire is once again wrapping itself around me and causing another orgasm to rise.

Theo pushes through my lips, and his taste floods my senses. My eyes roll to the back of my head as too much pleasure all at once fills me. He slides across my tongue in slow strokes, hitting the roof of my mouth with his tip and flooding my mouth with saliva. "Look at that pussy stretch. Fuck Mia, you look so good stretched wide with all of us inside of you." Carter groans.

Theo's grip tightens on my neck, and his thrusts increase in speed and force, pushing him closer to the edge. My body tightens, all of my limbs spasming as thunder roars through me and heat lights a blaze across my skin. I scream harshly across Theo's thick length at the back of my throat, pushing his cock further down my column and stopping any air from traveling back up.

"Fuck, her pussy is clamping us like a vice." Finn groans, his cock spearing through me with Carter's as his companion. Mateo's harsh breaths are booming in my ear. His breath catches in his throat as he thrusts one final time inside of my ass, and a moan rips from his chest.

Carter and Finn's gasps and moans are deafening when combined with my panting and cries. They both race towards their own completion, pushing forward together until another cry tries to leave my throat, Carter roars, and

Finn gasps. Both of them are flooding my pussy with their cum. I can feel them coating me deep inside, their cocks throbbing and jerking as they release and paint my core.

Theo's breathing picks up, and his eyes meet mine with a gleaming sultry look full of heat. He watched as his fellow kings came inside of me, filling me to the brim with their cum. There's color high on his cheeks and neck, and his nostrils flare as he plunges one last time to the back of my throat and releases.

Finn pulls out from within my swollen pussy, and Carter follows suit. I can immediately feel the cum sliding from inside of me as it trickles down to where Mateo is still deep inside my asshole. Theo pulls back, popping his cock from inside my lips and causing me to choke down on how much cum is in my mouth. I swallow and lick my lips, and he watches with heat in his gaze. Mateo goes to lift me up and off of himself, but Theo reaches forward and pushes me back down.

"I need her, Mat. Let me fuck her while you're still inside of her." Theo pops down from his position on the chair and gets on his knees before me as all of us watch. He leans forward and licks me from where Mateo's cock is still deep inside of me and still hard to my throbbing clit. Theo licks and sucks my folds, pushing his tongue into my pussy hole, and then stands up. Carter, Finn and my cum glistens on his lips. He leans over me, and I open my lips wide as he spits inside my mouth. "You taste delicious filled with all of our cum, Mia."

He pulls back and returns to his knees, pushing his cock inside my swollen, abused pussy and fucking me like a man about to take his last breath. His harsh strokes move me over and over again on Mateo's hard cock. Theo rubs his fingers methodically over my sore and engorged clit, and I detonate with another orgasm that has me seeing fireworks. A moan leaves my lips as he and Mateo both find their release within my tired and sore body.

"Now you are ours, Mia, forever." Theo grunts, leans over my body, and his lips catch mine in a brutal kiss.

"MIA! What the fuck are you doing in there? It sounds like the world is ending! Are y'all having more kinky fuckery? Lord, Jesus, y'all need to go to fuckin' church, you damn heathens!" Raegan banging on the door rips a chuckle from each of us. Church? I'm pretty sure I met God just now.

CHAPTER 47

Theo

"Being deeply loved by someone gives you strength, while loving someone deeply gives you courage." Lao Tzu

C laiming Mia with my brothers yesterday was the best fucking day of my life. Nothing could top her finally finding out the truth behind our actions, forgiving us, and acknowledging with her words, body, and heart that she is ours just as much as we are hers.

We spent the rest of the day in a sticky cocoon together in that room. The five of us were fearful that somehow the spell would be broken after our *"kinky fuckery"* as Raegan likes to call it. Rae was madder than a wet hen when we finally did escape the room and tried to get Mia past her so we could get cleaned up. The evil glare she gave each of us made my balls want to shrivel up and climb back inside my body.

We stayed up late into the night talking, discussing our fears, concerns, and plans for the future. Our future is wherever Mia is. There is no changing that, and honestly, none of us would have it any other way. Mia has decided to return to Manhattan. She was never happy here in Casbury, and this town holds too many sinister ghosts for all of us.

Mia accepted her placement at Brown University in the fall, and with our inheritances released, thanks to Stella, each of us will be leaving Casbury for good and moving to New York with her. Fuck, even Rae is coming with us. The little hellion is going to beat on us nonstop. Let's hope she finds someone else out there to keep her busy, like maybe an asshole named after a fucking bird that left her hanging. *He could use a beating or two.*

Carter has no intentions of going to university. He's going to take his place at the head of his family's company and move on from there now that Mack is dead and his mom is terrified of him.

Mateo has also decided to not return to school in the fall. He doesn't think he can manage it with his mental health, and school's never been his thing. All of us respect his choices and will be helping to keep an eye on him to ensure he doesn't fall back into the habit of self-harming. He wants to pursue other interests, and as long as he's still with us, he doesn't really care where he lives.

That leaves Finn and me to accompany Mia to Brown. At first, I thought Stella was going to outright refuse the whole idea of us staying with Mia and attending school with her and Raegan. It took some negotiating, pleading from Mia, and even some downright begging from Carter, who we know she has a soft spot for, to get her to relent. Stella threatened all of us with death at her hands if we hurt Mia again, but fuck, she agreed.

Now we just have to figure out a way to convince her to allow us to live outside the Stratford compound. No offense, but the thought of fucking Mia raw multiple times daily under Stella's roof brings me nothing but unease. I wouldn't put it past the queen of Manhattan to hear Mia scream from pleasure and use it as an excuse to shoot one of us.

Honestly, I think she relented so quickly because she has other issues to tend to. It seems Issy never made it back to Manhattan, and she and Diego have disappeared off the face of the planet. The tracker that she had embedded into Issy's arm was removed the day we sedated everyone, kidnapped Mia, and took her to Canada.

In fact, that fucker Diego left it as a souvenir for Stella to find. The guy really has a death wish. Now that Mia is safe from Ajax Pickering, there is only one more loose end to tie up, James Hamilton. Stella's leaving that in my vengeful queen's little hands. Stella's new focus is on killing Diego Cabano before the fucker makes her a great-grandmother. I wish him fucking luck; he's going to need it.

"Are we ready to go?" Finn asks as he approaches me, and we both turn to stare at our queen, who is pressed up against the wall by Carter's body as he ravishes her mouth with a scorching kiss. "If Carter would release Mia, we would be."

Mia wants to take her own revenge on James Hamilton, despite each of us demanding to do the honors so she didn't sully her hands with his filth. She very eloquently refused us by telling us all to go to hell and that she is a Stratford and they pay their own debts. She's going to be the death of my self-control; I just fucking know it. I'm going to end up as insane as fucking Carter is.

I have a feeling that shit with my girl is never going to be easy. She will never give up control to us; any small amount that she does gives us is just a smoke screen to soothe our caveman tendencies. Despite my demanding, possessive, and alpha fucker issues, I wouldn't want it any other way. Besides, I get to watch her bring each of us to our knees and have discovered that's where I prefer to spend my time, especially if I can have my lips on her pretty pussy.

"Killer, we got to go. Clark is already in the car with Stella and Tom, and I don't look forward to her ordering one of them to come in here and taser our asses."

Carter pulls back from Mia's swollen lips with an evil grin and releases her. "That's cause you're a weak bastard, Finn. I get tasered at least once daily, and I'm still fucking fine."

"Yup, you're fine. You're certifiable and should a hundred percent be fucking locked up, but you're fine, Carter." Mateo calls from the entrance way where he's standing waiting for us. I tried to convince him to stay behind. I didn't want him to be further affected by more darkness, but he refused. He said he needed to see this through to the end with Mia to give himself peace of mind that James was really gone.

"Miss Mia, your grandmother is becoming displeased and ordered me to shoot whichever king is holding us up," Tom calls from the open front doorway.

"See! I fucking told you, asshole. Naw, I'm out. I love you, killer, but my ass is heading to the car so the evil granny doesn't shoot it." Finn walks out the door, followed by a laughing Mateo. "Evil granny, fuck, she might just kill you for calling her that, Finn."

We walk into the warehouse behind Mia. Stella, Clark, and Tom are leading us in, and a few of the other security guys are closing ranks behind us. A cold chill rises up my back. I, for fucking sure, don't like how we are surrounded by Stella's henchmen, all armed to the teeth, while we were not allowed to bring any weapons of our own.

Is Stella going to dispose of the four of us after Mia is done with her revenge on James Hamilton? My eyes meet Finn's, and I see the wariness in his eyes. He's not liking the way this situation is playing out either.

"Grandma Stella, can I please set his body on fire after Mia is done with it?" Carter asks Stella in a pleading voice. I watch as she comes to a halt and turns her head to look over her shoulder at him. Her blue eyes stare back at him like a dark sky before a storm, filled with suppressed rage, daunting and terrifying. "I'm not your grandmother, Carter Pemberton. You had better hush that mouth of yours before I ask Tom to cut off your tongue."

"You will be one day soon," Carter replies with zero self-preservation as Mia shakes her head at both his and Stella's antics.

The room opens into a similar layout to a warehouse my father used to do his dirty work in. A place where mine and the guys' hands were stained by sins committed at the demand of that demon. The one whose body now lies in an unmarked grave, forgotten, unabsolved of his sins.

Carter seems way too comfortable in the space, which tells me this is where he came with Mia when they disposed of those fuckers that hid behind a screen and watched my girl get raped by the unconscious, naked fucker strapped to a metal table in front of us.

Carter walks past Stella and Mia and heads straight to the table to look down at James Hamilton. His body is a live wire with anticipation of getting to hurt this sick fuck. Carter's gray-blue eyes seem to glow on his face with a look of maniacal glee at all the damage he did to James. My body feels antsy and restless watching this scene go down, and some part of me wonders if I will walk out of this room.

Mia stops a few short feet away from them and turns to meet Stella's gaze. "My darling, you do not have to do this. You can still get your revenge without having to be the one that plunges the knife into his heart."

"What would be the fun in that grandmother? I'm a Stratford, we never forget, and we always pay our debts. This fucker owes me his life as debt for all the horrific horrors I suffered at his hands."

Stella's eyes brighten with satisfaction and pride. You can see it across her features as she releases her hold on the mask she wears. Mia's eerie statement allows no room for negotiations. She will be the one that ends James and removes the stain of his life from this world. My chest tightens as I watch her take the last steps forward to put herself next to the table.

She's stunning in her malevolent energy and determination. I only bow to those that deserve it, and in this lifetime, there will only be one person who will have that honor. She stands before me, radiant and filled with wrath for the man on the table. I want to fall down to my knees and worship at her altar. My queen, my deity, and the bearer of my beating heart.

Carter circles the table like a caged tiger. I can feel the hairs on the back of my neck standing on end at the way he is staring so intently at James. He can be so unpredictable and irrational. His control is always so precarious. I should know as the recipient of his rage for weeks.

I wouldn't put it past him to do something reckless and attack James again, killing him. Which would cause Mia to lose her shit and punish him for taking away her desire to meet justice with her own hand. I watch as Carter relaxes his muscles, a predator getting ready for attack, a frenzied look of anticipation and glee across his face. "Carter, fucking don't," I call out and pull his gaze to me. His strange eyes meet mine before he physically shakes himself and pulls back.

"Jesus, was he about to lose control?" Finn inquires at my side in a low tone.

"I don't want to be in an enclosed space with all these weapons when he does lose control. I have no desire to die today." Mateo answers from my other side.

Mia moves forward and grabs onto the bloody mess that should be James' chin. If Carter hadn't made his face look like a bunch of ground beef with the beating he gave him in the courtyard two days ago. Has it really only been two days? It feels so much longer. *That's what happens when you finally get to enjoy your girl; time has no meaning anymore,* my mind whispers.

"Is there a way to bring him back to a conscious state? I want him to be alert." Mia turns around and meets Clark's gaze. The big man watches everything with a quiet expression. He nods to one of the guys across the room, and he moves forward, holding a large syringe. My guess is that fucker is about to get a high dosage of adrenaline into his system. Then my girl gets to play.

The guard, Fisher, I think his name is, stabs the syringe into James' chest, right where his heart is. We wait in tense silence, and after a minute or two, James' whole body tightens, and a loud gasp leaves his lips. He tries to open the eye that Mia didn't stab and stare out, but Carter's beating did a number on it, and he can barely get it open more than a slit.

"Mmmm, whaaat...whe...where...am...I?" His words are garbled and low, but there isn't another sound in the room other than of us breathing, and even then, most of us are holding our breaths for what Mia will do next.

"You're at hell's door, James. Are you ready to go back to where you came from?"

"Am.....elia." The name slithers from his blood-soaked mouth, and instant anger rises inside my body. She's not that girl anymore; that's not her fucking name. *Is that because that name reminds you of your own sins against her?* My mind questions.

Yes, that name will always remind me of our tumultuous past and the harm I caused her with the need for control and my poor decisions. I will spend the rest of my life trying to make up for all the damage I caused. I will always be the man at her side, her defender, her warrior, and her king. I will make it my life's mission to ensure her happiness above all else.

"She died. Amelia doesn't exist. She hasn't for many years. You helped destroy that young girl with your disgusting touch. You tried to kill her and her momma, but you know what, James?" She leans closer to his face until he can see her, and she can stare into his one eye. An eye that is the same color as her own. "I was reborn in the fire of her death, and I am not weak. I am a Stratford. You should have thought about that before you came after me. We are the top apex predator, and you, you're just a worm waiting to die at my hands."

"Ple......ase."

A deranged laughing sound leaves Mia's lips. She throws her head back with it, and it echoes off the walls. "Oh, you're going to beg, James, it's time to do some entertaining, motherfucker." She throws his own words back at him, and it frightens me to my core to see her like this.

She steps back and walks over to the far wall, where a table is laid out with different implements of torture. Her hand reaches for a hammer, and I have to swallow a pained groan from leaving my lips. Darkness tries to creep up on me with the reminder of what my own father did to me with a hammer the last time he had me in his clutches.

She walks back over with it, swinging it in her hands until she reaches James' side. He's strapped down to the table by thick metal gray chains. One around his abdomen and arms, another confining his waist, and the last around his calves, preventing him from kicking out. We can see the damage that Mia did back in the cabin to his cock, someone sutured it back together, and he still bears the stitches.

She slams the hammer with force down on his hand, and he screams, his arm trying desperately to pull against the chains, but it's useless. Whoever tied him down ensured he could barely breathe, never mind move. Her arm swings again, slamming down on the same hand as we hear bones being crushed. Blood splatters on the long sleeve gray top she's wearing. She moves to the other side of the table and does the same damage to his other hand. James' head thrashes on the table, and his breathing becomes labored. He goes to pass out, but Mia reaches forward and fists his cock, tightening until he screams. "Don't go to sleep, James; there are boogeymen waiting in your nightmares."

She slams the hammer down on his left kneecap and then his right. Mateo moans next to me and turns away from the brutality. His eyes meet mine, and I note as he swallows the bile that has made it into his mouth. He's really pale, and there are beads of sweat along his forehead and upper lip. He looks like he might get sick. He doesn't make an attempt to leave, but he also doesn't watch. Carter's eyes, however, are trained on Mia as if she was an apparition of a saint come to life before him. One he prays to with devout benediction.

My eyes return to Mia, and I flinch at the sound of her slamming the hammer down on James' ankles and feet. He stops screaming and passes out, and Mia's lips actually pout in misery. "Bring him back. I'm not done." She orders. Fisher once again moves forward and injects James with another syringe. After another minute or so, James comes through again with a hoarse shout, and Mia chuckles. "Did you think we were done, James?"

She walks back to the table, drops the bloody hammer on the surface with a clang, and grabs a large blade. Her clothes are spattered with blood. There's even some across her chin and jaw. I want to call out and ask her to stop, to just end his life so I don't have to see her become this person who relishes in the pain of that sick fuck, but I bite my tongue. She has to do this in order to help her get past what was done to her. I never got the chance with Vincent, but she made sure to avenge me.

She trails the blade across his skin, splitting the flesh like a grotesque piece of fruit before she reaches his stomach and makes a massive gash along the surface. Her hands slide through the blood until her hand is covered, and the sleeve of her shirt is drenched. "This blood you carry is tainted, James. You tainted me with it too, and the only way I can purge myself of the sins you committed against me is to spill it."

She presses the blade down the middle of his chest, and another huge gash opens up. At this point, he will die from blood loss, and no amount of adrenaline shots will bring him back. Stella must see that Mia is lost in bloodlust too. She motions me forward, and I carefully approach my vicious little queen. "Mia, you need to end this before his heart stops on its own." Her ocean-blue eyes rise to mine, and tears appear, but she pulls back and refuses to shed them.

She moves behind his head; he's almost out now, barely breathing. With a final look down, her eyes rise and meet mine and then meet Stella's as she slides the blade across his neck and opens his throat until we can hear nothing but gurgling sounds and then a horrible rustling sound, as he takes his last breath and dies.

I don't hesitate, walking towards her, pulling the blade from her hand, and allowing it to fall on the ground. I grab her and lift her into my arms bridal style, tucking her blood-drenched form close to mine and walk out of the room, my fellow kings immediately following me out.

It's done. All of this misery has ended. It's now time for our new beginning.

CHAPTER 48
Mia

"The emotion that can break your heart is sometimes the very one that heals it." Nicholas Sparks, At First Sight

It's been a week since I slit James' throat and took my vengeance. You would think I would immediately feel better after vanquishing the monster from my nightmares, but unfortunately, he still lives there along with that fucker Vincent. When I wake up with my heart thundering in my chest and screams leaving my lips, one or more of my kings are always there to wrap me in their arms and reassure me that I am alive and they are not.

Graduation came and went, and none of us attended. I don't think that we were really in a celebrating mood. Although Carter, the fiend, ordered enough junk food to the house to feed an army. Raegan might have fallen slightly in love with Carter at the sight of all that food. Luckily for her, and for me, cause I don't share, it lasted five minutes until he opened his mouth, and she was right back to beating on him. The sight of all the high-calorie greasy food made me queasy. I still have food issues, despite knowing that I shouldn't and that I eat healthily and live an active lifestyle. Fuck, do I burn a lot of calories around these kings.

I made Carter return to the school to apologize to poor Cindy, who he scared half to death. The others were forced to utter apologies to Jessie, with expressions on their faces like I was making them eat dog shit. Jessie, the goof, stood there and smiled wide as each of my kings forced words from their mouths that I know they would have rather choked on than utter. They did it, however, and I was proud of them, so I rewarded them each with a fantastic blow job.

My grandmother left three days ago to return to Manhattan. My sister still hasn't been found, and in a shocking turn of events, Manuel Cabano offered to help her find his psychotic kidnapping son IF she went on a date with him. Honestly, we all held our collective breaths, thinking for sure she was going to kill him or, at the bare minimum, have Clark do it. She did nothing. Stella just stared at him with a menacing glare and walked out of the room. Mateo seems to think she might actually secretly like his uncle. I have my doubts, but if it means my grandmother gets another chance at happiness. I'm all for it.

Raegan went to spend time with her mom when Stella left, so we have had the house all to ourselves for three glorious days. Three days where we have spent almost all our waking moments with one of them constantly inside of me. Their fear that I may still change my mind and leave them is adorable. I have no intentions of going anywhere. My pussy, however, is thinking of running away and fucking hiding. I'm so sore that I'm now walking funny, and Carter keeps making jokes about me being bow legged by the time we make it to Manhattan.

We decided to leave early and spend the summer in the big apple and on my grandmother's estate in the Hamptons. There's nothing left for us here in Casbury, and the oppressive ghosts that linger around every corner threaten to steal our joy.

Carter's mom has gone into hiding, fearing that he may come after her for her neglect and abuse over the years. His baby brother is still in private school across the country in Seattle, but Carter has convinced him to visit us when we are in the Hamptons and come stay for a while. He's hoping to rekindle some brotherly emotion between them. He also spends his time looking longingly at his phone, missing his bromance with Diego.

Finn's parents were resistant to his decision to leave Casbury and head with us to the east coast, but Finn refused to budge on his decision, even when they threatened his trust fund. He laughed in his mother's face and told her he wasn't worried about being poor ever again. He has a sugar momma that is one of the world's wealthiest women, and he belongs to a harem filled with two billionaires and two multimillionaires, so he would be alright.

Although Mateo's parents aren't technically dead, Stella has them on the run with Manuel's help. Let me tell you how my jaw hit the floor when she divulged that information to us before she left. *I told you, the fucker has the hots for my grandmother.* Whatever dark hole Mateo's parents have crawled into, I hope they stay there and, finally, give their son a semblance of peace. Then again, I also hope Stella murders them and buries them in a deep grave, so yeah, I'm still a vindictive bitch.

Today we are heading for the private airport and getting on Carter's private plane to take us to our new beginning. Raegan will meet us in the Hamptons in a couple of weeks after we settle in. We still need to find a way to convince Stella to allow us to live independently outside of the estate, but for now, she's not having it. She still fears someone out there might try to hurt me.

The thing is, if someone were to try, they would have to contend with trying to pry my four ruthless and domineering caveman kings off of me long enough to get to me. Trust me when I tell you they all take my safety to nauseating extremes. What's that saying from *The Hunger Games?* *"May the odds be in your favor."* They won't be, I assure you.

"Blondie, I need to make a stop before we hit the plane." Carter turns around from the passenger front seat of Finn's car to stare at me in the back, squished between Mateo and Theo's broad fucking shoulders. Both of them completely invading my personal space and running their hands over parts of my body. Jesus, we haven't even left the driveway yet, and they all just fucking gangbanged me in the damn family room before we even left. *Will they never get enough?*

"Where, Carter?" I question and witness an uncomfortable look cross his face.

"Just something I meant to do weeks ago, but it slipped my mind. I can't leave Casbury without doing it, though." His words are a bit cryptic, but I guess as long as he doesn't plan to kill anyone, it doesn't truly matter when we get to the plane. It's not like it will leave without us. He gives Finn a nod, and I glimpse a smirk crossing Finn's face. *What the fuck are they up to?*

Fifteen minutes later, I have my answer. We pull up to my old house on the other side of the tracks. It's all boarded up and dilapidated, and there are signs proclaiming it as condemned. It brings me sadness to see it like this. When I first came back to Casbury, I had to resist the temptation to come here and look at where I had grown up for fear of someone recognizing me as Amelia Hamilton. Now that I am here, various happy memories with my mom filter through my mind.

My mom was devastated to learn of everything that occurred here while she was imprisoned under house arrest in Europe by my grandmother. Tears fell down her face on the Zoom call when I told her about being kidnapped and raped by James. She broke out in loud sobs, and I wish I could have wrapped her in my arms and comforted her. When I hinted that he was gone and would not ever be crossing our paths again in this lifetime, a look of relief appeared on her beautiful features.

It turns out my mother has fallen in love with someone out there and doesn't wish to return permanently to the States. It's right out of a romance novel. She fell in love with her guard that held her prisoner all these months. Like shit, I can't make this stuff up. Someone needs to write that story!

Carter gets out of the vehicle the minute we park, and the rest of us watch as he goes to the truck and pulls out a gift bag. *What the fuck?* He walks up to my old neighbor's house and knocks on the door, looking antsy and agitated. The rest of us quickly exit the vehicle and stand on the sidewalk with curiosity. When the door opens wide, and an older version of Mrs. Simpson pops out, a cry leaves my lips. Oh my God, she's still here, living in that run-down home. I thought for sure she would have moved on or even been in nursing care somewhere by now. The woman has got to be in her nineties now.

"Boy, what ya doin' on my porch with those demon eyes?"

"Ma'am. I...I came to bring you something."

This tiny white-haired stooped lady pops out of the door holding a broom and whacks Carter across the shoulder with it. We all groan and gasp as he stands there and takes the abuse.

"Where's the other fella at? The one that ain't so pretty?"

What other fella? Ain't so pretty? Is she talking about Diego Cabano?

"He's gone, ma'am. Stole a princess right out from under a vicious queen's nose. Not sure we will be seeing him again in this lifetime."

"Well, Lord have mercy, that poor girl then. I'll pray for her; yes, I will. I know he said he killed a demon, but boy, I think it might have tainted him some, ya hear." She moves forward a couple of steps in her thin pink-striped bathrobe with shuffling movements, and we see she's wearing a pair of rundown dog head slippers. This whole interaction is boggling my mind right now.

Carter lifts up the gift bag in front of him as a peace offering but keeps her broom in his sights. "This is for you, ma'am. I'm trying to do some good now, following the lord's way and all. I'm hoping that you can find some use for it to soften out your days." He rubs his hand across the back of his neck, and Finn elbows and winks at me. Trying to follow the lord's way? The fucker was just sharing me with three other men not an hour ago. I'm not sure if that's precisely what the lord had in mind when he said, *"Love thy brother."*

"Proverbs 22:2: "The rich and the poor meet together; the Lord is the maker of them all." Carter quotes the bible, and I see Mrs. Simpson's eyes light up. What in the ever-loving fuck is happening right now? Who is this man before me, quoting scripture, and what have you done with my reckless and unbalanced king?

She takes the bag from him and leans her broom against the wall nearby, just in case she needs to hit Carter again. A chuckle leaves my throat at watching him cower in front of a ninety-year-old woman. I swear my Carter is a damn contradiction. One that I have no doubt will keep me on my toes for the rest of my life.

Mrs. Simpson pulls out a pair of brand new Dalmation slippers stuffed with stacks of cash popping from inside them. "Ummm... see your house is falling down around you, beg your pardon, ma'am, and...I...I just thought maybe you could use an upgrade." He turns around and points to a white vehicle parked across the street. "That car is yours, and the guy sitting in the driver's seat is here to help you collect whatever you want to take with you. He's going to drive you around from now on and take you wherever you need to go. I got you a small apartment, so you have no stairs to climb."

Carter's ears go beet red, and he starts to sweat and shift from one foot to the other while Mrs. Simpson just stares at him. She breaks her look and squints my way. "Is that be you, Amelia, girl?"

I move forward and stand next to Carter, lacing my fingers through his and giving him a small smile. "Yes, ma'am."

"Ya look prettier than a peach, girl. What ya doing with a no-good trouble-maker? Jesus gave ya better sense, girl, even though he be showing an old woman some of the lord's compassion."

"Yes, ma'am, well, you see, he kind of loves me, and that love saved me from going down a dark path with no redemption."

"Well, I reckon the lord be workin' in some mysterious ways. Boy, I'm not a foolish woman. I be takin' ya up on your Christianity, ya hear. I'll just be gettin' my bible and goin' with that fine man in my new car."

We watch as she shuffles back into the house, taking her broom with her but holding on tight to the gift bag with her slippers and the cash Carter stuffed inside of them. She returns with a black purse around her tiny arm and a bible tucked under her armpit, wearing the new slippers on her feet and carrying her trusty broom. She stops in front of Carter and raises her hand, cradling his cheek in her small veiny hand. "The lord saw fit to send ya an angel, boy. Ya had best make sure ya treat her right, or Imma come back and hit you with this broom, ya hear?" Then she walks off and gets in the white car, and it drives away.

I look over, and Finn is rolling on the ground, with tears trailing down his face, clutching his middle. Mateo is bent forward, hands on his knees, laughing so hard that it's coming out in snorts and pants, and Theo's dark blue eyes are bright, and a wide smile is across his face.

"Harhar, fucking funny assholes. You're all laughing, but she packs a mean wallop with that broom." His face is filled with anger, but I see his lips twitching. He knows that was a hella of a funny sight to see.

"I love you, Carter Pemberton, you and your kind spirit. You can always be my demon, and I will always be your avenging angel." I lean up, kiss him on the lips, and then pull him back to the car before "somehow" we all end up having raunchy sex on my old front lawn. "Let's go home, my kings."

CHAPTER 49

Epilogue

"I will find you. In the farthest corner, I will find you."
Mary E. Pearson, The Kiss of Deception

O ne year Later.

"Jesus, Mia, we are going to break the fucking table, and then Rae-Rae will beat our asses." Theo groans into my neck as I ride him hard and dirty on the kitchen table, taking him with quick strokes that have electricity racing through my limbs.

Midnight blue eyes with thick lashes meet mine at half-mast, filled with desire. I undulate and thrust my hips forward until my throbbing clit is rubbing against the skin of his pubic bone, taking him deeper inside of me until his eyes start to roll to the back of his head. My hands on his shoulders clench as the beginning of an orgasm starts its climb inside of me. "Say it, Theo," I demand as my sharp red-tipped nails dig into his skin.

We are both home from school today and finally caught the condo empty of all the others. I couldn't help myself when I walked into the kitchen and saw him sitting in just a pair of tight blue boxers at the round wood breakfast table, eating cereal. He looked so domesticated and content that I had to come over and climb into his lap. It didn't help that I was naked underneath Finn's green

T-Shirt or that my pussy was still dripping cum from Carter filling it before he left for the day.

See, I have come to the realization that Theo actually has a sloppy seconds kink. He gets immensely turned on when he sees any of my holes filled with his fellow kings' cum. He likes to fuck me dirty with someone else's cum coating his cock, and if given a choice, he prefers to be the last one to take me and reclaim me from the others. It's convenient for him that one of the other three are always more than willing to oblige him.

He also likes it when he stops my breathing to the point that I almost pass out. Like right now, his fingers are tightening around my throat, leaving a hand necklace in his size that I will have to hide for school and dinner with my grandmother tomorrow, along with all the hickeys Carter blessed me with. These fucking four cavemen are only happy when I am constantly sporting their marks of possession for the world to see I belong to them.

"I'm yours. I belong to you, Mia."

Fuck, those words do silly things to me. They make my chest tighten, my stomach clench, and my heart flutter every single time I hear them. His other hand grasps the globe of my breast, squeezing the round flesh tightly and pinching my nipple between two of his digits until a moan leaves my lips. I'm so wet, between my own juices and Carter's cum, that the sound of our skin slapping together is borderline obscene.

My eyes narrow on the tattoo along the base of his neck with my name written in pretty script and a small crown. Each of the kings has one somewhere on their body. Mateo jokes that they branded themselves with ownership. When I first saw them all, I was shocked. Now, however, they bring me so much pleasure. *They belong to only me.*

Other girls try to hit on them; how could they not? Have you seen how ridiculously fucking sexy my four men are? Theo never engages with anyone who flirts with him. He just gives them death stares until they slither away. Finn is always polite but stern with shutting down any attempts. Carter and Mateo, however, like to immediately point to their ownership and divulge that their queen is a jealous psychopath. Ok, so I might have gotten into a few fights when we first returned to Manhattan. There were a lot of thirsty bitches out here that didn't know how to keep their hands off my men. I might have helped them remember with my fist.

"Fuck, baby, slow down. I want to still take your ass."

"Did someone say ass?"

Theo's grip loosens on my neck enough for me to look over my shoulder and catch Mateo already stripping down in the middle of the kitchen. Where did he even come from? I thought he had left for yoga? *Fuck, he is delicious.*

Mat has put on a lot of lean muscle in the last year, doing yoga, swimming, and weight training for the surfing competitions he's attending. Most of the lines he cut into his skin have faded away; he's no longer embarrassed by them. In fact, he has come such a long way in the last year. He does regular counseling, takes his meds for his anxiety, and has even started speaking to youth groups about his experiences with anxiety and panic attacks. *I'm so fucking proud of him.*

He saunters up to us with a massive smile across his elfen features. He's regrowing his long locks because he knows I like running my fingers through them. He leans forward and takes my mouth with a punishing kiss that steals my air and has me slowing my rhythm on Theo's cock. A slap vibrates through my ass, causing heat and pain to race to the fleshy globe. "Ride, Mia, or I won't let you cum." Theo grunts from below me, and I once again pick up my speed.

"*Mami*, are you wet enough for me to just slide in with Theo, or should I fuck your ass first?" Mateo questions as he pulls back from the kiss and moves behind me. He pushes down on the middle of my back until my chest meets Theo's and spreads my asscheeks with his hands. "Carter's or Finn's cum?" He questions as he slides a finger through the mess escaping my pussy that's clenching Theo's cock tightly.

"Mine, motherfucker!" Carter's voice echoes through the kitchen. All of our eyes turn to the entryway to see him standing there with his eyes narrowed on us.

"You...came...back?" I moan as Theo thrusts from below into my pussy, and Mateo's fingers reach between our bodies to rub my clit.

Carter moves slowly into the room, a sleek panther stalking his prey. His husky eyes meet mine, and I see anarchy and chaos in their depth. He will always have a bit of madness inside of him, and I wouldn't want it any other way. "I forgot my phone." He lifts said phone from the counter and waves it at us. "Fucking glad I did; it seems the three of you were about to enjoy breakfast, and I'm still starving."

His words have me clenching down on Theo's hard cock, and he releases a groan. Theo has taken over, thrusting with harsh strokes into my pussy as I became distracted with the other two. My eyes return to his as the sound of clothes rustling behind me signifies Carter is also getting naked. Well, I guess this threesome just became a foursome. I would complain, but fuck that shit. *They are about to rock my world.*

Mateo's fingers leave my swollen bundle of nerves and trail up to my puckered hole, slipping a wet finger inside and fucking me in synchrony with Theo's thrusts. His lips meet my shoulder with a slide of his tongue before trailing down my back, and I feel him bend down behind us before his pouty lips meet where his fingers are moving inside of me, and he slips his tongue inside of my back hole to join them.

Carter strolls forward to the side of the table, his piercing and a bead of precum catching the sunlight through the large windows that look out over Central Park West. He grips his stiff cock and gives it a few punishing strokes. "Babe, are you still hungry? Did my cock not do his job this morning and satisfy you?" He slides up on the table with Theo and me and kneels in front of my face with his cock protruding forward. We hear the sound of the wood give a slight groan beneath us. *Shit, we are a hundred percent breaking this table.*

"Let me give you something more to eat, blondie. Open wide for me." I open my lips wide, and he pushes his cock inside of my mouth. His piercing slides across my tongue before meeting the roof of my mouth and driving to the back of my throat with his shallow thrusts. Mateo stops licking my back hole and rises behind me, and his swollen crown meets my tight hole as Theo stops moving. He pushes forward into my pussy, already stuffed with Theo's cock, and my breath stalls in my chest at the sting of pain before he bottoms out inside of me. The sensation of both of them moving within my tight channel together, pleasure and pain mixed, makes my pussy throb and spasm and sparks a wildfire within my body as my temperature rises and sweat breaks out across my skin.

Carter thrusts to the back of my throat and holds himself there, his hands rising to either side of my face and cradling my jaw as the air lodges in my throat along with his length. Panic fills me at my stalled breath, and I start to struggle. Theo's grip on my throat returns to a punishing tightness, and Mateo's hand slips into my hair and pulls on the loose ponytail, wrapping my hair around his wrist with force.

"That's my good little slut; swallow me down, blondie. Show me you belong to me." My chest heaves as Mateo and Theo pick up speed, but Carter continues to hold me immobile as I gag over and over on his cock, and tears trail down my face to mix with the saliva slipping from my mouth and making a mess of my chin.

"What a messy girl you are, Mia, choking on Carter's monster cock." Theo grunts from below me as his fingers release their hold on my neck just before darkness threatens to take me, and Carter finally pulls back to just the tip. I cough and try to desperately bring copious amounts of air into my lungs through my nose. One of these days, these fuckers will end up killing me with this shit. *Shut up bitch, we love it,* my mind snickers.

"What the fuck, guys? Not cool! Y'all are having an orgy for breakfast without me?" Finn's deep voice sounds in the room, and it causes shivers to race across my skin. Fuck, he's home too. Did no one have anything to do today except fuck me raw? "I thought you had class this morning fucker?" Carter questions as he slams back into the back of my throat.

"Canceled. Prof is sick or something." Finn walks over to us and meets my gaze with his warm chocolate-brown eyes. I watch as he licks his full bottom lip and observes me deep-throating Carter's cock, and then he lifts his shirt off with one hand by the collar in that sexy way men do, putting his delectable abs on display. My pussy tightens down on the two cocks currently wrecking her. Groans fill the air from Theo and Mateo's mouths.

"Killer, your mouth stretches so pretty around a cock. Fuck, those lips look beautiful around Carter's veiny dick." Finn slides down the zipper of his pants and pulls out his girthy cock, stroking it in his large hand from root to tip.

I close my eyes tightly as tears continue to slide down my face. I'm going into sensory overload with all their touches and words. "Fuck, she's so tight, no matter how many times we all fuck her holes. Her pretty pussy is soaked, and it's dripping down my balls." Mateo groans.

"That's 'cause she's a perfect little whore, aren't you, blondie? You were made to take all our cocks." I hum in acknowledgment along his long length and feel Theo below me, getting closer to finding his release as his body tightens, and his strokes pick up, losing the rhythm with Mateo's.

The table shakes and groans below us as Mateo also races towards his own oblivion, and pounds in with fierceness against my core. Skin slapping skin is loud in the air, mixed in with groans and the sound of the table moving. "Fuck Mia!" Theo's hoarse voice groans as he finally comes inside my body and floods my pussy. Mateo follows him into rapture with a cry and slumps over my back, his sweaty chest meeting my skin.

"Fuck Mat, move brother, let me get in there while she's all loosened up like that. I'm gonna stretch her ass until it gapes for us." Finn pushes Mateo off of me. Mateo releases a groan, and his cock slips from inside of me, but Theo's remains semi-hard still within me, coated by their combined cum.

Finn's tip pushes against my tight entrance before he slips inside, both Theo and I moaning in unison at the feel of his hard cock inside my pussy. He thrusts a couple of times, lubricating his hard girthy dick in Theo and Mateo's combined mess, and pulls out. His crown prods my puckered hole before he pushes past the tight ring of muscle and fucks me with fast, hard strokes that force my body to move back and forward on Theo's hardening cock.

Theo's hands wrap around my hips, tightening their grip as he starts to move again within my pussy. I gag again and again on Carter's hard dick as he thrusts his hand into the hair at the top of my head, and fists my strands forcing his long cock so deep in my throat, that the tip of my nose almost touches his stomach. His other hand holds tight to my jaw, forcing me to take all of him.

Prickles of heat coat my limbs, and my body tightens with the friction of my clit rubbing on Theo's warm skin and the slapping sounds of Finn fucking my ass hard. Tingles explode all over my body, causing goosebumps to rise on my skin, my toes curl, and my hands tighten into fists as my body races towards the cliff of ecstasy and falls over the edge. Blinding prisms of light shine behind my eyes as they are forced to close from the sensation. My chest tightens, and I can hear my blood rushing in my ears. Shockwaves race through my body one after the other until, finally, I am spent and boneless. My body is so exhausted and languid that I can't even move a finger.

Carter pushes in one last time and holds me firmly as he cums down my throat with a deep animalistic groan. "Love you, blondie. Fuck, you are amazing."

"Fuck, killer. I will never get enough of you. You are mine. Ours." Finn thrusts one last time, and I feel him release inside my ass, causing small tremors of electricity to soar through my skin and my pussy to spasm around Theo's cock. I open my eyes and stare down at my king as Carter pulls out of my mouth, and cum dribbles down my chin and coats my lips. I lean forward, press my lips to Theo's, and let him taste Carter on my tongue. The combination of Finn's words and Carter's taste are Theo's undoing, and he comes with a heavy groan as his tongue lashes my mouth.

The table decides at that moment that it's had enough brutality inflicted on it, and one of the legs gives out, crashing down with Theo, Carter, and myself still on it and forcing Finn to pull out and grab for me. The sound is loud in the air as we tumble to the floor. Mateo's loud laugh breaks across the room and has the rest of us breaking into laughter. "Fuck, we're gonna need a new stronger table."

We all get up in a tangle of limbs, laughing at the state of the table. A moan leaves my lips at how sore all of my holes are. My pussy and ass throb as they leak cum between my legs, and it slides down the inside of my thighs. My abused throat makes it hard to swallow. I give Carter a nasty look, but he just waggles his eyebrows at me. "You know you love me, blondie." He smirks at me, making me want to pummel him with my fists.

"Now *Mami,* can we please revisit the discussion of you marrying one of us?" Mateo calls out from the fridge, where he's filling glasses with water from the dispenser for all of us. I watch as he pours honey and lemon into my mine and passes it to me across the island. Asshole, no doubt knows how sore my throat is right now. It's too bad they're not into each other. They all deserve to experience what it's like to deep-throat one of their massive cocks. Guaranteed they would be gentler if they did. *Who are you lying to bitch? We don't want gentle!*

"Nope. We have already had this discussion, Mateo, multiple times, in fact. It wouldn't be legal, and I have no intention of ever being anything but a Stratford. It's the name I will carry until the day I take my last breath."

"Maybe I could be a Stratford?" Mateo questions as I roll my eyes at his antics.

"Stella could also stab you in the throat for suggesting that, but you go right ahead with that pipe dream, buddy." Finn pats Mateo's shoulder as he grabs his glass of water from the counter.

Our life is not conventional. I will never be able to marry all of them, and because I can't do that, I refuse to marry any of them, despite them asking numerous times a week. My eyes stare down at my ring on my left hand. They presented it to me at Christmas. It's a beautiful diamond-encrusted eternity band with each of their names inscribed on the inside. A sign of their undying promise to love me for eternity.

The subject of them taking the Stratford name has come up before, but I shut them down. If and when we have kids in the far-off future, our kids will take the Stratford name and continue my grandmother's legacy so that my grandfather Jaxon's wishes for a Stratford empire never die. All four of my kings agreed to that clause. Fuck, Carter wanted to start making babies right away, the psycho.

My plan is to finish school and then join my grandmother at Stratford Industries until she is ready to retire, and Issy and I can take our rightful places as the next generation of Stratfords leading our vast empire. *Issy.* My sister's name pulls a smile to my face. That little princess brought a lot of trouble within the last year to my grandmother. That tale is for another time, though.

The five of us are comfortable and secure in our relationship. There will never be me with just one of them. I could never dream of having just one king in my life. Together, they are the perfect men to tame and repair my damaged heart. We are five strands of the same string, intertwined for life to make a strong rope. Without them, I would lose myself. With them, I have found all the fragmented pieces of my heart and put it back together to make this indestructible version of Mia Stratford.

The reign of the queen caused the fall of the kings and ended a corrupted kingdom. It brought with it a new adventure and a fresh start for five soul-weary and damaged people to become one. They tame my darkness, and I bring them light. Together we balance each other out.

I look forward to spending eternity with them. Even when this life ends, I know each of them will find me in the next. Fate has pulled us together, and we will never be apart again.

A horrified scream rents the air and pulls me from my poetic musings. "Carter Pemberton, hell no! I did not need to see that monster in front of my eyes! What the hell is that hanging off the end of it? Oh, my sweet baby Jesus, you have jewelry on it? God save us all."

Raegan stands in the entryway of our kitchen, her face red like a tomato as she stares at Carter's junk, and the fucker makes it jiggle before her shocked face causing her to take steps back and shield her eyes with her hands.

I think it's adorable that she still gets embarrassed when she catches us in compromising situations. She made each of us agree to keep our sexcapades behind closed doors when she moved in with us last year. Despite our promises and good intentions, none of us were able to keep them.

I spy what I think is a giant hickey on her neck, and it makes my eyebrows hit my hairline. Rae-Rae hasn't been coming home at night lately. She's been abnormally silent, not even really fighting with Carter as regularly. Which in this condo is a daily thing. Theo seems to think she's seeing someone. When I questioned her, she refused to answer any of my questions and told me to go mind my harem of men.

I have the sneaky suspicion I know who it is, and if he's smart, he better watch himself before I send all four of my kings after his ass. Who am I kidding? I'll murder him myself if he hurts her. There is no way that spoiled fucker is good enough for my ride or die biatch. I'm going to be watching her closely, and if I see any tears or misery, he will meet the end of my blade.

"Mia Stratford, you said you would keep your kinky fuckery out of the damn kitchen! There's food in here, girl!" Raegan stammers. She looks through her fingers at me and spies the broken table. "MIA, WHAT THE FUCK? What did y'all do to the table? Jesus, Mary, and Joseph, I am never eating in here again." She shrieks before turning around and walking out of the kitchen to rounds of rancorous laughter.

This is my life now. Mia Stratford has found her home, her people, and her destiny. Everything I suffered led me here to this world I was always meant to be the center of. My kings are my universe, and I am the very core of theirs. Love won despite all the obstacles it had to face.

Am I the victim? No, I conquered all my demons. Slayed them with my own hands. Am I the villain? Well, maybe. After all, it's a lot more fun on the dark side. Especially when you have four dark kings to keep you company. I have no regrets.

Love,

Mia

xoxo

If you want to hear more about Diego and Issy's story, you will find them in **The Queen's Serpent** out in late 2023. Preorder today:https://books2read.com/u/31VPRD

Long may a Stratford reign.

About Author

Her love of all things romance and paranormal has stayed with her over the years, and now she devours books at an alarming rate! Why she seems to always fall in love with the villains of the stories is anyone's wonder.

Drinker of gallons of coffee, lover of all things chocolate, and an avid gardener. You can find her wandering around her small town in Southwestern Ontario with her trusty writing assistant, the four-legged fur-demon, binge-watching Netflix, hands deep in the dirt of her gardens, or spending time with her two grown kids and her soulmate.

She writes about demanding, possessive, morally gray, and ruthless dark alpha-aholes and the strong women who bring them to their knees in her spicy dark romances.

Come Stalk Me!

Be sure to subscribe to her newsletter: https://www.authoralmaruga.com/
This will keep you updated on her craziness, book releases and giveaways!
Come join the naughty fun in her author's Facebook group!
A.L Maruga's Naughty Queen's Lair: https://www.face-
book.com/groups/httpslinktr.eeauthoralmaruga
Stalk her on:
Instagram: https://www.instagram.com/authoralmaruga/
TikTok: https://www.tiktok.com/@almarugaauthor?lang=en or check out her
LinkTree: https://linktr.ee/authoralmaruga

Also By

Reign of the Queen, A.L Maruga's debut, dark enemies to lovers, why choose/RH, bully romance. Available in Kindle Unlimited, paper back and coming soon in hardback!

Get your copy today! **https://books2read.com/u/mgPLn0**

Fall of a King, the second book in the Casbury Prep series. Available in Kindle Unlimited, paper back and coming soon in hardback!

Get your copy today! https://books2read.com/u/4ARvq0

Rise of a Kingdom, is a forced marriage, dark enemies to lovers standalone not in the Casbury series, but set in the same world. Available in Kindle Unlimited, paperback, and hardback.

Get your copy today! https://books2read.com/u/bMza2V

The Queen's Serpent, is a dark enemies to lovers, kidnapping and forced marriage standalone that features characters, Diego Cabano and Issy Stratford from the Casbury Prep series. It part of the same Casbury world. Coming November 2023. Available now for preorder. https://books2read.com/u/31VPRD

Acknowledgments

Lovelies!

Let me start by saying how I am incredibly grateful and honored that you read my books and have followed me on my journey!

Corrupted Kingdom was a roller coaster ride to write. It took everything out of me, left me weary and mentally, emotionally, and physically drained. These characters demand their story come to a closure with fireworks, and I could not disappoint them.

When I wrote the end, I had to sit and cry knowing that I had to part ways with them and that their voices would no longer be inside of my head. I hope that I have done justice to you, the readers with my closure. *Thank you for sticking with me.*

To the readers - thank you from the bottom of my heart and soul for reading my books. I am humbled and honored by each kind word, post, and video. I have made so many amazing friends amongst you. Thank you for being my tribe. Know that without you, there are no books! *Thanks for giving this Canadian indie author a chance!*

To my ride or die - I owe you a million kisses, and a vacation somewhere that has no internet and I don't utter a single word about a book I'm writing. *I love* *you.* Thank you for always supporting me, even when I'm crazy and loving me in real life like my favorite book boyfriends do in the books I write & read.

To my daughter, Katie - You are an inspiration to me. You inspire every single strong FMC I write. Thank you for being my biggest champion and pulling me back from the edge when my writing gets too dark. I could not continue to do this without you. Thank you for reading another one of your mom's dark, questionable and unhinged romances. I'm sorry for the nightmares. *I love you, little momma!*

To my handsome son - Who spilled the beans to his auntie about mom writing word p*rn and once again ignoring me through this whole book. While buying me Funko Pops when I was losing my mind and needed a ray of happiness. *Thank you!*

To my four-legged demon spawn - You inspired *Carter Pemberton* and if you could speak, I have no doubt you would sound exactly like him. Thank you for being mommy's demanding, possessive, insane and controlling ahole. *I love you, handsome fur demon.*

Anna, Lillie, Erin, Tawny, & Katelin - Thank you for reading this book during editing. You, ladies, are some of the most amazing, supportive woman I have had the pleasure to meet on this journey. Thank you for all your support and talking me down when I wanted to quit. *I am honored to have you in my life and call you friends.*

Darcy Bennett – You are an angel, sent to me in my hour of need. I could not have functioned the last few weeks without you. Thank you for all your help and support. *I could not have done this without you!*

Mia Fury – You are one of the most amazing people I have met on this journey. I am blessed to have met you. Thank you for all your kindness, support & help. *I could not have done this book without you.*

My lovely members of the Queen's Lair on F.B. - You make me smile & keep me sane every day! Thank you for being a part of my world, participating in book fairy events and making the world a brighter place with your kindness. I am honored to have met you! *Thank you for putting up with my cray-cray and still coming back daily!*

To my arc team - I love you! Thank you for putting up with me when I forget to post. For sharing my teasers and my books and bringing me so much happiness with your presence. *You are all amazing!*

To the group of Bookish Girls and Issa – You ladies are some of the most amazing women I have had the pleasure to meet. I am so honored to be a part of your tribe, thank you for welcoming me into your circle of book love. Thank you for sharing my worlds with other readers. You have my gratitude & heart forever. Issa, I love you! You are forever my fairy godmother!

Thank you, to the other amazing book community authors, PA, and readers who have been very supportive, inclusive, and patient with me.

Thank you, Cady Verdiramo, for making this gorgeous non-discrete cover!

Thank you, Mark Suan, for the formatting, and beautiful graphic details in this book.

Thank you, H.E. from B&R edits, for helping to polish my words, and reducing down my vivid profanity!

I have so many new worlds and books to be published. I hope you all stick with me and continue on this amazing journey.

I love ya, lovelies!

A.L. Maruga, xoxo

Resources

I recognize there were certain themes within this book that could have been triggering, please see available resources below. *Together we are stronger than our demons.*

If you or someone you know needs help for **assault crisis**, please view the following resources.

isurvive.org **USA & CANADA**

endingviolencecanada.org **Canada**

safehelpline.org **Universal**

myawayout.org **Universal**

If you or someone you know needs help with **mental health crisis**, please see the links below

wellnesstogethercanada **Canada**

mentalhealth.gov **USA**

988lifeline.org **USA**

checkpointorg.com/global **Universal**

Printed in Great Britain
by Amazon

26279077R00262